The Best Science Fiction
of the Year #10

is the latest installment of the famous standard anthology of the best short fiction in the science fiction field published annually. Reflecting the themes, styles, and ideas of the top science fiction writers today, this collection presents the most outstanding short stories, novelettes and novellas drawn from a field of astonishing scope and quality.

Here, once again—*the best* of the BESTs!

Books by Terry Carr

The Best Science Fiction of the Year #10
Fantasy Annual III

Published by TIMESCAPE BOOKS

TERRY CARR, EDITOR

THE BEST SCIENCE FICTION OF THE YEAR #10

PUBLISHED BY POCKET BOOKS NEW YORK

This collection is comprised of works of fiction. Names, characters, places and incidents are either the product of the authors' imaginations or are used fictitiously, and any resemblance to actual persons, living or dead, events or locales is entirely coincidental.

Another *Original* publication of TIMESCAPE BOOKS

A Timescape Book published by
POCKET BOOKS, a Simon & Schuster division of
GULF & WESTERN CORPORATION
1230 Avenue of the Americas, New York, N.Y. 10020

ISBN: 0-671-42262-6

First Timescape Books printing July, 1981

10 9 8 7 6 5 4 3 2 1

POCKET and colophon are trademarks of Simon & Schuster.

Use of the TIMESCAPE trademark under exclusive license
from trademark owner.

Printed in the U.S.A.

CREDITS

CONTENTS

THE BEST SCIENCE FICTION OF THE YEAR #10

INTRODUCTION

Terry Carr

THERE ARE GREAT CHANGES OCCURRING IN THE science fiction genre, and I'm sorry to say that most of them are bad. The recession has severely curtailed most readers' budgets for entertainment, with the result that book sales have lessened considerably. (As Robert A. Heinlein pointed out years ago, writers are competing for the readers' beer-money.) The situation is made worse by inflation, as production costs have forced publishers to raise the prices of their books. At the end of 1980, paper costs rose by 20 percent, so we'll have to expect further price raises.

Fortunately, the recession hasn't hit publishing quite as hard as other fields of entertainment, such as records and movies. A number of record-store chains have been forced out of business, and the movie companies are running scared: 1980's movie releases were lower in quality than those of any year in recent memory, an appalling proportion of them being sequels to or imitations of proven box-office hits.

A similar trend *has* been evidenced in science fiction, though: bookstore shelves are crowded with sequels, series novels and trilogies. Even the "individual" novels being published now show a much higher proportion of lowest-common-denominator styles and subjects, most of them adventure novels or "hard science" stories. Some of these are excellent—there's nothing innately wrong with these types—but the era of widespread innovation in sci-

1

ence fiction has disappeared, or at best been halted for the foreseeable future.

The science fiction magazines were hit hardest, and several of them had to cease publication during the past year, among them *Galaxy, Fantastic* and *Galileo.* The only sf magazine that is still a big commercial success is *Omni;* but that magazine publishes only a few stories per issue, concentrating on science articles and beautifully reproduced paintings and photos. Significantly, *Omni* has inspired a number of imitators, but none of them so far publishes science fiction along with its science articles and graphics.

It all sounds pretty grim, doesn't it? We can add the fact that new writers find it very difficult to break into print in this situation, and that most established writers receive considerably less payment for their works than they've had in recent years. Still, there is reason to be optimistic about the future of science fiction.

First and foremost: A great number of the best sf writers, new and old alike, write science fiction for pleasure as much as for money; they love science fiction. These people won't quit. Second: There are signs that the situation has reached and passed its nadir already, and though editors are still being cautious, many of them are predicting an upsurge in the next year or two.

Whether or not they're right, the troubled economics of sf publishing haven't reduced the number of excellent stories available for a best-of-the-year anthology such as this one, which I believe is one of the finest in the series. The price you pay for this book is now higher than it used to be, but you're getting a longer book than ever before. Three years ago I split the book in half, producing *The Best Science Fiction of the Year,* all short stories and novelettes, and *The Best Science Fiction Novellas of the Year,* which gathered the top stories of less than full-novel length. It seemed a good idea at the time, but evidently most readers want the greatest variety possible in subjects, styles *and* lengths.

So this year there's just one best sf anthology from me, but it's considerably longer so that I can offer the top novellas, novelettes and short stories in one book. Never mind the price: you won't find a better bargain.

—TERRY CARR

GROTTO OF THE
DANCING DEER

Clifford D. Simak

What if you were an archaeologist who found
a Cro-Magnon cave decorated with ancient
paintings and still containing the "palette"
used by the ancient painter . . . and what
if there were fingerprints on it that exactly
matched those of your Basque assistant?
Probably you'd suspect a hoax along the
lines of the Piltdown discoveries. But current scientific techniques can prove or dis-
prove such hoaxes; what if they showed
conclusively that this *wasn't* a hoax?

Clifford D. Simak has been writing science fiction for fifty years, and has been
one of the genre's top writers throughout
those years. His most famous book is *City*,
which won the International Fantasy Award;
he has also won the Hugo Award for his
novelette "The Big Front Yard" and his
novel *Way Station*. In 1976 the Science Fiction Writers of America made him the third
author to win the Grand Master Award.
(Robert A. Heinlein and Jack Williamson
had won the first two.) In his newest short
story he shows that he's lost none of his
skills for imagination, narration and, in particular, moving characterization.

LUIS WAS PLAYING HIS PIPE WHEN BOYD climbed the steep path that led up to the cave. There was no need to visit the cave again; all the work was done, mapping, measuring, photographing, extracting all possible information from the site. Not only the paintings, although the paintings were the important part of it. Also there had been the animal bones, charred, and the still remaining charcoal of the fire in which they had been charred; the small store of natural earths from which the pigments used by the painters had been compounded—a cache of valuable components, perhaps hidden by an artist who, for some reason that could not now be guessed, had been unable to use them; the atrophied human hand, severed at the wrist (why had it been severed and, once severed, left there to be found by men thirty millennia removed?); the lamp formed out of a chunk of sandstone, hollowed to accommodate a wad of moss, the hollow filled with fat, the moss serving as a wick to give light to those who painted. All these and many other things, Boyd thought with some satisfaction; Gavarnie had turned out to be, possibly because of the sophisticated scientific methods of investigation that had been brought to bear, the most significant cave painting site ever studied—perhaps not as spectacular, in some ways, as Lascaux, but far more productive in the data obtained.

No need to visit the cave again, and yet there was a reason—the nagging feeling that he had passed something

up, that in the rush and his concentration on the other
work, he had forgotten something. It had made small impression on him at the time, but now, thinking back on it,
he was becoming more and more inclined to believe it
might have importance. The whole thing probably was a
product of his imagination, he told himself. Once he saw
it again (if, indeed, he could find it again, if it were not
a product of retrospective worry), it might prove to be
nothing at all, simply an impression that had popped up
to nag him.

So here he was again, climbing the steep path, geol-
ogist's hammer swinging at his belt, large flashlight
clutched in hand, listening to the piping of Luis who
perched on a small terrace, just below the mouth of the
cave, a post he had occupied through all the time the
work was going on. Luis had camped there in his tent
through all kinds of weather, cooking on a camper's stove,
serving as self-appointed watch-dog, on alert against intruders, although there had been few intruders other than
the occasional curious tourist who had heard of the project and tramped miles out of the way to see it. The vil-
lagers in the valley below had been no trouble; they
couldn't have cared less about what was happening on
the slope above them.

Luis was no stranger to Boyd; ten years before, he had
shown up at the rock shelter project some fifty miles distant and there had stayed through two seasons of digging.
The rock shelter had not proved as productive as Boyd
initially had hoped, although it had shed some new light
on the Azilian culture, the tag-end of the great Western
European prehistoric groups. Taken on as a common
laborer, Luis had proved an apt pupil and as the work
went on had been given greater responsibility. A week after the work had started at Gavarnie, he had shown up
again.

"I heard you were here," he'd said. "What do you
have for me?"

As he came around a sharp bend in the trail, Boyd saw
him, sitting cross-legged in front of the weather-beaten
tent, holding the primitive pipe to his lips, piping away.

That was exactly what it was—piping. Whatever music
came out of the pipe was primitive and elemental.
Scarcely music, although Boyd would admit that he knew
nothing of music. Four notes—would it be four notes? he

wondered. A hollow bone with an elongated slot as a mouthpiece, two drilled holes for stops.

Once he had asked Luis about it. "I've never seen anything like it," he had said. Luis had told him, "You don't see many of them. In remote villages here and there, hidden away in the mountains."

Boyd left the path and walked across the grassy terrace, sat down beside Luis, who took down the pipe and laid it in his lap.

"I thought you were gone," Luis said. "The others left a couple of days ago."

"Back for one last look," said Boyd.

"You are reluctant to leave it?"

"Yes, I suppose I am."

Below them the valley spread out in autumn browns and tans, the small river a silver ribbon in the sunlight, the red roofs of the village a splash of color beside the river.

"It's nice up here," said Boyd. "Time and time again, I catch myself trying to imagine what it might have been like at the time the paintings were done. Not much different than it is now, perhaps. The mountains would be unchanged. There'd have been no fields in the valley, but it probably would have been natural pasture. A few trees here and there, but not too many of them. Good hunting. There'd have been grass for the grazing animals. I have even tried to figure out where the people would've camped. My guess would be where the village is now."

He looked around at Luis. The man still sat upon the grass, the pipe resting in his lap. He was smiling quietly, as if he might be smiling to himself. The small black beret sat squarely on his head, his tanned face was round and smooth, the black hair close-clipped, the blue shirt open at the throat. A young man, strong, not a wrinkle on his face.

"You love your work," said Luis.

"I'm devoted to it. So are you, Luis," Boyd said.

"It's not my work."

"Your work or not," said Boyd, "you do it well. Would you like to go with me? One last look around."

"I need to run an errand in the village."

"I thought I'd find you gone," said Boyd. "I was surprised to hear your pipe."

"I'll go soon," said Luis. "Another day or two. No reason to stay but, like you, I like this place. I have no place to go, no one needing me. Nothing's lost by staying a few more days."

"As long as you like," said Boyd. "The place is yours. Before too long, the government will be setting up a caretaker arrangement, but the government moves with due deliberation."

"Then I may not see you again," said Luis.

"I took a couple of days to drive down to Roncesvalles," said Boyd. "That's the place where the Gascons slaughtered Charlemagne's rearguard in 778."

"I've heard of the place," said Luis.

"I'd always wanted to see it. Never had the time. The Charlemagne chapel is in ruins, but I am told masses are still said in the village chapel for the dead paladins. When I returned from the trip, I couldn't resist the urge to see the cave again."

"I am glad of that," said Luis. "May I be impertinent?"

"You're never impertinent," said Boyd.

"Before you go, could we break bread once more together? Tonight, perhaps. I'll prepare an omelet."

Boyd hesitated, gagging down a suggestion that Luis dine with him. Then he said, "I'd be delighted, Luis. I'll bring a bottle of good wine."

2

Holding the flashlight centered on the rock wall, Boyd bent to examine the rock more closely. He had not imagined it; he had been right. Here, in this particular spot, the rock was not solid. It was broken into several pieces, but with the several pieces flush with the rest of the wall. Only by chance could the break have been spotted. Had he not been looking directly at it, watching for it as he swept the light across the wall, he would have missed it. It was strange, he thought, that someone else, during the time they had been working in the cave, had not found it. There'd not been much that they'd missed.

He held his breath, feeling a little foolish at the holding of it, for, after all, it might mean nothing. Frost cracks, perhaps, although he knew that he was wrong. It would be unusual to find frost cracks here.

He took the hammer out of his belt and, holding the

flashlight in one hand, trained on the spot, he forced the chisel end of the hammer into one of the cracks. The edge went in easily. He pried gently and the crack widened. Under more pressure, the piece of rock moved out. He laid down the hammer and flash, seized the slab of rock and pulled it free. Beneath it were two other slabs and they both came free as easily as the first. There were others as well and he also took them out. Kneeling on the floor of the cave, he directed the light into the fissure that he had uncovered.

Big enough for a man to crawl into, but at the prospect he remained for the moment undecided. Alone, he'd be taking a chance to do it. If something happened, if he should get stuck, if a fragment of rock should shift and pin him or fall upon him, there'd be no rescue. Or probably no rescue in time to save him. Luis would come back to the camp and wait for him, but should he fail to make an appearance, Luis more than likely would take it as a rebuke for impertinence or an American's callous disregard of him. It would never occur to him that Boyd might be trapped in the cave.

Still, it was his last chance. Tomorrow he'd have to drive to Paris to catch his plane. And this whole thing was intriguing; it was not something to be ignored. The fissure must have some significance; otherwise, why should it have been walled up so carefully? Who, he wondered, would have walled it up? No one, certainly, in recent times. Anyone, finding the hidden entrance to the cave, almost immediately would have seen the paintings and would have spread the word. So the entrance to the fissure must have been blocked by one who would have been unfamiliar with the significance of the paintings or by one to whom they would have been commonplace.

It was something, he decided, that could not be passed up; he would have to go in. He secured the hammer to his belt, picked up the flashlight and began the crawl.

The fissure ran straight and easy for a hundred feet or more. It offered barely room enough for crawling, but, other than that, no great difficulties. Then, without warning, it came to an end. Boyd lay in it, directing the flash beam ahead of him, staring in consternation at the smooth wall of rock that came down to cut the fissure off.

It made no sense. Why should someone go to the trouble of walling off an empty fissure? He could have missed something on the way, but thinking of it, he was fairly sure he hadn't. His progress had been slow and he had kept the flash directed ahead of him every inch of the way. Certainly if there had been anything out of the ordinary, he would have seen it.

Then a thought came to him and slowly, with some effort, he began to turn himself around, so that his back, rather than his front, lay on the fissure floor. Directing the beam upward, he had his answer. In the roof of the fissure gaped a hole.

Cautiously, he raised himself into a sitting position. Reaching up, he found handholds on the projecting rock and pulled himself erect. Swinging the flash around, he saw that the hole opened, not into another fissure, but into a bubblelike cavity—small, no more than six feet in any dimension. The walls and ceiling of the cavity were smooth, as if a bubble of plastic rock had existed here for a moment at some time in the distant geologic past when the mountains had been heaving upward leaving behind it as it drained away a bubble forever frozen into smooth and solid stone.

As he swung the flash across the bubble, he gasped in astonishment. Colorful animals capered around the entire expanse of stone. Bison played leapfrog. Horses cantered in a chorus line. Mammoths turned somersaults. All around the bottom perimeter, just above the floor, dancing deer, standing on their hind legs, joined hands and jigged, antlers swaying gracefully.

"For the love of Christ!" said Boyd.

Here was Stone Age Disney.

If it was the Stone Age. Could some jokester have crawled into the area in fairly recent times to paint the animals in this grotto? Thinking it over, he rejected the idea. So far as he had been able to ascertain, no one in the valley, nor in the entire region, for that matter, had known of the cave until a shepherd had found it several years before when a lamb had blundered into it. The entrance was small and apparently for centuries had been masked by a heavy growth of brush and bracken.

Too, the execution of the paintings had a prehistoric touch to them. Perspective played but a small part. The paintings had that curious flat look that distinguished most prehistoric art. There was no background—no horizon line, no trees, no grass or flowers, no clouds, no sense of sky. Although, he reminded himself, anyone who had any knowledge of cave painting probably would have been aware of all these factors and worked to duplicate them.

Yet, despite the noncharacteristic antics of the painted animals, the pictures did have the feeling of cave art. What ancient man, Boyd asked himself, what kind of ancient man, would have painted gamboling bison and tumbling mammoths? While the situation did not hold in all cave art, all the paintings in this particular cave were deadly serious—conservative as to form and with a forthright, honest attempt to portray the animals as the artists had seen them. There was no frivolity, not even the imprint of paint-smeared human hands as so often happened in other caves. The men who had worked in this cave had not as yet been corrupted by the symbolism that had crept in, apparently rather late in the prehistoric painting cycle.

So who had been this clown who had crept off by himself in this hidden cavern to paint his comic animals? That he had been an accomplished painter there could be no doubt. This artist's techniques and executions were without flaw.

Boyd hauled himself up through the hole, slid out onto the two-foot ledge that ran all around the hole, crouching, for there was no room to stand. Much of the painting, he realized, must have been done with the artist lying flat upon his back, reaching up to work on the curving ceiling.

He swept the beam of the flashlight along the ledge. Halfway around, he halted the light and jiggled it back and forth to focus upon something that was placed upon the ledge, something that undoubtedly had been left by the artist when he had finished his work and gone away.

Leaning forward, Boyd squinted to make out what it was. It looked like the shoulder blade of a deer; beside the shoulder blade lay a lump of stone.

Cautiously, he edged his way around the ledge. He had been right. It was the shoulder blade of a deer. Upon the flat surface of it lay a lumpy substance. Paint? he wondered, the mixture of animal fats and mineral earths the prehistoric artists used as paints? He focused the flash closer and there was no doubt. It was paint, spread over the surface of the bone which had served as a palette, with some of the paint lying in thicker lumps ready for use, but never used, paint dried and mummified and bearing imprints of some sort. He leaned close, bringing his face down to within a few inches of the paint, shining the light upon the surface. The imprints, he saw, were fingerprints, some of them sunk deep—the signature of that ancient, long-dead man who had worked here, crouching even as Boyd now crouched, shoulders hunched against the curving stone. He put out his hand to touch the palette, then pulled it back. Symbolic, yes, this move to touch, this reaching out to touch the man who painted—but symbolic only; a gesture with too many centuries between.

He shifted the flashlight beam to the small block of stone that lay beside the shoulder blade. A lamp—hollowed out sandstone, a hollow to hold the fat and the chunk of moss that served as a wick. The fat and wick were long since gone, but a thin film of soot still remained around the rim of the hollow that had held them.

Finishing his work, the artist had left his tools behind him, had even left the lamp, perhaps still guttering, with the fat almost finished—had left it here and let himself down into the fissure, crawling it in darkness. To him, perhaps, there was no need of light. He could crawl the tunnel by touch and familiarity. He must have crawled the route many times, for the work upon these walls had taken long, perhaps many days.

So he had left, crawling through the fissure, using the blocks of stone to close the opening to the fissure, then had walked away, scrambling down the slope to the valley where grazing herds had lifted their heads to watch him, then had gone back to grazing.

But when had this all happened? Probably, Boyd told himself, after the cave itself had been painted, perhaps even after the paintings in the cave had lost much of whatever significance they originally would have held— one lone man coming back to paint his secret animals in his secret place. Painting them as a mockery of the pompous, magical importance of the main cave paintings? Or as a protest against the stuffy conservatism of the original paintings? Or simply as a bubbling chuckle, an exuberance of life, perhaps even a joyous rebellion against the grimness and the simple-mindedness of the hunting magic? A rebel, he thought, a prehistoric rebel—an intellectual rebel? Or, perhaps, simply a man with a viewpoint slightly skewed from the philosophy of his time?

But this was that other man, that ancient man. Now how about himself? Having found the grotto, what did he do next? What would be the best way to handle it? Certainly he could not turn his back upon it and walk away, as the artist, leaving his palette and his lamp behind him, had walked away. For this was an important discovery. There could be no question of that. Here was a new and unsuspected approach to the prehistoric mind, a facet of ancient thinking that never had been guessed.

Leave everything as it lay, close up the fissure and make a phone call to Washington and another one to Paris, unpack his bags and settle down for a few more weeks of work. Get back the photographers and other members of the crew—do a job of it. Yes, he told himself, that was the way to do it.

Something lying behind the lamp, almost hidden by the sandstone lamp, glinted in the light. Something white and small.

Still crouched over, Boyd shuffled forward to get a better look.

It was a piece of bone, probably a leg bone from a small grazing animal. He reached out and picked it up and, having seen what it was, hunched unmoving over it, not quite sure what to make of it.

It was a pipe, a brother to the pipe that Luis carried in his jacket pocket, had carried in his pocket since that first day he'd met him, years ago. There was the mouthpiece slot, there the two round stops. In that long-gone day when the paintings had been done the artist had hunched here, in the flickering of the lamp, and had played softly to himself, those simple piping airs that Luis had played almost every evening, after work was done.

"Merciful Jesus," Boyd said, almost prayerfully, "it simply cannot be!"

He stayed there, frozen in his crouch, the thoughts hammering in his mind while he tried to push the thoughts away. They would not go away. He'd drive them away for just a little distance, then they'd come surging back to overwhelm him.

Finally, grimly, he broke the trance in which the thoughts had held him. He worked deliberately, forcing himself to do what he knew must be done.

He took off his windbreaker and carefully wrapped the shoulder blade palette and the pipe inside it, leaving the lamp. He let himself down into the fissure and crawled, carefully protecting the bundle that he carried. In the cave again, he meticulously fitted the blocks of stone together to block the fissure mouth, scraped together handfuls of soil from the cave floor and smeared it on the face of the blocks, wiping it away, but leaving a small clinging film to mask the opening to all but the most inquiring eye.

Luis was not at his camp on the terrace below the cave mouth; he was still on his errand into the village.

When he reached his hotel, Boyd made his telephone call to Washington. He skipped the call to Paris.

3

The last leaves of October were blowing in the autumn wind and a weak sun, not entirely obscured by the floating clouds, shone down on Washington.

John Roberts was waiting for him on the park bench. They nodded at one another, without speaking, and Boyd sat down beside his friend.

"You took a big chance," said Roberts. "What would have happened if the customs people . . ."

"I wasn't too worried," Boyd said. "I knew this man in Paris. For years he's been smuggling stuff into America. He's good at it and he owed me one. What have you got?"

"Maybe more than you want to hear."

"Try me."

"The fingerprints match," said Roberts.

"You were able to get a reading on the paint impressions?"

"Loud and clear."

"The FBI?"

"Yes, the FBI. It wasn't easy, but I have a friend or two."

"And the dating?"

"No problem. The bad part of the job was convincing my man this was top secret. He's still not sure it is."

"Will he keep his mouth shut?"

"I think so. Without evidence no one would believe him. It would sound like a fairy story."

"Tell me."

"Twenty-two thousand. Plus or minus three hundred years."

"And the prints do match. The bottle prints and . . ."

"I told you they match. Now will you tell me how in

hell a man who lived twenty-two thousand years ago could leave his prints on a wine bottle that was manufactured last year."

"It's a long story," said Boyd. "I don't know if I should. First, where do you have the shoulder blade?"

"Hidden," said Roberts. "Well hidden. You can have it back, and the bottle, any time you wish."

Boyd shrugged. "Not yet. Not for a while. Perhaps never."

"Never?"

"Look, John, I have to think it out."

"What a hell of a mess," said Roberts. "No one wants the stuff. No one would dare to have it. Smithsonian wouldn't touch it with a ten-foot pole. I haven't asked. They don't even know about it. But I know they wouldn't want it. There's something, isn't there, about sneaking artifacts out of a country . . ."

"Yes, there is," said Boyd.

"And now you don't want it."

"I didn't say that. I just said let it stay where it is for a time. It's safe, isn't it?"

"It's safe. And now . . ."

"I told you it is a long story. I'll try to make it short. There's this man—a Basque. He came to me ten years ago when I was doing the rock shelter . . ."

Roberts nodded. "I remember that one."

"He wanted work and I gave him work. He broke in fast, caught onto the techniques immediately. Became a valuable man. That often happens with native laborers. They seem to have the feel for their own antiquity. And then when we started work on the cave he showed up again. I was glad to see him. The two of us, as a matter of fact, are fairly good friends. On my last night at the cave he cooked a marvelous omelet—eggs, tomato, green pimentoes, onions, sausages and home-cured ham. I brought a bottle of wine."

"*The* bottle?"

"Yes, *the* bottle."

"So go ahead."

"He played a pipe. A bone pipe. A squeaky sort of thing. Not too much music in it . . ."

"There was a pipe . . ."

"Not that pipe. Another pipe. The same kind of pipe, but not the one our man has. Two pipes the same. One in

a living man's pocket, the other beside the shoulder blade.
There were things about this man I'm telling you of.
Nothing that hit you between the eyes. Just little things.
You would notice something and then, some time later,
maybe quite a bit later, there'd be something else, but by
the time that happened, you'd have forgotten the first incident and not tie the two together. Mostly it was that he
knew too much. Little things a man like him would not be
expected to know. Even things that no one knew. Bits and
pieces of knowledge that slipped out of him, maybe without his realizing it. And his eyes. I didn't realize that until
later, not until I'd found the second pipe and began to
think about the other things. But I was talking about his
eyes. In appearance he is a young man, a never-aging
man, but his eyes are old . . ."

"Tom, you said he is a Basque."

"That's right."

"Isn't there some belief that the Basques may have descended from the Cro-Magnons?"

"There is such a theory. I have thought of it."

"Could this man of yours be a Cro-Magnon?"

"I'm beginning to think he is."

"But think of it—twenty thousand years!"

"Yes, I know," said Boyd.

4

Boyd heard the piping when he reached the bottom of
the trail that led up to the cave. The notes were ragged,
torn by the wind. The Pyrenees stood up against the high
blue sky.

Tucking the bottle of wine more securely underneath
his arm, Boyd began the climb. Below him lay the redness
of the village rooftops and the sere brown of autumn that
spread across the valley. The piping continued, lifting and
falling as the wind tugged at it playfully.

Luis sat cross-legged in front of the tattered tent. When
he saw Boyd, he put the pipe in his lap and sat waiting.

Boyd sat down beside him, handing him the bottle. Luis
took it and began working on the cork.

"I heard you were back," he said. "How went the trip?"

"It went well," said Boyd.

"So now you know," said Luis.

Body nodded. "I think you wanted me to know. Why should you have wanted that?"

"The years grow long," said Luis. "The burden heavy. It is lonely, all alone."

"You are not alone."

"It's lonely when no one knows you. You now are the first who has really known me."

"But the knowing will be short. A few years more and again no one will know you."

"This lifts the burden for a time," said Luis. "Once you are gone, I will be able to take it up again. And there is something . . ."

"Yes, what is it, Luis?"

"You say when you are gone there'll be no one again. Does that mean . . ."

"If what you're getting at is whether I will spread the word, no, I won't. Not unless you wish it. I have thought on what would happen to you if the world were told."

"I have certain defenses. You can't live as long as I have if you fail in your defenses."

"What kind of defenses?"

"Defenses. That is all."

"I'm sorry if I pried. There's one other thing. If you wanted me to know, you took a long chance. Why, if something had gone wrong, if I had failed to find the grotto . . ."

"I had hoped, at first, that the grotto would not be necessary. I had thought you might have guessed, on your own."

"I knew there was something wrong. But this is so outrageous I couldn't have trusted myself even had I guessed. You know it's outrageous, Luis. And if I'd not found the grotto. . . . Its finding was pure chance, you know."

"If you hadn't, I would have waited. Some other time, some other year, there would have been someone else. Some other way to betray myself."

"You could have told me."

"Cold, you mean?"

"That's what I mean. I would not have believed you, of course. Not at first."

"Don't you understand? I could not have told you. The concealment now is second nature. One of the defenses I talked about. I simply could not have brought myself to tell you, or anyone."

"Why me? Why wait all these years until I came along?"

"I did not wait, Boyd. There were others, at different times. None of them worked out. I had to find, you must understand, someone who had the strength to face it. Not one who would run screaming madly. I knew you would not run screaming."

"I've had time to think it through," Boyd said. "I've come to terms with it. I can accept the fact, but not too well, only barely. Luis, do you have some explanation? How come you are so different from the rest of us?"

"No idea at all. No inkling. At one time, I thought there must be others like me and I sought for them. I found none. I no longer seek."

The cork came free and he handed the bottle of wine to Boyd. "You go first," he said steadily.

Boyd lifted the bottle and drank. He handed it to Luis. He watched him as he drank. Wondering, as he watched, how he could be sitting here, talking calmly with a man who had lived, who had stayed young through twenty thousand years. His gorge rose once again against acceptance of the fact—but it had to be a fact. The shoulder blade, the small amount of organic matter still remaining in the pigment, had measured out to 22,000 years. There was no question that the prints in the paint had matched the prints upon the bottle. He had raised one question back in Washington, hoping there might be evidence of hoax. Would it have been possible, he had asked, that the ancient pigment, the paint used by the prehistoric artist, could have been reconstituted, the fingerprints impressed upon it, and then replaced in the grotto? Impossible was the answer. Any reconstitution of the pigment, had it been possible, would have shown up in the analysis. There had been nothing of the sort—the pigment dated to 20,000 years ago. There was no question of that.

"All right, Cro-Magnon," said Boyd, "tell me how you did it. How does a man survive as long as you have? You do not age, of course. Your body will not accept disease. But I take it you are not immune to violence or to accident. You've lived in a violent world. How does a man sidestep accident and violence for two hundred centuries?"

"There were times early," Luis said, "when I came close

to not surviving. For a long time, I did not realize the kind of thing I was. Sure, I lived longer, stayed younger than all the others—I would guess, however, that I didn't begin to notice this until I began to realize that all the people I had known in my early life were dead—dead for a long, long time. I knew then that I was different from the rest. About the same time others began to notice I was different. They became suspicious of me. Some of them resented me. Others thought I was some sort of evil spirit. Finally I had to flee the tribe. I became a skulking outcast. That was when I began to learn the principles of survival."

"And those principles?"

"You keep a low profile. You don't stand out. You attract no attention to yourself. You cultivate a cowardly attitude. You are never brave. You take no risks. You let others do the dirty work. You never volunteer. You skulk and run and hide. You grow a skin that's thick; you don't give a damn what others think of you. You shed all your noble attributes, your social consciousness. You shuck your loyalty to tribe or folk or country. You're not a patriot. You live for yourself alone. You're an observer, never a participant. You scuttle around the edges of things. And you become so self-centered that you come to believe that no blame should attach to you, that you are living in the only logical way a man can live. You went to Roncesvalles the other day, remember?"

"Yes. I mentioned I'd been there. You said you'd heard of it."

"Heard of it. Hell, I was there the day it happened—August 15, 778. An observer, not a participant. A cowardly little bastard who tagged along behind that noble band of Gascons who did in Charlemagne. Gascons, hell. That's the fancy name for them. They were Basques, pure and simple. The meanest crew of men who ever drew the breath of life. Some Basques may be noble, but not this band. Not the kind of warriors who'd stand up face to face with the Franks. They hid up in the pass and rolled rocks down on all those puissant knights. But it wasn't the knights who held their interest. It was the wagon train. They weren't out to fight a war or to avenge a wrong. They were out for loot. Although little good it did them."

"Why do you say that?"

"It was this way," said Luis. "They knew the rest of

the Frankish army would return when the rearguard didn't come up and they had not the stomach for that. They stripped the dead knights of their golden spurs, their armor and fancy clothes, the money bags they carried and loaded all of it on the wagons and got out of there. A few miles further on, deep in the mountains, they holed up and hid. In a deep canyon where they thought they would be safe. But if they should be found, they had what amounted to a fort. A half mile or so below the place they camped, the canyon narrowed and twisted sharply. A lot of boulders had fallen down at that point, forming a barricade that could have been held by a handful of men against any assault that could be launched against it. By this time, I was a long way off. I smelled something wrong, I knew something most unpleasant was about to happen. That's another thing about this survival business. You develop special senses. You get so you can smell out trouble, well ahead of time. I heard what happened later."

He lifted the bottle and had another drink. He handed it to Boyd.

"Don't leave me hanging," said Boyd. "Tell me what did happen."

"In the night," said Luis, "a storm came up. One of those sudden, brutal summer thunderstorms. This time it was a cloudburst. My brave fellow Gascons died to the man. That's the price of bravery."

Boyd took a drink, lowered the bottle, held it to his chest, cuddling it.

"You know about this," he said. "No one else does. Perhaps no one had ever wondered what happened to those Gascons who gave Charlemagne the bloody nose. You must know of other things. Christ, man, you've lived history. You didn't stick to this area."

"No. At times I wandered. I had an itching foot. There were things to see. I had to keep moving along. I couldn't stay in one place any length of time or it would be noticed that I wasn't aging."

"You lived through the Black Death," said Boyd. "You watched the Roman legions. You heard first hand of Attila. You skulked along on Crusades. You walked the streets of ancient Athens."

"Not Athens," said Luis. "Somehow Athens was never to my taste. I spent some time in Sparta. Sparta, I tell you —that was really something."

"You're an educated man," said Boyd. "Where did you go to school?"

"Paris, for a time, in the fourteenth century. Later on at Oxford. After that at other places. Under different names. Don't try tracing me through the schools that I attended."

"You could write a book," said Boyd. "It would set new sales records. You'd be a millionaire. One book and you'd be a millionaire."

"I can't afford to be a millionaire. I can't be noticed and millionaires are noticed. I'm not in want. I've never been in want. There's always treasure for a skulker to pick up. I have caches here and there. I get along all right."

Luis was right, Boyd told himself. He couldn't be a millionaire. He couldn't write a book. In no way could he be famous, stand out in any way. In all things, he must remain unremarkable, always anonymous.

The principles of survival, he had said. And this was part of it, although not all of it. He had mentioned the art of smelling trouble, the hunch ability. There would be, as well, the wisdom, the street savvy, the cynicism that a man would pick up along the way, the expertise, the ability to judge character, an insight into human reaction, some knowledge concerning the use of power, power of every sort, economic power, political power, religious power.

Was the man still human, he wondered, or had he, in 20,000 years, become something more than human? Had he advanced that one vital step that would place him beyond humankind, the kind of being that would come after man?

"One thing more," said Boyd. "Why the Disney paintings?"

"They were painted some time later than the others," Luis told him. "I painted some of the earlier stuff in the cave. The fishing bear is mine. I knew about the grotto. I found it and said nothing. No reason I should have kept it secret. Just one of those little items one hugs to himself to make himself important. I know something you don't know—silly stuff like that. Later I came back to paint the grotto. The cave art was so deadly serious. Such terribly silly magic. I told myself painting should be fun. So I came back, after the tribe had moved and painted simply for the fun of it. How did it strike you, Boyd?"

"Damn good art," said Boyd.

"I was afraid you wouldn't find the grotto and I couldn't help you. I knew you had seen the cracks in the wall; I watched you one day looking at them. I counted on your remembering them. And I counted on you seeing the fingerprints and finding the pipe. All pure serendipity, of course. I had nothing in mind when I left the paint with the fingerprints and the pipe. The pipe, of course, was the tip-off and I was confident you'd at least be curious. But I couldn't be sure. When we ate that night, here by the campfire, you didn't mention the grotto and I was afraid you'd blew it. But when you made off with the bottle, sneaking it away, I knew I had it made. And now the big question. Will you let the world in on the grotto paintings?"

"I don't know. I'll have to think about it. What are your thoughts on the matter?"

"I'd just as soon you didn't."

"Okay," said Boyd. "Not for the time at least. Is there anything else I can do for you? Anything you want?"

"You've done the best thing possible," said Luis. "You know who I am, what I am. I don't know why that's so important to me, but it is. A matter of identity, I suppose. When you die, which I hope will be a long time from now, then, once again, there'll be no one who knows. But the knowledge that one man did know, and what is more important, understood, will sustain me through the centuries. A minute—I have something for you."

He rose and went into the tent, came back with a sheet of paper, handing it to Boyd. It was a topographical survey of some sort.

"I've put a cross on it," said Luis. "To mark the spot."

"What spot?"

"Where you'll find the Charlemagne treasure of Roncesvalles. The wagons and the treasure would have been carried down the canyon in the flood. The turn in the canyon and the boulder barricade I spoke of would have blocked them. You'll find them there, probably under a deep layer of gravel and debris."

Boyd looked up questioningly from the map.

"It's worth going after," said Luis. "Also it provides another check against the validity of my story."

"I believe you," said Boyd. "I need no further evidence."

"Ah, well!" said Luis, "it wouldn't hurt. And now, it's time to go."

"Time to go! We have a lot to talk about."

"Later, perhaps," said Luis. "We'll bump into one another time to time. I'll make a point we do. But now it's time to go."

He started down the path and Boyd sat watching him. After a few steps, Luis halted and half-turned back to Boyd.

"It seems to me," he said in explanation, "it's always time to go."

Boyd stood and watched him move down the trail toward the village. There was about the moving figure a deep sense of loneliness—the most lonely man in all the world.

SCORCHED SUPPER
ON NEW NIGER

Suzy McKee Charnas

Here's a rousing, and sometimes very funny, adventure story set on a far planet: a tale of a woman escaping a plot to rob her of her starship. She seeks sanctuary on the planet New Niger, whose unusual society presents surprises for her . . . and for her antagonists when they track her down.

Suzy McKee Charnas achieved instant fame in science fiction with her first novel, *Walk to the End of the World,* and its sequel, *Motherlines.* Her latest novel is *The Vampire Tapestry,* and she's currently writing the third book of the trilogy begun with her first two novels. (Charnas, not incidentally, spent two years working as a Peace Corps volunteer in Nigeria, so the extrapolated society of New Niger is based on first-hand knowledge.)

BOB W. NETCHKAY WANTED MY SHIP AND I
was damned if I was going to let him have it.

It was the last of the Steinway space fleet that my sister
Nita and I had inherited from our aunt Juno. Aunt Juno
had been a great tough lady of the old days and one hell
of an administrator, far better alone than us two Steinway
sisters together. I was young when she died, but smart
enough to know that I was a hell of a pilot; so I hired an
administrator to run the line for Nita and me.

Bob Netchkay administrated himself a large chunk of
our income, made a bunch of deliberately bad deals, and
secretly bought up all my outstanding notes after a disas-
trous trading season. I threw him out, but he walked away
with six of my ships. I lost nine moré on my own. Then
my sister Nita married the bastard and took away with her
all the remaining ships but one, my ship, the *Sealyham
Eggbeater*.

And I'd mortgaged that to raise money for a high risk,
high profit cargo in hopes of making a killing. But there
were delays on Droslo, repairs to be made at Coyote Station, and the upshot was that Bob had gotten his hands
on my mortgage. Now he was exercising his rights under
it to call it early, while I was still racing for the one
nearby dealer not trade-treatied to my competitors. His
message was waiting for me when I woke that morning
someplace between Rico and the Touchgate system.

Ripotee had checked in the message for me. He sat on

the console chewing imaginary burrs out from between his paw pads. No comment from him. He was probably in one of those moods in which he seemed to feel that the best way to preserve his catlike air of mystery was keeping his mouth shut and acting felinely aloof.

I read my message, smacked the console, and bounced around the cabin yelling and hugging my hand. Then I said, "This is short range, from 'The Steinway Legal Department,' which means that creep Rily in Cabin D of our flagship—I mean the Netchkay pirate ship. They're close enough to intercept me before I can reach my buyer on Touchgate Center. Bob will get my ship and my cargo and find a way to keep both."

Ripotee yawned delicately, curling his pink tongue.

I wiped the console and cut every signal, in or out, that might help Bob to home in on me again. Then I set an automatic jig course to complicate his life. Fast evasive tactics would cost me heavily in fuel but still leave me enough to get to Red Joy Power Station, an outpost on Touchgate Six that was closer to me than my original buyer. Red Joy is an arm of Eastern Glory, the China combine that is one of the great long-hauling companies. I could make Red Joy before Bob caught me, dump my cargo with the Chinese for the best price they would give me, and nip out again.

The Chinese run an admirable line, knowing how to live well on little in these times of depression. They're arrogant in a falsely humble way, lack daring and imagination as Aunt Juno taught me to define those terms, and think very little of anything not Chinese. But they are honest and I could count on them to give me fair value for my cargo.

On the other hand, though the Steinway ships are short haulers, they are the only short haulers that can travel among star systems without having to hitch costly rides with long haulers like the Chinese. We are in competition, of a sort. The Chinese don't like competition on principle; so they don't much like Steinways.

Ripotee was observing the course readouts glowing on the wall. "Red Joy," he remarked, "used to be the trademark of underwear marketed in China in the days of Great Mao."

"At worst they would impound my ship," I said, "but they'd still pay me for what's in it."

Ripotee coughed. "About our cargo," he said. His tail thumped the top of the console. "I was mouse hunting this morning in the hold." I kept mice on the *Eggbeater* to eat up my crumbs and to keep Ripotee fit and amused. "All that pod is souring into oatmeal."

I sat there and spattered my instruments with tears.

Pod is one of the few really valuable alien trade items to have been found in the known universe. It integrates with any living system it's properly introduced to and realigns that system into a new balance that almost always turns out to be beneficial. People are willing to pay a lot for a pod treatment. But if pod gets contaminated with organic matter it integrates on its own and turns into "oatmeal," a sort of self-digested sludge which quickly becomes inert and very smelly and hard to clean up.

I hadn't had the time or the money to compartmentalize the hold of the *Eggbeater*. If some of the pod was soured, it was all soured.

"New Niger," Ripotee murmured. His eyes were sleepy blue slits, contemplating the wall charts. "We could reach New Niger faster than Netchkay could. They would buy the *Eggbeater* and fight Bob afterward to keep it."

I sat paralyzed with indecision. The New Nigerians certainly would buy the *Sealyham Eggbeater*, given the chance.

It was to keep my ship out of such hands as theirs that Bob was so anxious to take it over. All the other Steinways are later models, set to blow themselves up if strangers go poking around in their guts. This protects the Steinway secret: what Aunt Juno did to fit her short haul ships for travel between systems without hitching rides at the extortioners' rates that long haulers charge. An engineer could dig into my ship, though, and come out unscathed to report that Aunt Juno had simply modified the straight-and-tally system in a particular manner with half a dozen counter-clock Holbein pins, without disturbing the linkup with the stabilizers and the degreasing works. Everybody knows the general principles, but nobody outside of us Steinways knows the exact arrangement.

The Chinese, long haulers exclusively, wouldn't be interested. They would only take my ship to tuck it away out of commission so its secret couldn't be used by anybody else to cut down their income from giving hitches.

But the Africans of New Niger ran short haul ships and were long time competitors of the Steinway Line on the in-system short haul routes. They could use Aunt Juno's secret, if they had it, to bounce from system to system cheap, as we did, and wipe out our advantage.

Ripotee said, "Or you could just give up and let Netchkay have the ship. A lot of people would say you should. He's a good administrator." I took a swipe at him, but he eluded me with a graceful leap onto the food synthesizer, which burped happily and offered me a cup of steaming ersatz. "He's a North American," Ripotee continued, "a go-getter, who's trying to rebuild North American prestige——"

"To build himself, you mean, on my ships and my sister's treachery!"

"The Captain's always right," Ripotee said, "in her own ship."

I drank the ersatz and glared at the wall, ignoring for the moment the instruments blinking disaster warnings at me: Bob's ship was following my jig course already. If I was starting to pick him up, he would be picking me up too, first in signals and then in reality.

Among the instruments that gave the walls their baroque look of overdone detail I had stuck a snapshot of a New Nigerian captain I had encountered once, closely. What were the chances that somebody down there would know where Barnabas was these days? It would make a difference to know that I had one friend on New Niger.

My console jumped on, and there was a splintery image of Bob Netchkey's swarthy, handsome face. He looked grave and concerned, which made me fairly pant with hatred.

"You got my offer, Dee," he said in a honey voice.

If I turned off again he would think I was too upset to deal with him. I looked him in the eye and did not smile.

"Did you?" he pressed. He faced me full on, obscuring the predatory thrust of his beaky features.

"I know all about this final stage of your grab project, yes," I said.

He shook his head. "No, Dee, you don't understand. I'm thinking about the family now." He had changed his name to Steinway on marrying Nita, which was good for business but bad for my blood pressure. "I've talked this over with Nita and she agrees; the only way to handle it right is together, as a family."

I said, "I have no family."

Nita came and looked over his shoulder at me, her round, tanned face reproachful. I almost gagged: Nita, charter member of the New Lambchop League, sweet and slinky and one pace behind "her" man, pretending she knew nothing about business. She had dumped me as a partner for this ambitious buccaneer because he would play along with her frills and her protect-me-I'm-weak line. I think Aunt Juno had hoped to lead her in another direction by leaving half of the Steinway fleet to her. But Nita was part of the new swing back to "romance," a little lost lambchop, not an admiral of the spaceways.

"We're still sisters, Dee." She blinked her black eyes at me under her naked brows. She had undergone face stiffening years ago to create the supposedly alluring effect of enormous, liquid orbs in a mysterious mask.

"You may be somebody's sister," I snapped. "I'm not."

She whispered something to Bob.

He nodded. "I know. You see how bad things have gotten, Dee, when you get into a worse temper than ever at the sight of your own sister. Sometimes I think it's a chemical imbalance, that temper of yours, it's not natural. Nita has to go, she's got things to do. I just wanted you to know that anything I suggest has already been run past her, and she's in complete agreement. Isn't that right, Nita?"

Nita nodded, fluttered her tapered fingers in my direction, and whisked her svelte, body-suited figure out of the picture. Where she had been I saw something I recognized behind Bob's shoulder: one of those stretched guts from the Wailies of Tchan that's supposed to show images of the future if you expose it to anti-gravity. It had never shown Aunt Juno these two connivers running her flagship.

"Well?" I said. I sipped the cold dregs of my ersatz.

Bob lowered sincerely at me. "Look, Dee, I'm older than you and a lot more experienced at a lot of things, like running a successful trade business. And I'm very concerned about the future of the Steinway name. You and I have been at odds for a long time, but you don't really think I've gone to all this trouble just to junk the line, do you? I did what I had to do, that's all."

He stopped and glared past me; I turned. Ripotee had a hind foot stuck up in the air and was licking his crotch. He paused to say loudly, "I'm doing what I have to do too."

"Get that filth off the console!" Bob yelled. I chortled. He got control of himself and plowed on: "Already I've restored your family's reputation; Steinway is once again a name held in commercial respect. And I can do more.

"You don't realize; things are going to get rougher than you can imagine, and it won't be any game for a free-lance woman with nobody to back her up. Look around you: times are changing, it's a tougher and tougher short haul market, and women are pulling back into softer, older ways. What will you be out there, one of a handful of female freaks left over from the days of Juno and her type? Freaks don't get work, not when there are good, sound men around to take it away from them. You'll be a pauper.

"I don't want that. Nita doesn't want it. You don't want it. Give up and face facts."

He paused, the picture of a man carried away by his own eloquence. And a pleasure to look at too, if I hadn't been burning up with loathing for his very tripes. Even without the frame of curling black hair and high collar, the subtly padded shoulders and chest—the New Lamb-chops weren't the only ones looking back in time to more romantic eras—Bob was handsome, and very masculine looking in a hard, sharp-cut way.

He knew it and used it, posing there all earnest drama, to give me a minute to react, to cue him as to how all this was setting with me. I said, deadpan, "What's the deal?"

He looked pained. "Not a deal; a way for us all to come out all right. You give me the *Sealyham Eggbeater*, pull out of the business, take a holiday someplace, grow out your hair. In exchange for your ship I'll give you a one-third inalienable interest in the Steinway stock and a nice desk job for income. But I get to run things my own way without interference. You keep your mouth shut and let me do what I know how to do, and I take care of you and your sister."

I was so mad I could hardly work my jaw loose enough to utter a sound. "But I don't get to do what *I* know how to do, which is to pilot a short haul ship. My answer is no."

I wiped the console and punched a new jig. Then I plugged in a tingle of electracalm and a light dose of antistress because I needed my head clear.

Ripotee lay stretched out along the sill of a viewport, curved within its curve, one paw hanging down. He liked to keep his distance when I was upset. His sapphire eyes rested on me, intent, unreadable. He had either found that he could not or decided that he would not learn to use his facial muscles for expressiveness on the human model. I couldn't interpret that masked, blunt-muzzled visage.

I said, "Ripotee, what do you know about New Niger?"

His tail started swinging, lashing. That was something he had never been able to control. He was excited, onto something.

"Jungle," he said. "Tall trees and vines and close underbrush. Good smells, earth and voidings and growth. Not like here."

"You've got cabin fever," I snorted. I was already setting up a fast but indirect course for Singlet, New Niger's main port. "Aren't your mice entertaining you enough any more?"

I reached out to pat his head, but he jerked away. He didn't say, Don't do that, though he could have. Sometimes he was pleased to show me the superfluity of that human invention, speech. We had been in space a longish while. Ripotee got just as irritable as anyone else—as me.

The autodrives took over at full speed on a wild zigzag course. Strapping in tight, I signalled Ripotee, over the shout of the engines, to get into his harness. I tried to cut the graveys, but the switch stuck: it was going to be a rough ride. I felt reckless. Bob was close; if he tried to grab the *Eggbeater* now, he'd run a good chance of collision and of getting himself killed, if not all of us.

There was a lot of buffeting and slinging as the ship shunted from course to course. I kept my eyes on Ripotee, not wanting to see evidence of impossible strain, of damage, of imminent ruin on the dials that encrusted the walls. He lay flat in his nest of straps secured to a padded niche over the internal monitor banks, his claws bradded into the fibres. He was Siamese, fawn beneath and seal-brown on top, a slight shading of stripes on his upper legs, cheeks, and forehead. He had street blood in him, none of your overbred mincing and neurosis there. I hoped he wasn't about to come to a crashing end on account of my feud with Netchkay.

I am a natural pilot but not what they call a sheep-herder, the kind who thrives on being alone in space. A good short haul ship can be managed by one operator and can carry more cargo that way, and I don't like crowding. So I had acquired Ripotee instead of a human partner.

He had been a gift as a kitten, along with a treatment contract on him for a place out in the Tic Tacs where they use pod infections to mutate animals upward—if humanizing their brains is actually a step in that direction. He came out of his pod fever with a good English vocab-ulary and a talent for being aggravating in pursuit of his own independence.

Even at his worst he was the companion I needed, a reminder of something besides the bright sterility of space and its stars. There wasn't anything else. We had yet to find alien life of true intelligence. Meanwhile, the few Earth animals that had survived the Oil Age were all the more important to us—to those of us who cared about such things, anyway.

The ship dropped hard, slewing around to a new head-ing. Straps bit my skin. I thought of the time when, after a brush with some name-proud settlers on Le Cloue, I had asked Ripotee, "Do you want to change your name? Maybe you don't like being called 'Ripotee?'" I was thinking that it was hard for him to pronounce it, as he had some trouble with t's.

He had said, "I don't care, I don't have to say it. I can say 'I,' just like a person. Anyway, Ripotee isn't my name; it's just your name for me."

Only later I wondered whether this proud statement covered not some private name he had for himself but the fact that he had no name except the one I had given him.

I could hardly draw breath to think with now, and I was very glad to have had no breakfast but that cup of ersatz.

Another hard swing, and I smelled rotting pod; a cargo seal must have broken and who knew what else. Ripotee let out a sudden wail—not pain, I hoped, just fear. I kept my eyes closed now. If he'd been shaken loose from his harness he could be slammed to death on the walls, just as I would be if I tried to go and help him.

One thing about Ripotee that neither of us nor his producers in the Tic Tacs knew was how long he had to live. He was approaching his first watermark, the eighth year, which if successfully passed normally qualifies a domestic cat for another seven or eight. In his case, we had no idea whether the pod infection had fitted him with a human life span to go with his amplified mind, or, given that, whether his physical small-animal frame would hold up to such extended usage. One thing was sure, enough of this battering around and he would end up just as punchy as any human pilot would.

I blacked out twice. Then everything smoothed down, and my power automatically cut as the landing beams locked on. A voice sang a peculiarly enriched English into my ears over the headset: looping vowels, a sonorous timbre—reminding me of Barnabas' voice. "Singlet Port. So now you will be boarded by a customs party. Please prepare to receive. . . ."

Prepare to give up—but never to Bob.

Ripotee was first out on New Niger. I sprung the forward hatch and a group of people came in; he padded right past them, tail in the air, none of your hanging about sniffing to decide whether or not it was worth his time to go through the doorway. Normally he's as cautious as any cat, but he is also given to wild fits of berserker courage that are part existential meanness and part tomcat.

He paused in his progress only to lay a delicate line of red down the back of a reaching hand—just an eyeblink swipe of one paw, an exclamation from the victim, and Ripotee was off, belly stretched in an ecstatic arc of all-out effort above the landing pad. Well out of reach, he paused with his tail quirked up in its play mode, glanced back, and then bounded sideways out of sight behind a heap of cartons and drums.

I had to pay a quarantine fine on him, of course. They were very annoyed to have lost any organisms he might have brought in with him that could be useful in pod experiments. The fine was partly offset by some prime wriglies they got out of me, leftovers from a visit to the swamps of Putt.

There were forms to fill out and a lot of "dash" to pay for hints on how to fill them out with the least chance of expensive mistakes. I stood in the security office, my head still fuzzy from the rough flight, and I wrote.

A young man with a long thin face like a deer's came and plucked me by the sleeve. He said in soft, accented English, "You are asked for, Missisi. Come with me please."

"Who?" I said, thinking damn it, Bob has landed, he's onto me already. I stalled. "I have these forms to finish—"

He looked at the official who had given me these books of papers and said, "Missisi Helen will see to it that everything is put right."

The official reached over, smiling, and eased the papers out from under my hand. "I did not know that Captain Steinway was a friend of Missisi Helen. Do not worry of your ship; it goes into our clean-out system because of the oatmeal."

My guide led me through corridors and once across a landing surface brilliant with sun. I wondered if this Missisi Helen was the famous Helen who had been trading from New Niger as far back as Aunt Juno's own times: a tough competitor.

We went to a hangar where a short hauler stood surrounded by half-unpacked bales and boxes and spilled fruit. For a barnyard flavor, chickens (the African lines would carry anything) ran among the feet of the passengers, who shouted and pawed through everything, looking, I supposed, for their own belongings mixed in with the scattered cargo. The mob, rumpled and steamy with their own noise and excitement, was all Black except for one skinny, shiny-bald White man in the stained white sari of a Holy Wholist missionary. He stood serenely above it all.

I picked my way along after my guide, trying not to wrinkle my nose; after all, I'd had no more opportunity for a thorough bath and fresh change of clothing than these folks had. To tell the truth, I felt nervous in that crush and scramble of people; there were so many, and I had lived without other humans for a long time.

A knot of argument suddenly burst, and a little woman in a long rose-colored dress stepped out to meet me, snapping angrily over her shoulder at a man who reached pleadingly to restrain her: "And I tell you, it is for you some of my cargo was dumped cheap at Lagos Port to make room for this, your cousin. I am surprised you did not want my very ancestor's bones thrown away so you could bring your whole family! You will pay back for my lost profits, or I will make you very sorry! Speak there to my secretary."

She faced me, one heavily braceleted arm cocked hand-on-hip, her bare, stubby feet planted wide. Her hair, a tight, springy pile of gray, was cut and shaped into an exaggerated part, like two steep hills on her head. She tipped her head back and looked down her curved, broad, delicate nose at me.

"Dee Steinway. You do not look at all like your aunt Juno."

"I favor my father's side."

"As well," she said. "Juno ran to fat in her later years. I knew her well; I am Helen Nwanyeruwa, head of Heaven Never Fail Short Hauling Limited. Why are you here, and why did Bob Netchkay land right behind you, waving pieces of paper under the noses of customs?"

Well, that was straight out, and it shook me up a little bit. Most trading people talk around things to see what all the orbits are before they set a plain course. I looked nervously at the intent faces surrounding us. I said, "He wants to take my ship."

She grimaced. "With papers; that means with laws."

"I'd rather sell the ship to you before he can slap those papers on me," I said.

"What ship?"

"Not just any ship. The Steinway *Eggbeater.*"

Her eyes were very bright. "Then it is good I have set some friends of mine here to wrapping Bob Netchkay in many, many yards of bright red tape. If you knew how often I tried to get Juno to trade me a ship of hers——" She looked me up and down, scowling now. "I don't want to have to discuss this over Netchkay's papers; so, we must hide you. Hey!" She spoke rapidly in her own language to one of her attendants, who hurried away.

Helen watched the attendant engage in an animated conversation with the Holy Wholist. "See that missionary," she commented, "how he waves his arms, he is all rattled about, he outrages as if back in his own place now, not a foreign planet. I tell you, some of these White priest people think they are still in Nineteenth Century Africa when they throw their weights around. Ah, there, something is agreed; now tell me about this ship."

I started to tell her. Somewhere in the second paragraph, one and then the other of my legs were tapped and lifted as if I were a horse being shod. I looked down. My space boots had been deftly removed. Before I could object I was wrapped in an odorous garment which I recognized disgustedly as the yards and yards of the Holy Wholist's grubby sari. The Wholist himself was gone.

"A trade," said Helen calmly, adjusting a fold of this raggedy toga into a pretty tuck at my waist.

"What, my mag shoes for his clothes? Come on!" Space boots—mag shoes, we call them—are valuable in industry for walking on metal walls and such.

"Not so simple," she said, "but in the end, yes. He said he would take nothing for his sari but a permit to preach in the markets where we do not like such interferences. I know an official who has long wanted a certain emblem for the roof of his air car, for which he would surely give a preaching permit. And among my own family there is a young man upon whose air-sled there is fixed this same fancy metal emblem—"

"Which he was willing to swap for my mag shoes," I said. "But how did you work it all out so fast?"

"Why, I am a trader, what else?" Helen said. "Did your aunt never teach you not to interrupt your elders in the middle of a story?"

"Sorry," I muttered, got annoyed with myself for being so easily chastened, and added defiantly, "But I'm not going to shave my head as bare as the Wholist's for the sake of this fool disguise." I go baldheaded in space rather than fuss with hairnets and stiffeners and caps to keep long hair from swimming into my eyes in non-gravey. Approaching landfall, I always start it growing out again.

Helen shrugged. Then she whirled on her attendants and clapped her hands, shouting, "Is there no car to take these passengers to town?"

The passengers grabbed their things and were herded toward an ancient gas truck parked outside. The Heaven Never Fail Short Hauling Line seemed to deal in some very small consignments. The area was still littered with boxes and sacks. These were being haggled over by Helen's people and the drivers of air-sleds who loaded up and drove off.

Helen caught my arm and took me with her to a raised loading platform from which she could observe the exodus while she asked me about the *Sealyham Eggbeater*. She knew all the right questions to ask, about construction, running costs, capacity, maintenance record, logged travel history (and unlogged). When she heard of the long hauls that the little ship had made, she nodded shrewdly.

"So it has Juno's modifications; unshielded, as I have heard—it can be examined?"

"Yes."

"You do not know the specifications of the modifications yourself, do you?"

"I'm a pilot, not an engineer," I said huffily. It embarrasses me that I can't keep that sort of thing in my head.

She asked about the name of the ship.

I shrugged. "I don't know about '*Sealyham*,'" but "*Eggbeater*' dates from when the Kootenay Line ran ships shaped like eggs and it became a great fashion. Aunt Juno didn't want to spend money to modify our own ships, so we stuck with our webby, messy look and renamed all of them some kind of eggbeater."

Helen smiled and nodded. "Now I remember. At the time I suggested taking slogans for her ships as we do here. You know my ships' names: *In God Starry Hand; No Rich Without Tears; Pearl of the Ocean Sky*. I have twenty-seven ships." She waved at the hangar floor. "You see how quickly my cargo is gone. I have a warehouse too but only small, and this is my one hangar. My goods move all the time, and my ships are moving them. Yams in the yam-house start no seedlings."

"Yams?" I said. I was beginning to feel a little feverish, probably from the antipoddies I'd taken before landing.

"You must scatter yams in the ground," Helen said impatiently. "In Old Africa. Yams don't grow here; we must import. But the saying is true everywhere, so my ships fly, my goods travel. I named the ships in old style pidgin talk from Africa, in honor of my beginnings—in my ancestors' lorry lines. All the lorries bore such fine slogans.

"My personal ship is *Let Them Say*. It means, I care nothing how people gossip on me, only how they work for me—"

She fell abruptly silent. Alarmed, I looked where she

was looking. A machine was in the doorway I'd come in by, its scanner turning to sweep the hangar while its sensor arm patted about on the floor and door jambs.

Helen signaled to one of the freight sleds with a furious gesture. It lifted toward us. She tapped at her ear—that was when I noticed the speaker clipped there in the form of an earring—and said bitingly into a mike on her collar, "Robot sniffers are working this port, why were they not spotted, why was I not told?"

Jerked out of the spell of her exotic authority, I remembered my danger and I remembered Ripotee: "I had a companion, a cat—"

"It must find you, then. These machines come from the Steinway flagship."

I looked around frantically for some sign of Ripotee. "Don't you have to stay a little to make sure everything gets done right here?"

"My people will do for me. Sit down, that sniffer is turned this way."

With surprising strength, Helen yanked me onto the sled beside her; the sled, driven by a heavy girl in a bright blue jumper, slewed around and sped us swiftly out into the bright sunshine.

We headed toward a cluster of domes and spires some distance away. The sled skimmed over broad stubbly fields between high, shaggy green walls that were stands of trees and undergrowth: outposts of the jungle Ripotee had spoken of. Other sleds followed and preceded ours, most of them fully loaded.

"Where are we going?" I said.

"To market, of course."

I remembered that Helen was an old opponent in the marketplaces of the worlds, and it occurred to me that perhaps she was simply keeping me scarce until she could trade me in for a good profit. I checked the driver's instruments out of the corner of my eye, gauging the possibility of jumping for it and hiding out on my own in the jungle or something, just in case I had to. Helen must have seen me because she laughed and patted my knee.

"Ah, my runaway White girl, what are you looking for? Is it that you are suspicious of me now? Netchkay flashes his papers about, claiming that you are space-sick and need to be protected from yourself, or why would you flee from your own family to the home of the trade rivals of the great Steinway Line? You think I might sell you to Bob Netchkay.

"Foolish! I am your friend here, and not only because of Juno and her invention, which can make me very much richer; not even only for the sake of the Steinway Line as it was in its heyday, all those bright, sharp little ships running rings around the big men and their big plans. Yes; not only for these reasons am I your friend, but because women know how to help each other here. The knowledge comes in the blood, from so many generations that lived as many wives to one man. They all competed like Hell, but if the husband treated one wife badly, the others made complaint, and were sick, and scorched his food, until he behaved nicely again. So, here is Bob Netchkay being nasty with you; I will play co-wife, and for you I will scorch bad Bob's supper."

Now, why couldn't my own sister Nita take that line?

"That man is a fungus," I muttered.

"Now, that is the proper tone," Helen said approvingly, "for a missionary talking about one of another sect." Then she added with serene and perfect confidence, "As for Netchkay, I will shortly think what to do about him.

"First tell me just what you yourself want out of it."

"My ship back and some money to start flying." On a sudden inspiration I added, "My mag shoes were worth much more than this Holy Wholey rag I'm wearing. You have to count them in any deal between us."

She let that pass and leaned forward to snap out an order to our driver. "There is the market," she said to me, indicating a high translucent dome with landing pads hitched round it in a circle like a halo on a bald head.

I scowled. "I know you have business there, but what good is the market to me?"

"Bob Netchkay's robot sniffers cannot enter on your trail. No servos are permitted on the market floor. They are not agile enough for the crowds and always get trampled and pushed about until they break, and then they sit there in the way with their screamers on for assistance, driving everyone mad. In there you must play missionary a little. White missionaries are not remarkable here on New Niger; if those sniffers ask of you outside the market from people coming out, they will learn nothing.

"Sit still and be quiet till we land, I must listen to the trading reports."

She turned up the volume on the button communicator in her earring and ignored me. I studied her as we neared the market building. She didn't look old enough to have known Aunt Juno, but it never occurred to me to doubt that she had. I thought I saw in her the restless, swift energy of my aunt. In Helen it was keen ambition, right out there on the surface for all to see. Helen even had the same alert, eager poise of the head that Aunt Juno had so noticeably developed along with her progressive nearsightedness.

She shooed me out onto a ribbon lift which lowered me to the edge of the immense seethe and roar of the jam-packed market floor. She herself boarded a little floater. That way she could oversee the trading at her booths, darting like an insect from one end of the hall to the other.

I took up a position as deep within the crowd as I could elbow myself room. On my right a fat woman hawked chili-fruits from Novi Nussbaum; on my left squawking chickens were passed over the heads of the crowd to their purchasers. Women carrying loads on their heads strode between buyers and sellers, yelling at each other in the roughly defined aisles between stalls.

I shouted myself what I imagined might be the spiel of a Holy Wholist: "The sky of New Niger is the sky of Old Earth; our souls are pieces of one great eggshell enclosing the universe!" and similar rubbish. Some of the crowd stopped around me; about a dozen women, and two men with red eyes and the swaying stance of drunks.

Suddenly there was a shriek from the chili-fruit woman. Over a milling of excited marketers I could just glimpse her slapping among her wares with her shoe.

Helen's floater zipped in; she seized the shouting woman by the arm and spoke harshly into her ear, reducing her to silence. I managed to insinuate myself through the crowd, which was already beginning to disperse in search of more interesting matters.

Helen said to me in a venomous whisper, "Did you hear it? This woman says she saw moving, maybe, a sweetsucker among the chili-fruits. A sweetsucker, can you imagine, carried all the way from Novi Nussbaum with my cargo!"

The vendor, eyes cast down, muttered, "I saw it, I am telling you—sweetsucker or not. A long thing like what they call snake in Iboland, but hairy, and making a nasty sound," and she drew her lips back and made clicking sounds with her tongue and widely chomping teeth, like a kid who hasn't learned yet to chew with its mouth closed. It was just the sound Ripotee makes when he's eating.

Helen rounded on the woman again, snarling threats: "If you spread rumors of sweetsuckers drying up my Novi Nussbaum fruits, I will see you not only never sell for me again but find every market on New Niger closed to you!"

I bent down and hunted quietly around the stand, calling Ripotee's name. Not quietly enough: some friendly people at the next stall over turned to watch and saw my religious attire. Identifying my behavior as some exotic prayer ceremony, they cheerfully took up my call as a chant, clapping their hands: "Rip-o-tee! Rip-o-tee!"

Helen took me firmly by the wrist. "What are you doing?"

"This vending woman must have seen my cat."

"And by now many people in the market have your cat's name in their mouths, which is very foolish and not good for us. Netchkay is clever, and I just now get word that seeing he could not introduce his machines here to find if you are at the market, he has sent instead your own sister, Nita Steinway. She will know that cat's name if she hears it spoken, and she will look for you. So we must go at once, though it means I break my business early, which I do not like at all."

She propelled me onto the floater with her, hovering there a moment to give curt orders to the vending woman: "Go take these chili-fruits to put water in them and plump them up, so no one will believe this nonsense about sweetsuckers!" We rose straight for one of the roof hatches.

I said, "Helen, my cat—"

"Oh, your cat, this cat is driving me mad!" she cried, shooting us out onto one of the landing pads again and bustling me sharply into a waiting town skipper. It was an elegant model with hardwood and bright silver fittings inside. She drove it herself, shying us through the sky in aggressive swoops that made other skippers edge nervously out of our way.

"Now listen, is it this cat you want to talk about or diddling Bob Netchkay? If you are interested, I have arranged it; I have set engineers to copying the Steinway modification from your ship. When plans are drawn we will show them to Netchkay. If he wants them sold to every short hauler in the business, he can continue to worry you. If he agrees to leave you alone, he will have only one competitor with the secret of long hauling in short haul ships: myself."

Chuckling, she sideslipped us past a steeple that had risen unexpectedly before us. "Oh, he will grind his teeth to powder, and I—I will be the one to carry on the true spirit of the Steinway Line."

I looked down at the bubble buildings we were skimming over, interspersed with what looked like not very satisfactorily transplanted palm trees, all brown and drooping. I felt lonesome and exposed in the hands of Helen Nwanyeruwa above that alien townscape.

We landed on the roof of a square, solid cement building. Helen shouted for attendants to come moor the skipper and for a guide to show me to my room. She said kindly, "Go there now, I have made a surprise for you. Maybe then you will stop wailing after this cat and enjoy my party tonight."

The surprise was Barnabas, sitting on the bed and grinning. He had grown a curl of beard along his jawline and wore not a captain's jumper but tan cord pants and a gown-like shirt of green and black.

"Barnabas!" I said. "What in the worlds—"

"Everybody here knows you and I have met and made connection before. New Niger is the market place of gossip."

"Better to make connection than to just talk about it," I said and began tossing off my clothes. I'd forgotten that peculiarly electrical expression of New Nigerian English; it set me off. I was suddenly so horny I could hardly see straight.

In space I forget; most of us do, though we like to keep up the legend of rampant pilots whooping it up in free fall. Actually, all that is inhibited out there, maybe by stress. But it comes back fast and furious when you are aground again.

Barnabas had the presence of mind to get up and shut the door. He knew right away what was happening and threw himself into it with a cheerful, warm gusto that had me almost in tears. I finally had to beg off because he was making me sore with all that driving, and he tumbled off me sideways, laughing: "Sorry, I didn't mean to hurt you, but it is long since I did this with a crew-cut woman!"

"It's the first thing I've done on New Niger that didn't feel all foreign and strange," I said. "Let's do it again, but this time I'll get on top."

Later on a small boy came padding in with his eyes downcast bringing us towels, and padded out again. Two towels.

Pilots tend to be a little prudish about these things, which are after all more important and isolated incidents for us than for your average planet-bunny with all his or her opportunities. "Don't you people know what servo-mechs are for?" I grumbled.

Barnabas was stroking my throat. "You have a beautiful neck, just like the belly of a snake. No, no, that is compliment! Don't mind the youngsters—Helen gives employment to many children of relatives. She is very rich, you know."

"How did he know there were two of us needing towels?"

"Everyone knows I was up here, and what else does a man do with a woman. They forget that I am a captain myself and might have business to talk with you. To people here, I am just a man, good only for fun and fathering. . . ."

At his sudden glance of inquiry and concern I shook my head. "Lord no, Barnabas, I shot myself full of antipoddies before leaving the ship. Otherwise I'd be nailed to the toilet with the runs." All pilots use antis on landfall. You have to make a special effort to conceive.

"I have several children now," Barnabas said, and his voice took a bitter edge. "But unfortunately no ship. A falling out with my employer." He smiled wrily. "I am sorry for myself. What have you been doing, Deedee? I hear you have a lot of trouble with Bob Netchkay and your sister."

I explained. He grimaced and shook his head, half condemning, half admiring "I told you long ago, that man is to be watched; he has plenty of brains and drive, and with your clever sister to help him he is making a great company to rival even the Chinese."

"He's a fungus," I said. I liked that word.

Barnabas laughed. "Let's not argue in the shower."

We stood in the wet corner under the fine spray shooting in from the walls and talked, rubbing and sponging each other and picking our hairs out of the drain. Then we toweled off, got back on the bed, and soon had to clean up all over again.

"Can you stay a while?" I asked, stroking the long muscles woven across his back. "You're doing me a lot of good, Barnabas."

"Me too," he said. "To be free of the worry, you know, of not making babies. . . . They like a man to be fertile here." He shrugged and changed the subject. "Tell me about Ripotee. I was thinking of him just now; he used to complain that it was disgusting, us two together—"

"I think he was just jealous, not really overcome with horror at our inordinate hugenesses rolling around together. I tried taking a female cat aboard for him, but he couldn't stand her." I started to cry.

Barnabas hugged me and made soothing sounds into my frizz of new grown hair. I blubbed out how Ripotee had left the ship before I could do anything, even shoot him with antis. "He was in one of his crazy derring-do fits. He kept up with me as far as the market, but since then I don't know—Helen doesn't care. Maybe she's already heard that he's been caught and eaten. From what I've seen, no animals survive here except humans and chickens. People must be crazy for a taste of red meat—"

"Not cat meat, it is awful!" Barnabas exploded.

We curled up together and talked about Ripotee. I told Barnabas how it made me feel so peculiar to think back to the days when Ripotee had been a dumb cat that I could shove around and tickle and yell at, as people do with cats, without a thought. I'd teased him, called him all kinds of names, grabbed him up, and scrubbed him under the chin 'til he half-fainted with delight.

I didn't do things like that any more.

"Don't be put off," Barnabas said. "It is only his pride that keeps him from flopping down for a chin rub just as he used to do, and he would love for you to push him over and rub his chin anyway."

I shook my head. "He's changed since you knew him. I think it's all that reading. When he lies relaxed with his eyes half shut looking at nothing, I know he's not falling asleep any more; now he's brooding. Like a person."

Barnabas stood up and pulled on his shorts. "He is luckier than a person. If he were a mere man, he would be protesting always how all he needs are his mates, he must have good fellows to drink with and gossip and play cards."

"This afternoon you and I certainly proved that's a lie," I said smugly.

He didn't smile; he wrinkled his nose and sat down again, putting his arm around my shoulders. "But this is what they say here, and the women of New Niger can make it stick, too, I tell you. You know, Dee, I might have inherited wealth as you did, but my great grandfather was too ambitious. He was seduced by the big trade of international business like many other men in Nigeria. He jumped to put his money into the big boom of Europe and America, just as he had jumped right into Christianity and having only one wife at a time.

"So then the wars and the bad weather came and broke all the high finance, and him with it, among all the rest. He was left nothing but a worn out yam farm in an over-crowded, overworked corner of Iboland in the Eastern Region. Nobody had much of anything in Nigeria then, except some of the women traders with lorry fleets—the lorry mammies—and those who went even on foot from market to market, dealing haircombs and matches and sugar by the cube. They became the ones with funds to put into space travel.

"So here I am on the world they settled, trying to get rich myself. And who do you think is my boss, the one that is giving me trouble and keeping me grounded?"

"A woman," I guessed.

"A cousin of Helen's, and a woman, yes." He slipped on one of his plastic sandals. "The other men say, take it easy, relax and enjoy some drinking."

I felt less than completely sympathetic; I heard that angry, self-pitying tone again and didn't like it. I said lightly, "These women of New Niger are some tough ladies."

He answered with a grudging pride: "Listen, long ago, when your ancestor-mothers were chaining themselves to the gates of politicians' houses, my ancestor-mothers were rousing each other to riot against the English colonials' plan to take census of women and women's property. It was thought this would lead to special taxing of these women, for even then there were many wives who were farmers and petty traders on their own. They made what is still called the Women's War. Thousands rose up in different places to catch the chiefs the English had appointed and to sit on them—it means to frighten and belittle a man with angry, insulting songs and to spoil his property. They tore some public buildings to the ground. In all some fifty women were shot dead by the authorities, and many more were wounded—that is how frightened the government were. No tax was applied, and the English had a big inquiry in their parliament on how to rule Iboland.

"Helen herself is named for the woman who began the War. On being told in her own yard to count her goats and children, this woman shouted to the official who said it, 'Was your mother counted?' and seized him by the throat."

I could well believe it and said so.

Barnabas got up again.

"Where are you off to?" I said. Talking with him like this was almost like old times together in space.

"I must get ready for the party; you should too. Tonight Helen Nwanyeruwa holds a feast for the spirit of her ancestor the lorry mammy. Wealthy Missisi Helen had the ancestor-bones brought here on one of her ships; the spirit would not dare to displease her by staying behind."

He bent and rested both hands on my shoulders, looking intently into my face. "It is very good to see you, Deedee."

The outer surfaces of the house were illuminated so that the walled courtyard was brilliantly lit for the party. Family and guests milled around on the quickie grass, grown for the evening in an hour to cover where the plastic paving had been rolled back.

Wrapped in my Holy Wholist sari, worn properly this time with nothing underneath—it didn't bother me, I often go naked in my ship—I milled around with the best of them. As a missionary I was not expected to join the dancing, for which I was grateful. I felt nervous and shy and alien, and I wandered over toward where Helen sat on a huge couch beside the shrine she had had erected: a concrete stele with the image of a truck on it. On the way I passed a line of men and a line of women dancing opposite each other, and Barnabas stepped to my side out of the men's line. His skin was shiny with sweat. He caught me around the waist and murmured in my ear, "You and I do our own private dancing, Deedee, later on."

As we approached, Helen patted the slowflow plastic next to her, making room for me but not for Barnabas. He joined the crowd of retainers on her right.

Helen wore African clothing of sparkling silverweave and a piece of the same cloth tied around her head into an elaborate turban. Even her white plastic sandals couldn't spoil the effect. She was beautiful; by comparison, those around her who affected the fashionable billowing Victorian look of the new Romanticism seemed puny and laughable.

Sitting beside her wiry, tense body on the surface that slowly moulded to my shape, I felt protected by her feisty energy. Yet her boldness in having me up there in full view endangered me; suppose Bob had spies here? The drums thundered in the spaces of the courtyard. I gulped down the drink she handed me. It tasted like lemonade filtered through flannel.

I shivered. "Helen, what if—an enemy hears the drums and comes to your party?"

She looked at me out of the corner of her eye and said with haughty dismissiveness, "No enemy has been invited."

This was repeated among the others around us and brought much laughter. Of course she must have robot guards, computer security systems and so on, I thought; but I felt edgy.

Barnabas leaned toward us. "Even so, Missisi Helen, it might be wise to take extra care. I myself and a few friends have devised a special power hookup—"

Helen set down her drink and turned to him. "Don't worry yourself about these things, Barnabas; you will only get in the way. You are a good, strong young man, and Missisi Alicia tells me you have fathered a fine baby in her family. Go and drink from my private casks, over there, you and your friends. Go amuse yourselves."

Barnabas spun and forced his way out through the crowd toward the dancers—then swerved sharply back toward the bar.

"Why are you so hard on him?" I said.

"These boys get too big ideas of themselves, especially the young ones who have been out in space," Helen replied, reaching for a fresh drink from a tray offered her. "They begin thinking their fathers ran fleets of lorries too."

Everybody whooped over this. Helen was excited, feeding off the high spirits of those who fed off her own. She flung out her arm, pointing at a young man in the forefront of a huddle of others who had been looking our way on and off for quite a while. He resisted his friends' efforts to push him forward.

"You see that boy there," she said, pitching her voice so that everyone near the ancestor shrine must hear; "he has been chasing after that girl, my Anne, who is still nearly a baby, but he has not taken up his courage to speak to me about her. And he boasts that his father hunts lions with a spear in Old Africa, where there are fewer lions than here on New Niger." She snatched up a pebble and pitched it not to strike but to startle into squawking flight one of the ubiquitous chickens pecking for scraps around a food table. "See what kind of lions we have here! Just such as that boy's father hunts, just so fierce!"

At last, something familiar—the suitor who didn't suit Mother. "Anne is one of your daughters?"

"Oh no," Helen replied proudly, "one of my wives."

I didn't know what to say. Helen grinned at me, plainly pleased with the effect of her words.

"I have lots of wives," she added with great satisfaction. "It was always Ibo custom that a woman rich enough to support wives could marry so; and I am very rich. My Anne will find herself a young man who makes her happy for a while. No fear, in time she will bring me a child of that union to be brother or sister to the children of my own body and my other wives'."

She gave me an affectionate hug, chuckling. "Just as you look now, so shocked, that is how your aunt looked when I married my first wife. Even once I told her, 'Juno, you should have daughters to comfort your old age and inherit your goods. Do as I do, there must be some White way with many documents.' But she said, 'I only have time for one creation, and that is the Steinway Line.' Then she laughed because it was the kind of grand talk men use to impress each other; we both knew the petty trading would go on as always, while the men heroes choke on their grand schemes.

"I live by that petty trading, and I live well, as you see. Come make fast to my own good fortune, as in one of our African sayings: if a person is not successful at trading in the market, it would be cowardly to run away; instead she should change her merchandise.

"Give up wishing to be Admiral of a trading fleet, and say you will come work for my company, my bold White flyer."

I was looking at Barnabas. He danced, his shoulders rippling like water shunting down a long container, first to one end and then to the other. A bit wobbly, in fact; as he turned without seeing me I realized that it was not only the ecstasy of the dance that sealed his eyes. He was drunk. I was alone among strangers.

I shook my head.

"You are too stubborn," Helen said, giving me a thump in the side with her elbow. But she didn't look unhappy. Maybe she thought I was just making a move in a complicated bargaining game, and approved. If I were any good at that kind of thing, I wouldn't have been in this spot with Bob. It's not the dealing I love, it's the piloting. Helen didn't know me well enough yet to really understand that. "Well," she added, "you must do what suits you, and let them say!"

Somebody screamed, there was a swirling in the crowd as one of the food tables crashed down and a girl came flying toward us, shrieking. I leaped up, thinking, Netchkay has come, someone has been hurt because of him; but I was fuddled with drink and couldn't think what to do.

Helen strode to meet the screaming girl.

"It spoke to me, the spirit of your ancestor," the girl gibbered, twisting her head to stare wide-eyed over her shoulder at the tumbled ruin of the food table. "I was serving food, Missisi Helen, as you told me, and a little high voice said from someplace down low, behind me, 'A piece of light meat please, cut up small on a plate.' I looked in the dark by the wall, I saw eyes like red hot coins."

I hurried unsteadily over to where two servos were already sucking up the mess and getting in each other's way.

Behind me I heard the girl: "I was afraid, Missisi. The spirit repeated, so I put down food, but then some one passed behind me and I heard the spirit cry, 'Get off my tail!' and it vanished. Mary thinks she stepped on it—Oh, Missisi Helen, will Mary and me be cursed?"

I shoved one of the servos aside, looking for the poor, crushed remains of Ripotee.

I found nothing but a hole in the wall, low, rounded, and utterly puzzling. I rapped on the nearest servo, which was busy wiping at some sauce with the trailing end of my sari, apparently under the impression that this was a large, handy rag.

"What's this?" I said into the speaker of the servo, pointing at the hole. "Where does it lead to?"

"Madame or sir, it is hole for fowl," creaked the servo. Madame or sir, it leads in for chickens seeking entry to this compound for the night and leads out for—"

"All right, all right," I said. While addressing me the tin fool had decided the sari was beyond salvage, and had begun ingesting it into its cannister body for disposal. I yanked.

The servo clicked disapprovingly and sheared off the swallowed portion of my garment with an interior blade. I made my way back through the crowd toward Helen, rearranging the remains of my clothing and swearing to myself.

"—Not possible that my ancestor has returned as *an animal*," Helen was saying in an ominous voice. "Felicity, remember this: I took you from your mother for a good bride price, I put you to school. I have adopted your children for my own. Now think what you are saying to me of my own ancestor here before all my guests."

Silence. I elbowed near enough to see just as the girl dropped suddenly full length on the ground, her hands spread flat beside her shoulders like some one doing the down part of a push-up.

The crowd gave a satisfied sigh; but Helen stamped her foot in exasperation and said, "We are not in Old Africa now, I will not have you prostrating to me. Just get up and ask my pardon nicely." She looked pleased though.

Felicity scrambled to her feet and whispered an apology. Helen came and linked her arm through mine, saying loudly, "If it was somebody's ancestor, it must go find food at the house of its proper descendants." In a lower voice she continued, "Monitors have been found under some of the spilled serving dishes; Netchkay will know you are here. You must leave for a mission church away from Singlet, just until my engineers have finished work on your ship. One of my freight sleds will take you. It goes at mid-morning tomorrow to tour the market towns. By the time you return——"

"Helen, listen, I can't just take off again like this. My cat is still hanging around here someplace——"

"Oh, cat, cat! You must get your mind to business now." She fiddled impatiently with her ear speaker. "Do you think I can keep track of all that happens here? I have a dozen wives to attend to. This is only an animal, after all."

"Ripotee is my friend."

"Then you must hope for the best for your friend, and meanwhile go and rest; you have a journey tomorrow."

And she walked away and stepped into the center of one of the lines of dancing women, stamping and whirling and flipping her head to the different parts of the complex beat, lithe as a girl.

When Barnabas came to my room, it was not to tumble into my bed.

I had fallen asleep, still in my sari, despite the music and voices from the courtyard. He shook me awake in the half-lit room—it was quiet now, near dawn—and whispered, "Dee—you can stop worrying about Ripotee. I have him safe for you, outside with a friend of mine who found him."

His breath smelled of liquor, but he seemed steady and alert, and I could have hugged him for the news he brought. I followed him downstairs. Some one murmured, from within another room with its door ajar, "Barnabas?" A woman's voice; and I thought, ha, he has other beds to sleep in at Helen's house than mine, no wonder he can visit as he likes.

I ran with him across the courtyard, holding up my hem to keep from tripping. As we passed out of the gateway, a long air car swept silently toward us and stopped. A door opened. I bent to look inside, and Barnabas grabbed both my arms from behind and thrust me forward into the interior, where not Ripotee but someone else waited. I tried to twist away, but Barnabas shoved in beside me, pinning me hard with his hip and shoulder. The other person was Nita, my sister.

While I was still caught in the first breathless explosion of shock and incredulous outrage, she slapped a little needle into my neck. She may be a lambchop, my sultry sister, but she is quick. Quicker than I am, who had never stopped to wonder in my sleepy daze why Barnabas hadn't just brought Ripotee up to me himself.

"—Too much in the needle," Barnabas was saying in underwater tones. I could feel breath on each cheek, and on one side was a tinge of wine odor: Barnabas. I was sitting wedged between them. It occurred to me that the antipoddies I had taken might have buffered the effect of the drug. I hoped so; and hoped that Barnabas, out of practice at the transition from space to land, would forget about the effects of antis.

"You've never fought with Dee," Nita said. "She's strong as a servo, and I'm not taking any chances." She fidgeted next to me, trying to get at something tucked into her clothing, doubtless another needle.

Barnabas said firmly, "If you give another needle, this is all finished. I will go back to Helen and tell everything. Mr. Netchkay and I made particular agreement that there would be no risk of harm to Dee."

A moment of frigid tenseness: good, good, fight or something. Shoot me again, Nita, it would be worth it, if only Barnabas would then go to Helen as he threatened.

She didn't, and he didn't. I smelled dust, smoke, and was that rocket fuel? The car stopped, and I slumped helplessly there until he hauled me out with a fair amount of grunting. True to her chosen style, Nita let Barnabas do the work: he was the man, after all. I was set down on a metal surface in what felt like an enclosed space. There was a nasty odor in the air.

Barnabas' hands moved mine to set them comfortably under my cheek, as if I lay sleeping. He whispered in my ear. I shut out the words, knowing what they would be: that he was sorry, that the only way he could go out as a pilot again was to work for a foreigner like Netchkay; that this was his only chance. That he would be sure nothing terrible happened to me. And so on.

I didn't blame him, exactly. I just felt sick and sorry. There isn't a captain alive who wouldn't understand the feeling of sitting on a planet for years, going soft in the head on a soft life, while good reflexes and knowledge soak away.

Nita was another story. I wondered if she hated me, if

she meant to do me some hideous injury while I lay there defenseless.

"Please leave me alone with my sister, Captain," she said. Barnabas made no more apologies to me; I heard his quiet steps recede.

Nita folded herself neatly, with poise, beside me. I didn't see her, but I knew, for her, there would be nothing so inelegent as a squat. Warm drops wet my cheek.

"You look awful," she groaned. "Dressed like a fanatic of some skinhead sect and smelling like a savage— Honestly, Dee, you are so crazy! Why don't you let us take care of you? Bob's not a bad man. He did take the Steinway Line, but he saved it from ruin, won't you credit him with that?"

She paused, snuffling forlornly. I wanted to cry myself. And in her accustomed manner, she was making it very hard for me to hate her. Nita never let anything happen the easy way for others, only for herself. It was very easy for her to betray me because she had fooled herself into believing she was doing the right thing.

"I hope there are no rats in here," she said miserably. "But I had to talk to you. Once Bob comes, it'll be all shouting and cursing and nobody getting in a sensible word.

"There's going to be a war. The independent short haul traders have had enough of being wrung dry by the Chinese long haulers, and Bob has finally gotten them together on a plan to take the Chinese long haul trade into American hands. So for a while there aren't going to be any nifty little short haul ships operating on their own, flitting around as they please, and calling themselves free-lancers —your way. It's going to be too dangerous. Everyone will have to choose a side and stick with it. But you've got no sense. You'll hold out on your own in some old ship and end getting blown up by us or the other side—and I'm not going to tolerate it."

She patted my fuzz of hair and pulled at my wrap, arranging me as a more modest heap on the floor. She blew her nose and added resentfully, "Bob says it's no more than you deserve, charging around the way you do. He should have known Aunt Juno, the awful example she set us—as if every girl could be like that, or should be! She may not have meant to get you killed, but that's just what it will turn out to be by leaving you space ships to run. She thought you were tough as a man, like her."

More sniffling. "She never thought much of me; but then I was always the realist."

Sure, if realism means you just coast along looking for somebody to notice how pretty you make yourself so they take the burden of your own life off your shoulders for you. I almost told her that, before reminding myself that my best chance was to fake being more knocked out by the drug than I was, so she wouldn't give me another shot. While I burned, she prattled on, fixing up my wayward life, and Aunt Juno's wayward life too for that matter, her own way.

"You and Bob and I would make a great team, once you got off your high horse and left the strategy to him. Bob's a natural leader. He'll do well, you'll see. But you have to come in with us, you have to stop fighting us and charging off in any crazy direction you feel like! Honestly, sometimes I think I must be the older one and you the younger.

"I haven't had even a minute to sit down and talk to you in more than four home years, do you realize that? I bet you don't even notice."

So she shot me after all, if only with guilt, an old lambchop trick. I was the older sister; it was all my fault, whatever "it" happened to be. BULLSHIT, I yelled silently. HELP, SOMEBODY!

"I'm warning you, Dee; if you insist on bucking Bob, I'll side with him. We'll see that you spend the war out of harm's way in nice, quiet seclusion somewhere, and so drugged up for your own good that you'll never get your pilot's license renewed again. Grounded forever. Think about it, Dee, please. This isn't just what you want and what I want any more. You've got to be realistic."

Then she leaned down and kissed me, my sister who knew how to set all my defense alarm systems roaring in a panic; and I swear the kiss was honest.

I was so glad when she got up and walked out that I nearly bawled with relief. A little while passed. I lay there trying to flex my sluggish muscles, thinking about being locked up, thinking about being grounded for good, so I shouldn't worry Nita or inconvenience Bob. I wondered if Barnabas would repent and go tell Helen what had happened; and what, if anything, Helen would or could do about me.

The place had a real stink to it, laced with the faint pungence of Barnabas' sweat and Nita's perfumes. Later on there was another smell: stinky cat breath, by the stars!

"Ripotee." I strained to see; by this time the drug had begun to wear off. There had to be some light in the place because there were the reflections in Ripotee's eyes, not a foot from my face: just as Felicity had said, two burning red coins. I couldn't reach out to him, and he came no closer. "Are you hurt?" I cried.

"I'm fine, but hungry. At your party someone tramped on my tail before I could get anything to eat, and there's nothing here—they cleaned out my mice with the oatmeal."

What a pleasure it was to hear his voice—any voice, most particularly two voices, instead of Nita's sugary tones foretelling my ruin. I tried to sit up. My hand encountered a line of rivets in the wall beside me.

"What is this? Where has Bob had me locked up?"

Ripotee said, "We're in the hold of the *Sealyham Eggbeater.*"

"Shit," I said. Now I recognized the smell, pod rot plus cleanzymes. So Bob had the *Eggbeater* and he had me, and he had Ripotee too now; which made me feel very stupid, very tired, and a little mean.

Ripotee elaborated. "Bob is outside. He took the flagship up last night. Now he's trying to buy clearance so he can take the *Eggbeater* up too, even though it's still officially in the cleaning process." He was angry. His tail kept slap-slapping the floor.

It annoyed me that he could see me in that darkness, and I couldn't see him. Sitting there blind, holding myself up against the wall, I said, "How was the jungle, Ripotee?"

"Hot," he said, "and tangled and full of bugs. Some of them are living in my ears. You smell of medicine."

"Drug. It's almost all worn off." I could hear his tail flailing away at the floor and the wall, and the faint click of his claws as he paced. I said, "Why did you stay away like that? I was worried to death about you."

"I just wanted to be on my own out there in the jungle, like the big cats used to be on Old Earth. It was lonesome. There was nobody there but chickens. I got mad and hun-

gry and I ate some. People chased me." He coughed, minute explosions. I could see the blurry red discs of his
eyes again. "I wanted to land here, but there isn't anything here for me; like there isn't anything here for you.

"What I really wanted," he added fiercely, "was a fight,
as a matter of fact; another cat to fight with." This was
solid ground. I knew how he loved to go tomming it at
any landfall we made, coming home bloody and limping and high on adrenalin. I think he liked the instinctual
speed and strength and ferocity of the contest, no chance
to think, let alone talk. Which contradicted the last thing
he'd said about the jungle, but he's just as capable of
wanting two opposing things at the same time as I am.

"You just couldn't stand it that I was out there on my
own," he raged, "you were scared I'd turn wild or something—a fish dropping back into the water will swim
away and forget, that's all you thought I'd do. Well, even
when my brain was just kitty brains it was bigger than
that!"

"I was worried about you!" I yelled.

"Poor Ripotee, dumb Ripotee can't possibly manage
on his own." He was pacing again. "In the jungle his ancestors ruled like kings, he needs his soft-bodied human
to look after him and protect him! Go marry some rich
man so you can retire from space and look after him!"

"Oh, Ripotee—"

"Don't talk to me!" His agitated voice wound right up
into a real old fashioned Siamese yowl.

That yowl was heard; the hatch was swung open, letting in a sweep of light, and Bob stood framed against the
afternoon outside. What a blast of energy it gave me to
see that tall, strong, masterful silhouette: just what I
needed to nerve me up for a fight.

"If it isn't the voice of the talking cat," he said. "I'd
know it anywhere, damned unnatural noise. Nita's worried about the shot she gave you, Dee, but if you're trading mouse stories with the jumped-up lap-warmer you
must be okay."

He didn't seem to have people with him, but I thought I
heard voices outside; or was it only the cackling of the in-
escapable chickens of New Niger?

He read my admittedly obvious thoughts. "I have
friends with me. Oh, yes, your friends are here too, I
wouldn't lie to you, but there's nothing they can do for

a foreigner in the face of trade federation papers—except obstruct and annoy me. When your friends run out of obstruction and annoyance, my friends will be free to come in here where you can't duck me again, and they'll be my witnesses and hold you down while I serve you with these papers."

One thing was certain, and that was that my friends couldn't help me as long as they were outside and I was trapped in here.

I said, "Go to Hell," while patting madly around on the floor in search of something, anything, to use as a weapon. All I had was the Holy Wholey sari; so I pulled that off and rested there on my knees with it in my hands, wondering how much Bob could see in the dimness of the hold.

I could see him fairly well. He was wearing one of those wide light capes popular in the upper ranks of federation office. It can disguise the fact that many of the members come from worlds where the human form has been pretty heavily engeneticked to fit alien environments. Bob let his hang loose to the floor so that anyone could see what a fine, straight figure of a man he was. And he was, too. Nita has good taste—in appearances.

Myself, I have good taste in disasters, which was what led me to be crouching naked in front of my enemy, nothing but a bunch of wrinkled cloth in my fists, nothing at all in my head.

Ripotee minced over and rubbed against Bob's ankle. I held my breath. He said, "Something to tell you, Uncle Bob," using the twee little voice and baby talk that Bob always wanted from him.

With his head up so that he could keep an eye on me, Bob sank onto his haunches. He wasn't dumb enough to try to pick Ripotee up, something that even I seldom did and never without an invitation. He hunkered there in the doorway, one hand braced on the floor, the other hooked into his belt; a dashing figure even on his hams.

Ripotee said, "I want to go away with you, Uncle Bob; will you take me, for a secret? A secret about the Steinway modification?"

Bob bent a little lower, bringing his dark Byronic curls closer to Ripotee's narrow face.

Ripotee did what a fighting tom does; he shot up so high on his hind legs that he stood for an instant on the tip of his extended tail, and he let go a left and right too swift to see. Bob screamed and reared up, both hands clapped to his face, and Ripotee leaped between his legs and out of the hatchway.

Holding my garment stretched out in front of me I flung myself at the light, bowling Bob out onto the ground with me, entangled in folds of cloth. I am not a giant, regardless of Ripotee's opinion, but I am solid and I landed on top, knees and elbows first.

People came rushing over and pried us apart, lifting me to my feet and trying to wrap me up. I think some thought Bob had gotten my clothes off me for some nefarious purpose and were somewhat miffed by my own lack of concern. As I said, I float around naked in space a lot, and I carried it off pretty coolly.

When Bob panted that he was all right, his eyes hadn't been touched, I thought, thank gods. It was enough to be able to laugh freely at the sight he made, scrubbing at his blood-smeared face with his prettily embroidered cuffs.

At my side Helen said rapidly, "He has a federation warrant to suspend your license and immobilize you pending mental exam. It applies at once, as you are not a citizen here."

Shaking bright drops onto the soiled white cloth heaped on the ground at his feet, Bob groped for the paper held out by one of his minions.

I spoke first. "Helen, you'd make any girl a wonderful husband. Will you marry me?"

Helen swooped down on a chicken that was scrabbling around by our feet. She bit off its head and spit it out, held up the fluttering corpse and sprinkled us both with blood. Then she tossed the bird away, threw her arms around my waist, and announced loudly, "Robert Wilkie Netchkay Steinway—that is your name on those papers? —you and your people are invited to my house tonight to celebrate this wedding I have just made here with Dee Steinway. It is sudden, but here in New Niger we have very hot blood and we do things suddenly. I myself am surprised to find that I have married again.

"As for your papers, they cannot be executed on a woman of New Niger. Try going through the local courts if you wish. You will find many of my relatives there hard at work; just as I have numbers of cousins and grown children working also here at Singlet Port, where you docked your big ship illegally yesterday."

"Docked illegally?" snapped Bob. "Your own port people let me in and let me out again."

"Someone made a mistake," said Helen blandly. "Your flagship was too big for our facilities. Some damage has been done and certain other traders were prevented from landing and have suffered losses on that account. There will be a large fine, I fear.

"If you do not come tonight," she added, "I will be very insulted, and so too will all my hard-working relatives. Also you would miss a fine trade we are arranging for you, to make you happy at our celebration."

As we walked away amid Helen's voluble crowd of supporters, I looked back; there was the *Eggbeater*, freshly plated and rewired, ports open to let in the air. There was Bob, trying to push Nita off him as she clung and wailed.

And there was Ripotee, trotting along behind us, a few feathers stuck to his whiskers.

As the bride, I didn't have anything to do at the wedding feast but dance around. Helen and a few of her kindred skilled in law and business sat at a table with Bob, Nita, a mess of papers, and a records terminal. They talked while platters of food were brought, notably the specialty of the evening. Yams Wriggly, an Oriental dish; the wrigglies came from a Red Joy tariff delegation. Bob himself didn't eat much; his face looked as if whatever they served him was burnt.

I danced, badly, with Ripotee clinging to my shoulders. We threw the whole line of dancers off.

Our guests from the flagship got up to leave rather early, seen out personally by their host and the beaming bride. Bob looked at me coolly, with an unbloodied eye—he'd had fast, first rate treatment of the scratches and showed not a mark—and said, "If you ever grow up, Dee, you'll be welcome at home."

I laughed in his face.

He was trembling ever so slightly—with pure rage, I sincerely hoped. As he turned and started to steer Nita away with him in an iron grip, she burst into tears and cried, "Oh, Dee, what will become of your life? My sister has turned into a naked savage—"

I was wearing my jumper, as a matter of fact,
trimmed with bright patterns that a couple of Helen's jun-
ior wives had applied to the chest, back, and bottom.
But I suppose Nita was still seeing me as I had burst from
the ship that afternoon, bare and blood-spattered.

Other guests began leaving, hurried out by Helen's
loud, laughing complaints that she was being ruined by
two parties on successive nights.

She drew me over to the long table where she and Bob
and Nita had feasted. Ripotee jumped down from my
shoulder.

"I'm going off for a walk. Don't get worried about me
this time. I'll meet you in the morning at the, ah, hole
for fowl."

Helen called sharply after him, "Food will be left out
for you. Please confine your eating to *cold* chicken."

She turned to me. "Here are your ship papers and your
debt agreements. Netchkay paid his fine with your ship,
since that was the only currency the port would accept;
and I did a bit of dealing so that the ownership papers
end in my hands—and now in yours."

I was pretty well bowled over by this; and I found that
now that we had done it, diddled Bob and saved my neck,
it wasn't going to be so simple just to accept my salvation
at the hands of an old trading rival. I was suddenly worried about some hidden twist, some pitfall, in the already
odd situation in which I had landed myself.

Into the awkward silence—awkward for me, though
Helen was grinning triumphantly—came noise from an
adjoining courtyard, where many of the guests seemed to
have congregated on their way out. Singing, it was, and
loud laughter.

"They are sitting on Barnabas," Helen said with relish.

"Helen, let him go work for Netchkay if that's what
he wants. He's earned it."

"His just desserts!" She laughed. "White people are terrible to work for. Oh, yes, I worked for your Aunt Juno
once, on the computer records of the Steinway Line—
making sure they were fit for the eyes of certain officials.
I learned a lot working for Juno, but she would not learn
much from me, or even about me—she was so surprised
when I went my own way, to make my own fleet! Perhaps
she thought I would spend my life as a faithful retainer!"

I took a deep breath. "Look, Helen, I like to hear

about Aunt Juno, but things can't be left like this between you and me. You paid no bride wealth for me, and maybe I can't bring you any children to add to your family, and I'll never learn local ways enough to be comfortable or to be a credit to you—"

Helen threw back her head and screamed with laughter. She slapped my arms, she hugged me. "Oh, you child you!" she crowed, dashing tears of mirth from her eyes. "Listen, you silly White girl; what do you think, we get married like that? A marriage is an alliance of families, planned long in advance. The bride comes and works for years first in the husband's house, so the husband's family can see is she worth marrying. We are not impulsive like you people, and we do not marry with chicken blood! But, that is what a man like Bob Netchkay would believe."

"Then I'm not—?"

"You are not. Nor am I so foolish as to marry a foreigner, bringing nothing but trouble and misunderstanding on all sides."

"But then it's all pure gift," I said, getting up from the table. "I can't accept, Helen—my freedom, my ship—"

"Sit down, sit, sit, sit," she said, pulling me back down beside her. "You forget, there are still the plans for the Steinway modifications, which are worth a great deal to me.

"Also I act in memory of certain debts to your Aunt Juno; and because you are a woman and not a puny weed like that sister of yours; and to black the eye of my rival Netchkay in front of everyone; and also for the pleasure of doing a small something for a White girl, whose race was once so useful in helping my people to get up.

"But I could also say, Dee, that I hope to make you just enough beholden to me so that you will bend your pride—not much, only small-small—and a Steinway will fly her ship for me out there in space that she loves better than any world."

I leaned forward and made wet circles on the plastic table with the bottom of my glass. An image of Aunt Juno came into my mind—a plump dynamo of a woman with her hair piled high on her head to make her look taller; and pretty, pretty even after her neck thickened and obliterated her shapely little chin, and age began to freckle her hands. She had come tripping into my shop class in the Learning Center where I was raised, and batting her long lashes above a dazzling smile that left the teaching team charmed and humbled, she had summoned me away with her because she believed I could become a pilot.

Helen murmured, "Do you know, I myself never fly. All my dealings are made from here, from landfall. In Iboland it was taboo forever for women to climb up above the level of any man's head, it brought sickness. Now we are bolder, we have discarded such notions, we climb easily to the top floors of tall buildings and nobody falls ill. But I am old fashioned, and I am still not comfortable climbing into black space among the stars."

I said, "I'll fly for you."

And so I have done ever since, with brief visits to my "family" on New Niger. I think sometimes how sharp Ripotee was to see that there was no living there for either of us. But I don't tell him; he thinks well enough of himself as it is.

GINUNGAGAP

≋≋≋≋≋≋≋≋≋≋≋≋≋≋≋

Michael Swanwick

Stories about humanity's first contact with
an alien species have been a staple of the
genre ever since science fiction began. At
first, non-human societies were devices by
which writers satirized our own world, or
utopias that served a similar function; later,
alien beings were depicted as marauding
monsters who were deadly enemies to humans. Recent decades have produced more
and more stories that seriously considered
what the psychologies of aliens might be
like; "Ginungagap" is one of the best of
these.

Michael Swanwick, one of the best writ-
ers to enter the science fiction field re-
cently, lives in Philadelphia, where he works
for the National Solar Heating and Cooling
Information Center at the Franklin Institute.
He's sold excellent stories to *Destinies,
New Dimensions, Universe* and, in this case,
TriQuarterly.

ABIGAIL CHECKED OUT OF MOTHER OF
Mercy and rode the translator web to Toledo Cylinder in
Juno Industrial Park. Stars bloomed, dwindled, disappeared five times. It was a long trek, halfway around the
sun.

Toledo was one of the older commercial cylinders, now
given over almost entirely to bureaucrats, paper pushers,
and free-lance professionals. It was not Abigail's favorite
place to visit, but she needed work and 3M had already
bought out of her contract.

The job broker had dyed his chest hairs blond and his
leg hairs red. They clashed wildly with his green *cache-
sexe* and turquoise jewelry. His fingers played on a keyout, bringing up an endless flow of career trivia. "Cute
trick you played," he said.

Abigail flexed her new arm negligently. It was a good
job, but pinker than the rest of her. And weak, of course,
but exercise would correct that. "Thanks," she said. She
laid the arm underneath one breast and compared the
colors. It matched the nipple perfectly. Definitely too
pink. "Work outlook any good?"

"Naw," the broker said. A hummingbird flew past his
ear, a nearly undetectable parting of the air. "I see here
that you applied for the Proxima colony."

"They were full up," Abigail said. "No openings for a
gravity bum, hey?"

"I didn't say that," the broker grumbled. "I'll find—

64

Hello! What's this?" Abigail craned her neck, couldn't get a clear look at the screen. "There's a tag on your employment record."

"What's that mean?"

"Let me read." A honeysuckle flower fell on Abigail's hair and she brushed it off impatiently. The broker had an open-air office, framed by hedges and roofed over with a trellis. Sometimes Abigail found the older Belt cylinders a little too lavish for her taste.

"Mmp." The broker looked up. "Bell-Sandia wants to hire you. Indefinite term one-shot contract." He swung the keyout around so she could see. *"Very* nice terms, but that's normal for a high risk contract."

"High risk? From B-S, the Friendly Communications People? What kind of risk?"

The broker scrolled up new material. "There." He tapped the screen with a finger. "The language is involved, but what it boils down to is they're looking for a test passenger for a device they've got that uses black holes for interstellar travel."

"Couldn't work," Abigail said. "The tidal forces—"

"Spare me. Presumably they've found a way around that problem. The question is, are you interested or not?"

Abigail stared up through the trellis at a stream meandering across the curved land overhead. Children were wading in it. She counted to a hundred very slowly, trying to look as if she needed to think it over.

Abigail strapped herself into the translation harness and nodded to the technician outside the chamber. The tech touched her console and a light stasis field immobilized Abigail and the air about her while the chamber wall irised open. In a fluid bit of technological sleight of hand, the translator rechanneled her inertia and gifted her with a velocity almost, but not quite, that of the speed of light.

Stars bloomed about her and the sun dwindled. She breathed in deeply and—was in the receiver device. Relativity had cheated her of all but a fraction of the transit time. She shrugged out of harness and frog-kicked her way to the lip station's tug dock.

The tug pilot grinned at her as she entered, then turned his attention to his controls. He was young and wore streaks of brown makeup across his chest and thighs

—only slightly darker than his skin. His mesh vest was almost in bad taste, but he wore it well and looked roguish rather than overdressed. Abigail found herself wishing she had more than a *cache-sexe* and nail polish on—some jewelry or makeup, perhaps. She felt drab in comparison.

The star-field wraparound held two inserts routed in by synchronous cameras. Alphanumerics flickered beneath them. One showed her immediate destination, the Bell-Sandia base *Arthur C. Clarke.* It consisted of five wheels, each set inside the other and rotating at slightly differing speeds. The base was done up in red-and-orange supergraphics. Considering its distance from the Belt factories, it was respectably sized.

Abigail latched herself into the passenger seat as the engines cut in. The second insert—

Ginungagap, the only known black hole in the sun's gravity field, was discovered in 2023, a small voice murmured. *Its presence explained the long-puzzling variations in the orbits of the outer planets. The* Arthur C. Clarke *was . . .*

"Is this necessary?" Abigail asked.

"Absolutely," the pilot said. "We abandoned the tourist program a year or so ago, but somehow the rules never caught up. They're very strict about the regs here." He winked at Abigail's dismayed expression. "Hold tight a minute while—" His voice faded as he tinkered with the controls.

. . . established forty years later and communications with the Proxima colony began shortly thereafter. Ginungagap . . .

The voice cut off. She grinned thanks. "Abigail Vanderhoek."

"Cheyney," the pilot said. "You're the gravity bum, right?"

"Yeah."

"I used to be a vacuum bum myself. But I got tired of it, and grabbed the first semipermanent contract that came along."

"I kind of went the other way."

"Probably what I should have done," Cheyney said amiably. "Still, it's a rough road. I picked up three scars along the way." He pointed them out: a thick slash across his abdomen, a red splotch beside one nipple, and a white crescent half obscured by his scalp. "I could've had them cleaned up, but the way I figure, life is just a process of picking up scars and experience. So I kept 'em."

If she had thought he was trying to impress her, Abigail would have slapped him down. But it was clearly just part of an ongoing self-dramatization, possibly justified, probably not. Abigail suspected that, tour trips to Earth excepted, the *Clarke* was as far down a gravity well as Cheyney had ever been. Still he did have an irresponsible, boyish appeal. "Take me past the net?" she asked.

Cheyney looped the tug around the communications net trailing the *Clarke*. Kilometers of steel lace passed beneath them. He pointed out a small dish antenna on the edge and a cluster of antennae on the back. "The loner on the edge transmits into Ginungagap," he said. "The others relay information to and from Mother."

"Mother?"

"That's the traditional name for the *Arthur C. Clarke*." He swung the tug about with a careless sweep of one arm, and launched into a long and scurrilous story about the origin of the nickname. Abigail laughed, and Cheyney pointed a finger. "There's Ginungagap."

Abigail peered intently. "Where? I don't see a thing." She glanced at the second wraparound insert, which displayed a magnified view of the black hole. It wasn't at all impressive: a red smear against black nothingness. In the star-field it was all but invisible.

"Disappointing, hey? But still dangerous. Even this far out, there's a lot of ionization from the accretion disk."

"Is that why there's a lip station?"

"Yeah. Particle concentration varies, but if the translator was right at the *Clarke*, we'd probably lose about a third of the passengers."

Cheyney dropped Abigail off at Mother's crew lock and looped the tug off and away. Abigail wondered where to go, what to do now.

"You're the gravity bum we're dumping down Ginungagap." The short, solid man was upon her before she saw him. His eyes were intense. His *cache-sexe* was a conservative orange. "I liked the stunt with the arm. It takes a lot of guts to do something like that." He pumped her arm. "I'm Paul Girard. Head of external security. In charge of your training. You play verbal Ping Pong?"

"Why do you ask?" she countered automatically.

"Don't you know?"

"Should I?"

"Do you mean now or later?"

"Will the answer be different later?"

A smile creased Paul's solid face. "You'll do." He took her arm, led her along a sloping corridor. "There isn't much prep time. The dry run is scheduled in two weeks. Things will move pretty quickly after that. You want to start your training now?"

"Do I have a choice?" Abigail asked, amused.

Paul came to a dead stop. "Listen," he said. "Rule number one: don't play games with *me*. You understand? Because I always win. Not sometimes, not usually—always."

Abigail yanked her arm free. "You maneuvered me into that," she said angrily.

"Consider it part of your training." He stared directly into her eyes. "No matter how many gravity wells you've climbed down, you're still the product of a near-space culture—protected, trusting, willing to take things at face value. This is a dangerous attitude, and I want you to realize it. I want you to learn to look behind the mask of events. I want you to grow up. And you will."

Don't be so sure. A small smile quirked Paul's face as if he could read her thoughts. Aloud, Abigail said, "That sounds a little excessive for a trip to Proxima."

"Lesson number two," Paul said: "don't make easy assumptions. You're not going to Proxima." He led her outward-down the ramp to the next wheel, pausing briefly at the juncture to acclimatize to the slower rate of revolution. "You're going to visit spiders." He gestured. "The crew room is this way."

The crew room was vast and cavernous, twilight gloomy, Keyouts were set up along winding paths that wandered aimlessly through the work space. Puddles of light fell on each board and operator. Dark-loving foliage was set between the keyouts.

"This is the heart of the beast," Paul said. "The green keyouts handle all Proxima communications—pretty routine by now. But the blue . . ." His eyes glinting oddly, he pointed. Over the keyouts hung silvery screens with harsh, grainy images floating on their surfaces, black-and-white blobs that Abigail could not resolve into recognizable forms.

"Those," Paul said, "are the spiders. We're talking to them in real-time. Response delay is almost all due to machine translation."

In a sudden shift of perception, the blobs became arachnid forms. That mass of black fluttering across the screen was a spider leg and *that* was its thorax. Abigail felt an immediate, primal aversion, and then it was swept away by an all-encompassing wonder.

"Aliens?" she breathed.

"Aliens."

They actually looked no more like spiders than humans looked like apes. The eight legs had an extra joint each, and the mandible configuration was all wrong. But to an untrained eye they would do.

"But this is—How long have you—? Why in God's name are you keeping this a secret?" An indefinable joy arose in Abigail. This opened a universe of possibilities, as if after a lifetime of being confined in a box someone had removed the lid.

"Industrial security," Paul said. "The gadget that'll send you through Ginungagap to *their* black hole is a spider invention. We're trading optical data for it, but the law won't protect our rights until we've demonstrated its use. We don't want the other corporations cutting in." He nodded toward the nearest black-and-white screen. "As you can see, they're weak on optics."

"I'd love to talk . . ." Abigail's voice trailed off as she realized how little-girl hopeful she sounded.

"I'll arrange an introduction."

There was a rustling to Abigail's side. She turned and saw a large black tomcat with white boots and belly emerge from the bushes. "This is the esteemed head of Alien Communications," Paul said sourly.

Abigail started to laugh, then choked in embarrassment as she realized that he was not speaking of the cat. "Julio Dominguez, section chief for translation," Paul said. "Abigail Vanderhoek, gravity specialist."

The wizened old man smiled professorially. "I assume our resident gadfly has explained how the communications net works, has he not?"

"Well—" Abigail began.

Dominguez clucked his tongue. He wore a yellow *cache-sexe* and matching bow tie, just a little too garish for a man his age. "Quite simple, actually. Escape velocity from a black hole is greater than the speed of light. Therefore, within Ginungagap the speed of light is no longer the limit to the speed of communications."

He paused just long enough for Abigail to look baffled. "Which is just a stuffy way of saying that when we aim a stream of electrons into the boundary of the stationary limit, they emerge elsewhere—out of another black hole. And if we aim them *just so*"—his voice rose whimsically—"they'll emerge from the black hole of our choosing. The physics is simple. The finesse is in aiming the electrons."

The cat stalked up to Abigail, pushed its forehead against her leg, and mewed insistently. She bent over and picked it up. "But nothing can emerge from a black hole," she objected.

Dominguez chuckled. "Ah, but anything can fall in, hey? A positron can fall in. But a positron falling into Ginungagap in positive time is only an electron falling out in negative time. Which means that a positron falling into a black hole in negative time is actually an electron falling out in positive time—exactly the effect we want. Think of Ginungagap as being the physical manifestation of an equivalence sign in mathematics."

"Oh," Abigail said, feeling very firmly put in her place. White moths flittered along the path. The cat watched, fascinated, while she stroked its head.

"At any rate, the electrons do emerge, and once the data are in, the theory has to follow along meekly."

"Tell me about the spiders," Abigail said before he could continue. The moths were darting up, sideward, down, a chance ballet in three dimensions.

"The *aliens*," Dominguez said, frowning at Paul, "are still a mystery to us. We exchange facts, descriptions, recipes for tools, but the important questions do not lend themselves to our clumsy mathematical codes. Do they know of love? Do they appreciate beauty? Do they believe in God, hey?"

"Do they want to eat us?" Paul threw in.

"Don't be ridiculous," Dominguez snapped. "Of course they don't."

The moths parted when they came to Abigail. Two went to either side; one flew over her shoulder. The cat batted at it with one paw. "The cat's name is Garble," Paul said. "The kids in Bio cloned him up."

Dominguez opened his mouth, closed it again.

Abigail scratched Garble under the chin. He arched his neck and purred all but noiselessly. "With your permission," Paul said. He stepped over to a keyout and waved its operator aside.

"Technically you're supposed to speak a convenience language, but if you keep it simple and non-idiomatic, there shouldn't be any difficulty." He touched the keyout. "Ritual greetings, spider." There was a blank pause. Then the spider moved, a hairy leg flickering across the screen.

"Hello, human."

"Introductions: Abigail Vanderhoek. She is our representative. She will ride the spinner." Another pause. More leg waving.

"Hello, Abigail Vanderhoek. Transition of vacuum garble resting garble commercial benefits garble still point in space."

"Tricky translation," Paul said. He signed to Abigail to take over.

Abigail hesitated, then said, "Will you come to visit us? The way we will visit you?"

"No, you see—" Dominguez began, but Paul waved him to silence.

"No, Abigail Vanderhoek. We are sulfur-based life."

"I do not understand."

"You can garble black hole through garble spinner because you are carbon-based life. Carbon forms chains easily but sulfur combines in lattices or rosettes. Our garble simple form garble. Sometimes sulfur forms short chains."

"We'll explain later," Paul said. "Go on, you're doing fine."

Abigail hesitated again. What do you say to a spider, anyway? Finally, she asked, "Do you want to eat us?"

"Oh, Christ, get her off that thing," Dominguez said, reaching for the keyout.

Paul blocked his arm. "No," he said. "I want to hear this."

Several of the spider legs wove intricate patterns. "The question is false. Sulfur-based life derives no benefit from eating carbon-based life."

"You see," Dominguez said.

"But if it were possible," Abigail persisted. "If you *could* eat us and derive benefit. Would you?"

"Yes, Abigail Vanderhoek. With great pleasure."

Dominguez pushed her aside. "We're terribly sorry," he said to the alien. "This is a horrible, horrible misunderstanding. You!" he shouted to the operator. "Get back on and clear this mess up."

Paul was grinning wickedly. "Come," he said to Abigail. "We've accomplished enough here for one day."

As they started to walk away, Garble twisted in Abigail's arms and leaped free. He hit the floor on all fours and disappeared into the greenery. "Would they really eat us?" Abigail asked. Then amended it to, "Does that mean they're hostile?"

Paul shrugged. "Maybe they thought we'd be insulted if they *didn't* offer to eat us." He led her to her quarters. "Tomorrow we start training for real. In the meantime, you might make up a list of all the ways the spiders could hurt us if we set up transportation and they *are* hostile. Then another list of all the reasons we shouldn't trust them." He paused. "I've done it myself. You'll find that the lists get rather extensive."

Abigail's quarters weren't flashy, but they fit her well. A full star field was routed to the walls, floor, and ceiling, only partially obscured by a trellis inner frame that supported fox-grape vines. Somebody had done research into her tastes.

"Hi." The cheery greeting startled her. She whirled, saw that her hammock was occupied.

Cheyney sat up, swung his legs over the edge of the hammock, causing it to rock lightly. "Come on in." He touched an invisible control and the star field blueshifted down to a deep, erotic purple.

"Just what do you think you're doing here?" Abigail asked.

"I had a few hours free," Cheyney said, "so I thought I'd drop by and seduce you."

"Well, Cheyney, I appreciate your honesty," Abigail said. "So I won't say no."

"Thank you."

"I'll say maybe some other time. Now get lost. I'm tired."

"Okay." Cheyney hopped down, walked jauntily to the door. He paused. "You said 'Later,' right?"

"I said *maybe* later."

"Later. Gotcha." He winked and was gone.

Abigail threw herself into the hammock, red-shifted the star field until the universe was a sparse smattering of dying embers. Annoying creature! There was no hope for anything more than the most superficial of relationships with him. She closed her eyes, smiled. Fortunately, she wasn't currently in the market for a serious relationship.

She slept.

She was falling . . .

Abigail had landed the ship an easy walk from 3M's robot laboratory. The lab's geodesic dome echoed white clouds to the north, where Nix Olympus peeked over the horizon. Otherwise all—land, sky, rocks—was standard issue Martian orange. She had clambered to the ground and shrugged on the supply backpack.

Resupplying 3M-RL stations was a gut contract, easy but dull. So perhaps she was less cautious than usual going down the steep, rock-strewn hillside, or perhaps the rock would have turned under her no matter how carefully she placed her feet. Her ankle twisted and she lurched sideways, but the backpack had shifted her center of gravity too much for her to be able to recover.

Arms windmilling, she fell.

The rock slide carried her downhill in a panicky flurry of dust and motion, tearing her flesh and splintering her bones. But before she could feel pain, her suit shot her full of a nerve synesthetic, translating sensation into colors—reds, russets, and browns, with staccato yellow spikes when a rock smashed into her ribs. So that she fell in a whirling rainbow of glorious light.

She came to rest in a burst of orange. The rocks were settling about her. A spume of dust drifted away, out toward the distant red horizon. A large, jagged slab of stone slid by, gently shearing off her backpack. Tools, supplies, airpacks flew up and softly rained down.

A spanner as long as her arm slammed down inches from Abigail's helmet. She flinched, and suddenly events became real. She kicked her legs and sand and dust fountained up. Drawing her feet under her body—the one ankle bright gold—she started to stand.

And was jerked to the ground by a sudden tug on one arm. Even as she turned her head, she became aware of a deep purple sensation in her left hand. It was pinioned to a rock not quite large enough to stake a claim to. There was no color in the fingers.

"Cute," she muttered. She tugged at the arm, pushed at the rock. Nothing budged.

Abigail nudged the radio switch with her chin. "Grounder to Lip Station," she said. She hesitated, feeling foolish, then said, "Mayday. Repeat, Mayday. Could you guys send a rescue party down for me?"

There was no reply. With a sick green feeling in the pit of her stomach, Abigail reached a gloved hand around the back of her helmet. She touched something jagged, a sensation of mottled rust, the broken remains of her radio.

"I think I'm in trouble." She said it aloud and listened to the sound of it. Flat, unemotional—probably true. But nothing to get panicky about.

She took quick stock of what she had to work with. One intact suit and helmet. One spanner. A worldful of rocks, many close at hand. Enough air for—she checked the helmet readout—almost an hour. Assuming the lip station ran its checks on schedule and was fast on the uptake, she had almost half the air she needed.

Most of the backpack's contents were scattered too far away to reach. One rectangular gaspack, however, had landed nearby. She reached for it but could not touch it, squinted but could not read the label on its nozzle. It was almost certainly liquid gas—either nitrogen or oxygen—for the robot lab. There was a slim chance it was the spare airpack. If it was, she might live to be rescued.

Abigail studied the landscape carefully, but there was nothing more. "Okay, then, it's an airpack." She reached as far as her tethered arm would allow. The gaspack remained a tantalizing centimeter out of reach.

For an instant she was stymied. Then, feeling like an idiot, she grabbed the spanner. She hooked it over the gaspack. Felt the gaspack move grudgingly. Slowly nudged it toward herself.

By the time Abigail could drop the spanner and draw in the gaspack, her good arm was blue with fatigue. Sweat running down her face, she juggled the gaspack to read its nozzle markings.

It was liquid oxygen—useless. She could hook it to her suit and feed in the contents, but the first breath would freeze her lungs. She released the gaspack and lay back, staring vacantly at the sky.

Up there was civilization: tens of thousands of human stations strung together by webs of communication and transportation. Messages flowed endlessly on laser cables. Translators borrowed and lent momentum, moving streams of travelers and cargo at almost (but not quite) the speed of light. A starship was being readied to carry a third load of colonists to Proxima. Up there, free from gravity's relentless clutch, people lived in luxury and ease. Here, however . . .

"I'm going to die." She said it softly and was filled with wondering awe. Because it was true. She was going to die.

Death was a black wall. It lay before her, extending to infinity in all directions, smooth and featureless and mysterious. She could almost reach out an arm and touch it. Soon she would come up against it and, if anything lay beyond, pass through. Soon, very soon, she would *know*.

She touched the seal to her helmet. It felt gray— smooth and inviting. Her fingers moved absently, tracing the seal about her neck. With sudden horror, Abigail realized that she was thinking about undoing it, releasing her air, throwing away the little time she had left. . . .

She shuddered. With sudden resolve, she reached out and unsealed the shoulder seam of her captive arm.

The seal clamped down, automatically cutting off air loss. The flesh of her damaged arm was exposed to the raw Martian atmosphere. Abigail took up the gaspack and cradled it in the pit of her good arm. Awkwardly, she opened the nozzle with the spanner.

She sprayed the exposed arm with liquid oxygen for over a minute before she was certain it had frozen solid. Then she dropped the gaspack, picked up the spanner, and swung.

Her arm shattered into a thousand fragments.

She stood up.

Abigail awoke, tense and sweaty. She blue-shifted the walls up to normal light, and sat up. After a few minutes of clearing her head, she set the walls to cycle from red to blue in a rhythm matching her normal pulse. Eventually the womb-cycle lulled her back to sleep.

"Not even close," Paul said. He ran the tape backward, froze it on a still shot of the spider twisting two legs about each other. "That's the morpheme for 'extreme disgust,' remember. It's easy to pick out, and the language kids say that any statement with this gesture should be reversed in meaning. Irony, see? So when the spider says that the strong should protect the weak, it means——"

"How long have we been doing this?"

"Practically forever," Paul said cheerfully. "You want to call it a day?"

"Only if it won't hurt my standing."

"Hah! Very good." He switched off the keyout. "Nicely thought out. You're absolutely right; it would have. However, as reward for realizing this, you can take off early *without* it being noted on your record."

"Thank you," Abigail said sourly.

Like most large installations, the *Clarke* had a dozen or so smaller structures tagging along after it in minimum maintenance orbits. When Abigail discovered that these included a small wheel gymnasium, she had taken to putting in an hour's exercise after each training shift. Today she put in two.

The first hour she spent shadowboxing and practicing *savate* in heavy-gee to work up a sweat. The second hour she spent in the axis room, performing free-fall gymnastics. After the first workout, it made her feel light and nimble and good about her body.

She returned from the wheel gym sweaty and cheerful to find Cheyney in her hammock again. "Cheyney," she said, "this is not the first time I've had to kick you out of there. Or even the third, for that matter."

Cheyney held his palms up in mock protest. "Hey, no," he said. "Nothing like that today. I just came by to watch the raft debate with you."

Abigail felt pleasantly weary, decidedly uncerebral. "Paul said something about it, but . . ."

"Turn it on, then. You don't want to miss it." Cheyney touched her wall, and a cluster of images sprang to life at the far end of the room.

"Just what is a raft debate anyway?" Abigail asked, giving in gracefully. She hoisted herself onto the hammock, sat beside him. They rocked gently for a moment.

"There's this raft, see? It's adrift and powerless and there's only enough oxygen on board to keep one person alive until rescue. Only there are three on board—two humans and a spider."

"Do spiders breathe oxygen?"

"It doesn't matter. This is a hypothetical situation." Two thirds of the image area was taken up by Dominguez and Paul, quietly waiting for the debate to begin. The remainder showed a flat spider image.

"Okay, what then?"

"They argue over who gets to survive. Dominguez argues that he should, since he's human and human culture is superior to spider culture. The spider argues for itself and its culture." He put an arm around her waist. "You smell nice."

"Thank you." She ignored the arm. "What does Paul argue?"

"He's the devil's advocate. He argues that no one deserves to live and they should dump the oxygen."

"Paul would enjoy that role," Abigail said. Then, "What's the point to this debate?"

"It's an entertainment. There isn't supposed to be a point."

Abigail doubted it was that simple. The debate could reveal a good deal about the spiders and how they thought, once the language types were done with it. Conversely, the spiders would doubtless be studying the human responses. *This could be interesting,* she thought. Cheyney was stroking her side now, lightly but with great authority. She postponed reaction, not sure whether she liked it or not.

Louise Chang, a vaguely high-placed administrator, blossomed in the center of the image cluster. "Welcome," she said, and explained the rules of the debate. "The winner will be decided by acclaim," she said, "with half the vote being human and half alien. Please remember not to base your vote on racial chauvinism, but on the strengths of the arguments and how well they are presented." Cheyney's hand brushed casually across her nipples; they stiffened. The hand lingered. "The debate will begin with the gentleman representing the aliens presenting his thesis."

The image flickered as the spider waved several legs.

"Thank you, Ms. Chairman. I argue that I should survive. My culture is superior because of our technological advancement. Three examples. Humans have used translation travel only briefly, yet we have used it for sixteens of garble. Our black hole technology is superior. And our garble has garble for the duration of our society."

"Thank you. The gentleman representing humanity?"

"Thank you, Ms. Chairman." Dominguez adjusted an armlet. Cheyney leaned back and let Abigail rest against him. Her head fit comfortably against his shoulder. "My argument is that technology is neither the sole nor the most important measure of a culture. By these standards dolphins would be considered brute animals. The aesthetic considerations—the arts, theology, and the tradition of philosophy—are of greater import. As I shall endeavor to prove."

"He's chosen the wrong tactic," Cheyney whispered in Abigail's ear. "That must have come across as pure garble to the spiders."

"Thank you. Mr. Girard?"

Paul's image expanded. He theatrically swigged from a small flask and hoisted it high in the air. "Alcohol! There's the greatest achievement of the human race!" Abigail snorted. Cheyney laughed out loud. "But I hold that neither Mr. Dominguez nor the distinguished spider deserves to live, because of the disregard both cultures have for sentient life." Abigail looked at Cheyney, who shrugged. "As I shall endeavor to prove." His image dwindled.

Chang said, "The arguments will now proceed, beginning with the distinguished alien."

The spider and then Dominguez ran through their arguments, and to Abigail they seemed markedly lackluster. She didn't give them her full attention, because Cheyney's hands were moving most interestingly across unexpected parts of her body. He might not be too bright, but he was certainly good at some things. She nuzzled her face into his neck, gave him a small peck, returned her attention to the debate.

Paul blossomed again. He juggled something in his palm, held his hand open to reveal three ball bearings. "When I was a kid I used to short out the school module and sneak up to the axis room to play marbles." Abigail smiled, remembering similar stunts she had played. "For the sake of those of us who are spiders, I'll explain that marbles is a game played in free-fall for the purpose of developing coordination and spatial perception. You make a six-armed star of marbles in the center . . ."

One of the bearings fell from his hand, bounced noisily, and disappeared as it rolled out of camera range. "Well, obviously it can't be played here. But the point is that when you shoot the marble just right, it hits the end of one arm and its kinetic energy is transferred from marble to marble along that arm. So that the shooter stops and the marble at the far end of the arm flies away." Cheyney was stroking her absently now, engrossed in the argument.

"Now, we plan to send a courier into Ginungagap and out the spiders' black hole. At least, that's what we say we're going to do.

"But what exits from a black hole is not necessarily the same as what went into its partner hole. We throw an electron into Ginungagap and another one pops out elsewhere. It's identical. It's a direct causal relationship. But it's like the marbles—they're identical to each other and have the same kinetic force. It's simply not the same electron."

Cheyney's hand was still, motionless. Abigail prodded him gently, touching his inner thigh. "Anyone who's interested can see the equations. Now, when we send messages, this doesn't matter. The message is important, not the medium. However, when we send a human being in . . . what emerges from the other hole will be cell for cell, gene for gene, atom for atom identical. *But it will not be the same person.*" He paused a beat, smiled.

"I submit, then, that this is murder. And further, that by conspiring to commit murder, both the spider and human races display absolute disregard for intelligent life. In short, no one on the raft deserves to live. And I rest my case."

"Mr. Girard!" Dominguez objected, even before his image was restored to full size. "The simplest mathematical proof is an identity: that A equals A. Are you trying to deny this?"

Paul held up the two ball bearings he had left. "These marbles are identical too. But they are not the same marble."

"We know the phenomenon you speak of," the spider

said. "It is as if garble the black hole bulges out simultaneously. There is no violation of continuity. The two entities are the same. There is no death."

Abigail pulled Cheyney down, so that they were both lying on their sides, still able to watch the images. "So long as you happen to be the second marble and not the first," Paul said. Abigail tentatively licked Cheyney's ear.

"He's right," Cheyney murmured.

"No he's not," Abigail retorted. She bit his earlobe.

"You mean that?"

"Of course I mean that. He's confusing semantics with reality." She engrossed herself in a study of the back of his neck.

"Okay."

Abigail suddenly sensed that she was missing something. "Why do you ask?" She struggled into a sitting position. Cheyney followed.

"No particular reason." Cheyney's hands began touching her again. But Abigail was sure something had been slipped past her.

They caressed each other lightly while the debate dragged to an end. Not paying much attention, Abigail voted for Dominguez, and Cheyney voted for Paul. As a result of a nearly undivided spider vote, the spider won. "I told you Dominguez was taking the wrong approach," Cheyney said. He hopped off the hammock. "Look, I've got to see somebody about something. I'll be right back."

"You're not leaving now?" Abigail protested, dumbfounded. The door irised shut.

Angry and hurt, she leaped down, determined to follow him. She couldn't remember ever feeling so insulted.

Cheyney didn't try to be evasive; it apparently did not occur to him that she might follow. Abigail stalked him down a corridor, up an in-ramp, and to a door that irised open for him. She recognized that door.

Thoughtfully she squatted on her heels behind an untrimmed boxwood and waited. A minute later, Garble wandered by, saw her, and demanded attention. "Scat!" she hissed. He butted his head against her knee. "Then be quiet, at least." She scooped him up. His expression was smug.

The door irised open and Cheyney exited, whistling. Abigail waited until he was gone, stood, went to the door, and entered. Fish darted between long fronds under a transparent floor. It was an austere room, almost featureless. Abigail looked, but did not see a hammock.

"So Cheyney's working for you now," she said coldly. Paul looked up from a corner keyout.

"As a matter of fact, I've just signed him to permanent contract in the crew room. He's bright enough. A bit green. Ought to do well."

"Then you admit that you put him up to grilling me about your puerile argument in the debate?" Garble struggled in her arms. She juggled him into a more comfortable position. "And that you staged the argument for my benefit in the first place?"

"Ah," Paul said. "I knew the training was going somewhere. You've become very wary in an extremely short time."

"Don't evade the question."

"I needed your honest reaction," Paul said. "Not the answer you would have given me, knowing your chances of crossing Ginungagap rode on it."

Garble made an angry noise. "You tell him, Garble!" she said. "That goes double for me." She stepped out the door. "You lost the debate," she snapped.

Long after the door had irised shut, she could feel Paul's amused smile burning into her back.

Two days after she returned to kick Cheyney out of her hammock for the final time, Abigail was called to the crew room. "Dry run," Paul said. "Attendance is mandatory." And cut off.

The crew room was crowded with technicians, triple the number of keyouts. Small knots of them clustered before the screens, watching. Paul waved her to him.

"There," he motioned to one screen. "That's Clotho —the platform we built for the transmission device. It's a hundred kilometers off. I wanted more, but Dominguez overruled me. The device that'll unravel you and dump you down Ginungagap is that doohickey in the center." He tapped a keyout and the platform zoomed up to fill the screen. It was covered by a clear, transparent bubble. Inside, a space-suited figure was placing something into a machine that looked like nothing so much as a giant armor-clad clamshell. Abigail looked, blinked, looked again.

"That's Garble," she said indignantly.

"Complain to Dominguez. I wanted a baboon."

The clamshell device closed. The space-suited tech left in his tug, and alphanumerics flickered, indicating the device was in operation. As they watched, the spider-designed machinery immobilized Garble, transformed his molecules into one long continuous polymer chain, and spun it out an invisible opening at near light speed. The water in his body was separated out, piped away, and preserved. The electrolyte balances were recorded and simultaneously transmitted in a parallel stream of electrons. It would reach the spider receiver along with the lead end of the cat-polymer, to be used in the reconstruction.

Thirty seconds passed. Now Garble was only partially in Clotho. The polymer chain, invisible and incredibly long, was passing into Ginungagap. On the far side the spiders were beginning to knit it up.

If all was going well . . .

Ninety-two seconds after they flashed on, the alphanumerics stopped twinkling on the screen. Garble was gone from Clotho. The clamshell opened and the remote cameras showed it to be empty. A cheer arose.

Somebody boosted Dominguez atop a keyout. Intercom cameras swiveled to follow. He wavered fractionally, said "My friends," and launched into a speech. Abigail didn't listen.

Paul's hand fell on her shoulder. It was the first time he had touched her since their initial meeting. "He's only a scientist," he said. "He had no idea how close you are to that cat."

"Look, I *asked* to go. I knew the risks. But Garble's just an animal; he wasn't given the choice."

Paul groped for words. "In a way, this is what your training has been about—the reason you're going across instead of someone like Dominguez. He projects his own reactions onto other people. If—"

Then, seeing that she wasn't listening, he said, "Anyway, you'll have a cat to play with in a few hours. They're only keeping him long enough to test out the life systems."

There was a festive air to the second gathering. The spiders reported that Garble had translated flawlessly. A brief visual display showed him stalking about Clotho's sister platform, irritable but apparently unharmed.

"There," somebody said. The screen indicated that the receiver net had taken in the running end of the cat's polymer chain. They waited a minute and a half and the operation was over.

It was like a conjuring trick: the clamshell closed on emptiness. Water was piped in. Then it opened and Garble floated over its center, quietly licking one paw.

Abigail smiled at the homeliness of it. "Welcome back, Garble," she said quietly. "I'll get the guys in Bio to brew up some cream for you."

Paul's eyes flicked in her direction. They lingered for no time at all, long enough to file away another datum for future use, and then his attention was elsewhere. She waited until his back was turned and stuck out her tongue at him.

The tub docked with Clotho and a technician floated in. She removed her helmet self-consciously, aware of her audience. One hand extended, she bobbed toward the cat, calling softly.

"Get that jerk on the line," Paul snapped. "I want her helmet back on. That's sloppy. That's real—"

And in that instant Garble sprang.

Garble was a black-and-white streak that flashed past the astonished tech, through the air lock, and into the open tug. The cat pounced on the pilot panel. Its forelegs hit the controls. The hatch slammed shut, and the tug's motors burst into life.

Crew room techs grabbed wildly at their keyouts. The tech on Clotho frantically tried to fit her helmet back on. And the tug took off, blasting away half the protective dome and all the platform's air.

The screens showed a dozen different scenes, lenses shifting from close to distant and back. "Cheyney," Paul said quietly. Dominguez was frozen, looking bewildered. "Take it out."

"It's coming right at us!" somebody shouted.

Cheyney's fingers flicked: rap-tap-rap.

A bright nuclear flower blossomed.

There was silence, dead and complete, in the crew room. *I'm missing something,* Abigail thought. *We just blew up 5 percent of our tug fleet to kill a cat.*

"*Pull* that transmitter!" Paul strode through the crew

room, scattering orders. "Nothing goes out! You, you, and you"—he yanked techs away from their keyouts—"*off* those things. I want the whole goddamned net shut *down*."

"Paul, . . ." an operator said.

"Keep on receiving." He didn't bother to look. "Whatever they want to send. Dump it all in storage and don't merge any of it with our data until we've gone over it."

Alone and useless in the center of the room, Dominguez stuttered, "What—what happened?"

"You blind idiot!" Paul turned on him viciously. "Your precious aliens have just made their first hostile move. The cat that came back was nothing like the one we sent. They made changes. They retransmitted it with instructions wet-wired into its brain."

"But why would they want to steal a tug?"

"*We don't know!*" Paul roared. "Get that through your head. We don't know their motives and we don't know how they think. But we would have known a lot more about their intentions than we wanted if I hadn't rigged that tug with an abort device."

"You didn't—" Dominguez began. He thought better of the statement.

"—have the authority to rig that device," Paul finished for him. "That's right. I didn't." His voice was heavy with sarcasm.

Dominguez seemed to shrivel. He stared bleakly, blankly, about him, then turned and left, slightly hunched over. Thoroughly discredited in front of the people who worked for him.

That was cold, Abigail thought. She marveled at Paul's cruelty. Not for an instant did she believe that the anger in his voice was real, that he was capable of losing control.

Which meant that in the midst of confusion and stress, Paul had found time to make a swift play for more power. To Abigail's newly suspicious eye, it looked like a successful one, too.

For five days Paul held the net shut by sheer willpower and force of personality. Information came in but did not go out. Bell-Sandia administration was not behind him; too much time and money had been sunk into Clotho to abandon the project. But Paul had the support of the tech crew, and he knew how to use it.

"Nothing as big as Bell-Sandia runs on popularity," Paul explained. "But I've got enough sympathy from above, and enough hesitation and official cowardice to keep this place shut down long enough to get a message across."

The incoming information flow fluctuated wildly, shifting from subject to subject. Data sequences were dropped halfway through and incomplete. Nonsense came in. The spiders were shifting through strategies in search of the key that would reopen the net.

"When they start repeating themselves," Paul said, "we can assume they understand the threat."

"But we *wouldn't* shut the net down permanently," Abigail pointed out.

Paul shrugged. "So it's a bluff."

They were sharing an after-shift drink in a fifth-level bar. Small red lizards scuttled about the rock wall behind the bartender. "And if your bluff doesn't work?" Abigail asked. "If it's all for nothing—what then?"

Paul's shoulders sagged, a minute shifting of tensions. "Then we trust in the goodwill of the spiders," he said. "We let them call the shots. And they will treat us benevolently or not, depending. In either case," his voice became dark, "I'll have played a lot of games and manipulated a lot of people for no reason at all." He took her hand. "If that happens, I'd like to apologize." His grip was tight, his knuckles pale.

That night Abigail dreamed she was falling.

Light rainbowed all about her, in a violent splintering of bone and tearing of flesh. She flung out an arm and it bounced on something warm and yielding.

"Abigail."

She twisted and tumbled and something smashed into her ribs. Bright spikes of yellow darted up.

"Abigail!" Someone was shaking her, speaking loudly into her face. The rocks and sky went gray, were overlaid by unresolved images. Her eyelids struggled apart, fell together, opened.

"Oh," she said.

Paul rocked back on his heels. Fish darted about in the water beneath him. "There now," he said. Blue-green lights shifted gently underwater, moving in long, slow arcs. "Dream over?"

Abigail shivered, clutched his arm, let go of it almost immediately. She nodded.

"Good. Tell me about it."

"I—" Abigail began. "Are you asking me as a human being or in your official capacity?"

"I don't make that distinction."

She stretched out a leg and scratched her big toe, to gain time to think. She really didn't have any appropriate thoughts. "Okay," she said, and told him the entire dream.

Paul listened intently, rubbed a thumb across his chin thoughtfully when she was done. "We hired you on the basis of that incident, you know," he said. "Coolness under stress. Weak body image. There were a lot of gravity bums to choose from. But I figured you were just a hair tougher, a little bit grittier."

"What are you trying to tell me? That I'm replaceable?"

Paul shrugged. "Everybody's replaceable. I just wanted to be sure you knew that you could back out if you want. It wouldn't wreck our project."

"I don't want to back out." Abigail chose her words carefully, spoke them slowly, to avoid giving vent to the anger she felt building up inside. "Look, I've been on the gravity circuit for ten years. I've been everywhere in the system there is to go. Did you know that there are less than two thousand people alive who've set foot on Mercury *and* Pluto? We've got a little club; we get together once a year." Seaweed shifted about her; reflections of the floor lights formed nebulous swimming shapes on the walls. "I've spent my entire life going around and around and around the sun, and never really getting anywhere. I want to travel, and there's nowhere left for me to go. So you offer me a way out and then ask if I want to back down. Like hell I do!"

"Why don't you believe that going through Ginungagap is death?" Paul asked quietly. She looked into his eyes, saw cool calculations going on behind them. It frightened her, almost. He was measuring her, passing judgment, warping events into long logical chains that did not take human factors into account. He was an alien presence.

"It's—common sense, is all. I'll be the same when I exit as when I go in. There'll be no difference, not an atom's worth, not a scintilla."

"The *substance* will be different. Every atom will be different. Not a single electron in your body will be the same one you have now."

"Well, how does that differ so much from normal life?" Abigail demanded. "All our bodies are in constant flux. Molecules come and go. Bit by bit, we're replaced. Does that make us different people from moment to moment? 'All that is body is as coursing vapors,' right?"

Paul's eyes narrowed. "Marcus Aurelius. Your quotation isn't complete, though. It goes on: 'All that is of the soul is dreams and vapors.' "

"What's that supposed to mean?"

"It means that the quotation doesn't say what you claimed it did. If you care to read it literally, it argues the opposite of what you're saying."

"Still, you can't have it both ways. Either the me that comes out of the spider black hole is the same as the one who went in, or I'm not the same person as I was an instant ago."

"I'd argue differently," Paul said. "But no matter. Let's go back to sleep."

He held out a hand, but Abigail felt no inclination to accept it. "Does this mean I've passed your test?"

Paul closed his eyes, stretched a little. "You're still reasonably afraid of dying, and you don't believe that you will," he said. "Yeah. You pass."

"Thanks a heap," Abigail said. They slept, not touching, for the rest of the night.

Three days later Abigail woke up, and Paul was gone. She touched the wall and spoke his name. A recording appeared. "Dominguez has been called up to Administration," it said. Paul appeared slightly distracted; he had not looked directly into the recorder and his image avoided Abigail's eyes. "I'm going to reopen the net before he returns. It's best we beat him to the punch." The recording clicked off.

Abigail routed an intercom call through to the crew room. A small chime notified him of her call, and he waved a hand in combined greeting and direction to remain silent. He was hunched over a keyout. The screen above it came to life.

"Ritual greetings, spider," he said.

"Hello, human. We wish to pursue our previous inquiry: the meaning of the term 'art' which was used by the human Dominguez six-sixteenths of the way through his major presentation."

"This is a difficult question. To understand a definition of art, you must first know the philosophy of aesthetics. This is a comprehensive field of knowledge comparable to the study of perception. In many ways it is related."

"What is the trade value of this field of knowledge?"

Dominguez appeared, looking upset. He opened his mouth, and Paul touched a finger to his own lips, nodding his head toward the screen.

"Significant. Our society considers art and science as being of roughly equal value."

"We will consider what to offer in exchange."

"Good. We also have a question for you. Please wait while we select the phrasing." He cut the translation lines, turned to Dominguez. "Looks like your raft gambit paid off. Though I'm surprised they bit at that particular piece of bait."

Dominguez looked weary. "Did they mention the incident with the cat?"

"No, nor the communications blackout."

The old man sighed. "I always felt close to the aliens," he said. "Now they seem—cold, inhuman." He attempted a chuckle. "That was almost a pun, wasn't it?"

"In a human, we'd call it a professional attitude. Don't let it spoil your accomplishment," Paul said. "This could be as big as optics." He opened the communications line again. "Our question is now phrased." Abigail noted he had not told Dominguez of her presence.

"Please go ahead."

"Why did you alter our test animal?"

Much leg waving. "We improved the ratios garble centers of perception garble wetware garble making the animal twelve-sixteenths as intelligent as a human. We thought you would be pleased."

"We were not. Why did the test animal behave in a hostile manner toward us?"

The spider's legs jerked quickly and it disappeared from the screen. Like an echo, the machine said, "Please wait."

Abigail watched Dominguez throw Paul a puzzled look. In the background, a man with a leather sack looped over one shoulder was walking slowly along the twisty access path. His hand dipped into the sack, came out, sprinkled fireflies among the greenery. Dipped in, came out again. Even in the midst of crisis the trivia of day-to-day existence went on.

The spider reappeared, accompanied by two of its own kind. Their legs interlaced and retreated rapidly, a visual pantomime of an excited conversation. Finally one of their number addressed the screen.

"We have discussed the matter."

"So I see."

"It is our conclusion that the experience of translation through Ginungagap had a negative effect on the test animal. This was not anticipated. It is new knowledge. We know little of the psychology of carbon-based life."

"You're saying the test animal was driven mad?"

"Key word did not translate. We assume understanding. Steps must be taken to prevent a recurrence of this damage. Can you do this?"

Paul said nothing.

"Is this the reason why communications were interrupted?"

No reply.

"There is a cultural gap. Can you clarify?"

"Thank you for your cooperation," Paul said, and switched the screen off. "You can set your people to work," he told Dominguez. "No reason why they should answer the last few questions, though."

"Were they telling the truth?" Dominguez asked wonderingly.

"Probably not. But at least now they'll think twice before trying to jerk us around again." He winked at Abigail, and she switched off the intercom.

They re-ran the test using a baboon shipped out from the Belt Zoological Gardens. Abigail watched it arrive from the lip station, crated and snarling.

"They're a lot stronger than we are," Paul said. "Very agile. If the spiders want to try any more tricks, we couldn't offer them better bait."

The test went smooth as silk. The baboon was shot through Ginungagap, held by the spiders for several hours, and returned. Exhaustive testing showed no tampering with the animal.

Abigail asked how accurate the tests were. Paul hooked his hands behind his back. "We're returning the baboon to the Belt. We wouldn't do that if we had any doubts. But—" He raised an eyebrow, asking Abigail to finish the thought.

"But if they're really hostile, they won't underestimate us twice. They'll wait for a human to tamper with."

Paul nodded.

The night before Abigail's send-off they made love. It was a frenzied and desperate act, performed wordlessly and without tenderness. Afterward they lay together, Abigail idly playing with Paul's curls.

"Gail . . ." His head was hidden in her shoulder; she couldn't see his face. His voice was muffled.

"Mmmm?"

"Don't go."

She wanted to cry. Because as soon as he said it, she knew it was another test, the final one. And she also knew that Paul wanted her to fail it. That he honestly believed transversing Ginungagap would kill her, and that the woman who emerged from the spiders' black hole would not be herself.

His eyes were shut; she could tell by the creases in his forehead. He knew what her answer was. There was no way he could avoid knowing.

Abigail sensed that this was as close to a declaration of emotion as Paul was capable of. She felt how he despised himself for using his real emotions as yet another test, and how he could not even pretend to himself that there were circumstances under which he would *not* so test her. *This must be how it feels to think as he does,* she thought. *To constantly scrabble after every last implication, like eternally picking at a scab.*

"Oh, Paul," she said.

He wrenched about, turning his back to her. "Sometimes I wish"—his hands rose in front of his face like claws; they moved toward his eyes, closed into fists— "that for just ten goddamned minutes I could turn my mind off." His voice was bitter.

Abigail huddled against him, looped a hand over his side and onto his chest. "Hush," she said.

The tug backed away from Clotho, dwindling until it was one of a ring of bright sparks pacing the platform. Mother was a point source lost in the star field. Abigail shivered, pulled off her arm bands and shoved them into a storage sack. She reached for her *cache-sexe,* hesitated.

The hell with it, she thought. *It's nothing they haven't seen before.* She shucked it off, stood naked. Gooseflesh rose on the backs of her legs. She swam to the transmittal device, feeling awkward under the distant watching eyes.

Abigail groped into the clamshell. "Go," she said.

The metal closed about her seamlessly, encasing her in darkness. She floated in a lotus position, bobbing slightly.

A light, gripping field touched her, stilling her motion. On cue, hypnotic commands took hold in her brain. Her breathing became shallow; her heart slowed. She felt her body ease into stasis. The final command took hold.

Abigail weighed 50 keys. Even though the water in her body would not be transmitted, the polymer chain she was to be transformed into would be 275 kilometers long. It would take 15 minutes and 17 seconds to unravel at light speed, negligibly longer at translation speed. She would still be sitting in Clotho when the spiders began knitting her up.

It was possible that Garble had gone mad from a relatively swift transit. Paul doubted it, but he wasn't taking any chances. To protect Abigail's sanity, the meds had wet-wired a travel fantasy into her brain. It would blind her to external reality while she traveled.

She was an eagle. Great feathered wings extended out from her shoulders. Clotho was gone, leaving her alone in space. Her skin was red and leathery, her breasts hard and unyielding. Feathers covered her thighs, giving way at the knees to talons.

She moved her wings, bouncing lightly against the thin solar wind swirling down into Ginungagap. The vacuum felt like absolute freedom. She screamed a predator's exultant shrill. Nothing enclosed her; she was free of restrictions forever.

Below her lay Ginungagap, the primal chasm, an invisible challenge marked by a red smudge of glowing gases. It was inchoate madness, a gibbering, impersonal force that wanted to draw her in, to crush her in its embrace. Its hunger was fierce and insatiable.

Abigail held her place briefly, effortlessly. Then she folded her wings and dove.

A rain of X rays stung through her, the scattering of

Ginungagap's accretion disk. They were molten iron passing through a ghost. Shrieking defiance, she attacked, scattering sparks in her wake.

Ginungagap grew, swelled until it swallowed up her vision. It was purest black, unseeable, unknowable, a thing of madness. It was Enemy.

A distant objective part of her knew that she was still in Clotho, the polymer chain being unraveled from her body, accelerated by a translator, passing through two black holes, and simultaneously being knit up by the spiders. It didn't matter.

She plunged into Ginungagap as effortlessly as if it were the film of a soap bubble.

In—

—And out.

It was like being reversed in a mirror, or watching an entertainment run backward. She was instantly flying out the way she came. The sky was a mottled mass of violet light.

The stars before her brightened from violet to blue. She craned her neck, looked back at Ginungagap, saw its disk-shaped nothingness recede, and screamed in frustration because it had escaped her. She spread her wings to slow her flight and—

—was sitting in a dark place. Her hand reached out, touched metal, recognized the inside of a clamshell device.

A hairline crack of light looped over her, widened. The clamshell opened.

Oceans of color bathed her face. Abigail straightened, and the act of doing so lifted her up gently. She stared through the transparent bubble at a phosphorescent foreverness of light.

My God, she thought. *The stars.*

The stars were thicker, more numerous than she was used to seeing them—large and bright and glittery rich. She was probably someplace significant, in a star cluster or the center of the galaxy; she couldn't guess. She felt irrationally happy to simply *be;* she took a deep breath, then laughed.

"Abigail Vanderhoek."

She turned to face the voice, and found that it came from a machine. Spiders crouched beside it, legs moving silently. Outside, in the hard vacuum, were more spiders.

"We regret any pain this may cause," the machine said.

Then the spiders rushed forward. She had no time to react. Sharp mandibles loomed before her, then dipped to her neck. Impossibly swift, they sliced through her throat, severed her spine. A sudden jerk and her head was separated from her body.

It happened in an instant. She felt brief pain, and the dissociation of actually *seeing* her decapitated body just beginning to react. And then she died.

A spark. A light. *I'm alive,* she thought. Consciousness returned like an ancient cathode tube warming up. Abigail stretched slowly, bobbing gently in the air, collecting her thoughts. She was in the sister-Clotho again—not in pain, her head and neck firmly on her shoulders. There were spiders in the platform, and a few floating outside.

"Abigail Vanderhoek," the machine said. "We are ready to begin negotiations."

Abigail said nothing.

After a moment, the machine said, "Are you damaged? Are your thoughts impaired?" A pause, then, "Was your mind not protected during transit?"

"Is that you waving the legs there? Outside the platform?"

"Yes. It is important that you talk with the other humans. You must convey our questions. They will not communicate with us."

"I have a few questions of my own," Abigail said. "I won't cooperate until you answer them."

"We will answer any questions provided you neither garble nor garble."

"What do you take me for?" Abigail asked. "Of course I won't."

Long hours later she spoke to Paul and Dominguez. At her request the spiders had withdrawn, leaving her alone. Dominguez looked drawn and haggard. "I swear we had no idea the spiders would attack you," Dominguez said. "We saw it on the screens. I was certain you'd been killed. . . ." His voice trailed off.

"Well, I'm alive, no thanks to you guys. Just what *is* this crap about an explosive substance in my bones, anyway?"

"An explosive—I swear we know nothing of anything of the kind."

"A close relative to plastique," Paul said. "I had a small editing device attached to Clotho's translator. It altered roughly half the bone marrow in your sternum, pelvis, and femurs in transmission. I'd hoped the spiders wouldn't pick up on it so quickly."

"You actually did," Abigail marveled. "The spiders weren't lying; they decapitated me in self-defense. What the holy hell did you think you were *doing?*"

"Just a precaution," Paul said. "We wet-wired you to trigger the stuff on command. That way, we could have taken out the spider installation if they'd tried something funny."

"Um," Dominguez said, "this *is* being recorded. What I'd like to know, Ms. Vanderhoek, is how you escaped being destroyed."

"I didn't," Abigail said. "The spiders killed me. Fortunately, they anticipated the situation, and recorded the transmission. It was easy for them to recreate me—after they edited out the plastique."

Dominguez gave her a odd look. "You don't—feel anything particular about this?"

"Like what?"

"Well—" He turned to Paul helplessly.

"Like the real Abigail Vanderhoek died and you're simply a very realistic copy," Paul said.

"Look, we've been through this garbage before," Abigail began angrily.

Paul smiled formally at Dominguez. It was hard to adjust to seeing the two in flat black-and-white. "She doesn't believe a word of it."

"If you guys can pull yourselves up out of your navels for a minute," Abigail said, "I've got a line on something the spiders have that you want. They claim they've sent probes through their black hole."

"Probes?" Paul stiffened. Abigail could sense the thoughts coursing through his skull, of defenses and military applications.

"Carbon-hydrogen chain probes. Organic probes. Self-constructing transmitters. They've got a carbon-based secondary technology."

"Nonsense," Dominguez said. "How could they convert back to coherent matter with a receiver?"

Abigail shrugged. "They claim to have found a loop-hole."

"How does it work?" Paul snapped.

"They wouldn't say. They seemed to think you'd pay well for it."

"That's very true," Paul said slowly. "Oh, yes."

The conference took almost as long as her session with the spiders had. Abigail was bone weary when Dominguez finally said, "That ties up the official minutes. We now stop recording." A line tracked across the screen, was gone. "If you want to speak to anyone off the record, now's your chance. Perhaps there is someone close to you . . ."

"Close? No." Abigail almost laughed. "I'll speak to Paul alone, though."

A spider floated by outside Clotho II. It was a golden, crablike being, its body slightly opalescent. It skittered along unseen threads strung between the open platforms of the spider star-city. "I'm listening," Paul said.

"You turned me into a *bomb*, you freak."

"So?"

"I could have been killed."

"Am I supposed to care?"

"You damn well ought to, considering the liberties you've taken with my fair white body."

"Let's get one thing understood," Paul said. "The woman I slept with, the woman I cared for, is dead. I have no feelings toward or obligations to you whatsoever."

"Paul," Abigail said. *"I'm not dead.* Believe me, I'd know if I were."

"How could I possibly trust what you think or feel? It could all be attitudes the spiders wet-wired into you. We know they have the technology."

"How do you know that *your* attitudes aren't wet-wired in? For that matter, how do you know anything is real? I mean, these are the most sophomoric philosophic ideas there are. But I'm the same woman I was a few hours ago. My memories, opinions, feelings—they're all the same as they were. There's absolutely no difference between me and the woman you slept with on the *Clarke.*"

"I know." Paul's eyes were cold. "That's the horror of it." He snapped off the screen.

Abigail found herself staring at the lifeless machinery. *God, that hurt,* she thought. *It shouldn't, but it hurt.* She went to her quarters.

The spiders had done a respectable job of preparing for her. There were no green plants, but otherwise the room was the same as the one she'd had on the *Clarke*. They'd even been able to spin the platform, giving her an adequate down-orientation. She sat in her hammock, determined to think pleasanter thoughts. About the offer the spiders had made, for example. The one she hadn't told Paul and Dominguez about.

Banned by their chemistry from using black holes to travel, the spiders needed a representative to see to their interests among the stars. They had offered her the job.

Or perhaps the plural would be more appropriate— they had offered her the jobs. Because there were too many places to go for one woman to handle them all. They needed a dozen—in time, perhaps, a hundred— Abigail Vanderhoeks.

In exchange for licensing rights to her personality, the right to make as many duplicates of her as were needed, they were willing to give her the rights to the self-reconstructing black hole platforms.

It would make her a rich woman—a hundred rich women—back in human space. And it would open the universe. She hadn't committed herself yet, but there was no way she was going to turn down the offer. The chance to see a thousand stars? No, she would not pass it by.

When she got old, too, they could create another Abigail from their recording, burn her new memories into it, and destroy her old body.

I'm going to see the stars, she thought. *I'm going to live forever.* She couldn't understand why she didn't feel elated, wondered at the sudden rush of melancholy that ran through her like the precursor of tears.

Garble jumped into her lap, offered his belly to be scratched. The spiders had recorded him, too. They had been glad to restore him to his unaltered state when she made the request. She stroked his stomach and buried her face in his fur.

"Pretty little cat," she told him. "I thought you were dead."

FROZEN JOURNEY

〰〰〰〰〰〰〰〰〰〰〰〰〰〰〰〰〰

Philip K. Dick

Trips to other star-systems will, in the fore-seeable future, require many years; in this situation it will be sensible for the passengers to remain in "cold sleep" while the ship is run by a sophisticated computer. But what if one cryonic tank malfunctions, leaving its occupant conscious but paralyzed for the duration of the ten-year flight? Could any computer, no matter how extensive its abilities, keep him sane?

Philip K. Dick has been one of sf's major writers for nearly thirty years; his intense, sometimes darkly humorous, explorations of the relationships between human psychology and "reality" have established him as almost a "cult author" in the United States and Europe. His most famous novel is *The Man in the High Castle,* which won the Hugo Award in 1963.

AFTER TAKE-OFF, THE SHIP ROUTINELY
monitored the condition of the 60 people sleeping in its
cryonic tanks. One malfunction showed, that of person
nine. His EEG revealed brain activity.

Shit, the ship said to itself.

Complex homeostatic devices locked into circuit feed,
and the ship contacted person nine.

"You are slightly awake," the ship said, utilizing the
psychotronic route; there was no point in rousing person
nine to full consciousness. After all, the flight would last
a decade.

Virtually unconscious but, unfortunately, still able to
think, person nine thought, Someone is addressing me.
He said, "Where am I located? I don't see anything."

"You're in faulty cryonic suspension."

He said, "Then I shouldn't be able to hear you."

"Faulty, I said. That's the point; you can hear me. Do
you know your name?"

"Victor Kemmings. Bring me out of this."

"We are in flight."

"Then put me under."

"Just a moment." The ship examined the cryonic
mechanisms; it scanned and surveyed, and then it said,
"I will try."

Time passed. Victor Kemmings, unable to see anything, unaware of his body, found himself still conscious.
"Lower my temperature," he said. He could not hear his

voice; perhaps he only imagined he spoke. Colors floated
toward him and then rushed at him. He liked the colors;
they reminded him of a child's paintbox, the semi-
animated kind, an artificial life form. He had used them
in school, 200 years ago.

"I can't put you under," the voice of the ship sounded
inside Kemmings' head. "The malfunction is too elaborate; I can't correct it and I can't repair it. You will be
conscious for ten years."

The semi-animated colors rushed toward him, but now
they possessed a sinister quality, supplied to them by his
own fear. "Oh, my God," he said. Ten years! The colors
darkened.

As Victor Kemmings lay paralyzed, surrounded by
dismal flickerings of light, the ship explained to him its
strategy. This strategy did not represent a decision on its
part; the ship had been programmed to seek this solution
in case of a malfunction of this sort.

"What I will do," the voice of the ship came to him, "is
feed you sensory stimulation. The peril to you is sensory
deprivation. If you are conscious for ten years without
sensory data, your mind will deteriorate. When we reach
the LR4 system, you will be a vegetable."

"Well, what do you intend to feed me?" Kemmings
said in panic. "What do you have in your information
storage banks? All the video soap operas of the last century? Wake me up and I'll walk around."

"There is no air in me," the ship said. "Nothing for
you to eat. No one to talk to, since everyone else is under."

Kemmings said, "I can talk to you. We can play
chess."

"Not for ten years. Listen to me; I say, I have no food
and no air. You must remain as you are . . . a bad com-
promise, but one forced on us. You are talking to me
now. I have no particular information stored. Here is
policy in these situations: I will feed you your own buried
memories, emphasizing the pleasant ones. You possess
two hundred and six years of memories and most of them
have sunk down into your unconscious. This is a splendid
source of sensory data for you to receive. Be of good cheer.
This situation, which you are in, is not unique. It has
never happened within my domain before, but I am pro-

grammed to deal with it. Relax and trust me. I will see that you are provided with a world."

"They should have warned me," Kemmings said, "before I agreed to emigrate."

"Relax," the ship said.

He relaxed, but he was terribly frightened. Theoretically, he should have gone under, into the successful cryonic suspension, then awakened a moment later at his star of destination; or, rather, the planet, the colony-planet, of that star. Everyone else aboard the ship lay in an unknowing state; he was the exception, as if bad karma had attacked him for obscure reasons. Worst of all, he had to depend totally on the good will of the ship. Suppose it elected to feed him monsters. The ship could terrorize him for ten years—ten objective years and undoubtedly more from a subjective standpoint. He was, in effect, totally in the ship's power. Did interstellar ships enjoy such a situation? He knew little about interstellar ships; his field was microbiology. Let me think, he said to himself. My first wife, Martine; the lovely little French girl who wore jeans and a red shirt open to the waist and cooked delicious crêpes.

"I hear," the ship said. "So be it."

The rushing colors resolved themselves into coherent, stable shapes. A building: a little old yellow wooden house that he had owned when he was 19 years old, in Wyoming. "Wait," he said in panic. "The foundation was bad; it was on a mud sill. And the roof leaked." But he saw the kitchen, with the table that he had built himself. And he felt glad.

"You will not know, after a little while," the ship said, "that I am feeding you your own buried memories."

"I haven't thought of that house in a century," he said, wonderingly; entranced, he made out his old electric drip coffeepot with the box of paper filters beside it. This is the house where Martine and I lived, he realized. "Martine!" he said aloud.

"I'm on the phone," Martine said, from the living room.

The ship said, "I will cut in only when there is an emergency. I will be monitoring you, however, to be sure you are in a satisfactory state. Don't be afraid."

"Turn down the right rear burner on the stove," Martine called. He could hear her and yet not see her. He made his way from the kitchen through the dining room and into the living room. At the VF, Martine stood in rapt conversation with her brother; she wore shorts and she was barefoot. Through the front windows of the living room, he could see the street; a commercial vehicle was trying to park, without success.

It's a warm day, he thought. I should turn on the air conditioner.

He seated himself on the old sofa as Martine continued her VF conversation, and he found himself gazing at his most cherished possession, a framed poster on the wall above Martine: Gilbert Shelton's *Fat Freddy Says* drawing in which Freddy Freak sits with his cat on his lap and Fat Freddy is trying to say, "Speed kills," but he is so wired on speed—he holds in his hand every kind of amphetamine tablet, pill, Spansule and capsule that exists— that he can't say it, and the cat is gritting its teeth and wincing in a mixture of dismay and disgust. The poster is signed by Gilbert Shelton himself; Kemmings' best friend, Ray Torrance, gave it to him and Martine as a wedding present. It is worth thousands. It was signed by the artist back in the 1980s. Long before either Victor Kemmings or Martine lived.

If we ever run out of money, Kemmings thought to himself, we could sell the poster. It was not *a* poster; it was *the* poster. Martine adored it. The Fabulous Furry Freak Brothers—from the golden age of a long-ago society. No wonder he loved Martine so; she herself loved back, loved the beauties of the world, and treasured and cherished them as she treasured and cherished him; it was a protective love that nourished but did not stifle. It had been her idea to frame the poster; he would have tacked it up on the wall, so stupid was he.

"Hi," Martine said, off the VF now. "What are you thinking?"

"Just that you keep alive what you love," he said.

"I think that's what you're supposed to do," Martine said. "Are you ready for dinner? Open some red wine, a cabernet."

"Will an '07 do?" he said, standing up; he felt, then, like taking hold of his wife and hugging her.

"Either an '07 or a '12." She trotted past him, through the dining room and into the kitchen.

Going down into the cellar, he began to search among

the bottles, which, of course, lay flat. Musty air and dampness; he liked the smell of the cellar, but then he noticed the redwood planks lying half-buried in the dirt and he thought, I know I've got to get a concrete slab poured. He forgot about the wine and went over to the far corner, where the dirt was piled highest; bending down, he poked at a board . . . he poked with a trowel and then he thought, Where did I get this trowel? I didn't have it a minute ago. The board crumbled against the trowel. This whole house is collapsing, he realized. Christ sake. I better tell Martine.

Going back upstairs, the wine forgotten, he started to say to her that the foundation of the house was dangerously decayed; but Martine was nowhere in sight. And nothing cooked on the stove, no pots, no pans. Amazed, he put his hand on the stove and found it cold. Wasn't she just now cooking? he asked himself.

"Martine!" he said loudly.

No response. Except for himself, the house was empty. Empty, he thought, and collapsing. Oh, my God. He seated himself at the kitchen table and felt the chair give slightly under him; it did not give much, but he felt it, he felt the sagging.

I'm afraid, he thought. Where did she go?

He returned to the living room. Maybe she went next door to borrow some spices or butter or something, he reasoned. Nonetheless, panic now filled him.

He looked at the poster. It was unframed. And the edges had been torn.

I know she framed it, he thought; he ran across the room to it, to examine it closely. Faded . . . the artist's signature had faded; he could scarcely make it out. She insisted on framing it and under glare-free, reflection-free glass. But it isn't framed and it's torn! The most precious thing we own!

Suddenly, he found himself crying. It amazed him, his tears. Martine is gone; the poster is deteriorated; the house is crumbling away; nothing is cooking on the stove. This is terrible, he thought. And I don't understand it.

The ship understood it. The ship had been carefully monitoring Victor Kemmings' brain-wave patterns, and the ship knew that something had gone wrong. The wave forms showed agitation and pain. I must get him out of this feed circuit or I will kill him, the ship decided. Where does the flaw lie? it asked itself. Worry dormant in the man; underlying anxieties. Perhaps if I intensify the signal. I will use the same source but amp up the charge. What has happened is that massive subliminal insecurities have taken possession of him; the fault is not mine but lies, instead, in his psychological make-up.

I will try an earlier period in his life, the ship decided. Before the neurotic anxieties got laid down.

In the back yard, Victor scrutinized a bee that had gotten itself trapped in a spider's web. The spider wound up the bee with great care. That's wrong, Victor thought. I'll let the bee loose. Reaching up, he took hold of the encapsulated bee, drew it from the web and, scrutinizing it carefully, began to unwrap it.

The bee stung him; it felt like a little patch of flame.

Why did it sting me? he wondered. I was letting it go.

He went indoors to his mother and told her, but she did not listen; she was watching television. His finger hurt where the bee had stung it, but, more important, he did not understand why the bee would attack its rescuer. I won't do that again, he said to himself.

"Put some Bactine on it," his mother said at last, roused from watching the TV.

He had begun to cry. It was unfair. It made no sense. He was perplexed and dismayed and he felt a hatred toward small living things, because they were dumb. They didn't have any sense.

He left the house, played for a time on his swings, his slide, in his sandbox, and then he went into the garage, because he heard a strange flapping, whirring sound, like a kind of fan. Inside the gloomy garage, he found that a bird was fluttering against the cobwebbed rear window, trying to get out. Below it, the cat, Dorky, leaped and leaped, trying to reach the bird.

He picked up the cat; the cat extended its body and its front legs, it extended its jaws and bit into the bird. At once, the cat scrambled down and ran off with the still-fluttering bird.

Victor ran into the house. "Dorky caught a bird!" he told his mother.

"That goddamn cat." His mother took the broom from

the closet in the kitchen and ran outside, trying to find Dorky. The cat had concealed itself under the bramble-bushes; she could not reach it with the broom. "I'm going to get rid of that cat," his mother said.

Victor did not tell her that he had arranged for the cat to catch the bird: he watched in silence as his mother tried and tried to pry Dorky out from her hiding place; Dorky was crunching up the bird; he could hear the sound of breaking bones, small bones. He felt a strange feeling, as if he should tell his mother what he had done, and yet, if he told her, she would punish him. I won't do that again, he said to himself. His face, he realized, had turned red. What if his mother figured it out? What if she had some secret way of knowing? Dorky couldn't tell her and the bird was dead. No one would ever know. He was safe.

But he felt bad. That night, he could not eat his dinner. Both his parents noticed. They thought he was sick; they took his temperature. He said nothing about what he had done. His mother told his father about Dorky and they decided to get rid of Dorky. Seated at the table, listening, Victor began to cry.

"All right," his father said gently. "We won't get rid of her. It's natural for a cat to catch a bird."

The next day, he sat playing in his sandbox. Some plants grew up through the sand. He broke them off. Later, his mother told him that had been a wrong thing to do.

Alone in the back yard, in his sandbox, he sat with a pail of water, forming a small mound of wet sand. The sky, which had been blue and clear, became by degrees overcast. A shadow passed over him and he looked up. He sensed a presence around him, something vast that could think.

You are responsible for the death of the bird, the presence thought; he could understand its thoughts.

"I know," he said. He wished, then, that he could die. That he could replace the bird and die for it, leaving it as it had been, fluttering against the cobwebbed window of the garage.

The bird wanted to fly and eat and live, the presence thought.

"Yes," he said, miserably.

You must never do that again, the presence told him.
"I'm sorry," he said, and wept.

This is a very neurotic person, the ship realized. I am
having an awful lot of trouble finding happy memories.
There is too much fear in him and too much guilt. He
has buried it all, and yet it is still there, worrying him
like a dog worrying a rag. Where can I go in his memories to find him solace? I must come up with ten years
of memories, or his mind will be lost.

Perhaps, the ship thought, the error that I am making
is in the area of choice on my part; I should allow him to
select his own memories. However, the ship realized, this
will allow an element of fantasy to enter. And that is not
usually good. Still. . . .

I will try the segment dealing with his first marriage
once again, the ship decided. He really loved Martine.
Perhaps this time, if I keep the intensity of the memories
at a greater level, the entropic factor can be abolished.
What happened was a subtle vitiation of the remembered
world, a decay of structure. I will try to compensate for
that. So be it.

"Do you suppose Gilbert Shelton really signed this?"
Martine said pensively; she stood before the poster, her
arms folded; she rocked back and forth slightly, as if
seeking a better perspective on the brightly colored drawing hanging on their living-room wall. "I mean, it could
have been forged. By a dealer somewhere along the line.
During Shelton's lifetime or after."

"The letter of authentication," Victor Kemmings reminded her.

"Oh, that's right!" She smiled her warm smile. "Ray
gave us the letter that goes with it. But suppose the letter
is a forgery? What we need is another letter certifying
that the first letter is authentic." Laughing, she walked
away from the poster.

"Ultimately," Kemmings said, "we would have to have
Gilbert Shelton here to personally testify that he signed
it."

"Maybe he wouldn't know. There's that story about the
man taking the Picasso picture to Picasso and asking him
if it was authentic, and Picasso immediately signed it
and said, 'Now it's authentic.' " She put her arm around

Kemmings and, standing on tiptoe, kissed him on the cheek. "It's genuine. Ray wouldn't have given us a forgery. He's the leading expert on counterculture art of the Twentieth Century. Do you know that he owns an actual lid of dope? It's preserved under———"

"Ray is dead," Victor said.

"What?" She gazed at him in astonishment. "Do you mean something happened to him since we last———"

"He's been dead two years," Kemmings said. "I was responsible. I was driving the buzz car. I wasn't cited by the police, but it was my fault."

"Ray is living on Mars!" She stared at him.

"I know I was responsible. I never told you. I never told anyone. I'm sorry. I didn't mean to do it. I saw it flapping against the window, and Dorky was trying to reach it, and I lifted Dorky up, and I don't know why, but Dorky grabbed it———"

"Sit down, Victor." Martine led him to the overstuffed chair and made him seat himself. "Something's wrong," she said.

"I know," he said. "Something terrible is wrong. I'm responsible for the taking of a life, a precious life that can never be replaced. I'm sorry. I wish I could make it OK, but I can't."

After a pause, Martine said, "Call Ray."

"The cat———" he said.

"What cat?"

"There." He pointed. "In the poster. On Fat Freddy's lap. That's Dorky. Dorky killed Ray."

Silence.

"The presence told me," Kemmings said. "It was God. I didn't realize it at the time, but God saw me commit the crime. The murder. And He will never forgive me."

His wife stared at him numbly.

"God sees everything you do," said Kemmings. "He sees even the falling sparrow. Only in this case, it didn't fall; it was grabbed. Grabbed out of the air and torn down. God is tearing this house down which is my body, to pay me back for what I've done. We should have had a building contractor look this house over before we bought it. It's just falling goddamn to pieces. In a year, there won't be anything left of it. Don't you believe me?"

Martine faltered, "I———"

"Watch." Kemmings reached up his arms toward the

ceiling; he stood; he reached; he could not touch the ceiling. He walked to the wall and then, after a pause, put his hand through the wall.

Martine screamed.

The ship aborted the memory retrieval instantly. But the harm had been done.

He has integrated his early fears and guilt into one interwoven grid, the ship said to itself. There is no way I can serve up a pleasant memory to him, because he instantly contaminates it. However pleasant the original experience in itself was. This is a serious situation, the ship decided. The man is already showing signs of psychosis. And we are hardly into the trip; years lie ahead of him.

After allowing itself time to think the situation through, the ship decided to contact Victor Kemmings once more.

"Mr. Kemmings," the ship said.

"I'm sorry," Kemmings said. "I didn't mean to foul up those retrievals. You did a good job, but I———"

"Just a moment," the ship said. "I am not equipped to do psychiatric reconstruction of you; I am a simple mechanism, that's all. What is it you want? Where do you want to be and what do you want to be doing?"

"I want to arrive at our destination," Kemmings said. "I want this trip to be over."

Ah, the ship thought. That is the solution.

One by one, the cryonic systems shut down. One by one, the people returned to life, among them Victor Kemmings. What amazed him was the lack of a sense of the passage of time. He had entered the chamber, lain down, had felt the membrane cover him and the temperature begin to drop———

And now he stood on the ship's external platform, the unloading platform, gazing down at a verdant planetary landscape. This, he realized, is LR4-six, the colony world to which I have come in order to begin a new life.

"Looks good," a heavy-set woman beside him said.

"Yes," he said, and felt the newness of the landscape rush up at him, its promise of a beginning. Something better than he had known the past 200 years. I am a fresh person in a fresh world, he thought. And he felt glad.

Colors raced at him, like those of a child's semi-animate

kit. St. Elmo's fire, he realized. That's right; there is a great deal of ionization in this planet's atmosphere. A free light show, such as they had back in the 20th Century.

"Mr. Kemmings," a voice said. An elderly man had come up beside him, to speak to him. "Did you dream?"

"During the suspension?" Kemmings said. "No, not that I can remember."

"I think I dreamed," the elderly man said. "Would you take my arm on the descent ramp? I feel unsteady. The air seems thin. Do you find it thin?"

"Don't be afraid," Kemmings said to him. He took the elderly man's arm. "I'll help you down the ramp. Look; there's a guide coming this way. He'll arrange our processing for us; it's part of the package. We'll be taken to a resort hotel and given first-class accommodations. Read your brochure." He smiled at the uneasy older man to reassure him.

"You'd think our muscles would be nothing but flab after ten years in suspension," the elderly man said.

"It's just like freezing peas," Kemmings said. Holding on to the timid older man, he descended the ramp to the ground. "You can store them forever if you get them cold enough."

"My name's Shelton," the elderly man said.

"What?" Kemmings said, halting. A strange feeling moved through him.

"Don Shelton." The elderly man extended his hand; reflexively, Kemmings accepted it and they shook. "What's the matter, Mr. Kemmings? Are you all right?"

"Sure," he said. "I'm fine. But hungry. I'd like to get something to eat. I'd like to get to our hotel, where I can take a shower and change my clothes." He wondered where their baggage could be found. Probably it would take the ship an hour to unload it. The ship was not particularly intelligent.

In an intimate, confidential tone, elderly Mr. Shelton said, "You know what I brought with me? A bottle of Wild Turkey bourbon. The finest bourbon on Earth. I'll bring it over to your hotel room and we'll share it." He nudged Kemmings.

"I don't drink," Kemmings said. "Only wine." He wondered if there were any good wines here on this distant colony world. Not distant now, he reflected. It is Earth that's distant. I should have done like Mr. Shelton and brought a few bottles with me.

Shelton. What did the name remind him of? Something in his far past, in his early years. Something precious, along with good wine and a pretty, gentle young woman making crepes in an old-fashioned kitchen. Aching memories; memories that hurt.

Presently, he stood by the bed in his hotel room, his suitcase open; he had begun to hang up his clothes. In the corner of the room, a TV hologram showed a newscaster; he ignored it, but liking the sound of a human voice, he kept it on.

Did I have any dreams? he asked himself. During these past ten years?

His hand hurt. Gazing down, he saw a red welt, as if he had been stung. A bee stung me, he realized. But when? How? While I lay in cryonic suspension? Impossible. Yet he could see the welt and he could feel the pain. I'd better get something to put on it, he realized. There's undoubtedly a robot doctor in the hotel; it's a first-rate hotel.

When the robot doctor arrived and began treating the bee sting, Kemmings said, "I got this as punishment for killing the bird."

"Really?" the robot doctor said.

"Everything that ever meant anything to me has been taken away from me," Kemmings said. "Martine, the poster—my little old house with the wine cellar. We had everything and now it's gone. Martine left me because of the bird."

"The bird you killed," the robot doctor said.

"God punished me. He took away all that was precious to me because of my sin. It wasn't Dorky's sin; it was my sin."

"But you were just a little boy," the robot doctor said.

"How did you know that?" Kemmings said. He pulled his hand away from the robot doctor's grasp. "Something's wrong. You shouldn't have known that."

"Your mother told me," the robot doctor said.

"My mother didn't know!"

The robot doctor said, "She figured it out. There was no way the cat could have reached the bird without your help."

"So all the time that I was growing up, she knew. But she never said anything."

"You can forget about it," the robot doctor said.

Kemmings said, "I don't think you exist. There is no possible way that you could know these things. I'm still in cryonic suspension and the ship is still feeding me my own buried memories. So I won't become psychotic from sensory deprivation."

"You could hardly have a memory of completing the trip."

"Wish fulfillment, then. It's the same thing. I'll prove it to you. Do you have a screwdriver?"

"Why?"

Kemmings said, "I'll remove the back of the TV set and you'll see; there's nothing inside it, no components, no parts, no chassis—nothing."

"I don't have a screwdriver."

"A small knife, then. I can see one in your surgical-supply bag." Bending, Kemmings lifted up a small scalpel. "This will do. If I show you, will you believe me?"

"If there's nothing inside the TV cabinet——"

Squatting down, Kemmings removed the screws holding the back panel of the TV set in place. The panel came loose and he set it down on the floor.

There was nothing inside the TV cabinet. And yet the color hologram continued to fill a quarter of the hotel room and the voice of the newscaster issued forth from his three-dimensional image.

"Admit you're the ship," Kemmings said to the robot doctor.

"Oh, dear," the robot doctor said.

Oh, dear, the ship said to itself. And I've got almost ten years of this lying ahead of me. He is hopelessly contaminating his experiences with childhood guilt; he imagines that his wife left him because, when he was four years old, he helped a cat catch a bird. The only solution would be for Martine to return to him; but how am I going to arrange that? She may not still be alive. On the other hand, the ship reflected, maybe she *is* alive. Maybe she could be induced to do something to save her former husband's sanity. People by and large have very positive traits. And ten years from now, it will take a lot to save—

or, rather, restore—his sanity; it will take something drastic, something I myself cannot do alone.

Meanwhile, there was nothing to be done but recycle the wish-fulfillment arrival of the ship at its destination. I will run him through the arrival, the ship decided, then wipe his conscious memory clean and run him through it again. The only positive aspect of this, it reflected, is that it will give me something to do, which may help preserve *my* sanity.

Lying in cryonic suspension—faulty cryonic suspension—Victor Kemmings imagined, once again, that the ship was touching down and he was being brought back to consciousness.

"Did you dream?" a heavy-set woman asked him as the group of passengers gathered on the outer platform. "I have the impression that I dreamed. Early scenes from my life . . . over a century ago."

"None that I can remember," Kemmings said. He was eager to reach his hotel; a shower and a change of clothes would do wonders for his morale. He felt slightly depressed and wondered why.

"There's our guide," an elderly lady said. "They're going to escort us to our accommodations."

"It's in the package," Kemmings said. His depression remained. The others seemed so spirited, so full of life, but over him only a weariness lay, a weighing-down sensation, as if the gravity of this colony-planet were too much for him. Maybe that's it, he said to himself. But according to the brochure, the gravity here matched Earth's; that was one of the attractions.

Puzzled, he made his way slowly down the ramp, step by step, holding on to the rail. I don't really deserve a new chance at life anyhow, he realized. I'm just going through the motions . . . I am not like these other people. There is something wrong with me; I cannot remember what it is, but nonetheless, it is there. In me. A bitter sense of pain. Of lack of worth.

An insect landed on the back of Kemmings' right hand, an old insect, weary with flight. He halted, watched it crawl across his knuckles. I could crush it, he thought. It's so obviously infirm; it won't live much longer, anyhow.

He crushed it—and felt great inner horror. What have

I done? he asked himself. My first moment here and I have wiped out a little life. Is this my new beginning?

Turning, he gazed back up at the ship. Maybe I ought to go back, he thought. Have them freeze me forever. I am a man of guilt, a man who destroys. Tears filled his eyes.

And within its sentient works, the interstellar ship moaned.

During the ten long years remaining of the trip to the LR4 system, the ship had plenty of time to track down Martine Kemmings. It explained the situation to her. She had emigrated to a vast orbiting dome in the Sirius system, found her situation unsatisfactory and was en route back to Earth. Roused from her own cryonic suspension, she listened intently and then agreed to be at the colony world at LR4 when her ex-husband arrived—if it was at all possible.

Fortunately, it was possible.

"I don't think he'll recognize me," Martine said to the ship. "I've allowed myself to age. I don't really approve of entirely halting the aging process."

He'll be lucky if he recognizes anything, the ship thought.

At the intersystem spaceport on the colony world of LR4, Martine stood waiting for the people aboard the ship to appear on the outer platform. She wondered if she would recognize her former husband. She was a little afraid, but she was glad that she had gotten to LR4 in time. It had been close. Another week and his ship would have arrived before hers. Luck is on my side, she said to herself, and scrutinized the newly landed interstellar ship.

People appeared on the platform. She saw him. Victor had changed very little.

As he came down the ramp, holding on to the railing as if weary and hesitant, she went up to him, her hands thrust deep in the pockets of her coat; she felt shy, and when she spoke, she could hardly hear her own voice.

"Hi, Victor," she managed to say.

He halted, gazed at her. "I know you," he said.

"It's Martine," she said.

Holding out his hand, he said, smiling, "You heard about the trouble on the ship?"

"The ship contacted me." She took his hand and held it. "What an ordeal."

"Yeah," he said. "Recirculating memories forever. Did I ever tell you about a bee that I was trying to extricate from a spider's web when I was four years old? The idiotic bee stung me." He bent down and kissed her. "It's good to see you," he said.

"Did the ship——"

"It said it would try to have you here. But it wasn't sure if you could make it."

As they walked toward the terminal building, Martine said, "I was lucky; I managed to get a transfer to a military vehicle, a high-velocity-drive ship that just shot along like a mad thing. A new propulsion system entirely."

Victor Kemmings said, "I have spent more time in my own unconscious mind than any other human in history. Worse than early Twentieth Century psychoanalysis. And the same material over and over again. Did you know I was scared of my mother?"

"*I* was scared of your mother," Martine said. They stood at the baggage depot, waiting for his luggage to appear. "This looks like a really nice little planet. Much better than where I was. . . . I haven't been happy at all."

"So maybe there's a cosmic plan," he said, grinning. "You look great."

"I'm old."

"Medical science."

"It was my decision. I like older people." She surveyed him. He has been hurt a lot by the cryonic malfunction, she said to herself. I can see it in his eyes. They look broken. Broken eyes. Torn down into pieces of fatigue and—defeat. As if his buried, early memories swam up and destroyed him. But it's over, she thought. And I did get here in time.

At the bar in the terminal building, they sat having a drink.

"This old man got me to try Wild Turkey bourbon," Victor said. "It's amazing bourbon. He says it's the best on Earth. He brought a bottle with him from. . . ." His voice died into silence.

"One of your fellow passengers," Martine finished.

"I guess so," he said.

"Well, you can stop thinking of the birds and the bees," Martine said.

"Sex?" he said, and laughed.

"Being stung by a bee; helping a cat catch a bird. That's all past."

"That cat," Victor said, "has been dead one hundred and eighty-two years. I figured it out while they were bringing us all out of suspension. Probably just as well. Dorky. Dorky the killer cat. Nothing like Fat Freddy's cat."

"I had to sell the poster," Martine said. "Finally."

He frowned.

"Remember?" she said. "You let me have it when we split up. Which I always thought was really good of you."

"How much did you get for it?"

"A lot. I should pay you something like. . . ." She calculated. "Taking inflation into account, I should pay you about two million dollars."

"Would you consider," he said, "instead, in place of the money, my share of the sale of the poster, spending some time with me? Until I get used to this planet?"

"Yes," she said. And she meant it. Very much.

They finished their drinks and then, with his luggage transported by robot spacecap, made their way to his hotel room.

"This is a nice room," Martine said, perched on the edge of the bed. "And it has a hologram TV. Turn it on."

"There's no use turning it on," Victor Kemmings said. He stood by the open closet, hanging up his shirts.

"Why not?"

Kemmings said, "There's nothing in it."

Going over to the TV set, Martine turned it on. A hockey game materialized, projected out into the room, in full color, and the sound of the game assailed her ears.

"It works fine," she said.

"I know," he said. "I can prove it. If you have a nail file or something, I'll unscrew the back plate and show you."

"But I can——"

"Look at this." He paused in his work of hanging up his clothes. "Watch me put my hand through the wall." He placed the palm of his right hand against the wall. "See?"

His hand did not go through the wall, because hands do not go through walls; his hand remained pressed against the wall, unmoving.

"And the foundation," he said, "is rotting away."

"Come and sit down by me," Martine said.

"I've lived this often enough to know," he said. "I've lived this over and over again. I come out of suspension; I walk down the ramp; I get my luggage; sometimes I have a drink at the bar and sometimes I come directly to my room. Usually, I turn on the TV and then. . . ." He went over and held his hand toward her. "See where the bee stung me?"

She saw no mark on his hand; she took his hand and held it.

"There is no bee sting there," she said.

"And when the robot doctor comes, I borrow a tool from him and take off the back plate of the TV set. To prove to him that it has no chassis, no components in it. And then the ship starts me over again."

"Victor," she said. "Look at your hand."

"This is the first time you've been here, though," he said.

"Sit down," she said.

"OK." He seated himself on the bed, beside her, but not too close to her.

"Won't you sit closer to me?" she said.

"It makes me too sad," he said. "Remembering you. I really loved you. I wish this was real."

Martine said, "I will sit with you until it is real for you."

"I'm going to try reliving the part with the cat," he said, "and this time *not* pick up the cat and *not* let it get the bird. If I do that, maybe my life will change so that it turns into something happy. Something that is real. My real mistake was separating from you. Here; I'll put my hand through you." He placed his hand against her arm. The pressure of his muscles was vigorous; she felt the weight, the physical presence of him, against her. "See?" he said. "It goes right through you."

"And all this," she said, "because you killed a bird when you were a little boy."

"No," he said. "All this because of a failure in the temperature-regulating assembly aboard the ship. I'm not down to the proper temperature. There's just enough warmth left in my brain cells to permit cerebral activity."

He stood up, then, stretched, smiled at her. "Shall we go get some dinner?" he asked.

She said, "I'm sorry. I'm not hungry."

"I am. I'm going to have some of the local seafood. The brochure says it's terrific. Come along, anyhow; maybe when you see the food and smell it, you'll change your mind."

Gathering up her coat and purse, she went with him.

"This is a beautiful little planet," he said. "I've explored it dozens of times. I know it thoroughly. We should stop downstairs at the pharmacy for some Bactine, though. For my hand. It's beginning to swell and it hurts like hell." He showed her his hand. "It hurts more this time than ever before."

"Do you want me to come back to you?" Martine said.

"Are you serious?"

"Yes," she said. "I'll stay with you as long as you want. I agree; we should never have been separated."

Victor Kemmings said, "The poster is torn."

"What?" she said.

"We should have framed it," he said. "We didn't have sense enough to take care of it. Now it's torn. And the artist is dead."

THE UGLY CHICKENS

Howard Waldrop

Ornithology isn't one of the usual sciences employed in science fiction, but it's certainly a legitimate one. In any case, Howard Waldrop's stories are seldom of the usual kind, and during the past half-dozen years sf readers have come to expect the unexpected from him . . . such as in this fascinating, funny and poignant tale of an ornithologist who discovers that the dodo species did *not* become extinct over two hundred years ago, and who sets out on the trail of the last covey of the dodo.

Waldrop has written a good number of excellent sf short stories and novelettes, and collaborated with Jake Saunders on the novel *The Texas-Israeli War*. He lives in Austin, Texas.

MY CAR WAS BROKEN, AND I HAD A CLASS TO teach at eleven. So I took the city bus, something I rarely do.

I spent last summer crawling through the Big Thicket with cameras and tape recorder, photographing and taping two of the last ivory-billed woodpeckers on the earth. You can see the films at your local Audubon Society showroom.

This year I wanted something just as flashy but a little less taxing. Perhaps a population study on the Bermuda cahow, or the New Zealand takahe. A month or so in the warm (not hot) sun would do me a world of good. To say nothing of the advancement of science.

I was idly leafing through Greenway's *Extinct and Vanishing Birds of the World*. The city bus was winding its way through the ritzy neighborhoods of Austin, stopping to let off the chicanas, black women, and Vietnamese who tended the kitchens and gardens of the rich.

"I haven't seen any of those ugly chickens in a long time," said a voice close by.

A gray-haired lady was leaning across the aisle toward me.

I looked at her, then around. Maybe she was a shopping-bag lady. Maybe she was just talking. I looked straight at her. No doubt about it, she was talking to me. She was waiting for an answer.

"I used to live near some folks who raised them when I was a girl," she said. She pointed.

I looked down at the page my book was open to.

What I should have said was: That is quite impossible, madam. This is a drawing of an extinct bird of the island of Mauritius. It is perhaps the most famous dead bird in the world. Maybe you are mistaking this drawing for that of some rare Asiatic turkey, peafowl, or pheasant. I am sorry, but you *are* mistaken.

I should have said all that.

What she said was, "Oops, this is my stop." And got up to go.

My name is Paul Lindberl. I am twenty-six years old, a graduate student in ornithology at the University of Texas, a teaching assistant. My name is not unknown in the field. I have several vices and follies, but I don't think foolishness is one of them.

The stupid thing for me to do would have been to follow her.

She stepped off the bus.

I followed her.

I came into the departmental office, trailing scattered papers in the whirlwind behind me. "Martha! Martha!" I yelled.

She was doing something in the supply cabinet.

"Jesus, Paul! What do you want?"

"Where's Courtney?"

"At the conference in Houston. You know that. You missed your class. What's the matter?"

"Petty cash. Let me at it!"

"Payday was only a week ago. If you can't—"

"It's business! It's fame and adventure and the chance of a lifetime! It's a long sea voyage that leaves . . . a plane ticket. To either Jackson, Mississippi, or Memphis. Make it Jackson, it's closer. I'll get receipts! I'll be famous. Courtney will be famous. *You'll* even be famous! This university will make even *more* money! I'll pay you back. Give me some paper. I gotta write Courtney a note. When's the next plane out? Could you get Marie and Chuck to take over my classes Tuesday and Wednesday? I'll try to be back Thursday unless something happens. Courtney'll be back tomorrow, right? I'll call him from, well, wherever. Do you have some coffee?"

And so on and so forth. Martha looked at me like I was crazy. But she filled out the requisition anyway.

"What do I tell Kemejian when I ask him to sign these?"

"Martha, babe, sweetheart. Tell him I'll get his picture in *Scientific American*."

"He doesn't read it."

"*Nature,* then!"

"I'll see what I can do," she said.

The lady I had followed off the bus was named Jolyn (Smith) Jimson. The story she told me was so weird that it had to be true. She knew things only an expert or someone with firsthand experience could know. I got names from her, and addresses, and directions, and tidbits of information. Plus a year: 1927.

And a place. Northern Mississippi.

I gave her my copy of the Greenway book. I told her I'd call her as soon as I got back into town. I left her standing on the corner near the house of the lady she cleaned up for twice a week. Jolyn Jimson was in her sixties.

Think of the dodo as a baby harp seal with feathers. I know that's not even close, but it saves time.

In 1507 the Portuguese, on their way to India, found the (then unnamed) Mascarene Islands in the Indian Ocean—three of them a few hundred miles apart, all east of Madagascar.

It wasn't until 1598, when that old Dutch sea captain Cornelius van Neck bumped into them, that the islands received their names—names that changed several times through the centuries as the Dutch, French, and English changed them every war or so. They are now known as Rodriguez, Réunion, and Mauritius.

The major feature of these islands was large, flightless, stupid, ugly, bad-tasting birds. Van Neck and his men named them *dod-aarsen*, "stupid asses," or *dodars*, "silly birds," or solitaires.

There were three species: the dodo of Mauritius, the real gray-brown, hooked-beak, clumsy thing that weighed twenty kilos or more; the white, somewhat slimmer, dodo of Réunion; and the solitaires of Rodriguez and Réunion, which looked like very fat, very dumb light-colored geese.

The dodos all had thick legs, big squat bodies twice as large as a turkey's, naked faces, and big long downcurved beaks ending in a hook like a hollow linoleum knife. Long ago they had lost the ability to fly, and their wings had degenerated to flaps the size of a human hand with only three or four feathers in them. Their tails were curly and fluffy, like a child's afterthought at decoration. They had absolutely no natural enemies. They nested on the open ground. They probably hatched their eggs wherever they happened to lay them.

No natural enemies until Van Neck and his kind showed up. The Dutch, French, and Portuguese sailors who stopped at Mascarenes to replenish stores found that, besides looking stupid, dodos *were* stupid. The men walked right up to the dodos and hit them on the head with clubs. Better yet, dodos could be herded around like sheep. Ships' logs are full of things like: "Party of ten men ashore. Drove half a hundred of the big turkey-like birds into the boat. Brought to ship, where they are given the run of the decks. Three will feed a crew of 150."

Even so, most of the dodo, except for the breast, tasted bad. One of the Dutch words for them was *walghvogel*, "disgusting bird." But on a ship three months out on a return from Goa to Lisbon, well, food was where you found it. It was said, even so, that prolonged boiling did not improve the flavor.

Even so, the dodos might have lasted, except that the Dutch, and later the French, colonized the Mascarenes. The islands became plantations and dumping places for religious refugees. Sugarcane and other exotic crops were raised there.

With the colonists came cats, dogs, hogs, and the cunning *Rattus norvegicus* and the Rhesus monkey from Ceylon. What dodos the hungry sailors left were chased down (they were dumb and stupid, but they could run when they felt like it) by dogs in the open. They were killed by cats as they sat on their nests. Their eggs were stolen and eaten by monkeys, rats, and hogs. And they competed with the pigs for all the low-growing goodies of the islands.

The last Mauritius dodo was seen in 1681, less than a hundred years after humans first saw them. The last white dodo walked off the history books around 1720. The solitaires of Rodriguez and Réunion, last of the genus as well as the species, may have lasted until 1790. Nobody knows.

Scientists suddenly looked around and found no more of the Didine birds alive, anywhere.

This part of the country was degenerate before the first Snopes ever saw it. This road hadn't been paved until the late fifties, and it was a main road between two county seats. That didn't mean it went through civilized country. I'd traveled for miles and seen nothing but dirt banks red as Billy Carter's neck and an occasional church. I expected to see Burma Shave signs, but realized this road had probably never had them.

I almost missed the turnoff onto the dirt and gravel road the man back at the service station had marked. It led onto the highway from nowhere, a lane out of a field. I turned down it, and a rock the size of a golf ball flew up over the hood and put a crack three inches long in the windshield of the rental car I'd gotten in Grenada.

It was a hot, muggy day for this early. The view was obscured in a cloud of dust every time the gravel thinned. About a mile down the road, the gravel gave out completely. The roadway turned into a rutted dirt pathway just wider than the car, hemmed in on both sides by a sagging three-strand barbed-wire fence.

In some places the fence posts were missing for a few meters. The wire lay on the ground and in some places disappeared under it for long stretches.

The only life I saw was a mockingbird raising hell with something under a thornbush the barbed wire had been nailed to in place of a post. To one side now was a grassy field that had gone wild, the way everywhere will look after we blow ourselves off the face of the planet. The other was fast becoming woods—pine, oak, some black gum, and wild plum, fruit not out this time of the year.

I began to ask myself what I was doing here. What if Ms. Jimson were some imaginative old crank who—but no. Wrong, maybe, but even the wrong was worth checking. But I knew she hadn't lied to me. She had seemed incapable of lies—a good ol' girl, backbone of the South, of the earth. Not a mendacious gland in her being.

I couldn't doubt her, or my judgment either. Here I was, creeping and bouncing down a dirt path in Mississippi, after no sleep for a day, out on the thin ragged edge of a dream. I *had* to take it on faith.

The back of the car sometimes slid where the dirt had loosened and gave way to sand. The back tire stuck once, but I rocked out of it. Getting back out again would be another matter. Didn't anyone ever use this road?

The woods closed in on both sides like the forest primeval, and the fence had long since disappeared. My odometer said ten kilometers, and it had been twenty minutes since I'd turned off the highway. In the rearview mirror, I saw beads of sweat and dirt in the wrinkles of my neck. A fine patina of dust covered everything inside the car. Clots of it came through the windows.

The woods reached out and swallowed the road. Branches scraped against the windows and the top. It was like falling down a long, dark, leafy tunnel. It was dark and green in there. I fought back an atavistic urge to turn on the headlights. The roadbed must be made of a few centuries of leaf mulch. I kept constant pressure on the accelerator and bulled my way through.

Half a log caught and banged and clanged against the car bottom. I saw light ahead. Fearing for the oil pan, I punched the pedal and sped out.

I almost ran through a house.

It was maybe ten meters from the trees. The road ended under one of the windows. I saw somebody waving from the corner of my eye.

I slammed on the brakes.

A whole family was on the porch, looking like a Walker Evans Depression photograph, or a fever dream from the mind of a "Hee Haw" producer. The house was old. Strips of peeling paint a meter long tapped against the eaves.

"Damned good thing you stopped," said a voice. I looked up. The biggest man I had ever seen in my life leaned down into the driver-side window.

"If we'd have heard you sooner, I'd've sent one of the kids down to the end of the driveway to warn you," he said.

Driveway?

His mouth was stained brown at the corners. I figured he chewed tobacco until I saw the sweet-gum snuff brush sticking from the pencil pocket in the bib of his overalls. His hands were the size of catchers' mitts. They looked like they'd never held anything smaller than an ax handle.

"How y'all?" he said, by way of introduction.

"Just fine," I said. I got out of the car.

"My name's Lindberl," I said, extending my hand. He took it. For an instant, I thought of bear traps, sharks' mouths, closing elevator doors. The thought went back to wherever it is they stay.

"This the Gudger place?" I asked.

He looked at me blankly with his gray eyes. He wore a diesel truck cap and had on a checked lumberjack shirt beneath the coveralls. His rubber boots were the size of the ones Karloff wore in *Frankenstein*.

"Naw. I'm Jim Bob Krait. That's my wife, Jenny, and there's Luke and Skeeno and Shirl." He pointed to the porch.

The people on the porch nodded.

"Lessee. Gudger? No Gudgers round here I know of. I'm sorta new here." I took that to mean he hadn't lived here for more than twenty years or so.

"Jennifer!" he yelled. "You know of anybody named Gudger?" To me he said, "My wife's lived around heres all her life."

His wife came down onto the second step of the porch landing. "I think they used to be the ones what lived on the Spradlin place before the Spradlins. But the Spradlins left around the Korean War. I didn't know any of the Gudgers myself. That's while we was living over to Water Valley."

"You an insurance man?" asked Mr. Krait.

"Uh . . . no," I said I imagined the people on the porch leaning toward me, all ears. "I'm a . . . I teach college."

"Oxford?" asked Krait.

"Uh, no. University of Texas."

"Well, that's a damn long way off. You say you're looking for the Gudgers?"

"Just their house. The area. As your wife said, I understand they left. During the Depression, I believe."

"Well, they musta had money," said the gigantic Mr. Krait. "Nobody around here was rich enough to *leave* during the Depression."

"Luke!" he yelled. The oldest boy on the porch sauntered down. He looked anemic and wore a shirt in vogue with the Twist. He stood with his hands in his pockets.

"Luke, show Mr. Lindberg—"

"Lindberl."

". . . Mr. Lindberl here the way up to the old Spradlin place. Take him as far as the old log bridge, he might get lost before then."

"Log bridge broke down, Daddy."

"When?"

"October, Daddy."

"Well, hell, somethin' else to fix! Anyway, to the creek."

He turned to me. "You want him to go along on up there, see you don't get snakebit?"

"No, I'm sure I'll be fine."

"Mind if I ask what you're going up there for?" he asked. He was looking away from me. I could see having to come right out and ask was bothering him. Such things usually came up in the course of conversation.

"I'm a—uh, bird scientist. I study birds. We had a sighting—someone told us the old Gudger place—the area around here—I'm looking for a rare bird. It's hard to explain."

I noticed I was sweating. It was hot.

"You mean like a good God? I saw a good God about twenty-five years ago, over next to Bruce," he said.

"Well, no." (A good God was one of the names for an ivory-billed woodpecker, one of the rarest in the world. Any other time I would have dropped my jaw. Because they were thought to have died out in Mississippi by the teens, and by the fact that Krait knew they *were* rare.)

I went to lock my car up, then thought of the protocol of the situation. "My car be in your way?" I asked.

"Naw. It'll be just fine," said Jim Bob Krait. "We'll look for you back by sundown, that be all right?"

For a minute, I didn't know whether that was a command or an expression of concern.

"Just in case I get snakebit," I said. "I'll try to be careful up there."

"Good luck on findin' them rare birds," he said. He walked up to the porch with his family.

"Les go," said Luke.

Behind the Krait house were a hen house and a pigsty where hogs lay after their morning slop like islands in a muddy bay, or some Zen pork sculpture. Next we passed broken farm machinery gone to rust, though there was nothing but uncultivated land as far as the eye could see. How the family made a living I don't know. I'm told you can find places just like this throughout the South.

We walked through woods and across fields, following a sort of path. I tried to memorize the turns I would have to take on my way back. Luke didn't say a word the whole twenty minutes he accompanied me, except to curse once when he stepped into a bull nettle with his tennis shoes.

We came to a creek that skirted the edge of a woodsy hill. There was a rotted log forming a small dam. Above it the water was nearly a meter deep; below it, half that much.

"See that path?" he asked.

"Yes."

"Follow it up around the hill, then across the next field. Then you cross the creek again on the rocks, and over the hill. Take the left-hand path. What's left of the house is about three-quarters the way up the next hill. If you come to a big, bare rock cliff, you've gone too far. You got that?"

I nodded.

He turned and left.

The house had once been a dog-run cabin, as Ms. Jimson had said. Now it was fallen in on one side, what they call sigoglin. (Or was it anti-sigoglin?) I once heard a hymn on the radio called "The Land Where No Cabins Fall." This was the country songs like that were written in.

Weeds grew everywhere. There were signs of fences, a flattened pile of wood that had once been a barn. Farther behind the house were the outhouse remains. Half a rusted pump stood in the backyard. A flatter spot showed where the vegetable garden had been; in it a single wild tomato, pecked by birds, lay rotting. I passed it. There was lumber from three outbuildings, mostly rotten and green with algae and moss. One had been a smokehouse and woodshed combination. Two had been chicken roosts. One was larger than the other. It was there I started to poke around and dig.

Where? Where? I wish I'd been on more archaeological digs, knew the places to look. Refuse piles, midden heaps, kitchen scrap piles, compost boxes. Why hadn't I been born on a farm so I'd know instinctively where to search?

I prodded around the grounds. I moved back and forth like a setter casting for the scent of quail. I wanted more, more. I still wasn't satisfied.

Dusk. Dark, in fact. I trudged into the Kraits' front yard. The tote sack I carried was full to bulging. I was hot, tired, streaked with fifty years of chicken shit. The Kraits were on their porch. Jim Bob lumbered down like a friendly mountain.

I asked him a few questions, gave them a Xerox of one of the dodo pictures, left them addresses and phone numbers where they could reach me.

Then into the rental car. Off to Water Valley, acting on information Jennifer Krait gave me. I went to the postmaster's house at Water Valley. She was getting ready for bed. I asked questions. She got on the phone. I bothered people until one in the morning. Then back into the trusty rental car.

On to Memphis as the moon came up on my right. Interstate 55 was a glass ribbon before me. WLS from Chicago was on the radio.

I hummed along with it, I sang at the top of my voice.

The sack full of dodo bones, beaks, feet, and eggshell fragments kept me company on the front seat.

Did you know a museum once traded an entire blue whale skeleton for one of a dodo?

Driving, driving.

The Dance of the Dodos

I used to have a vision sometimes—I had it long before this madness came up. I can close my eyes and see it by thinking hard. But it comes to me most often, most vividly, when I am reading and listening to classical music, especially Pachelbel's *Canon in D.*

It is near dusk in The Hague, and the light is that of Frans Hals, of Rembrandt. The Dutch royal family and their guests eat and talk quietly in the great dining hall. Guards with halberds and pikes stand in the corners of the room. The family is arranged around the table: the King, Queen, some princesses, a prince, a couple of other children, an invited noble or two. Servants come out with plates and cups, but they do not intrude.

On a raised platform at one end of the room an orchestra plays dinner music—a harpsichord, viola, cello, three violins, and woodwinds. One of the royal dwarfs sits on the edge of the platform, his foot slowly rubbing the back of one of the dogs sleeping near him.

As the music of Pachelbel's *Canon in D* swells and rolls through the hall, one of the dodos walks in clumsily, stops, tilts its head, its eyes bright as a pool of tar. It sways a little, lifts its foot tentatively, one, then another, rocks back and forth in time to the cello.

The violins swirl. The dodo begins to dance, its great ungainly body now graceful. It is joined by the other two dodos who come into the hall, all three turning in a sort of circle.

The harpsichord begins its counterpoint. The fourth dodo, the white one from Réunion, comes from its place under the table and joins the circle with the others.

It is most graceful of all, making complete turns where the others only sway and dip on the edge of the circle they have formed.

The music rises in volume; the first violinist sees the dodos and nods to the King. But he and the others at the table have already seen. They are silent, transfixed—even the servants stand still, bowls, pots, and kettles in their hands, forgotten.

Around the dodos dance with bobs and weaves of their ugly heads. The white dodo dips, takes a half step, pirouettes on one foot, circles again.

Without a word the King of Holland takes the hand of the Queen, and they come around the table, children before the spectacle. They join in the dance, waltzing (anachronism) among the dodos while the family, the guests, the soldiers watch and nod in time with the music.

Then the vision fades, and the afterimage of a flickering fireplace and a dodo remains.

The dodo and its kindred came by ships to the ports of Europe. The first we have record of is that of Captain van Neck, who brought back two in 1599—one for the ruler of Holland, and one that found its way through Cologne to the menagerie of Emperor Rudolf II.

This royal aviary was at Schloss Negebau, near Vienna.

It was here that the first paintings of the dumb old birds were done by Georg and his son Jacob Hoefnagel, between 1602 and 1610. They painted it among more than ninety species of birds that kept the Emperor amused.

Another Dutch artist named Roelandt Savery, as someone said, "made a career out of the dodo." He drew and painted the birds many times, and was no doubt personally fascinated by them. Obsessed, even. Early on, the paintings are consistent; the later ones have inaccuracies. This implies he worked from life first, then from memory as his model went to that place soon to be reserved for all its species. One of his drawings has two of the Raphidae scrambling for some goody on the ground. His works are not without charm.

Another Dutch artist (they seemed to sprout up like mushrooms after a spring rain) named Peter Withoos also stuck dodos in his paintings, sometimes in odd and exciting places—wandering around during their owner's music lessons, or stuck with Adam and Eve in some Edenic idyll.

The most accurate representation, we are assured, comes from half a world away from the religious and political turmoil of the seafaring Europeans. There is an Indian miniature painting of the dodo that now rests in a museum in Russia. The dodo could have been brought by the Dutch or Portuguese in their travels to Goa and the coasts of the Indian subcontinent. Or it could have been brought centuries before by the Arabs who plied the Indian Ocean in their triangular-sailed craft, and who may have discovered the Mascarenes before the Europeans cranked themselves up for the First Crusade.

At one time early in my bird-fascination days (after I stopped killing them with BB guns but before I began to work for a scholarship), I once sat down and figured out where all the dodos had been.

Two with van Neck in 1599, one to Holland, one to Austria. Another was in Count Solms's park in 1600. An account speaks of "one in Italy, one in Germany, several in England, eight or nine to Holland." William Boentekoe van Hoorn knew of "one shipped to Europe in 1640, another in 1685," which he said was "also painted by Dutch artists." Two were mentioned as "being kept in Surrat House in India as pets," perhaps one of which is the one in the painting. Being charitable, and considering "several" to mean at least three, that means twenty dodos in all.

There had to be more, when boatloads had been gathered at the time.

What do we know of the Didine birds? A few ships' logs, some accounts left by travelers and colonists. The English were fascinated by them. Sir Hamon Lestrange, a contemporary of Pepys, saw exhibited "a Dodar from the Island of Mauritius . . . it is not able to flie, being so bigge." One was stuffed when it died, and was put in the Museum Tradescantum in South Lambeth. It eventually found its way into the Ashmolean Museum. It grew ratty and was burned, all but a leg and the head, in 1750. By then there were no more dodos, but nobody had realized that yet.

Francis Willughby got to describe it before its incineration. Earlier, old Carolus Clusius in Holland studied the one in Count Solms's park. He collected everything known about the Raphidae, describing a dodo leg Pieter Pauw kept in his natural-history cabinet, in *Exoticarium libri decem* in 1605, seven years after their discovery.

François Leguat, a Huguenot who lived on Réunion for some years, published an account of his travels in which he mentioned the dodos. It was published in 1708 (after the Mauritius dodo was extinct) and included the information that "some of the males weigh forty-five pound. . . . One egg, much bigger than that of a goos is laid by the female, and takes seven weeks hatching time."

The Abbé Pingré visited the Mascarenes in 1761. He saw the last of the Rodriguez solitaires and collected what information he could about the dead Mauritius and Réunion members of the genus.

After that, only memories of the colonists and some scientific debate as to *where* the Raphidae belonged in the great taxonomic scheme of things—some said pigeons, some said rails—were left. Even this nitpicking ended. The dodo was forgotten.

When Lewis Carroll wrote *Alice in Wonderland* in 1865, most people thought he had invented the dodo.

The service station I called from in Memphis was busier than a one-legged man in an ass-kicking contest. Between bings and dings of the bell, I finally realized the call had gone through.

The guy who answered was named Selvedge. I got nowhere with him. He mistook me for a real estate agent, then a lawyer. Now he was beginning to think I was some sort of a con man. I wasn't doing too well, either. I hadn't slept in two days. I must have sounded like a speed freak. My only progress was that I found that Ms. Annie Mae Gudger (childhood playmate of Jolyn Jimson) was now, and had been, the respected Ms. Annie Mae Radwin. This guy Selvedge must have been a secretary or toady or something.

We were having a conversation comparable to that between a shrieking macaw and a pile of mammoth bones. Then there was another click on the line.

"Young man?" said the other voice, an old woman's voice, southern, very refined but with a hint of the hills in it.

"Yes? Hello! Hello!"

"Young man, you say you talked to a Jolyn somebody? Do you mean Jolyn Smith?"

"Hello! Yes! Ms. Radwin, Ms. Annie Mae Radwin who used to be Gudger? She lives in Austin now. Texas. She used to live near Water Valley, Mississippi, Austin's where I'm from. I—"

"Young man," asked the voice again, "are you sure you haven't been put up to this by my hateful sister Alma?"

"Who? No, ma'am. I met a woman named Jolyn—"

"I'd like to talk to you, young man," said the voice. Then, offhandedly, "Give him directions to get here, Selvedge."

Click.

I cleaned out my mouth as best I could in the service station restroom, tried to shave with an old clogged Gillette disposable in my knapsack, and succeeded in gapping up my jawline. I changed into a clean pair of jeans and the only other shirt I had with me, and combed my hair. I stood in front of the mirror.

I still looked like the dog's lunch.

The house reminded me of Elvis Presley's mansion, which was somewhere in the neighborhood. From a shack on the side of a Mississippi hill to this, in forty years. There are all sorts of ways of making it. I wondered what Annie Mae Gudger's had been. Luck? Predation? Divine intervention? Hard work? Trover and replevin?

Selvedge led me toward the sun room. I felt like Philip Marlowe going to meet a rich client. The house was filled with that furniture built sometime between the turn of the century and the 1950s—the ageless kind. It never looks great, it never looks ratty, and every chair is comfortable.

I think I was expecting some formidable woman with sleeve blotters and a green eyeshade hunched over a roll-top desk with piles of paper whose acceptance or rejection meant life or death for thousands.

Who I met was a charming lady in a green pantsuit. She was in her sixties, her hair still a straw-wheat color. It didn't look dyed. Her eyes were blue as my first-grade teacher's had been. She was wiry and looked as if the word *fat* was not in her vocabulary.

"Good morning, Mr. Lindberl." She shook my hand. "Would you like some coffee? You look as if you could use it."

"Yes, thank you."

"Please sit down." She indicated a white wicker chair at a glass table. A serving tray with coffeepot, cups, tea bags, croissants, napkins, and plates lay on the tabletop.

After I swallowed half a cup of coffee at a gulp, she said, "What you wanted to see me about must be important."

"Sorry about my manners," I said. "I know I don't look it, but I'm a biology assistant at the University of Texas. An ornithologist. Working on my master's. I met Ms. Jolyn Jimson two days ago—"

"How is Jolyn? I haven't seen her in, oh Lord, it must be on to fifty years. The time gets away."

"She seemed to be fine. I only talked to her half an hour or so. That was—"

"And you've come to see me about . . . ?"

"Uh. The . . . about some of the poultry your family used to raise, when they lived near Water Valley."

She looked at me a moment. Then she began to smile.

"Oh, you mean the ugly chickens?" she said.

I smiled. I almost laughed. I knew what Oedipus must have gone through.

It is now four-thirty in the afternoon. I am sitting in the downtown Motel 6 in Memphis. I have to make a phone call and get some sleep and catch a plane.

Annie Mae Gudger Radwin talked for four hours, answering my questions, setting me straight on family history, having Selvege hold all her calls.

The main problem was that Annie Mae ran off in 1928, the year *before* her father got his big break. She went to Yazoo City, and by degrees and stages worked her way northward to Memphis and her destiny as the widow of a rich mercantile broker.

But I get ahead of myself.

Grandfather Gudger used to be the overseer for Colonel Crisby on the main plantation near McComb, Mississippi. There was a long story behind that. Bear with me.

Colonel Crisby himself was the scion of a seafaring family with interests in both the cedars of Lebanon (almost all cut down for masts for His Majesty's and others' navies) and Egyptian cotton. Also teas, spices, and any other salable commodity that came his way.

When Colonel Crisby's grandfather reached his majority in 1802, he waved good-bye to the Atlantic Ocean at Charleston, S.C., and stepped westward into the forest. When he stopped, he was in the middle of the Chickasaw Nation, where he opened a trading post and introduced slaves to the Indians.

And he prospered, and begat Colonel Crisby's father, who sent back to South Carolina for everything his father owned. Everything—slaves, wagons, horses, cattle, guinea fowl, peacocks, and dodos, which everybody thought of as atrociously ugly poultry of some kind. One of the seafaring uncles had bought them off a French merchant in 1721. (I surmised these were white dodos from Réunion, unless they had been from even earlier stock. The dodo of Mauritius was already extinct by then.)

All this stuff was herded out west to the trading post in the midst of the Chickasaw Nation. (The tribes around there were of the confederation of the Dancing Rabbits.)

And Colonel Crisby's father prospered, and so did the guinea fowl and the dodos. Then Andrew Jackson came along and marched the Dancing Rabbits off up the Trail of Tears to the heaven of Oklahoma. And Colonel Crisby's father begat Colonel Crisby, and put the trading post in the hands of others, and moved his plantation westward still to McComb.

Everything prospered but Colonel Crisby's father, who died. And the dodos, with occasional losses to the avengin' weasel and the egg-sucking dog, reproduced themselves also.

Then along came Granddaddy Gudger, a Simon Legree role model, who took care of the plantation while Colonel Crisby raised ten companies of men and marched off to fight the War for Southern Independence. Colonel Crisby came back to the McComb plantation earlier than most, he having stopped much of the same volley of Minié balls that caught his commander, General Beauregard Hanlon, on a promontory bluff during the Siege of Vicksburg. He wasn't dead, but death hung around the place like a gentlemanly bill collector for a month. The Colonel languished, went slapdab crazy, and freed all his slaves the week before he died (the war lasted another two years after that). Not now having any slaves, he didn't need an overseer.

Then comes the Faulkner part of the tale, straight out of *As I Lay Dying,* with the Gudger family returning to the area of Water Valley (before there was a Water Valley), moving through the demoralized and tattered displaced persons of the South, driving their dodos before them. For Colonel Crisby had given them to his former overseer for his faithful service. Also followed the story of the bloody murder of Granddaddy Gudger at the hands of the Freedman's militia during the rising of the first Klan, and of the trials and tribulations of Daddy Gudger in the years between 1880 and 1910, when he was between the ages of four and thirty-four.

Alma and Annie Mae were the second and fifth of Daddy Gudger's brood, born three years apart. They seem to have hated each other from the very first time Alma looked into little Annie Mae's crib. They were kids by Daddy Gudger's second wife (his desperation had killed the first) and their father was already on his sixth career. He had been a lumberman, a stump preacher, a plowman-for-hire (until his mules broke out in farcy buds and died of the glanders), a freight hauler (until his horses died of overwork and the hardware store repossessed the wagon), a politician's roadie (until the politician lost the election). When Alma and Annie Mae were born, he was failing as a sharecropper. Somehow Gudger had made it through the depression of 1898 as a boy, and was too poor after that to notice more about economics than the price of Beech-Nut tobacco at the store.

Alma and Annie Mae fought, and it helped none at all that Alma, being the oldest daughter, was both her mother's and her father's darling. Annie Mae's life was the usual unwanted-poor-white-trash-child's hell. She vowed early to run away, and recognized her ambition at thirteen.

All this I learned this morning. Jolyn Smith Jimson was Annie Mae's only friend in those days—from a family even poorer than the Gudgers. But somehow there was food, and an occasional odd job. And the dodos.

"My father hated those old birds," said the cultured Annie Mae Radwin, née Gudger, in the solarium. "He always swore he was going to get rid of them someday, but just never seemed to get around to it. I think there was more to it than that. But they were so much *trouble*. We always had to keep them penned up at night, and go check for their eggs. They wandered off to lay them, and forgot where they were. Sometimes no new ones were born at all in a year.

"And they got so *ugly*. Once a year. I mean, terrible-looking, like they were going to die. All their feathers fell off, and they looked like they had mange or something. Then the whole front of their beaks fell off, or worse, hung halfway on for a week or two. They looked like big old naked pigeons. After that they'd lose weight, down to twenty or thirty pounds, before their new feathers grew back.

"We were always having to kill foxes that got after them in the turkey house. That's what we called their roost at night. I don't think they could have found it standing ten feet from it."

She looked at me.

"I think much as my father hated them, they meant something to him. As long as he hung on to them, he knew he was as good as Granddaddy Gudger. You may not know it, but there was a certain amount of family pride about Granddaddy Gudger. At least in my father's eyes. His rapid fall in the world had a sort of grandeur to it. He'd gone from a relatively high position in the old order, and maintained some grace and stature after the Emancipation. And though he lost everything, he managed to keep those ugly old chickens the Colonel had given him as sort of a symbol.

"And as long as he had them, too, my daddy thought himself as good as his father. He kept his dignity, even when he didn't have anything else."

I asked what happened to them. She didn't know, but told me who did and where I could find her.

That's why I'm going to make a phone call.

"Hello. Dr. Courtney. Dr. Courtney? This is Paul. Memphis, Tennessee. It's too long to go into. No, of course not, not yet. But I've got evidence. What? Okay, how do trochanters, coracoids, tarsometatarsi, and beak sheaths sound? From their hen house, where else? Where would you keep *your* dodos, then?

"Sorry. I haven't slept in a couple of days. I need some help. Yes, yes. Money. Lots of money.

"Cash. Three hundred dollars, maybe. Western Union, Memphis, Tennessee. Whichever one's closest to the airport. Airport. I need the department to set up reservations to Mauritius for me. . . .

"No. No. Not a wild-goose chase, wild-*dodo* chase. Tame-dodo chase. I *know* there aren't any dodos on Mauritius! I know that. I could explain. I know it'll mean a couple of grand—if—but—

"Look, Dr. Courtney. Do you want *your* picture in *Scientific American,* or don't you?"

I am sitting in the airport café in Port Louis, Mauritius. It is now three days later, five days since that fateful morning my car wouldn't start. God bless the Sears Diehard people. I have slept sitting up in a plane seat, on and off, different planes, different seats, for twenty-four hours, Kennedy to Paris, Paris to Cairo, Cairo to Madagascar. I felt like a brand-new man when I got here.

Now I feel like an infinitely sadder and wiser brand-new man. I have just returned from the hateful sister Alma's house in the exclusive section of Port Louis, where all the French and British officials used to live.

Courtney will get his picture in *Scientific American,* all right. Me too. There'll be newspaper stories and talk shows for a few weeks for me, and I'm sure Annie Mae Gudger Radwin on one side of the world and Alma

Chandler Gudger Molière on the other will come in for their share of glory.

I am putting away cup after cup of coffee. The plane back to Tananarive leaves in an hour. I plan to sleep all the way back to Cairo, to Paris, to New York, pick up my bag of bones, sleep back to Austin.

Before me on the table is a packet of documents, clippings, and photographs. I have come across half the world for this. I gaze from the package, out the window across Port Louis to the bulk of Mont Pieter Both, which overshadows the city and its famous racecourse.

Perhaps I should do something symbolic. Cancel my flight. Climb the mountain and look down on man and all his handiworks. Take a pitcher of martinis with me. Sit in the bright semitropical sunlight (it's early dry winter here). Drink the martinis slowly, toasting Snuffo, God of Extinction. Here's one for the great auk. This is for the Carolina parakeet. Mud in your eye, passenger pigeon. This one's for the heath hen. Most important, here's one each for the Mauritius dodo, the white dodo of Réunion, the Réunion solitaire, the Rodriguez solitaire. Here's to the Raphidae, great Didine birds that you were.

Maybe I'll do something just as productive, like climbing Mont Pieter Both and pissing into the wind.

How symbolic. The story of the dodo ends where it began, on this very island. Life imitates cheap art. Like the Xerox of the Xerox of a bad novel. I never expected to find dodos still alive here (this is the one place they would have been noticed). I still can't believe Alma Chandler Gudger Molière could have lived here twenty-five years and not *know* about the dodo, never set foot inside the Port Louis Museum, where they have skeletons and a stuffed replica the size of your little brother.

After Annie Mae ran off, the Gudger family found itself prospering in a time the rest of the country was going to hell. It was 1929. Gudger delved into politics again and backed a man who knew a man who worked for Theodore "Sure Two-Handed Sword of God" Bilbo, who had connections everywhere. Who introduced him to Huey "Kingfish" Long just after that gentleman lost the Louisiana governor's election one of the times. Gudger stumped around Mississippi, getting up steam for Long's Share the Wealth plan, even before it had a name.

The upshot was that the Long machine in Louisiana

knew a rabble-rouser when it saw one, and invited
Gudger to move to the Sportsman's Paradise, with his
family, all expenses paid, and start working for the Kingfish at the unbelievable salary of $62.50 a week. Which
prospect was like turning a hog loose under a persimmon
tree, and before you could say Backwoods Messiah, the
Gudger clan was on its way to the land of pelicans, graft,
and Mardi Gras.

Almost. But I'll get to that.

Daddy Gudger prospered all out of proportion to his
abilities, but many men did that during the Depression.
First a little, thence to more, he rose in bureaucratic (and
political) circles of the state, dying rich and well hated
with his fingers in *all* the pies.

Alma Chandler Gudger became a debutante (she says
Robert Penn Warren put her in his book) and met and
married Jean Carl Molière, only heir to rice, indigo, and
sugarcane growers. They had a happy wedded life, moving first to the West Indies, later to Mauritius, where the
family sugarcane holdings were among the largest on the
island. Jean Carl died in 1959. Alma was his only survivor.

So local family makes good. Poor sharecropping Mississippi people turn out to have a father dying with a
smile on his face, and two daughters who between them
own a large portion of the planet.

I open the envelope before me. Ms. Alma Molière had
listened politely to my story (the university had called
ahead and arranged an introduction through the director
of the Port Louis Museum, who knew Ms. Molière so-
cially) and told me what she could remember. Then she
sent a servant out to one of the storehouses (large as a
duplex) and he and two others came back with boxes of
clippings, scrapbooks, and family photos.

"I haven't looked at any of this since we left St.
Thomas," she said. "Let's go through it together."

Most of it was about the rise of Citizen Gudger.

"There's not many pictures of us before we came to
Louisiana. We were so frightfully poor then, hardly anyone we knew had a camera. Oh, look. Here's one of Annie Mae. I thought I threw all those out after Momma
died."

This is the photograph. It must have been taken about
1927. Annie Mae is wearing some unrecognizable piece

of clothing that approximates a dress. She leans on a hoe, smiling a snaggle-toothed smile. She looks to be ten or eleven. Her eyes are half-hidden by the shadow of the brim of a gapped straw hat she wears. The earth she is standing in barefoot has been newly turned. Behind her is one corner of the house, and the barn beyond has its upper hay windows open. Out-of-focus people are at work there.

A few feet behind her, a huge male dodo is pecking at something on the ground. The front two-thirds of it shows, back to the stupid wings and the edge of the upcurved tail feathers. One foot is in the photo, having just scratched at something, possibly an earthworm, in the new-plowed clods. Judging by its darkness, it is the gray, or Mauritius, dodo.

The photograph is not very good, one of those 3½ x 5 jobs box cameras used to take. Already I can see this one, and the blowup of the dodo, taking up a double-page spread in *S.A.* Alma told me that around then they were down to six or seven of the ugly chickens, two whites, the rest a gray-brown.

Besides this photo, two clippings are in the package, one from the Bruce *Banner-Times*, the other from the Oxford newspaper; both are columns by the same woman dealing with "Doings in Water Valley." Both mention the Gudger family's moving from the area to seek its fortune in the swampy state to the west, and tell how they will be missed. Then there's a yellowed clipping from the front page of the Oxford paper with a small story about the Gudger Family Farewell Party in Water Valley the Sunday before (dated October 19, 1929).

There's a handbill in the package, advertising the Gudger Family Farewell Party, Sunday Oct. 15, 1929 Come One Come All. The people in Louisiana who sent expense money to move Daddy Gudger must have overestimated the costs by an exponential factor. I said as much.

"No," Alma Molière said. "There was a lot, but it wouldn't have made any difference. Daddy Gudger was like Thomas Wolfe and knew a shining golden opportunity when he saw one. Win, lose, or draw, he was never coming back *there* again. He would have thrown some kind of soiree whether there had been money for it or not. Besides, people were much more sociable then, you mustn't forget."

I asked her how many people came.

"Four or five hundred," she said. "There's some pictures here somewhere." We searched awhile, then we found them.

Another thirty minutes to my flight. I'm not worried sitting here. I'm the only passenger, and the pilot is sitting at the table next to mine talking to an RAF man. Life is much slower and nicer on these colonial islands. You mustn't forget.

I look at the other two photos in the package. One is of some men playing horseshoes and washer toss, while kids, dogs, and women look on. It was evidently taken from the east end of the house looking west. Everyone must have had to walk the last mile to the old Gudger place. Other groups of people stand talking. Some men, in shirt sleeves and suspenders, stand with their heads thrown back, a snappy story, no doubt, just told. One girl looks directly at the camera from close up, shyly, her finger in her mouth. She's about five. It looks like any snapshot of a family reunion that could have been taken anywhere, anytime. Only the clothing marks it as backwoods 1920s.

Courtney will get his money's worth. I'll write the article, make phone calls, plan the talk-show tour to coincide with publication. Then I'll get some rest. I'll be a normal person again—get a degree, spend my time wading through jungles after animals that will all be dead in another twenty years, anyway.

Who cares? The whole thing will be just another media event, just this year's Big Deal. It'll be nice getting normal again. I can read books, see movies, wash my clothes at the laundromat, listen to Johnathan Richman on the stereo. I can study and become an authority on some minor matter or other.

I can go to museums and see all the wonderful dead things there.

"That's the memory picture," said Alma. "They always took them at big things like this, back in those days. Everybody who was there would line up and pose for the camera. Only we couldn't fit everybody in. So we had two made. This is the one with us in it."

The house is dwarfed by people. All sizes, shapes, dress, and age. Kids and dogs in front, women next, then men at the back. The only exceptions are the bearded patriarchs seated toward the front with the children—men whose eyes face the camera but whose heads are still ringing with something Nathan Bedford Forrest said to them one time on a smoke-filled field. This photograph is from another age. You can recognize Daddy and Mrs. Gudger if you've seen their photographs before. Alma pointed herself out to me.

But the reason I took the photograph is in the fore-ground. Tables have been built out of sawhorses, with doors and boards nailed across them. They extend the entire width of the photograph. They are covered with food, more food than you can imagine.

"We started cooking three days before. So did the neighbors. Everybody brought something," said Alma.

It's like an entire Safeway had been cooked and set out to cool. Hams, quarters of beef, chickens by the tub-ful, quail in mounds, rabbit, butter beans by the bushel, yams, Irish potatoes, an acre of corn, eggplants, peas, turnip greens, butter in five-pound molds, cornbread and biscuits, gallon cans of molasses, red-eye gravy by the pot.

And five huge birds—twice as big as turkeys, legs capped as for Thanksgiving, drumsticks are the size of Schwarzenegger's biceps, whole-roasted, lying on their backs on platters large as cocktail tables.

The people in the crowd sure look hungry.

"We ate for days," said Alma.

I already have the title for the *Scientific American* article. It's going to be called "The Dodo Is *Still* Dead."

NIGHTFLYERS

George R. R. Martin

This is a science fiction novella of terror on a starship whose mission is to track and find an ancient race of star-faring aliens. The ship's mysterious captain never shows himself except by hologram projections; and the members of the crew are being killed, one by one. . . . In some startling ways, the plot and structure of this story parallel those of the movie *Alien*—but though I enjoyed the movie, I believe "Nightflyers" is much better.

(Martin hadn't yet seen *Alien* when he wrote this story; when he did see the movie, he was stunned by the similarities—as much as you will be by the differences.)

George R. R. Martin became an extremely popular writer of science fiction during the late 1970s, and has won several Hugo and Nebula Awards. His books include the novel *Dying of the Light* and two story collections, *A Song for Lya* and *Songs of Stars and Shadows*.

WHEN JESUS OF NAZARETH HUNG DYING ON his cross, the *volcryn* passed within a light-year of his agony, headed outward. When the Fire Wars raged on Earth, the *volcryn* sailed near Old Poseidon, where the seas were still unnamed and unfished. By the time the stardrive had transformed the Federated Nations of Earth into the Federal Empire, the *volcryn* had moved into the fringes of Hrangan space. The Hrangans never knew it. Like us they were children of the small bright worlds that circled their scattered suns, with little interest and less knowledge of the things that moved in the gulfs between.

War flamed for a thousand years and the *volcryn* passed through it, unknowing and untouched, safe in a place where no fires could ever burn. Afterwards the Federal Empire was shattered and gone, and the Hrangans vanished in the dark of the Collapse, but it was no darker for the *volcryn*.

When Kleronomas took his survey ship out from Avalon, the *volcryn* came within ten light-years of him. Kleronomas found many things, but he did not find the *volcryn*. Not then did he and not on his return to Avalon a lifetime later.

When I was a child of three, Kleronomas was dust, as distant and dead as Jesus of Nazareth and the *volcryn* passed close to Daronne. That season all the Crey sensitives grew strange and sat staring at the stars with luminous, flickering eyes.

When I was grown, the *volcryn* had sailed beyond
Tara, past the range of even the Crey, still heading outward.

And now I am old and the *volcryn* will soon pierce the
Tempter's Veil where it hangs like a black mist between
the stars. And we follow, we follow. Through the dark
gulfs where no one goes, through the emptiness, through
the silence that goes on and on, my *Nightflyer* and I give
chase.

From the hour the *Nightflyer* slipped into stardrive,
Royd Eris watched his passengers.

Nine riders had boarded at the orbital docks above
Avalon; five women and four men, each an Academy
scholar, their backgrounds as diverse as their fields of
study. Yet, to Royd, they dressed alike, looked alike, even
sounded alike. On Avalon, most cosmopolitan of worlds,
they had become as one in their quest for knowledge.

The *Nightflyer* was a trader, not a passenger vessel. It
offered one double cabin, one closet-sized single. The
other academicians rigged sleepwebs in the four great
cargo holds, some in close confinement with the instruments and computer systems they had packed on board.
When restive, they could wander two short corridors, one
leading from the driveroom and the main airlock up past
the cabins to a well-appointed lounge-library-kitchen, the
other looping down to the cargo holds. Ultimately it did
not matter where they wandered. Even in the sanitary
stations, Royd had eyes and ears.

And always and everywhere, Royd watched.

Concepts like a right of privacy did not concern him,
but he knew they might concern his passengers, if they
knew of his activities. He made certain that they did not.

Royd's own quarters, three spacious chambers forward
of the passenger lounge, were sealed and inviolate; he
never left them. To his riders, he was a disembodied voice
over the communicators that sometimes called them for
long conversations, and a holographic spectre that joined
them for meals in the lounge. His ghost was a lithe, pale-
eyed young man with white hair who dressed in filmy
pastel clothing twenty years out of date, and it had the
disconcerting habit of looking past the person Royd was
addressing, or in the wrong direction altogether, but after

a few days the academicians grew accustomed to it. The holograph walked only in the lounge, in any event.

But Royd, secretly, silently, lived everywhere, and ferreted out all of their little secrets.

The cyberneticist talked to her computers, and seemed to prefer their company to that of humans.

The xenobiologist was surly, argumentative, and a solitary drinker.

The two linguists, lovers in public, seldom had sex and snapped bitterly at each other in private.

The psipsych was a hypochondriac given to black depressions, which worsened in the close confines of the *Nightflyer.*

Royd watched them work, eat, sleep, copulate; he listened untiringly to their talk. Within a week, the nine of them no longer seemed the same to him at all. Each of them was strange and unique, he had concluded.

By the time the *Nightflyer* had been under drive for two weeks, two of the passengers had come to engage even more of his attention. He neglected none of them, watched all, but now, specially, he focused on Karoly d'Branin and Melantha Jhirl.

"Most of all, I want to know the *why* of them," Karoly d'Branin told him one false night the second week out from Avalon. Royd's luminescent ghost sat close to d'Branin in the darkened lounge, watching him drink bittersweet chocolate. The others were all asleep. Night and day are meaningless on a starship, but the *Nightflyer* kept the usual cycles, and most of the passengers followed them. Only Karoly d'Branin, administrator and generalist, kept his own solitary time.

"The *if* of them is important as well, Karoly," Royd replied, his soft voice coming from the communicator panels in the walls. "Can you be truly certain if these aliens of yours exist?"

"*I* can be certain," Karoly d'Branin replied. "That is enough. If everyone else were certain as well, we would have a fleet of research ships instead of your little *Nightflyer.*" He sipped at his chocolate, and gave a satisfied sigh. "Do you know the Nor T'alush, Royd?"

The name was strange to him, but it took Royd only a moment to consult his library computer. "An alien race on the other side of human space, past the Fyndii worlds and the Damoosh. Possibly legendary."

D'Branin chuckled. "Your library is out-of-date. You must supplement it the next time you are on Avalon. Not legends, no, real enough, though far away. We have little information about the Nor T'alush, but we are sure they exist, though you and I may never meet one. They were the start of it all.

"I was coding some information into the computers, a packet newly arrived from Dam Tullian after twenty standard years in transit. Part of it was Nor T'alush folk-lore. I had no idea how long that had taken to get to Dam Tullian, or by what route it had come, but it was fascinating material. Did you know that my first degree was in xenomythology?"

"I did not," Royd said. "Please continue."

"The *volcryn* story was among the Nor T'alush myths. It awed me; a race of sentients moving out from some mysterious origin in the core of the galaxy, sailing towards the galactic edge and, it was alleged, eventually bound for intergalactic space itself, meanwhile keeping always to the interstellar depths, no planetfalls, seldom coming within a light-year of a star. And doing it all *without a stardrive,* in ships moving only a fraction of the speed of light! That was the detail that obsessed me! Think how *old* they must be, those ships!"

"Old," Royd agreed. "Karoly, you said *ships.* More than one?"

"Oh, yes, there are," d'Branin said. "According to the Nor T'alush, one or two appeared first, on the innermost edges of their trading sphere, but others followed. Hundreds of them, each solitary, moving by itself, bound outward, always the same. For fifteen thousand standard years they moved between the Nor T'alush stars, and then they began to pass out from among them. The myth said that the last *volcryn* ship was gone three thousand years ago."

"Eighteen thousand years," Royd said, adding, "are your Nor T'alush that old?"

D'Branin smiled. "Not as star-travellers, no. According to their own histories, the Nor T'alush have only been civilized for about half that long. That stopped me for a while. It seemed to make the *volcryn* story clearly a legend. A wonderful legend, true, but nothing more.

"Ultimately, however, I could not let it alone. In my spare time, I investigated, cross-checking with other alien cosmologies to see whether this particular myth was shared by any races other than the Nor T'alush. I thought perhaps I would get a thesis out of it. It was a fruitful line of inquiry.

"I was startled by what I found. Nothing from the Hrangans, or the Hrangan slaveraces, but that made sense, you see. They were *out* from human space, the *volcryn* would not reach them until after they had passed through our own sphere. When I looked *in,* however, the *volcryn* story was everywhere. The Fyndii had it, the Damoosh appeared to accept it as literal truth—and the Damoosh, you know, are the oldest race we have ever encountered—and there was a remarkably similar story told among the gethsoids of Aath. I checked what little was known about the races said to flourish further in still, beyond even the Nor T'alush, and they had the *volcryn* story too."

"The legend of the legends," Royd suggested. The spectre's wide mouth turned up in a smile.

"Exactly, exactly," d'Branin agreed. "At that point, I called in the experts, specialists from the Institute for the Study of Nonhuman Intelligence. We researched for two years. It was all there, in the files and the libraries at the Academy. No one had ever looked before, or bothered to put it together.

"The *volcryn* have been moving through the manrealm for most of human history, since before the dawn of spaceflight. While we twist the fabric of space itself to cheat relativity, they have been sailing their great ships right through the heart of our alleged civilization, past our most populous worlds, at stately slow sublight speeds, bound for the Fringe and the dark between the galaxies. Marvelous, Royd, marvelous!"

"Marvelous," Royd agreed.

Karoly d'Branin set down his chocolate cup and leaned forward eagerly towards Royd's projection, but his hand passed through empty light when he tried to grasp his companion by the forearm. He seemed disconcerted for a moment, before he began to laugh at himself. "Ah, my *volcryn.* I grow overenthused, Royd. I am so close now. They have preyed on my mind for a dozen years, and within a month I will have them. Then, *then,* if only I can open communication, if only my people can reach them, then at last I will know the *why* of it!"

The ghost of Royd Eris, master of the *Nightflyer*, smiled for him and looked on through calm unseeing eyes.

Passengers soon grow restless on a starship under drive, sooner on one as small and spare as the *Nightflyer*. Late in the second week, the speculation began. Royd heard it all.

"Who is this Royd Eris, really?" the xenobiologist complained one night when four of them were playing cards. "Why doesn't he come out? What's the purpose of keeping himself sealed off from the rest of us?"

"Ask him," the linguist suggested.

No one did.

When he was not talking to Karoly d'Branin, Royd watched Melantha Jhirl. She was good to watch. Young, healthy, active, Melantha Jhirl had a vibrancy about her that the others could not touch. She was big in every way; a head taller than anyone else on board, large-framed, large-breasted, long-legged, strong, muscles moving fluidly beneath shiny coal-black skin. Her appetites were big as well. She ate twice as much as any of her colleagues, drank heavily without ever seeming drunk, exercised for hours every day on equipment she had brought with her and set up in one of the cargo holds. By the third week out she had sexed with all four of the men on board and two of the other women. Even in bed she was always active, exhausting most of her partners. Royd watched her with consuming interest.

"I am an improved model," she told him once as she worked out on her parallel bars, sweat glistening on her bare skin, her long black hair confined in a net.

"Improved?" Royd said. He could not send his holographic ghost down to the holds, but Melantha had summoned him with the communicator to talk while she exercised, not knowing he would have been there anyway.

She paused in her routine, holding her body aloft with the strength of her arms. "Altered, Captain," she said. She had taken to calling him that. "Born on Prometheus among the elite, child of two genetic wizards. Improved, Captain. I require twice the energy you do, but I use it all. A more efficient metabolism, a stronger and more durable body, an expected lifespan half again the normal human's. My people have made some terrible mistakes when they try to radically redesign the lessers, but the small improvements they do well."

She resumed her exercises, moving quickly and easily, silent until she had finished. Then, breathing heavily, she crossed her arms and cocked her head and grinned. "Now you know my life story, Captain, unless you care to hear the part about my defection to Avalon, my extraordinary work in nonhuman anthropology, and my tumultuous and passionate lovelife. Do you?"

"Perhaps some other time," Royd said, politely.

"Good," Melantha Jhirl replied. She snatched up a towel and began to dry the sweat from her body. "I'd rather hear your life story, anyway. Among my modest attributes is an insatiable curiosity. Who are you, Captain? Really?"

"One as improved as you," Royd replied, "should certainly be able to guess.

Melantha laughed, and tossed her towel at the communicator grill.

By that time all of them were guessing, when they did not think Royd was listening. He enjoyed the rumors.

"He talks to us, but he can't be seen," the cyberneticist said. "This ship is uncrewed, seemingly all automated except for him. Why not entirely automated, then? I'd wager Royd Eris is a fairly sophisticated computer system, perhaps an Artificial Intelligence. Even a modest program can carry on a blind conversation indistinguishable from a human's."

The telepath was a frail young thing, nervous, sensitive, with limp flaxen hair and watery blue eyes. He sought out Karoly d'Branin in his cabin, the cramped single, for a private conversation. "I feel it," he said excitedly. "Something is wrong, Karoly, something is very wrong. I'm beginning to get frightened."

D'Branin was startled. "Frightened? I don't understand, my friend. What is there for you to fear?"

The young man shook his head. "I don't know, I don't know. Yet it's there, I feel it. Karoly, I'm picking up something. You know I'm good, I am, that's why you picked me. Class one, tested, and I tell you I'm afraid. I sense it. Something dangerous. Something volatile—and alien."

"My *volcryn?*" d'Branin said.

"No, no, impossible. We're in drive, they're light-years away." The telepath's laugh was desperate. "I'm not *that* good, Karoly. I've heard your Crey story, but I'm only a human. No, this is close. On the ship."

"One of us?"

"Maybe," the telepath said. "I can't sort it out."

D'Branin sighed and put a fatherly hand on the young man's shoulder. "I thank you for coming to me, but I cannot act unless you have something more definite. This feeling of yours—could it be that you are just tired? We have all of us been under strain. Inactivity can be taxing."

"This is real," the telepath insisted, but he left peacefully.

Afterward d'Branin went to the psipsych, who was lying in her sleepweb surrounded by medicines, complaining bitterly of aches. "Interesting," she said when d'Branin told her. "I've felt something too, a sense of threat, very vague, diffuse. I thought it was me, the confinement, the boredom, the way I feel. My moods betray me at times. Did he say anything more specific?"

"No."

"I'll make an effort to move around, read him, read the others, see what I can pick up. Although, if this is real, he should know it first. He's a one, I'm only a three."

D'Branin nodded, reassured. Later, when the rest had gone to sleep, he made some chocolate and talked to Royd through the false night. But he never mentioned the telepath once.

"Have you noticed the clothes on that holograph he sends us?" the xenobiologist said to the others. "A decade out of style, at least. I don't think he really looks like that. What if he's deformed, sick, ashamed to be seen the way he really looks? Perhaps he has some disease. The Slow Plague can waste a person terribly, but it takes decades to kill, and there are other contagions, manthrax and new leprosy and Langamen's Disease. Could it be that Royd's self-imposed quarantine is just that. A quarantine. Think about it."

In the fifth week out, Melantha Jhirl pushed her pawn to the sixth rank and Royd saw it was unstoppable and resigned. It was his eighth straight defeat at her hands in as many days. She was sitting cross-legged on the floor of the lounge, the chessmen spread out before her on a view-screen, its receiver dark. Laughing, she swept them away. "Don't feel bad, Royd," she told him. "I'm an improved model. Always three moves ahead."

"I should tie in my computer," he replied. "You'd never know." His holographic ghost materialized suddenly, standing in front of the viewscreen, and smiled at her.

"I'd know within three moves," Melantha Jhirl said. "Try it." She stood up and walked right through his projection on her way to the kitchen, where she found herself a bulb of beer. "When are you going to break down and let me behind your wall for a visit, Captain?" she asked, talking up to a communicator grill. She refused to treat his ghost as real. "Don't you get lonely there? Sexually frustrated? Claustrophobic?"

"I've flown the *Nightflyer* all my life, Melantha," Royd said. His projection ignored, winked out. "If I were subject to claustrophobia, sexual frustration, or loneliness, such a life would have been impossible. Surely that should be obvious to you, being as improved a model as you are?"

She took a squeeze of her beer and laughed her mellow, musical laugh at him. "I'll solve you yet, Captain," she warned.

"Fine," he said. "Meanwhile, tell me some more lies about your life."

"Have you ever heard of Jupiter?" the xenotech demanded of the others. She was drunk, lolling in her sleep-web in the cargo hold.

"Something to do with Earth," one of the linguists said. "The same myth system originated both names, I believe."

"Jupiter," the xenotech announced loudly, "is a gas giant in the same solar system as Old Earth. Didn't know that, did you? They were on the verge of exploring it when the stardrive was discovered, oh, way back. After that, nobody bothered with gas giants. Just slip into drive and find the habitable worlds, settle them, ignore the comets and the rocks and the gas giants—there's another star just a few light-years away, and it has more habitable planets. But there were people who thought those Jupiters might have life, you know. Do you see?"

The xenobiologist looked annoyed. "If there is intelligent life on the gas giants, it shows no interest in leaving them," he snapped. "All of the sentient species we have met up to now have originated on worlds similar to Earth, and most of them are oxygen breathers. Unless you suggest that the *volcryn* are from a gas giant?"

The xenotech pushed herself up to a sitting position and smiled conspiratorially. "Not the *volcryn*," she said. "Royd Eris. Crack that forward bulkhead in the lounge, and watch the methane and ammonia come smoking out." Her hand made a sensuous waving motion through the air, and she convulsed with giddy laughter.

"I dampened him," the psipsych reported to Karoly d'Branin during the sixth week. "Psionine-4. It will blunt his receptivity for several days, and I have more if he needs it."

D'Branin wore a stricken look. "We talked several times, he and I. I could see that he was becoming ever more fearful, but he could never tell me the why of it. Did you absolutely have to shut him off?"

The psipsych shrugged. "He was edging into the irrational. You should never have taken a class one telepath, d'Branin. Too unstable."

"We must communicate with an alien race. I remind you that is no easy task. The *volcryn* are perhaps more alien than any sentients we have yet encountered. Because of that we needed class one skills."

"Glib," she said, "but you might have no working skills at all, given the condition of your class one. Half the time he's catatonic and half the time crazy with fear. He insists that we're all in real physical danger, but he doesn't know why or from what. The worst of it is I can't tell if he's really sensing something or simply having an acute attack of paranoia. He certainly displays some classic paranoid symptoms. Among other things, he believes he's being watched. Perhaps his condition is completely unrelated to us, the *volcryn*, and his talent. I can't be sure at this point in time."

"What of your own talent?" d'Branin said. "You are an empath, are you not?"

"Don't tell me my job," she said sharply. "I sexed with

him last week. You don't get more proximity or better rapport for esping than that. Even under those conditions, I couldn't be sure of anything. His mind is a chaos, and his fear is so rank it stank up the sheets. I don't read anything from the others either, besides the ordinary tensions and frustrations. But I'm only a three, so that doesn't mean much. My abilities are limited. You know I haven't been feeling well, d'Branin. I can barely breathe on this ship. My head throbs. Ought to stay in bed."

"Yes, of course," d'Branin said hastily. "I did not mean to criticize. You have been doing all you can under difficult circumstances. Yet, I must ask, is it vital he be dampened? Is there no other way? Royd will take us out of drive soon, and we will make contact with the *volcryn*. We will need him."

The psipsych rubbed her temple wearily. "My other option was an injection of esperon. It would have opened him up completely, tripled his psionic receptivity for a few hours. Then, hopefully, he could home in on this danger he's feeling. Exorcise it if it's false, deal with it if it's real. But psionine-4 is a lot safer. The physical side effects of esperon are debilitating, and emotionally I don't think he's stable enough to deal with that kind of power. The psionine should tell us something. If his paranoia continues to persist, I'll know it has nothing to do with his telepathy."

"And if it does not persist?" Karoly d'Branin said.

She smiled wickedly. "Then we'll know that he really was picking up some sort of threat, won't we?"

False night came, and Royd's wraith materialized while Karoly d'Branin sat brooding over his chocolate. "Karoly," the apparition said, "would it be possible to tie in the computer your team brought on board with my shipboard system? Those *volcryn* stories fascinate me, and I'd like to be able to study them at my leisure."

"Certainly," d'Branin replied in an offhand, distracted manner. "It is time we got our system up and running in any case. Soon, now, we will be dropping out of drive."

"Soon," Royd agreed. "Approximately seventy hours from now."

At dinner the following day, Royd's projection did not appear. The academicians ate uneasily, expecting their host to materialize at any moment, take his accustomed place, and join in the mealtime conversation. Their expectations were still unfulfilled when the afterdinner pots of chocolate and spiced tea and coffee were set on the table before them.

"Our captain seems to be occupied," Melantha Jhirl observed, leaning back in her chair and swirling a snifter of brandy.

"We will be shifting out of drive soon," Karoly d'Branin said. "There are preparations to make."

Some of the others looked at one another. All nine of them were present, although the young telepath seemed lost in his own head. The xenobiologist broke the silence. "He doesn't eat. He's a damned holograph. What does it matter if he misses a meal? Maybe it's just as well. Karoly, a lot of us have been getting uneasy about Royd. What do you know about this mystery man anyway?"

D'Branin looked at him with wide, puzzled eyes. "Know, my friend?" he said, leaning forward to refill his cup with the thick, bittersweet chocolate. "What is there to know?"

"Surely you've noticed that he never comes out to play with us," the female linguist said drily. "Before you engaged his ship, did anyone remark on this quirk of his?"

"I'd like to know the answer to that too," her partner said. "A lot of traffic comes and goes through Avalon. How did you come to choose Eris? What were you told about him?"

D'Branin hesitated. "Told about him? Very little, I must admit. I spoke to a few port officials and charter companies, but none of them were acquainted with Royd. He had not traded out of Avalon originally, you see."

"Where *is* he from?" the linguists demanded in unison. They looked at each other, and the woman continued. "We've listened to him. He has no discernible accent, no idiosyncrasies of speech to betray his origins. Tell us, where did this *Nightflyer* come from?"

"I—I don't know, actually," d'Branin admitted, hesitating. "I never thought to ask him about it."

The members of his research team glanced at each other incredulously. "You never thought to *ask?*" the xenotech said. "How did you select this ship, then?"

"It was available. The administrative council approved my project and assigned me personnel, but they could not spare an Academy ship. There were budgetary constraints as well." All eyes were on him.

"What d'Branin is saying," the psipsych interrupted, "is that the Academy was pleased with his studies in xeno-myth, with the discovery of the *volcryn* legend, but less than enthusiastic about his plan to prove the *volcryn* real. So they gave him a small budget to keep him happy and productive, assuming that this little mission would be fruit-less, and they assigned him workers who wouldn't be missed back on Avalon." She looked around at each per-son. "Except for d'Branin," she said, "not a one of us is a first-rate scholar."

"Well, you can speak for yourself," Melantha Jhirl said. "I volunteered for this mission."

"I won't argue the point," the psipsych said. "The crux is that the choice of the *Nightflyer* is no large enigma. You engaged the cheapest charter you could find, didn't you, d'Branin?"

"Some of the available ships would not even consider my proposition," d'Branin said. "The sound of it is odd, we must admit. And many ship masters seemed to have a superstitious fear of dropping out of drive in interstellar space, without a planet near. Of those who agreed to the conditions, Royd Eris offered the best terms, and he was able to leave at once."

"And we *had* to leave at once," said the female linguist. "Otherwise the *volcryn* might get away. They've only been passing through this region for ten thousand years, give or take a few thousand," she said sarcastically.

Someone laughed. D'Branin was nonplussed. "Friends, no doubt I could have postponed departure. I admit I was eager to meet my *volcryn,* to ask them the questions that have haunted me, to discover the why of them, but I must also admit that a delay would have been no great hard-ship. But *why?* Royd is a gracious host, a skilled pilot, he has treated us well."

"He has made himself a cipher," someone said.

"What is he hiding?" another voice demanded.

Melantha Jhirl laughed. When all eyes had moved to her, she grinned and shook her head. "Captain Royd is perfect, a strange man for a strange mission. Don't any of you love a mystery? Here we are flying light-years to in-tercept a hypothetical alien starship from the core of the galaxy that has been outward bound for longer than humanity has been having wars, and all of you are upset because you can't count the warts on Royd's nose." She leaned across the table to refill her brandy snifter. "My mother was right," she said lightly. "Normals are subnormal."

"Melantha is correct," Karoly d'Branin said quietly. "Royd's foibles and neuroses are his business, if he does not impose them on us."

"It makes me uncomfortable," someone complained weakly.

"For all we know, Karoly," said the xenotech, "we might be travelling with a criminal or an alien."

"*Jupiter*," someone muttered. The xenotech flushed red, and there was sniggering around the long table.

But the young, pale-haired telepath looked up suddenly and stared at them all with wild, nervous eyes. "An *alien*," he said.

The psipsych swore. "The drug is wearing off," she said quickly to d'Branin. "I'll have to go back to my room to get some more."

All of the others looked baffled; d'Branin had kept his telepath's condition a careful secret. "What drug?" the xenotech demanded. "What's going on here?"

"Danger," the telepath muttered. He turned to the cyberneticist sitting next to him, and grasped her forearm in a trembling hand. "We're in danger, I tell you, I'm reading it. Something *alien*. And it means us ill."

The psipsych rose. "He's not well," she announced to the others. "I've been dampening him with psionine, trying to hold his delusions in check. I'll get some more." She started towards the door.

"Wait," Melantha Jhirl said. "Not psionine. Try esperon."

"Don't tell me my job, woman."

"Sorry," Melantha said. She gave a modest shrug. "I'm one step ahead of you, though. Esperon might exorcise his delusions, no?"

"Yes, but—"

'And it might let him focus on this threat he claims to detect, correct?"

"I know the characteristics of esperon," the psipsych said testily.

Melantha smiled over the rim of her brandy glass. "I'm sure you do," she said. "Now listen to me. All of you are

anxious about Royd, it seems. You can't stand not knowing what he's concealing about himself. You suspect him
of being a criminal. Fears like that won't help us work together as a team. Let's end them. Easy enough." She
pointed. "Here sits a class one telepath. Boost his power
with esperon and he'll be able to recite our captain's life
history to us, until we're all suitably bored with it. Meanwhile he'll also be vanquishing his personal demons."

"He's watching us," the telepath said in a low, urgent
voice.

"Karoly," the xenobiologist said, "this has gone too far.
Several of us are nervous, and this boy is terrified. I think
we all need an end to the mystery of Royd Eris. Melantha
is right."

D'Branin was troubled. "We have no right—"

"We have the *need,*" the cyberneticist said.

D'Branin's eyes met those of the psipsych, and he
sighed. "Do it," he said. "Get him the esperon."

"He's going to kill me," the telepath screamed and
leapt to his feet. When the cyberneticist tried to calm him
with a hand on his arm, he seized a cup of coffee and
threw it square in her face. It took three of them to hold
him down. "Hurry," one commanded, as the youth struggled.

The psipsych shuddered and quickly left the lounge.

Royd was watching.

When the psipsych returned, they lifted the telepath to
the table and forced him down, pulling aside his hair to
bare the arteries in his neck.

Royd's ghost materialized in its empty chair at the foot
of the long dinner table. "Stop that," it said calmly.
"There is no need."

The psipsych froze in the act of slipping an ampule of
esperon into her injection gun, and the xenotech startled
visibly and released one of the telepath's arms. But the
captive did not pull free. He lay on the table, breathing
heavily, too frightened to move, his pale blue eyes fixed
glassily on Royd's projection.

Melantha Jhirl lifted her brandy glass in salute. "Boo,"
she said. "You've missed dinner, Captain."

"Royd," said Karoly d'Branin, "I am sorry."

The ghost stared unseeing at the far wall. "Release

him," said the voice from the communicators. "I will tell you my great secret, if my privacy intimidates you so."

"He *has* been watching us," the male linguist said.

"Tell, then," the xenotech said suspiciously. "What are you?"

"I liked your guess about the gas giants," Royd said. "Sadly, the truth is less dramatic. I am an ordinary *Homo sapien* in late middle-age. Sixty-eight standard, if you require precision. The holograph you see before you was the real Royd Eris, although some years ago. I am older now."

"Oh?" The cyberneticist's face was red where the coffee had scalded her. "Then why the secrecy?"

"I will begin with my mother," Royd replied. "The *Nightflyer* was her ship originally, custom-built to her design in the Newholme spaceyards. My mother was a free-trader, a notably successful one. She made a fortune through a willingness to accept the unusual consignment, fly off the major trade routes, take her cargo a month or a year or two years beyond where it was customarily transferred. Such practices are riskier but more profitable than flying the mail runs. My mother did not worry about how often she and her crews returned home. Her ships were her home. She seldom visited the same world twice if she could avoid it."

"Adventurous," Melantha said.

"No," said Royd. "Sociopathic. My mother did not like people, you see. Not at all. Her one great dream was to free herself from the necessity of crew. When she grew rich enough, she had it done. The *Nightflyer* was the result. After she boarded it at Newholme, she never touched a human being again, or walked a planet's surface. She did all her business from the compartments that are now mine. She was insane, but she did have an interesting life, even after that. The worlds she saw, Karoly! The things she might have told you! Your heart would break. She destroyed most of her records, however, for fear that other people might get some use or pleasure from her experience after her death. She was like that."

"And you?" the xenotech said.

"I should not call her my mother," Royd continued. "I am her cross-sex clone. After thirty years of flying this ship alone, she was bored. I was to be her companion and lover. She could shape me to be a perfect diversion. She had no patience with children, however, and no desire to raise me herself. As an embryo, I was placed in a nurturant tank. The computer was my teacher. I was to be released when I had attained the age of puberty, at which time she guessed I would be fit company.

"Her death, a few months after the cloning, ruined the plan. She had programmed the ship for such an eventuality, however. It dropped out of drive and shut down, drifted in interstellar space for eleven years while the computer made a human being out of me. That was how I inherited the *Nightflyer*. When I was freed, it took me some years to puzzle out the operation of the ship and my own origins."

"Fascinating," said d'Branin.

"Yes," said the female linguist, "but it doesn't explain why you keep yourself in isolation."

"Ah, but it does," Melantha Jhirl said. "Captain, perhaps you should explain further for the less improved models?"

"My mother hated planets," Royd said. "She hated stinks and dirt and bacteria, the irregularity of the weather, the sight of other people. She engineered for us a flawless environment, as sterile as she could possibly make it. She disliked gravity as well. She was accustomed to weightlessness, and preferred it. These were the conditions under which I was born and raised.

"My body has no natural immunities to anything. Contact with any of you would probably kill me, and would certainly make me very sick. My muscles are feeble, atrophied. The gravity the *Nightflyer* is now generating is for your comfort, not mine. To me it is agony. At the moment I am seated in a floating chair that supports my weight. I still hurt, and my internal organs may be suffering damage. It is one reason why I do not often take on passengers."

"You share your mother's opinion of the run of humanity, then?" the psipsych said.

"I do not. I like people. I accept what I am, but I did not choose it. I experience human life in the only way I can, vicariously, through the infrequent passengers I dare to carry. At those times, I drink in as much of their lives as I can."

"If you kept your ship under weightlessness at all

times, you could take on more riders, could you not?"
suggested the xenobiologist.

"True," Royd said politely. "I have found, however,
that most people choose not to travel with a captain who
does not use his gravity grid. Prolonged free-fall makes
them ill and uncomfortable. I could also mingle with my
guests, I know, if I kept to my chair and wore a sealed
environment suit. I have done so. I find it lessens my par-
ticipation instead of increasing it. I become a freak, a
maimed thing, one who must be treated differently and
kept at a distance. I prefer isolation. As often as I dare,
I study the aliens I take on as riders."

"Aliens?" the xenotech said, in a confused voice.

"You are all aliens to me," Royd answered.

Silence then filled the *Nightflyer's* lounge.

"I am sorry this had to happen, my friend," Karoly
d'Branin said to the ghost.

"Sorry," the psipsych said. She frowned and pushed
the ampule of esperon into the injection chamber. "Well,
it's glib enough, but is it the truth? We still have no proof,
just a new bedtime story. The holograph could have
claimed it was a creature from Jupiter, a computer, or a
diseased war criminal just as easily." She took two quick
steps forward to where the young telepath still lay on the
table. "He still needs treatment, and we still need confirmation. I don't care to live with all this anxiety, when
we can end it all now." Her hand pushed the unresisting
head to one side, she found the artery, and pressed the
gun to it.

"No," the voice from the communicator said sternly.
"Stop. I order it. This is my ship. Stop."

The gun hissed loudly, and there was a red mark when
she lifted it from the telepath's neck.

He raised himself to a half-sitting position, supported
by his elbows, and the psipsych moved close to him.
"Now," she said in her best professional tones, "focus on
Royd. You can do it, we all know how good you are.
Wait just a moment, the esperon will open it all up for
you."

His pale blue eyes were clouded. "Not close enough,"
he muttered. "One, I'm one, tested. Good, you know
I'm good, but I got to be *close*." He trembled.

She put an arm around him, stroked him, coaxed him.
"The esperon will give you range," she said. "Feel it, feel

yourself grow stronger. Can you feel it? Everything's getting clear, isn't it?" Her voice was a reassuring drone. "Remember the danger now, remember, go find it. Look beyond the wall, tell us about it. Tell us about Royd. Was he telling the truth? Tell us. You're good, we all know that, you can tell us." The phrases were almost an incantation.

He shrugged off her support and sat upright by himself. "I can feel it," he said. His eyes were suddenly clearer. "Something—my head hurts—I'm *afraid!*"

"Don't be afraid," the psipsych said. "The esperon won't make your head hurt, it just makes you better. Nothing to fear." She stroked his brow. "Tell us what you see."

The telepath looked at Royd's ghost with terrified little-boy eyes, and his tongue flicked across his lower lip. "He's—'"

Then his skull exploded.

It was three hours later when the survivors met again to talk.

In the hysteria and confusion of the aftermath, Melantha Jhirl had taken charge. She gave orders, pushing her brandy aside and snapping out commands with the ease of one born to it, and the others seemed to find a numbing solace in doing as they were told. Three of them fetched a sheet, and wrapped the headless body of the young telepath within, and shoved it through the driveroom airlock at the end of the ship. Two others, on Melantha's order, found water and cloth and began to clean up the lounge. They did not get far. Mopping the blood from the table-top, the cyberneticist suddenly began to retch violently. Karoly d'Branin, who had sat still and shocked since it happened, woke and took the blood-soaked rag from her hand and led her away, back to his cabin.

Melantha Jhirl was helping the psipsych, who had been standing very close to the telepath when he died. A sliver of bone had penetrated her cheek just below her right eye, she was covered with blood and pieces of flesh and bone and brain, and she had gone into shock. Melantha removed the bone splinter, led her below, cleaned her, and put her to sleep with a shot of one of her own drugs.

And, at length, she got the rest of them together in the largest of the cargo holds, where three of them slept.

Seven of the surviving eight attended. The psipsych was still asleep, but the cyberneticist seemed to have recovered. She sat cross-legged on the floor, her features pale and drawn, waiting for Melantha to begin.

It was Karoly d'Branin who spoke first, however, "I do not understand," he said. "I do not understand what has happened. What could . . ."

"Royd killed him, is all," the xenotech said bitterly. "His secret was endangered, so he just—just blew him apart."

"I cannot believe that," Karoly d'Branin said, anguished. "I cannot. Royd and I, we have talked, talked many a night when the rest of you were sleeping. He is gentle, inquisitive, sensitive. A dreamer. He understands about the *volcryn*. He would not do such a thing."

"His holograph certainly winked out quick enough when it happened," the female linguist said. "And you'll notice he hasn't had much to say since."

"The rest of you haven't been usually talkative either," Melantha Jhirl said. "I don't know what to think, but my impulse is to side with Karoly. We have no proof that the captain was responsible for what happened."

The xenotech make a loud rude noise. "Proof."

"In fact," Melantha continued unperturbed, "I'm not even sure anyone is responsible. Nothing happened until he was given the esperon. Could the drug be at fault?"

"Hell of a side effect," the female linguist muttered.

The xenobiologist frowned. "This is not my field, but I know esperon is an extremely potent drug, with severe physical effects as well as psionic. The instrument of death was probably his own talent, augmented by the drug. Besides boosting his principal power, his telepathic sensitivity, esperon would also tend to bring out other psi-talents that might have been latent in him."

"Such as?" someone demanded.

"Biocontrol. Telekinesis."

Melantha Jhirl was way ahead of him. "Increase the pressure inside his skull sharply, by rushing all the blood in his body to his brain. Decrease the air pressure around his head simultaneously, using teke to induce a short-lived vacuum. Think about it."

They thought about it, and none of them liked it.

"It could have been self-induced," Karoly d'Branin said.

"Or a stronger talent could have turned his power against him," the xenotech said stubbornly.

"No human telepath has talent on that order, to seize control of someone else, body and mind and soul, even for an instant."

"Exactly," the xenotech said. "No *human* telepath."

"Gas giant people?" The cyberneticist's tone was mocking.

The xenotech stared her down. "I could talk about Crey sensitives or *githyanki* soulsucks, name a half-dozen others off the top of my head, but I don't need to. I'll only name one. A Hrangan Mind."

That was a disquieting thought. All of them fell silent and moved uneasily, thinking of the vast, inimicable power of a Hrangan Mind hidden in the command chambers of the *Nightflyer,* until Melantha Jhirl broke the spell. "That is ridiculous," she said. "Think of what you're saying, if that isn't too much to ask. You're supposed to be xenologists, the lot of you, experts in alien languages, psychology, biology, technology. You don't act the part. We warred with Old Hranga for a thousand years, but we *never* communicated successfully with a Hrangan Mind. If Royd Eris is a Hrangan, they've certainly improved their conversational skills in the centuries since the Collapse."

The xenotech flushed. "You're right," she mumbled. "I'm jumpy."

"Friends," Karoly d'Branin said, "we must not panic or grow hysterical. A terrible thing has happened. One of our colleagues is dead, and we do not know why. Until we do, we can only go on. This is no time for rash actions against the innocent. Perhaps, when we return to Avalon, an investigation will tell us what happened. The body is safe, is it not?"

"We cycled it through the airlock into the driveroom," said the male linguist. "Vacuum in there. It'll keep."

"And it can be examined on our return," d'Branin said, satisfied.

"That return should be immediate," the xenotech said. "Tel Eris to turn this ship around."

D'Branin looked stricken. "But the *volcryn!* A week more, and we will know them, if my figures are correct. To return would take us six weeks. Surely it is worth one week additional to know that they exist?"

The xenotech was stubborn. "A man is dead. Before he died, he talked about aliens and danger. Maybe we're in danger too. Maybe these *volcryn* are the cause, maybe they're more potent than even a Hrangan Mind. Do you care to risk it? And for what? Your sources may be fictional or exaggerated or wrong, your interpretations and computations may be incorrect, or they may have changed course—the *volcryn* may not even be within light-years of where we'll drop out!"

"Ah," Melantha Jhirl said, "I understand. Then we shouldn't go on because they won't be there, and besides, they might be dangerous."

D'Branin smiled and the female linguist laughed. "Not funny," said the xenotech, but she argued no more.

"No," Melantha continued, "any danger we are in will not increase significantly in the time it will take us to drop out of drive and look about for *volcryn*. We would have to drop out anyway, to reprogram. Besides, we have come a long way for these *volcryn*, and I admit to being curious." She looked at each of them in turn, but none of them disagreed. "We continue, then."

"And what do we do with Royd?" D'Branin asked.

"Treat the captain as before, if we can," Melantha said decisively. "Open lines to him and talk. He's probably as shocked and dismayed by what happened as we are, and possibly fearful that we might blame him, try to hurt him, something like that. So we reassure him. I'll do it, if no one else wants to talk to him." There were no volunteers. "All right. But the rest of you had better try to act normally."

"Also," said d'Branin, "we must continue with our preparations. Our sensory instruments must be ready for deployment as soon as we shift out of drive and reenter normal space, our computer must be functioning."

"It's up and running," the cyberneticist said quietly. "I finished this morning, as you requested." She had a thoughtful look in her eyes, but d'Branin did not notice. He turned to the linguists and began discussing some of the preliminaries he expected from them, and in a short time the talk had turned to the *volcryn*, and little by little the fear drained out of the group.

Royd, listening, was glad.

She returned to the lounge alone.

Someone had turned out the lights. "Captain?" she said, and he appeared to her, pale, glowing softly, with eyes that did not really see. His clothes, filmy and out-of-date, were all shades of white and faded blue. "Did you hear, Captain?"

His voice over the communicator betrayed a faint hint of surprise. "Yes. I hear and I see everything on my *Nightflyer*, Melantha. Not only in the lounge. Not only when the communicators and viewscreens are on. How long have you known?"

"Known?" She laughed. "Since you praised the gas giant solution to the Roydian mystery."

"I was under stress. I have never made a mistake before."

"I believe you, Captain," she said. "No matter. I'm the improved model, remember? I'd guessed weeks ago."

For a time Royd said nothing. Then: "When do you begin to reassure me?"

"I'm doing so right now. Don't you feel reassured yet?"

The apparition gave a ghostly shrug. "I am pleased that you and Karoly do not think I murdered that man."

She smiled. Her eyes were growing accustomed to the room. By the faint light of the holograph, she could see the table where it had happened, dark stains across its top. Blood. She heard a faint dripping, and shivered. "I don't like it in here."

"If you would like to leave, I can be with you wherever you go."

"No," she said. "I'll stay. Royd, if I asked you to, would you shut off your eyes and ears throughout the ship? Except for the lounge? It would make the others feel better, I'm sure."

"They don't know."

"They will. You made that remark about gas giants in everyone's hearing. Some of them have probably figured it out by now."

"If I told you I had cut myself off, you would have no way of knowing whether it was the truth."

"I could trust you," Melantha said.

Silence. The spectre looked thoughtful. "As you wish," Royd's voice said finally. "Everything off. Now I see and hear only in here."

"I believe you."

"Did you believe my story?" Royd asked.

"Ah," she said. "A strange and wondrous story, Captain. If it's a lie, I'll swap lies with you any time. You do it well. If it's true, then you are a strange and wondrous man."

"It's true," the ghost said quietly. "Melantha—" His voice hesitated.

"Yes."

"I watched you copulating."

She smiled. "Ah," she said. "I'm good at it."

"I wouldn't know," Royd said. "You're good to watch."

Silence. She tried not to hear the dripping. "Yes," she said after a long hesitation.

"Yes? What?"

"Yes, Royd, I would probably sex with you if it were possible."

"How did you know what I was thinking?"

"I'm an improved model," she said. "And no, I'm not a telepath. It wasn't so difficult to figure out. I told you, I'm three moves ahead of you."

Royd considered that for a long time. "I believe I'm reassured," he said at last.

"Good," said Melantha Jhirl. "Now reassure me."

"Of what?"

"What happened in here? Really?"

Royd said nothing.

"I think you know something," Melantha said. "You gave up your secret to stop us from injecting him with esperon. Even after your secret was forfeit, you ordered us not to go ahead. Why?"

"Esperon is a dangerous drug," Royd said.

"More than that, Captain," Melantha said. "What killed him?"

"I didn't."

"One of us? The *volcryn?"*

Royd said nothing.

"Is there an alien aboard your ship, Captain?" she asked. "Is that it?"

Silence.

"Are we in danger? Am *I* in danger, Captain? I'm not afraid. Does that make me a fool?"

"I like people," Royd said at last. "When I can stand it, I like to have passengers. I watch them, yes. It's not so terrible. I like you and Karoly especially. You have nothing to fear. I won't let anything happen to you."

"What might happen?" she asked.

Royd said nothing.

"And what about the others, Royd? Are you taking care of them, too? Or only Karoly and me?"

No reply.

"You're not very talkative tonight," Melantha observed.

"I'm under strain," his voice replied. "Go to bed, Melantha Jhirl. We've talked long enough."

"All right, Captain," she said. She smiled at his ghost and lifted her hand. His own rose to meet it. Warm dark flesh and pale radiance brushed, melded, were one. Melantha Jhirl turned to go. It was not until she was out in the corridor, safe in the light once more, that she began to tremble.

False midnight. The talks had broken up, the nightmares had faded, and the academicians were lost in sleep. Even Karoly d'Branin slept, his appetite for chocolate quelled by his memories of the lounge.

In the darkness of the largest cargo hold, three sleepwebs hung, sleepers snoring softly in two. The cyberneticist lay awake, thinking, in the third. Finally she rose, dropped lightly to the floor, pulled on her jumpsuit and boots, and shook the xenotech from her slumber. "Come," she whispered, beckoning. They stole off into the corridor, leaving Melantha Jhirl to her dreams.

"What the hell," the xenotech muttered when they were safely beyond the door. She was half-dressed, disarrayed, unhappy.

"There's a way to find out if Royd's story was true," the cyberneticist said carefully. "Melantha won't like it, though. Are you game to try?"

"What?" the other asked. Her face betrayed her interest.

"Come," the cyberneticist said.

One of the three lesser cargo holds had been converted into a computer room. They entered quietly; all empty. The system was up, but dormant. Currents of light ran silkily down crystalline channels in the data grids, meeting, joining, splitting apart again; rivers of wan multihued radiance crisscrossing a black landscape. The chamber was dim, the only noise a low buzz at the edge of human hearing, until the cyberneticist moved through it, touching keys, tripping switches, directing the silent luminescent currents. Slowly the machine woke.

"What are you *doing?*" the xenotech said.

"Karoly told me to tie in our system with the ship," the cyberneticist replied as she worked. "I was told Royd wanted to study the *volcryn* data. Fine, I did it. Do you understand what that means?"

Now the xenotech was eager. "The two systems are tied together!"

"Exactly. So Royd can find out about the *volcryn*, and we can find out about Royd." She frowned. "I wish I knew more about the *Nightflyer*'s hardware, but I think I can feel my way through. This is a pretty sophisticated system d'Branin requisitioned."

"Can you take over?" the xenotech asked excitedly.

"Take over?" The cyberneticist sounded puzzled. "You been drinking again?"

"No, I'm serious. Use your system to break into the ship's control, overwhelm Eris, countermand his orders, make the *Nightflyer* respond to us, down here."

"Maybe," the cyberneticist said doubtfully, slowly. "I could try, but why do that?"

"Just in case. We don't have to use the capacity. Just so we have it, if an emergency arises."

The cyberneticist shrugged. "Emergencies and gas giants. I only want to put my mind at rest about Royd." She moved over to a readout panel, where a half-dozen meter-square viewscreens curved around a console, and brought one of them to life. Long fingers brushed across holographic keys that appeared and disappeared as she touched them, the keyboard changing shape even as she used it. Characters began to flow across the viewscreen, red flickerings encased in glassy black depths. The cyberneticist watched, and finally froze them. "Here," she said, "here's my answer about the hardware. You can dismiss your takeover idea, unless those gas giant people of yours are going to help. The *Nightflyer*'s bigger and smarter than our little system here. Makes sense, when you stop to think about it. Ship's all automated, except for Royd." She whistled and coaxed her search program with soft words of encouragement. "It looks as though there *is* a Royd, though. Configurations are all wrong for a robot ship.

Damn, I would have bet anything." The characters began to flow again, the cyberneticist watching the figures as they drifted by. "Here's life support specs, might tell us something." A finger jabbed, and the screen froze once more.

"Nothing unusual," the xeonotech said in disappointment.

"Standard waste disposal. Water recycling. Food processor, with protein and vitamin supplements in stores." She began to whistle. "Tanks of Renny's moss and neograss to eat up the CO_2. Oxygen cycle, then. No methane or ammonia. Sorry about that."

"Go sex with a computer."

The cyberneticist smiled. "Ever tried it?" Her fingers moved again. "What else should I look for? Give me some ideas."

"Check the specs for nurturant tanks, cloning equipment, that sort of thing. Find Royd's life history. His mother's. Get a readout on the business they've done, all this alleged trading." Her voice grew excited, and she took the cyberneticist by her shoulder. "A log, a ship's log! There's got to be a log. Find it! You must!"

"All right." She whistled, happy, one with her systems, riding the data winds, in control, curious. The readout screen turned a bright red and began to blink at her, but she only smiled. "Security," she said, her fingers a blur. As suddenly as it had come, the blinking red field was gone. "Nothing like slipping past another system's security. Like slipping onto a man."

Down the corridor, an alarm sounded a whooping call. "Damn," the cyberneticist said, "that'll wake everyone." She glanced up when the xenotech's fingers dug painfully into her shoulder, squeezing, hurting.

A gray steel panel slid almost silently across the access to the corridor. "Wha—?" the cyberneticist said.

"That's an emergency airseal," the xenotech said in a dead voice. She knew starships. "It closes when they're about to load or unload cargo in vacuum."

Their eyes went to the huge curving outer airlock above their heads. The inner lock was almost completely open, and as they watched it clicked into place, and the seal on the outer door cracked, and now it was open half a meter, sliding, and beyond was twisted nothingness so bright it burned the eyes.

"Oh," the cyberneticist said. She had stopped whistling.

Alarms were hooting everywhere. The passengers began to stir. Melantha Jhirl leapt from her sleepweb and darted into the corridor, nude, concerned, alert. Karoly d'Branin sat up drowsily. The psipsych muttered fitfully in her drug-induced sleep. The xenobiologist cried out in alarm.

Far away metal crunched and tore, and a violent shudder ran through the ship, throwing the linguists out of their sleepwebs, knocking Melantha from her feet.

In the command quarters of the *Nightflyer* was a spherical room with featureless white walls, a lesser sphere—control console—suspended in its center. The walls were always blank when the ship was in drive; the warped and glaring underside of spacetime was painful to behold.

But now darkness woke in the room, a holoscape coming to life, cold black and stars everywhere, points of icy unwinking brilliance, no up and no down and no direction, the floating control sphere the only feature in the simulated sea of night.

The *Nightflyer* had shifted out of drive.

Melantha Jhirl found her feet again and thumbed on a communicator. The alarms were still hooting, and it was hard to hear. "Captain," she shouted, "what's happening?"

"I don't know," Royd's voice replied. "I'm trying to find out. Wait here. Gather the others to you."

She did as he had said and only when they were all together in the corridor did she slip back to her web to don some clothing. She found only six of them. The psipsych was still unconscious and could not be roused, and they had to carry her. And the xenotech and cyberneticist were missing. The rest looked uneasily at the seal that blocked cargo hold three.

The communicator came back to life as the alarms died. "We have returned to normal space," Royd's voice said, "but the ship is damaged. Hold three, your computer room, was breached while we were under drive. It was ripped apart by the flux. The computer automatically dropped us out of drive, or the drive forces might have torn my entire ship apart."

"Royd," d'Branin said, "two of my team are . . ."

"It appears that your computer was in use when the hold was breached," Royd said carefully. "We can only assume that they are dead. I cannot be sure. At Melantha's request, I have deactivated most of my eyes and ears, retaining only the lounge inputs. I do not know what happened. But this is a small ship, Karoly, and if they are not with you, we must assume the worst." He paused briefly. "If it is any consolation, they died quickly and painlessly."

The two linguists exchanged a long, meaningful look. The xenobiologist's face was red and angry, and he started to say something. Melantha Jhirl slipped her hand over his mouth firmly. "Do we know how it happened, Captain?" she asked.

"Yes," he said, reluctantly.

The xenobiologist had taken the hint, and Melantha took away her hand to let him breathe. "Royd?" she prompted.

"It sounds insane, Melantha," his voice replied, "but it appears your colleagues opened the hold's loading lock. I doubt that they did so deliberately, of course. They were apparently using the system interface to gain entry to the *Nightflyer*'s data storage and controls."

"I see," Melantha said. "A terrible tragedy."

"Yes," Royd agreed. "Perhaps more terrible than you think. I have yet to assess the damage to my ship."

"We should not keep you, Captain, if you have duties to perform," Melantha said. "All of us are shocked, and it is difficult to talk now. Investigate the condition of your ship, and we'll continue our discussion in the morning. All right?"

"Yes," Royd said.

Melantha thumbed the communicator plate. Now officially, the device was off. Royd could not hear them.

Karoly d'Branin shook his large, grizzled head. The linguists sat close to one another, hands touching. The psipsych slept. Only the xenobiologist met her gaze. "Do you believe him?" he snapped abruptly.

"I don't know," Melantha Jhirl said, "but I do know that the other three cargo holds can all be flushed just as hold three was. I'm moving my sleepweb into a cabin. I suggest those who are living in hold two do the same."

"Good idea," the female linguist said. "We can crowd in. It won't be comfortable, but I don't think I'd sleep the sleep of angels in the holds anymore."

"We should also take our suits out of storage in four and keep them close at hand," her partner suggested.

"If you wish," Melantha said. "It's possible that all the locks might pop open simultaneously. Royd can't fault us for taking precautions." She flashed a grim smile. "After today, we've earned the right to act irrationally."

"This is no time for your damned jokes, Melantha," the xenobiologist said, fury in his voice. "Three dead, a fourth maybe deranged or comatose, the rest of us endangered—"

"We still have no idea what is happening," she pointed out.

"Royd Eris is killing us!" he shouted, pounding his fist into an open palm to emphasize his point. "I don't know who or what he is and I don't know if that story he gave us is true, and I don't *care*. Maybe he's a Hrangan Mind or the avenging angel of the *volcryn* or the second coming of Jesus Christ. What the hell difference does it make? *He's killing us!"*

"You realize," Melantha said gently, "that we cannot actually know whether the good captain has turned off his inputs down here. He could be watching and listening to us right now. He isn't, of course. He told me he wouldn't and I believe him. But we have only his word on that. Now, *you* don't appear to trust Royd. If that's so, you can hardly put any faith in his promises. It follows that from your point of view it might not be wise to say the things that you're saying." She smiled slyly.

The xenobiologist was silent.

"The computer is gone, then," Karoly d'Branin said in a low voice before Melantha could resume.

She nodded. "I'm afraid so."

He rose unsteadily to his feet. "I have a small unit in my cabin," he said. "A wrist model, perhaps it will suffice. I must get the figures from Royd, learn where we have dropped out. The *volcryn*—" He shuffled off down the corridor and disappeared into his cabin.

"Think how distraught he'd be if *all* of us were dead,"

the female linguist said bitterly. "Then he'd have no one to help him look for *volcryn*."

"Let him go," Melantha said. "He is as hurt as any of us, maybe more so. He wears it differently. His obsessions are his defense."

"What's *our* defense?"

"Ah," said Melantha. "Patience, maybe. All of the dead were trying to breach Royd's secret when they died. We haven't tried. Here we sit discussing their deaths."

"You don't find that suspicious?"

"Very," Melantha Jhirl said. "I even have a method of testing my suspicions. One of us can make yet another attempt to find out whether our captain told us the truth. If he or she dies, we'll know." She stood up abruptly. "Forgive me, however, if I'm not the one who tries. But don't let me stop you if you have the urge. I'll note the results with interest. Until then, I'm going to move out of the cargo area and get some sleep."

"Arrogant bitch," the male linguist observed almost conversationally after Melantha had left.

"Do you think he can hear us?" the xenobiologist whispered quietly.

"Every pithy word," the female linguist said, rising. They all stood up. "Let's move our things and put her" —she jerked a thumb at the psipsych—"back to bed." Her partner nodded.

"Aren't we going to *do* anything?" the xenobiologist said. "Make plans. Defenses."

The linguist gave him a withering look, and pulled her companion off in the other direction.

"Melantha? Karoly?"

She woke quickly, alert at the mere whisper of her name, and sat up in the narrow bunk. Next to her, Karoly d'Branin moaned softly and rolled over, yawning.

"Royd?" she asked. "Is it morning now?"

"Yes," replied the voice from the walls. "We are drifting in interstellar space three light-years from the nearest star, however. In such a context, does morning have meaning?"

Melantha laughed. "Debate it with Karoly, when he wakes up enough to listen. Royd, you said *drifting*? How bad . . . ?"

"Serious," he said, "but not dangerous. Hold three is a

complete ruin, hanging from my ship like a broken metal eggshell, but the damage was confined. The drives themselves are intact, and the *Nightflyer's* computers did not seem to suffer from your machine's destruction. I feared they might. Electronic death trauma."

D'Branin said, "Eh? Royd?"

Melantha patted him. "I'll tell you later, Karoly," she said. "Royd, you sound serious. Is there more?"

"I am worried about our return flight, Melantha," he said. "When I take the *Nightflyer* back into drive, the flux will be playing directly on portions of the ship that were never engineered to withstand it. The airseal across hold three is a particular concern. I've run some projections, and I don't know if it can take the stress. If it bursts, my whole ship will split apart in the middle. My engines will go shunting off by themselves, and the rest . . ."

"I see. Is there anything we can do?"

"Yes. The exposed areas would be easy enough to reinforce. The outer hull is armored to withstand the warping forces, of course. We could mount it in place, a crude shield, but it would suffice. Large portions of the hull were torn loose when the locks opened, but they are still out there, floating within a kilometer or two, and could be used."

At some point, Karoly d'Branin had come awake. "My team has four vacuum sleds. We can retrieve these pieces for you."

"Fine, Karoly, but that is not my primary concern. My ship is self-repairing within certain limits, but this exceeds those limits. I will have to do this myself."

"You?" d'Branin said. "Friend, you said—that is, your muscles, your weakness—cannot we help with this?"

"I am only a cripple in a gravity field, Karoly," Royd said. "Weightless, I am in my element, and I will be killing our gravity grid momentarily, to try to gather my own strength for the repair work. No, you misunderstand. I am capable of the work. I have the tools, and my own heavy-duty sled."

"I think I know what you are concerned about," Melantha said.

"I'm glad," Royd said. "Perhaps, then, you can answer my question. If I emerge from the safety of my chambers, can you keep your friends from killing me?"

Karoly d'Branin was shocked. "Royd, Royd, we are

scholars, we are not soldiers or criminals, we do not—we are human, how can you think that we would threaten you?"

"Human," Royd repeated, "but alien to me, suspicious of me. Give me no false assurances, Karoly."

The administrator sputtered. Melantha took his hand and bid him quiet. "Royd," she said, "I won't lie to you. You'd be in some danger. But I'd hope that, by coming out, you'd make the rest of them joyously happy. They'd be able to see that you told the truth, wouldn't they?"

"They would," Royd said, "but would it be enough to offset their suspicions? They believe I killed your friends, do they not?"

"Some, perhaps. Half believe it, half fear it. They are frightened, Captain. *I* am frightened."

"No more than I."

"I would be less frightened if I knew what *did* happen. Do you know?"

Silence.

"Royd, if . . ."

"I tried to stop the esperon injection," he said. "I might have saved the other two, if I had seen them, heard them, known what they were about. But you made me turn off my monitors, Melantha. I cannot help what I cannot see." Hesitation. "I would feel safer if I could turn them back on. I am blind and deaf. It is frustrating. I cannot help if I am blind and deaf."

"Turn them on, then," Melantha said suddenly. "I was wrong. I did not understand. Now I do, though."

"Understand what?" Karoly said.

"You do not understand," Royd said. "You do *not*. Don't pretend that you do, Melantha Jhirl. *Don't!*" The calm voice from the communicator was shrill with emotion.

"What?" Karoly said. "Melantha, I do not understand."

Her eyes were thoughtful. "Neither do I," she said. "Neither do I, Karoly." She kissed him lightly. "Royd," sbe resumed, "it seems to me you must make this repair, regardless of what promises we can give you. You won't risk your ship by slipping back into drive in your present condition. The only other option is to drift here until we all die. What choice do we have?"

"I have a choice," Royd said with deadly seriousness.

"I could kill all of you, if that were the only way to save my ship."

"You could try," Melantha said.

"Let us have no more talk of death," d'Branin said.

"You are right, Karoly," Royd said. "I do not wish to kill any of you. But I must be protected."

"You will be," Melantha said. "Karoly can set the others to chasing your hull fragments. I'll never leave your side. I'll assist you; the work will be done three times as fast."

Royd was polite. "In my experience, most planet-bound are clumsy and easily tired in weightlessness. It would be more efficient if I worked alone."

"It would not," she replied. "I remind you that I'm the improved model, Captain. Good in free-fall as well as in bed. I'll help."

"As you will. In a few moments, I shall depower the gravity grid. Karoly, go and prepare your people. Unship your sled and suit up. I will exit *Nightflyer* in three hours after I have recovered from the pains of your gravity. I want all of you outside the ship when I leave."

It was as though some vast animal had taken a bite out of the universe.

Melantha Jhirl waited on her sled close by the *Nightflyer,* and looked at stars. It was not so very different out here, in the depths of interstellar space. The stars were cold, frozen points of light; unwinking, austere, more chill and uncaring somehow than the same suns made to dance and twinkle by an atmosphere. Only the absence of a landmark primary reminded her of where she was: in the places between, where men do not stop, where the *volcryn* sail ships impossibly ancient. She tried to pick out Avalon's sun, but she did not know where to search. The configurations were strange to her, and she had no idea of how she was oriented. Behind her, before her, above, all around, the starfields stretched endlessly. She glanced down, beneath her sled and the *Nightflyer,* expecting still more alien stars, and the bite hit her with an almost physical force.

Melantha fought off a wave of vertigo. She was suspended above a pit, a yawning chasm in the universe, black, starless, vast.

Empty.

She remembered then: the Tempter's Veil. Just a cloud of dark gas, nothing really, galactic pollution that obscured the light from the stars of the Fringe. But this close at hand, it looked immense, terrifying. She had to break her gaze when she began to feel as if she were falling. It was a gulf beneath her and the frail silver-white shell of the *Nightflyer*, a gulf about to swallow them.

Melantha touched one of the controls on the sled's forked handle, swinging around so the Veil was to her side instead of beneath her. That seemed to help somehow. She concentrated on the *Nightflyer*. It was the largest object in her universe, brightly-lit, ungainly; three small eggs side-by-side, two larger spheres beneath and at right angles, lengths of tube connecting it all. One of the eggs was shattered now, giving the craft an unbalanced cast.

She could see the other sleds as they angled through the black, tracking the missing pieces of eggshell, grappling with them, bringing them back. The linguistic team worked together, as always, sharing a sled. The xenobiologist was alone. Karoly d'Branin had a silent passenger; the psipsych, freshly drugged, asleep in the suit they had dressed her in. Royd had insisted that the ship be cleared completely, and it would have taken time and care to rouse the psipsych to consciousness; this was the safer course.

While her colleagues labored, Melantha Jhirl waited for Royd Eris, talking to the others occasionally over the comm link. The two linguists, unaccustomed to weightlessness, were complaining a lot. Karoly tried to soothe them. The xenobiologist worked in silence, argued out. He had been vehement earlier in his opposition to going outside, but Melantha and Karoly had finally worn him down and it seemed as if he had nothing more to say. Melantha now watched him flit across her field of vision, a stick figure in form-fitting black armor standing stiff and erect at the controls of his sled.

At last the circular airlock atop the foremost of the *Nightflyer's* major spheres dilated, and Royd Eris emerged. She watched him approach, wondering what he would look like. She had so many different pictures. His genteel, cultured, too-formal voice sometimes reminded her of the dark aristocrats of her native Prometheus, the wizards who toyed with human genes. At other times his naïvete made her think of him as an inexperienced youth. His ghost was a tired looking thin young man, and he was supposed to be considerably older than that pale shadow, but Melantha found it difficult to hear an old man talking when he spoke.

Royd's sled was larger than theirs and of a different design; a long oval plate with eight jointed grappling arms bristling from its underside like the legs of a metal spider, and the snout of a heavy-duty cutting laser mounted above. His suit was odd too, more massive than the Academy worksuits, with a bulge between its shoulder blades that was probably a powerpack, and rakish radiant fins atop shoulders and helmet.

But when he was finally near enough for Melantha to see his face, it was just a face. White, very white, that was the predominant impression she got; white hair cropped very short, a white stubble around the sharply-chiseled lines of his jaw, almost invisible eyebrows beneath which blue eyes moved restlessly. His skin was pale and unlined, scarcely touched by time.

He looked wary, she thought. And perhaps a bit frightened.

He stopped his sled close to hers, amid the twisted ruin that had been cargo hold three, and surveyed the damage, the pieces of floating wreckage that once had been flesh and blood, glass, metal, plastic. Hard to distinguish now, all of them fused and burned and frozen together. "We have a good deal of work to do, Melantha," he said.

"First let's talk," she replied. She shifted her sled closer and reached out to him, but the distance was still too great, the width of the two vacuum sleds keeping them apart. Melantha backed off, and turned herself over completely, so that Royd hung upside down in her world and she upside down in his. Then she moved towards him again, positioning her sled directly over/under his. Their gloved hands met, brushed, parted. Melantha adjusted her altitude. Their helmets touched.

"I don't—" Royd began to say uncertainly.

"Turn off your comm," she commanded. "The sound will carry through the helmets."

He blinked and used his tongue controls and it was done.

"Now we can talk," she said.

"I do not like this, Melantha," he said. "This is too obvious. This is dangerous."

"There's no other way," she said. "Royd, I *do* know."

"Yes," he said. "I knew you did. Three moves ahead, Melantha. I remember the way you play chess. You are safer if you feign ignorance, however."

"I understand that, Captain. Other things I'm less sure about. Can we talk about it?"

"No. Don't ask me to. Just do as I tell you. You are in danger, all of you, but I can protect you. The less you know, the better I can protect you." Through the transparent faceplates, his expression was grim.

She stared into his upside-down eyes. "Your ship is killing us, Captain. That's my suspicion, anyway. Not you. It. Only that doesn't make sense. You command the *Nightflyer*. How can it act independently? And why? What motive? How was that psionic murder accomplished? It can't be the ship. Yet it can't be anything else. Help me, Captain."

He blinked; there was anguish behind his eyes. "I should never have accepted Karoly's charter. Not with a telepath among you. It was risky. But I wanted to see the *volcryn*.

"You understand too much already, Melantha," Royd continued. "I can't tell you more. The ship is malfunctioning, that is all you need know. It is not safe to push too hard. As long as I am at the controls, however, you and your colleagues are in small danger. Trust me."

"Trust is a two-way bond," Melantha said steadily.

Royd lifted his hand and pushed her away, then tongued his comm back to life. "Enough gossip," he briskly announced. "We have repairs to make. Come. I want to see just how improved you are."

In the solitude of her helmet, Melantha Jhirl swore softly.

The xenobiologist watched Royd Eris emerge on his oversized work sled, watched Melantha Jhirl move to him, watched as she turned over and pressed her faceplate to his. He could scarcely contain his rage. Somehow they were all in it together, Royd and Melantha and possibly old d'Branin as well, he thought sourly. She had protected him from the first, when they might have taken action together, stopped him, found out who or what he was. And now three were dead, killed by the cipher in the misshapen spacesuit, and Melantha hung upside down, her face pressed to his like lovers kissing.

He tongued off his comm and cursed. The others were out of sight, off chasing spinning wedges of half-slagged metal. Royd and Melantha were engrossed in each other, the ship abandoned and vulnerable. This was his chance. No wonder Eris had insisted that all of them precede him into the void; outside, isolated from the controls of the *Nightflyer,* he was only a man. A weak one at that.

Smiling a thin hard smile, the xenobiologist brought his sled around in a wide circle and vanished into the gaping maw of the driveroom. His lights flickered past the ring of nukes and sent long bright streaks along the sides of the closed cylinders of the stardrives, the huge engines that bent the stuff of spacetime, encased in webs of metal and crystal. Everything was open to the vacuum. It was better that way; atmosphere corroded and destroyed.

He set the sled down, dismounted, moved to the airlock. This was the hardest part, he thought. The headless body of the young telepath was tethered loosely to a massive support strut, a grisly guardian by the door. The xenobiologist had to stare at it while he waited for the lock to cycle. Whenever he glanced away, somehow he would find his eyes creeping back to it. The body looked almost natural, as if it had never had a head. The xenobiologist tried to remember the young man's face, and failed, but then the lock door slid open and he gratefully pushed the thought away and entered.

He was alone in the *Nightflyer.*

A cautious man, he kept his suit on, though he collapsed the helmet and yanked loose the suddenly-limp metallic fabric so it fell behind his back like a hood. He could snap it in place quickly enough if the need arose. In cargo hold four, where they had stored their equipment, the xenobiologist found what he was looking for; a portable cutting laser, charged and ready. Low power, but it would do.

Slow and clumsy in weightlessness, he pulled himself through the corridor into the darkened lounge.

It was chilly inside, the air cold on his cheeks. He tried not to notice. He braced himself at the door and pushed off across the width of the room, sailing above the furniture, which was all safely bolted into place.

As he drifted toward his objective, something wet and cold touched his face. It startled him, but it was gone before he could make out what it was.

When it happened again, he snatched at it, caught it, and felt briefly sick. He had forgotten. No one had cleaned the lounge yet. The—*remains* were still there, floating now, blood and flesh and bits of bone and brain. All around him.

He reached the far wall, stopped himself with his arms, pulled himself down to where he wanted to go. The bulkhead. The wall. No doorway was visible, but the metal couldn't be very thick. Beyond was the control room, the computer access, safety, power. The xenobiologist did not think of himself as a vindictive man. He did not intend to harm Royd Eris, that judgment was not his to make. He would take control of the *Nightflyer*, warn Eris away, make certain the man stayed sealed in his suit. He would take them all back without any more mysteries, any more killings. The Academy arbiters could listen to the story, and probe Eris, and decide the right and wrong of it, guilt and innocence, what should be done.

The cutting laser emitted a thin pencil of scarlet light. The xenobiologist smiled and applied it to the bulkhead. It was slow work, but he had patience. They would not have missed him, quiet as he'd been, and if they did they would assume he was off sledding after some hunk of salvage. Eris' repairs would take hours, maybe days, to finish. The bright blade of the laser smoked where it touched the metal. He applied himself diligently.

Something moved on the periphery of his vision, just a little flicker, barely seen. A floating bit of brain, he thought. A sliver of bone. A bloody piece of flesh, hair still hanging from it. Horrible things, but nothing to worry about. He was a biologist, he was used to blood and brains and flesh. And worse, and worse; he had dissected many an alien in his day.

Again the motion caught his eye, teased at it. Not wanting to, he found himself drawn to look. He could not *not* look, somehow, just as he had been unable to ignore the headless telepath in the airlock. He looked.

It was an eye.

The xenobiologist trembled and the laser slipped

sharply off to one side, so he had to wrestle with it to bring it back to the channel he was cutting. His heart raced. He tried to calm himself. Nothing to be frightened of. No one was home, and if Royd should return, well, he had the laser as a weapon and he had his suit on if an airlock blew.

He looked at the eye again, willing away his fear. It was just an eye, the eye of the young telepath, intact, bloody but intact, the same watery blue eye the boy had when alive, nothing supernatural. A piece of dead flesh, floating in the lounge amid other pieces of dead flesh. Someone should have cleaned up the lounge, he thought angrily. It was indecent to leave it like this, it was uncivilized.

The eye did not move. The other grisly bits were drifting on the air currents that flowed across the room, but the eye was still. Fixed on him. Staring.

He cursed himself and concentrated on the laser, on his cutting. He had burned an almost straight line up the bulkhead for about a meter. He began another at right angles.

The eye watched dispassionately. The xenobiologist suddenly found he could not stand it. One hand released its grip on the laser, reached out, caught the eye, flung it across the room. The action made him lose balance. He tumbled backward, the laser slipping from his grasp, his arms flapping like the wings on some absurd heavy bird. Finally he caught an edge of the table and stopped himself.

The laser hung in the center of the room, still firing, turning slowly where it floated. That did not make sense. It should have ceased fire when he released it. A malfunction, he thought. Smoke rose from where the thin line of the laser traced a path across the carpet.

With a shiver of fear, the xenobiologist realized that the laser was turning towards him.

He raised himself, put both hands flat against the table, pushed off out of the way.

The laser was turning more swiftly now.

He slammed into a wall, grunted in pain, bounced off the floor, kicked. The laser was spinning quickly, chasing him. He soared, braced himself for a ricochet off the ceiling. The beam swung around, but not fast enough.

He'd get it while it was still firing off in the other direction.

He moved close, reached, and saw the eye.

It hung just above the laser. Staring.

The xenobiologist made a small whimpering sound low in his throat, and his hand hesitated—not long, but long enough—and the scarlet beam came up and around.

Its touch was a light, hot caress across his neck.

It was more than an hour later before they missed him. Karoly d'Branin noticed his absence first, called for him over the comm net, and got no answer. He discussed it with the others.

Royd Eris moved his sled back from the armor plate he had just mounted, and through his helmet Melantha Jhirl could see the lines around his mouth grow hard. His eyes were sharply alert.

It was just then that the screaming began.

A shrill bleat of pain and fear, followed by choked, anguished sobbing. They all heard it. It came over the comm net and filled their helmets.

"It's him," a woman's voice said. The linguist.

"He's hurt," her partner added. "He's crying for help. Can't you hear it?"

"Where?" someone started.

"The ship," the female linguist said. "He must have returned to the ship."

Royd Eris said, "No. I warned—"

"We're going to go check," the linguist said. Her partner cut free the hull fragment they had been towing, and it spun away, tumbling. Their sled angled down towards the *Nightflyer*.

"Stop," Royd said. "I'll return to my chambers and check from there, if you wish. Stay outside until I give you clearance."

"Go to hell," the linguist snapped at him over the open circuit.

"Royd, my friend, what can you mean?" Karoly d'Branin said. His sled was in motion too, hastening after the linguists, but he had been further out and it was a long way back to the ship. "He is hurt, perhaps seriously. We must help."

"No," Royd said. "Karoly, *stop*. If your colleague went back to the ship alone, he is dead."

"How do you know that?" the male linguist demanded. "Did you arrange it? Set traps?"

"Listen to me," Royd continued. "You can't help him now. Only I could have helped him, and he did not listen to me. Trust me. Stop."

In the distance, d'Branin's sled slowed. The linguists did not. "We've already listened to you too damn much, I'd say," the woman said. She almost had to shout to be heard above the sobs and whimpers, the agonized sounds that filled their universe. "Melantha," she said, "keep Eris right where he is. We'll go carefully, find out what is happening inside, but I don't want him getting back to his controls. Understood?"

Melantha Jhirl hesitated. Sounds of terror and agony beat against her ears; it was hard to think.

Royd swung his sled around to face her, and she could feel the weight of his stare. "Stop them," he said. "Melantha, Karoly, order it. They do not know what they are doing." His voice was edged with despair.

In his face, Melantha found decision. "Go back inside quickly, Royd. Do what you can, I'm going to try to intercept them."

He nodded to her across the gulf, but Melantha was already in motion. Her sled backed clear of the work area, congested with hull fragments and other debris, then accelerated briskly as she raced toward the rear of the *Nightflyer*.

But even as she approached, she knew it was too late. The linguists were too close, and already moving much faster than she was.

"*Don't*," she said, authority in her tone. "The ship isn't safe, damn it."

"Bitch," was all the answer she got.

Karoly's sled pursued vainly. "Friends, you must stop, please, I beg it of you, let us talk this out together."

The unending whimpers were his only reply.

"I am your superior," he said. "I order you to wait outside. Do you hear me? I order it, I invoke the authority of the Academy. Please, my friends, please listen to me."

Melantha watched as the linguists vanished down the long tunnel of the driveroom.

A moment later she halted her sled near the waiting black mouth, debating whether she should follow them into the *Nightflyer*. She might be able to catch them before the airlock opened.

Royd's voice, hoarse counterpoint to the crying, answered her unvoiced question. "Stay, Melantha. Proceed no further."

She looked behind her. Royd's sled was approaching.

"What are you doing?" she demanded. "Royd, use your own lock. You have to get back inside!"

"Melantha," he said calmly, "I cannot. The ship will not respond to me. The control lock will not dilate. I don't want you or Karoly inside the ship until I can return to my controls."

Melantha Jhirl looked down the shadowed barrel of the driveroom, where the linguists had vanished.

"What will——?"

"Beg them to come back, Melantha. Plead with them. Perhaps there is still time, if they will listen to you."

She tried. Karoly d'Branin tried too. The crying, the moaning, the twisted symphony went on and on. But they could not raise the two linguists at all.

"They've cut out their comm," Melantha said furiously. "They don't want to listen to us. Or that . . . that *sound*."

Royd's sled and Karoly d'Branin's reached her at the same time. "I do not understand," Karoly said. "What is happening?"

"It is simple, Karoly," Royd replied. "I am being kept outside until——until Mother is done with them."

The linguists left their vacuum sled next to the one the xenobiologist had abandoned and cycled through the airlock in unseemly haste, with hardly a glance for the grim doorman.

Inside they paused briefly to collapse their helmets. "I can still hear him," the man said.

The woman nodded. "The sound is coming from the lounge. Hurry."

They kicked and pulled their way down the corridor in less than a minute. The sounds grew steadily louder, nearer. "He's in there," the woman said when they reached the chamber door.

"Yes," her partner said, "but is he alone? We need a weapon. What if . . . Royd had to be lying. There *is* someone else on board. We need to defend ourselves."

The woman would not wait. "There are two of us," she

said. "Come *on!*" With that she launched herself through the doorway and into the lounge.

It was dark inside. What little light there was spilled through the door from the corridor. Her eyes took a long moment to adjust. "Where are you?" she cried in confusion. The lounge seemed empty, but maybe it was only the light.

"Follow the sound," the man suggested. He stood in the door, glancing warily about for a minute, before he began to feel his way down a wall, groping with his hands.

The woman, impatient, propelled herself across the room, searching. She brushed against a wall in the kitchen area, and that made her think of weapons. She knew where the utensils were stored. "Here," she said, "Here, I've got a knife, that should thrill you." She waved it, and brushed against a floating bubble of blood as big as her fist. It burst and reformed into a hundred smaller globules.

"Oh, merciful God," the man said in a voice thick with fear.

"What?" she demanded. "Did you find him? Is he—?"

He was fumbling his way back towards the door, creeping along the wall the way he had come. "Get out of here," he warned. "Oh, *hurry.*"

"Why?" She trembled despite herself.

"I found the source," he said. "The screams, the crying. Come *on!*"

"Wha—"

He whimpered, "It was the grill. Oh, don't you see? It's coming from the communicator!" He reached the door, and sighed audibly, and he did not wait for her. He bolted down the corridor and was gone.

She braced herself and positioned herself in order to follow him.

The sounds stopped. Just like that: turned off.

She kicked, floated towards the door, knife in hand.

Something dark crawled from beneath the dinner table and rose to block her path. She saw it clearly for a moment, outlined in the light from the corridor. The xenobiologist, still in his vacuum suit, but with his helmet pulled off. He had something in his hands that he raised to point at her. It was a laser, she saw, a simple cutting laser.

She was moving straight towards him. She flailed and tried to stop herself, but she could not.

When she got quite close, she saw that he had a second mouth below his chin, and it was grinning at her, and little droplets of blood flew from it, wetly, as he moved.

The man rushed down the corridor in a frenzy of fear, bruising himself as he smashed into walls. Panic and weightlessness made him clumsy. He kept glancing over his shoulder as he fled, hoping to see his lover coming after him, but terrified of what he might see in her stead.

It took a long, *long* time for the airlock to open. As he waited, trembling, his pulse began to slow. He steadied himself with an effort. Once inside the chamber, with the inner door sealed between him and the lounge, he began to feel safe.

Suddenly he could barely remember why he had been so terrified.

And he was ashamed; he had run, abandoned her. And for what? What had frightened him so? An empty lounge? Noises from a communicator? Why, that only meant the xenobiologist was alive somewhere else in the ship, in pain, spilling his agony into a comm unit.

Resolute, he reached out and killed the cycle on the airlock, then reversed it. The air that had been partially sucked out came gusting back into the chamber.

The man shook his head ruefully. He'd hear no end of this, he knew. She would never let him forget it. But at least he would return, and apologize. That would count for something.

As the inner door rolled back, he felt a brief flash of fear again, an instant of stark terror when he wondered what might have emerged from the lounge to wait for him in the corridors of the *Nightflyer*. He willed it away.

When he stepped out, she was waiting for him.

He could see neither anger nor disdain in her curiously calm features, but he pushed himself toward her and tried to frame a plea for forgiveness anyway. "I don't know why I—"

With languid grace, her hand came out from behind her back. The knife was in it. That was when he finally noticed the hole burned in her suit, just between her breasts.

"Your *mother*?" Melantha Jhirl said incredulously as they hung helpless in the emptiness beyond the ship.

"She can hear everything we say," Royd replied. "But at this point, it no longer makes any difference. Your friend must have done something very foolish, very threatening. Now she is determined to kill you all."

"She, she, what do you mean?" D'Branin's voice was puzzled. "Royd, surely you do not tell us that your mother is still alive. You said she died even before you were born."

"She did, Karoly," Royd said. "I did not lie to you."

"No," Melantha said. "I didn't think so. But you did not tell us the whole truth, either."

Royd nodded. "Mother is dead, but her—ghost still lives, and animates my *Nightflyer*. My control is tenuous at best."

"Royd," d'Branin said, "My *volcryn* are more real than any ghosts." His voice chided gently.

"I don't believe in ghosts either," Melantha Jhirl said with a frown.

"Call it what you will, then," Royd said. "My term is as good as any. The reality is unchanged. My mother, or some part of my mother, lives in the *Nightflyer*, and she is killing you all as she has killed others before."

"Royd, you do not make sense," d'Branin said. "I—"

"Karoly, let the captain explain."

"Yes," Royd said. "The *Nightflyer* is very—very *advanced,* you know. Automated, self-repairing, large. It had to be, if Mother were to be freed from the necessity of crew. It was built on Newholme, you will recall. I have never been there, but I understand that Newholme's technology is quite sophisticated. Avalon could not duplicate this ship, I suspect. There are few worlds that could."

"The point, Captain?"

"The point—the point is the computers, Melantha. They had to be extraordinary. They are, believe me, they are. Crystal-matrix cores, lasergrid data retrieval, and other—other features."

"Are you telling us that the *Nightflyer* is an Artificial Intelligence?"

"No," Royd said, "not as I understand it. But it is something close. Mother had a capacity for personality impress built in. She filled the central crystal with her own memories, desires, quirks, her loves and her—hates. That was why she trusted the computer with my education, you see? She knew it would raise me as she herself would, had she the patience. She programmed it in certain other ways as well."

"And you cannot deprogram, my friend?" Karoly asked.

Royd's voice was despairing. "I have *tried,* Karoly. But I am a weak hand at systems work, and the programs are very complicated, the machines very sophisticated. At least three times I have eradicated her, only to have her surface once again. She is a phantom program, and I cannot track her. She comes and goes as she will. A ghost, do you see? Her memories and her personality are so intertwined with the programs that run the *Nightflyer* that I cannot get rid of her without wiping the entire system. But that would leave me helpless. I could never reprogram, and with the computers down the entire ship would fail, drives, life support, everything. I would have to leave the *Nightflyer,* and that would kill me."

"You should have told us, my friend," Karoly d'Branin said. "On Avalon, we have many cyberneticists, some very great minds. We might have aided you. We could have provided expert help."

"Karoly, I have *had* expert help. Twice I have brought systems specialists on board. The first one told me what I have just told you; that it was impossible without wiping the programs completely. The second had trained on Newholme. She thought she could help me. Mother killed her."

"You are still omitting something," Melantha Jhirl said. "I understand how your cybernetic ghost can open and close airlocks at will and arrange other accidents of that nature. But that first death, our telepath, how do you explain that?"

"Ultimately I must bear the guilt," Royd replied. "My loneliness led me to a grievous error. I thought I could safeguard you, even with a telepath among you. I have carried other riders safely. I watch them constantly, warn them away from dangerous acts. If Mother attempts to interfere, I countermand her directly from the control room. That usually works. Not always. Usually. Before you she had killed only five times, and the first three died when I was quite young. That was how I learned about her. That party included a telepath too.

"I should have known better, Karoly. My hunger for

life has doomed you all to death. I overestimated my own abilities, and underestimated her fear of exposure. She strikes out when she is threatened, and telepaths are always a threat. They sense her, you see. A malign, looming presence, they tell me, something cool and hostile and inhuman."

"Yes," Karoly d'Branin said, "yes, that was what he said. An alien, he was certain of it."

"No doubt she feels alien to a telepath used to the familiar contours of organic minds. Hers is not a human brain, after all. What it is I cannot say—a complex of crystalline memories, a hellish network of interlocking programs, a meld of circuitry and spirit. Yes, I can understand why she might feel alien."

"You still haven't explained how a computer program could explode a man's skull," Melantha said patiently.

"Have you ever held a whisper-jewel?" Royd Eris asked her.

"Yes," she replied. She had even owned one once; a dark blue crystal, packed with the memories of a particularly satisfying bout of lovemaking. It had been esper-etched on Avalon, her feelings impressed onto the jewel, and for more than a year she had only to touch it to grow randy. It had finally faded, though, and afterwards she had lost it.

"Then you know that psionic power can be stored," Royd said. "The central core of my computer system is resonant crystal. I think Mother impressed it as she lay dying."

"Only an esper can etch a whisper-jewel," Melantha said.

"You never asked me the *why* of it, Karoly," Royd said. "Nor you, Melantha. You never asked why Mother hated people so. She was born gifted, you see. On Avalon, she might have been a class one, tested and trained and honored, her talent nurtured and rewarded. I think she might have been very famous. She might have been stronger than a class one, but perhaps it is only after death that she acquired such power, linked as she is to the *Nightflyer.*

"The point is moot. She was not born on Avalon. On her birth world, her ability was seen as a curse, something alien and fearful. So they cured her of it. They used drugs and electroshock and hypnotraining that made her violently ill whenever she tried to use her talent. She never lost her power, of course, only the ability to use it effectively, to control it with her conscious mind. It remained part of her, suppressed, erratic, a source of shame and pain. And half a decade of institutional cure almost drove her insane. No wonder she hated people."

"What was her talent? Telepathy?"

"No. Oh, some rudimentary ability perhaps. I have read that all psi talents have several latent abilities in addition to their one developed strength. But Mother could not read minds. She had some empathy, although her cure had twisted it curiously, so that the emotions she felt literally sickened her. But her major strength, the talent they took five years to shatter and destroy, was teke."

Melantha Jhirl swore. "No wonder she hated gravity. Telekinesis under weightlessness is—"

"Yes," Royd finished. "Keeping the *Nightflyer* under gravity tortures me, but it limits Mother."

In the silence that followed that comment, each of them looked down the dark cylinder of the driveroom. Karoly d'Branin moved awkwardly on his sled. "They have not returned," he said finally.

"They are probably dead," Royd said dispassionately.

"What will we do, friend Royd? We must plan. We cannot wait here indefinitely."

"The first question is what can *I* do," Royd Eris replied. "I have talked freely, you'll note. You deserved to know. We have passed the point where ignorance was a protection. Obviously things have gone too far. There have been too many deaths and you have been witness to all of them. Mother cannot allow you to return to Avalon alive."

"Ah," said Melantha, "true. But what shall she do with *you?* Is your own status in doubt, Captain?"

"The crux of the problem," Royd admitted. "You are still three moves ahead, Melantha. I wonder if it will suffice. Your opponent is four ahead this game, and most of your pawns are already captured. I fear checkmate is imminent."

"Unless I can persuade my opponent's king to desert, no?"

She could see Royd smile at her wanly. "She would probably kill me too if I choose to side with you."

Karoly d'Branin was slow to grasp the point. "But—but what else could you—"

"My sled has a laser. Yours do not. I could kill you both, right now, and thereby earn my way into the *Nightflyer's* good graces."

Across the three meters that lay between their sleds, Melantha's eyes met Royd's. Her hands rested easily on the thruster controls. "You could try, Captain. Remember, the improved model isn't easy to kill."

"I would not kill you, Melantha Jhirl," Royd said seriously. "I have lived sixty-eight standard years and I have never lived at all. I am tired, and you tell grand gorgeous lies. If we lose, we will all die together. If we win, well, I shall die anyway, when they destroy the *Nightflyer*—either that or live as a freak in an orbital hospital, and I would prefer death—"

"We will build you a new ship, Captain," Melantha said.

"Liar," Royd replied. But his tone was cheerful. "No matter. I have not had much a life anyway. Death does not frighten me. If we win, you must tell me about your *volcryn* once again, Karoly. And you, Melantha, you must play chess with me once more, and . . ." His voice trailed off.

"And sex with you?" she finished, smiling.

"If you would," he said quietly. "I have never— *touched,* you know. Mother died before I was born." He shrugged. "Well, Mother has heard all of this. Doubtless she will listen carefully to any plans we might make, so there is no sense making them. There is no chance now that the control lock will admit me, since it is keyed directly into the ship's computer. So we must follow your colleagues through the driveroom, and enter through the manual lock, and take what chances we are given. If I can reach consoles and restore gravity, perhaps we—"

He was interrupted by a low groan.

For an instant Melantha thought the *Nightflyer* was wailing at them again, and she was surprised that it was so stupid as to try the same tactic twice. Then the groan sounded a second time, and in the back of Karoly d'Branin's sled the forgotten fourth survivor struggled against the bonds that held her down. D'Branin hastened to free her, and the psipsych tried to rise to her feet and almost floated off the sled, until he caught her hand and pulled her back.

"Are you well?" he asked. "Can you hear me? Have you pain?"

Imprisoned beneath a transparent faceplate, wide frightened eyes flicked rapidly from Karoly to Melantha to Royd, and then to the broken *Nightflyer,* Melantha wondered whether the woman was insane, and started to caution d'Branin, when the psipsych spoke suddenly.

"The *volcryn,*" was all she said, "the *volcryn.* Oh, oh, the *volcryn!*"

Around the mouth of the driveroom, the ring of nuclear engines took on a faint glow. Melantha Jhirl heard Royd suck in his breath sharply. She gave the thruster controls of her sled a violent twist. "Hurry," she said, "the *Nightflyer* is preparing to move."

A third of the way down the long barrel of the driveroom, Royd pulled abreast of her, stiff and menacing in his black, bulky armor. Side by side they sailed past the cylindrical stardrives and the cyberwebs; ahead, dimly lit, was the main airlock and its ghastly sentinel.

"When we reach the lock, jump over to my sled," Royd said. "I want to stay armed and mounted, and the chamber is not large enough for two sleds."

Melantha Jhirl risked a quick glance behind her. "Karoly," she called. "Where are you?"

"I am outside, Melantha," the answer came. "I cannot come, my friend. Forgive me."

"But we have to stay together," she said.

"No," d'Branin's voice replied, "no, I could not risk it, not when we are so close. It would be so tragic, so futile, Melantha, to come so close and fail. Death I do not mind, but I must see them first, finally, after all these years." His voice was firm and calm.

Royd Eris cut in. "Karoly, my mother is going to move the ship. Don't you understand? You will be left behind, lost."

"I will wait," d'Branin replied. "My *volcryn* are coming, and I will wait for them."

Then there was no more time for conversation, for the airlock was almost upon them. Both sleds slowed and stopped, and Royd Eris reached out and began the cycle while Melantha moved to the rear of the huge oval work-sled. When the outer door moved aside, they glided through into the lock chamber.

"When the inner door opens, it will begin," Royd told her evenly. "Most of the permanent furnishings are either built in or welded or bolted into place, but the things that your team brought on board are not. Mother will use those things as weapons. And beware of doors, airlocks, any equpiment tied in to the *Nightflyer*'s computer. Need I warn you not to unseal your suit?"

"Hardly," she replied.

Royd lowered the sled a little, and its grapplers made a metallic sound as they touched against the chamber floor.

The inner door opened, and Royd applied his thrusters.

Inside the linguists were waiting, swimming in a haze of blood. The man had been slit from crotch to throat and his intestines moved like a nest of pale, angry anakes. The woman still held the knife. They swam closer with a grace they had never possessed in life.

Royd lifted his foremost grapplers and smashed them to the side. The man caromed off a bulkhead, leaving a wide wet mark where he struck, and more of his guts came sliding out. The woman lost control of the knife. Royd accelerated past them, driving up the corridor, through the cloud of blood.

"I'll watch behind," Melantha said, and she turned and put her back to his. Already the two corpses were safely behind them. The knife was floating uselessly in the air. She started to tell Royd that they were all right when the blade abruptly shifted and came after them, as if some invisible force had taken hold of it.

"*Swerve!*" she shouted.

The sled shot wildly to one side. The knife missed by a full meter, and glanced ringingly off a bulkhead.

But it did not drop. It came at them again.

The lounge loomed ahead. Dark.

"The door is too narrow," Royd said. "We will have to abandon the sled, Melantha." Even as he spoke, they hit: he wedged the sled squarely into the doorframe, and the sudden impact jarred them loose.

For a moment Melantha floated clumsily in the corridor, trying to get her balance. The knife slashed at her, opening her suit and her shoulder. She felt sharp pain and the warm flush of bleeding "*Damn*," she shrieked. The knife came around again, spraying droplets of blood.

Melantha's hand darted out and caught it.

She muttered something under her breath, and wrenched the blade free of the force that had been gripping it.

Royd had regained the controls of his sled and seemed intent on some manipulation. Beyond, in the dimness of the lounge, Melantha saw a dark semi-human shape float into view.

"Royd!" she warned, but as she did the thing activated its laser. The pencil beam caught Royd square in the chest.

He touched his own firing stud. The sled's heavy-duty laser cindered the xenobiologist's weapon and burned off his right arm and part of his chest. Its pulsing shaft hung in the air, and smoked against the far bulkhead.

Royd made some adjustments and began cutting a hole. "We'll be through in five minutes or less," he said curtly, without stopping or looking up.

"Are you all right?" Melantha asked.

"I'm uninjured," he replied. "My suit is better armored than yours, and his laser was a low-powered toy."

Melantha turned her attention back to the corridor. The linguists were pulling themselves toward her, one on each side of the passage, to come at her from two directions at once. She flexed her muscles. Her shoulder throbbed where she had been cut. Otherwise she felt strong, almost reckless. "The corpses are coming after us again," she told Royd. "I'm going to take them."

"Is that wise?" he asked. "There are two of them."

"I'm an improved model," Melantha said, "and they're dead." She kicked herself free of the sled and sailed toward the man. He raised his hands to block her. She slapped them aside, bent one arm back and heard it snap, and drove her knife deep into his throat before she realized what a useless gesture that was. The man continued to flail at her. His teeth snapped grotesquely.

Melantha withdrew her blade, seized him, and with all her considerable strength threw him bodily down the corridor. He tumbled, spinning wildly, and vanished into the haze of his own blood.

Melantha then flew in the opposite direction.

The woman's hands went around her from behind.

Nails scrabbled against her faceplate until they began to bleed, leaving red streaks on the plastic.

Melantha spun to face her attacker, grabbed a thrashing arm, and flung the woman down the passageway to crash into her struggling companion.

"I'm through," Royd announced.

She turned to see. A smoking meter-square opening had been cut through one wall of the lounge. Royd killed the laser, gripped both sides of the door-frame, and pushed himself towards it.

A piercing blast of sound drilled through her head. She doubled over in agony. Her tongue flicked out and clicked off the comm; then there was blessed silence.

In the lounge it was raining. Kitchen utensils, glasses and plates, pieces of human bodies all lashed violently across the room, and glanced harmlessly off Royd's armored form. Melantha—eager to follow—drew back helplessly. That rain of death would cut her up to pieces in her lighter, thinner vacuum suit. Royd reached the far wall and vanished into the secret control section of the ship. She was alone.

The *Nightflyer* lurched, and sudden acceleration provided a brief semblance of gravity. She was thrown to one side. Her injured shoulder smashed painfully against the sled.

All up and down the corridor doors were opening.

The linguists were moving toward her once again.

The *Nightflyer* was a distant star sparked by its nuclear engines. Blackness and cold enveloped them, and below was the unending emptiness of the Tempter's Veil, but Karoly d'Branin did not feel afraid. He felt strangely transformed.

The void was alive with promise.

"They *are* coming," he whispered. "Even I, who have no psi at all, even I can feel it. The Crey story must be so, even from light-years off they can be sensed. Marvelous!"

The psipsych seemed very small. "The *volcryn*," she muttered. "What good can they do us. I hurt. The ship is gone. D'Branin, my head aches." She made a small frightened noise. "The boy said that, just after I injected him, before . . . before . . . you know. He said that his head hurt."

"Quiet, my friend. Do not be afraid. I am here with you. Wait. Think only of what we shall witness, think only of that!"

"I can sense them," the psipsych said.

D'Branin was eager. "Tell me, then. We have the sled. We shall go to them. Direct me."

"Yes," she agreed. "Yes. Oh, yes."

Gravity returned: in a flicker, the universe became almost normal.

Melantha fell to the deck, landed easily and rolled, and was on her feet cat-quick.

The objects that had been floating ominously through the open doors along the corridor all came clattering down.

The blood was transformed from a fine mist to a slick covering on the corridor floor.

The two corpses dropped heavily from the air, and lay still.

Royd spoke to her. His voice came from the communicator grills built into the walls, not over her suit comm. "I made it," he said.

"I noticed," she replied.

"I'm at the main control console," he continued. "I have restored the gravity with a manual override, and I'm cutting off as many computer functions as possible. We're still not safe, though. She will try to find a way around me. I'm countermanding her by sheer force, as it were. I cannot afford to overlook anything, and if my attention should lapse for even a moment . . . Melantha, was your suit breached?"

"Yes. Cut at the shoulder."

"Change into another one. *Immediately.* I think the counter programming I'm doing will keep the locks sealed, but I can't take any chances."

Melantha was already running down the corridor, towards the cargo hold where the suits and equipment were stored.

"When you have changed," Royd continued, "dump the corpses into the mass conversion unit. You'll find the appropriate hatch near the driveroom, just to the left of the main lock. Convert any other loose objects that are not indispensable as well; scientific instruments, books, tapes, tableware—"

"Knives," suggested Melantha.

"By all means."

"Is teke still a threat, Captain?"

"Mother is vastly weaker in a gravity field," Royd said. "She has to fight it. Even boosted by the *Nightflyer*'s power, she can only move one object at a time, and she has only a fraction of the lifting force she wields under weightless conditions. But the power is still there, remember. Also, it is possible she will find a way to circumvent me and cut out the gravity again. From here I can restore it in an instant, but I don't want any weapons lying around even for that brief period of time."

Melantha had reached the cargo area. She stripped off her vacuum suit and slipped into another one in record time. Then she gathered up the discarded suit and a double armful of instruments and dumped them into the conversion chamber. Afterwards she turned her attention to the bodies. The man was no problem. The woman crawled down the hall after her as she pushed him through, and thrashed weakly when it was her own turn, a grim reminder that the *Nightflyer*'s powers were not all gone. Melantha easily overcame her feeble struggles and forced her through.

The corpse of the xenobiologist was less trouble, but while she was cleaning out the lounge a kitchen knife came spinning at her head. It came slowly, though, and Melantha just batted it aside, then picked it up and added it to the pile for conversion.

She was working through the second cabin, carrying the psipsych's abandoned drugs and injection gun under her arm, when she heard Royd cry out.

A moment later, a force like a giant invisible hand wrapped itself around her chest and squeezed and pulled her, struggling, to the floor.

Something was moving across the stars.

Dimly and far off, d'Branin could see it, though he could not yet make out details. But it was there, that was unmistakable, some vast shape that blocked off a section of the starscape. It was coming at them dead on.

How he wished he had his team with him now, his telepath, his experts, his instruments.

He pressed harder on the thrusters.

Pinned to the floor, hurting, Melantha Jhirl risked opening her suit's comm. She had to talk to Royd. "Are you there?" she asked. "What's happening?" The pressure was awful, and it was growing steadily worse. She could barely move.

The answer was pained and slow in responding. ". . . outwitted . . . me," Royd's voice managed. ". . . hurts . . . to . . . talk."

"Royd——"

". . . she . . . teked . . . dial . . . up . . . two . . . gees . . . three . . . higher . . . right . . . here . . . on . . . the . . . board . . . all . . . I . . . have to . . . to do . . . turn it . . . back . . . back . . . let me. . . ."

Silence. Then, finally, when Melantha was near despair, Royd's voice again. One word: ". . . can't . . ."

Melantha's chest felt as if it were supporting ten times her own weight. She could imagine the agony Royd must be in; Royd, for whom even one gravity was painful and dangerous. Even if the dial was an arm's length away she knew his feeble musculature would never let him reach it. "Why," she started, having somewhat less trouble talking than Royd, "why would she turn *up* the . . . gravity . . . it . . . weakens her too, yes?"

". . . yes . . . but . . . in a . . . a . . . time . . . hour . . . minute . . . my . . . my heart . . . will burst . . . and . . . and then . . . you alone . . . she . . . will . . . kil gravity . . . kill you . . ."

Painfully, Melantha reached out her arm and dragged herself half a length down the corridor. "Royd . . . hold on . . . I'm coming . . ." She dragged herself forward again. The psipsych's drug kit was still under her arm, impossibly heavy. She eased it down and started to shove it aside, then reconsidered. Instead she opened its lid.

The ampules were all neatly labeled. She glanced over them quickly, searching for adrenaline or synthastim, anything that might give her the strength she needed to reach Royd. She found several stimulants, selected the strongest, and was loading it into the injection gun with awkward, agonized slowness when her eyes chanced on the supply of esperon.

Melantha did not know why she hesitated. Esperon was only one of a half-dozen psionic drugs in the kit, but something about seeing it bothered her, reminded her of something she could not quite lay her finger on. She was trying to sort it out when she heard the noise.

"Royd," she said, "your mother . . . could she move . . .

she couldn't move anything . . . teke it . . . in this high a gravity . . . could she?"

"Maybe," he answered, " . . . if . . . concentrate . . . all her . . . power . . . hard . . . maybe possible . . . why?"

"Because," Melantha Jhirl said grimly, "because some-thing . . . some*one* . . . is cycling through the airlock."

The *volcryn* ship filled the universe.

"It is not truly a ship, not as I thought it would be," Karoly d'Branin was saying. His suit, Academy-designed, had a built-in encoding device, and he was recording his comments for posterity, strangely secure in the certainty of his impending death. "The scale of it is difficult to imagine, difficult to estimate. Vast, vast. I have noth-ing but my wrist computer, no instruments, I cannot make accurate measurements, but I would say, oh, a hundred kilometers, perhaps as much as three hundred, across. No solid mass, of course, not at all. It is delicate, airy, no ship as we know ships. It is—oh, beautiful—it is crystal and gossamer, alive with its own dim lights, a vast intricate kind of spiderwebby craft—it reminds me a bit of the old starsail ships they used once, in the days before drive, but this great construct, it is not solid, it cannot be driven by light. It is no ship at all, really. It is all open to vac-uum, it has no sealed cabins or life-support spheres, none visible to me, unless blocked from my line of sight in some fashion, and no, I cannot believe that, it is too open, too fragile. It moves quite rapidly. I would wish for the instrumentation to measure its speed, but it is enough to be here. I am taking our sled at right angles to it, to get clear of its path, but I cannot say that I will make it. It moves so much faster than we. Not at light speed, no, far below it, but still faster than the *Nightflyer* and its nuclear engines, I would guess. Only a guess.

"The *volcryn* craft has no visible means of propulsion. In fact, I wonder how—perhaps it *is* a light-sail, laser-launched millennia ago, now torn and rotted by some un-imaginable catastrophe—but no, it is too symmetrical, too beautiful, the webbings, the great shimmering veils near the nexus, the beauty of it.

"I must describe it, I must be more accurate, I know. It is difficult, I grow too excited. It is large, as I have said, kilometers across. Roughly—let me count—yes, roughly octagonal in shape. The nexus, the center, is a bright area, a small darkness surrounded by a much greater area of light, but only the dark portion seems entirely solid—the lighted areas are translucent, I can see stars through them, though discolored, shifted towards the purple. Veils, I call those the veils. From the nexus and the veils eight long—oh, vastly long—spurs project, not quite spaced evenly, so it is not a true geometric octagon—ah, I see better now, one of the spurs is shifted, oh, very slowly, the veils are rippling—they are mobile then, those projections, and the webbing runs from one spur to the next, around and around, but there are— patterns, odd patterns, it is not at all the simple webbing of a spider. I cannot quite see order in the patterns, in the traceries of the webs, but I feel sure that the order is there, the meaning is waiting to be found.

"There are lights. Have I mentioned the lights? The lights are brightest around the center nexus, but they are nowhere very bright, a dim violet. Some visible radiation, then, but not much. I would like to take an ultraviolet reading of this craft, but I do not have the instrumentation. The lights move. The veils seem to ripple, and lights run constantly up and down the length of the spurs, at differing rates of speed, and sometimes other lights can be seen traversing the webbing, moving across the patterns. I do not know what the lights are or whether they emanate from inside the craft or outside.

"The *volcryn* myths, this is really not much like the legends, not truly. Though, as I think, now I recall a Nor T'alush report that the *volcryn* ships were impossibly large, but I took that for exaggeration. And lights, the *volcryn* have often been linked to lights, but those reports were so vague, they might have meant anything, described anything from a laser propulsion system to simple exterior lighting, I could not know it meant this. Ah, what mysteries! The ship is still too far away for me to see the finer detail. I think perhaps the darker area in the center *is* a craft, a life capsule. The *volcryn* must be inside it. I wish my team was with me, my telepath. He was a class one, we might have made contact, might have communicated with them. The things we would learn! The things they have seen! To think how old this craft is, how ancient this race, how long they have been outbound! It fills me with awe. Communication would be such a gift, such an impossible gift, but they are so alien."

"*D'Branin,*" the psipsych said in a low, urgent voice. "Can't you feel?"

Karoly d'Branin looked at his companion as if seeing her for the first time. "Can *you* feel them? You are a three, can you sense them now, strongly?"

"Long ago," the psipsych said. "Long ago."

"Can you project? Talk to them. Where are they? In the center area?"

"Yes," she replied, and she laughed. Her laugh was shrill and hysterical, and d'Branin had to recall that she was a very sick woman. "Yes, in the center, d'Branin, that's where the pulses come from. Only you're wrong about them. It's not 'a *them* at all, your legends are all lies, lies, I wouldn't be surprised if we were the first to ever see your *volcryn,* to ever come this close. The others, those aliens of yours, they merely *felt,* deep and distantly, sensed a bit of the nature of the *volcryn* in their dreams and visions, and fashioned the rest to suit themselves. Ships, and wars, and a race of eternal travellers, it is all—all—"

"What do you mean, my friend?" Karoly said, baffled. "You do not make sense. I do not understand."

"No," the psipsych said, her voice suddenly gentle. "You do not, do you? You cannot feel it, as I can. So clear now. This must be how a one feels, all the time. A one full of esperon."

"*What* do you feel? *What?*"

"It's not a *them,* Karoly," the psipsych said. "It's an *it.* Alive, Karoly, and quite mindless, I assure you."

"Mindless?" d'Branin said. "No, you must be wrong, you are not reading correctly. I will accept that it is a single creature if you say so, a single great marvelous star-traveller, but how can it be mindless? You sensed it, its mind, its telepathic emanations. You and the whole of the Crey sensitives and all the others. Perhaps its thoughts are too alien for you to read."

"Perhaps," the psipsych admitted, "but what I do read is not so terribly alien at all. Only animal. Its thoughts are slow and dark and strange, hardly thoughts at all, faint. The brain must be huge, I grant you that, but it can't be devoted to conscious thought."

"What do you mean?"

"The propulsion system, d'Branin. Don't you *feel?* The pulses? They are threatening to rip off the top of my skull. Can't you guess what is driving your damned *volcryn* across the galaxy? Why they avoid gravity wells? Can't you guess how it is moving?"

"No," d'Branin said, but even as he denied it a dawn of comprehension broke across his face, and he looked away from his companion, back at the swelling immensity of the *volcryn,* its lights moving, its veils a-ripple, as it came on and on, across light-years, light-centuries, across eons.

When he looked back to her, he mouthed only a single word: "Teke," he said. Silence filled their world.

She nodded.

Melantha Jhirl struggled to lift the injection gun and press it against an artery. It gave a single loud hiss, and the drug flooded her system. She lay back and gathered her strength, tried to think. Esperon, esperon, why was that important? It had killed the telepath, made him a victim of his own abilities, tripled his power and his vulnerability. Psi. It all came back to psi.

The inner door of the airlock opened. The headless corpse came through.

It moved with jerks, unnatural shufflings, never lifting its legs from the floor. It sagged as it moved, half-crushed by the weight upon it. Each shuffle was crude and sudden; some grim force was literally yanking one leg forward, then the next. It moved in slow motion, arms stiff by its sides.

But it moved.

Melantha summoned her own reserves and began to crawl away from it, never taking her eyes off its advance.

Her thoughts went round and round, searching for the piece out of place, the solution to the chess problem, finding nothing.

The corpse was moving faster than she was. Clearly, visibly, it was gaining.

Melantha tried to stand. She got to her knees, her heart pounding. Then one knee. She tried to force herself up, to lift the impossible burden on her shoulders. She was strong, she told herself. She was the improved model.

But when she put all her weight on one leg, her muscles

would not hold her. She collapsed, awkwardly, and when she smashed against the floor it was as if she had fallen from a building. She heard a sharp *snap,* and a stab of agony flashed up the arm she had tried to use to break her fall. She blinked back tears and choked on her own scream.

The corpse was halfway up the corridor. It must be walking on two broken legs, she realized. It didn't care.

"Melantha . . . heard you . . . are . . . you . . . Melantha?"

"Quiet," she snapped at Royd. She had no breath to waste on talk.

Now she had only one arm. She used the disciplines she had taught herself, willed away the pain. She kicked feebly, her boots scraping for purchase, and she pulled herself forward with her good arm.

The corpse came on and on.

She dragged herself across the threshold of the lounge, worming her way under the crashed sled, hoping it would delay the cadaver.

It was a meter behind her.

In the darkness, in the lounge, there where it had all begun, Melantha Jhirl ran out of strength.

Her body shuddered, and she collapsed on the damp carpet, and she knew that she could go no further.

On the far side of the door, the corpse stood stiffly. The sled began to shake. Then, with the scrape of metal against metal, it slid backwards, moving in tiny sudden increments, jerking itself free and out of the way.

Psi. Melantha wanted to curse it, and cry. Vainly she wished for a psi power of her own, a weapon to blast apart the teke-driven corpse that stalked her. She was improved, she thought angrily, but not improved enough. Her parents had given her all the genetic gifts they could arrange, but psi was beyond them. The gene was astronomically rare, recessive, and—

—and suddenly it came to her.

"Royd!" she yelled, put all of her remaining will into her words. "The dial . . . *teke it.* Royd, teke it!"

His reply was very faint, troubled. ". . . can't . . . I don't . . . Mother . . . only . . . her . . . not me . . . no . . ."

"Not mother," she said, desperate. "You always . . . say . . . *mother.* I forgot . . . forgot. Not your mother

. . . listen . . . you're a *clone* . . . same genes . . . you
have it, too. The power."

"Don't," he said. "Never . . . must be . . sex-linked."

"*No!* It *isn't*. I know . . . Promethean, Royd . . .
don't tell a Promethean . . . about genes . . . turn it!"

The sled jumped a third of a meter, and listed to the
side. A path was clear.

The corpse came forward.

". . . trying," Royd said. "Nothing . . . I *can't!*"

"She *cured* you," Melantha said bitterly. "Better than
. . . she was . . . cured . . . pre-natal . . . but it's only
. . . suppressed . . . you *can!*"

"I . . . don't . . . know . . . how."

The corpse now stood above her. Stopped. Pale-fleshed
hands trembled spasticly. Began to rise.

Melantha swore, and wept, and made a futile fist.

And all at once the gravity was gone. Far, far away, she
heard Royd cry out and then fall silent.

The corpse bobbed awkwardly into the air, its hands
hanging limply before it. Melantha, reeling in the weightlessness, tried to ready herself for its furious assault.

But the body did not move again. It floated dead and
still. Melantha moved to it, pushed it, and it sailed
across the room.

"Royd?" she said uncertainly.

There was no answer.

She pulled herself through the hole into the control
chamber.

And found Royd Eris, master of the *Nightflyer*, prone
on his back in his armored suit, dead. His heart had given
out.

But the dial on the gravity grid was set at zero.

I have held the *Nightflyer*'s crystalline soul within my
hands.

It is deep and red and multifaceted, large as my head,
and icy to the touch. In its scarlet depths, two small sparks
of light burn fiercely and sometimes seem to whirl.

I have crawled through the consoles, wound my way
carefully past safeguards and cybernets, taking care to
damage nothing, and I have laid rough hands on that
great crystal, knowing that it is where *she* lives.

And I cannot bring myself to wipe it.

Royd's ghost has asked me not to.

Last night we talked about it once again, over brandy and chess in the lounge. Royd cannot drink, of course, but he sends his spectre to smile at me, and he tells me where he wants his pieces moved.

For the thousandth time he offered to take me back to Avalon, or any world of my choice, if only I would go outside and complete the repairs we abandoned so many years ago, so that the *Nightflyer* might safely slip into stardrive.

For the thousandth time I refused.

He is stronger now, no doubt. Their genes are the same, after all. Their power is the same. Dying, he too found the strength to impress himself upon the great crystal. The ship is alive with both of them, and frequently they fight. Sometimes she outwits him for a moment, and the *Nightflyer* does odd, erratic things. The gravity goes up or down or off completely. Blankets wrap themselves around my throat when I sleep. Objects come hurtling out of dark corners.

Those times have come less frequently of late, though. When they do come, Royd stops her, or I do. Together, the *Nightflyer* is ours.

Royd claims he is strong enough alone, that he does not really need me, that he can keep her under check. I wonder. Over the chessboard, I still beat him nine games out of ten.

And there are other considerations. Our work, for one. Karoly would be proud of us.

The *volcryn* will soon enter the mists of the Tempter's Veil, and we follow close behind. Studying, recording, doing all that old d'Branin would have wanted us to do. It is all in the computer. It is also on tape and on paper, should the computer ever be wiped. It will be interesting to see how the *volcryn* thrives in the Veil. Matter is so thick there, compared to the thin diet of interstellar hydrogen on which the creature has fed for endless eons.

We have tried to communicate with it, with no success. I do not believe it is sentient at all.

And lately Royd has tried to imitate its ways, gathering all his energies in an attempt to move the *Nightflyer* by teke. Sometimes, oddly, his mother even joins him in those efforts. So far they have failed, but we will keep trying.

So the work goes on, and it *is* important work, though not the field I trained for, back on Avalon. We know that our results will reach humanity. Royd and I have discussed it. Before I die, I will destroy the central crystal and clear the computers, and afterwards I will set course manually for the close vicinity of an inhabited world. I know I can do it. I have all the time I need, and I am an improved model.

I will not consider the other option, though it means much to me that Royd suggests it again and again. No doubt I could finish the repairs. Perhaps Royd could control the ship without me, and continue the work. But that is not important.

When I finally touched him, for the first and last and only time, his body was still warm. But *he* was gone already. He never felt my touch. I could not keep that promise.

But I can keep my other.

I will not leave him alone with her.

Ever.

BEATNIK BAYOU

John Varley

Science fiction in recent decades has in
creasingly turned to exploration of idea
about future societies. There are many di
ferent ways by which we might conduct ou
lives, and the establishment of colonies i
space or on other planets will certainl
bring innovations in those new cultures
(The colonization of the Americas resulte
in revolutionary ideas that changed th
whole world; consider the probability c
even greater societal changes in the ne
environments of space.) John Varley ha
been at the forefront of such sf explora
tions, and in this novelette he consider
different methods of education, new sys
tems of law . . . but people will probabl
remain the same, and there will be inevi
table conflicts between the new and the old

Varley was unquestionably one of the tw
most important new sf writers of the 1970
(the other being James Tiptree, Jr.). Hi
first novel was *The Ophiuchi Hotline,* fo
lowed by *Titan, Wizard* and the forthcom
ing *Demon,* which will complete this trilogy
He won both the Hugo and Nebula Award
for his novella "The Persistence of Vision,"
which became the title story for his firs
collection.

THE PREGNANT WOMAN HAD BEEN FOLLOWING
us for over an hour when Cathay did the unspeakable
thing.

At first it had been fun. Me and Denver didn't know
what it was about, just that she had some sort of beef with
Cathay. She and Cathay had gone off together and talked.
The woman started yelling, and it was not too long before
Cathay was yelling too. Finally Cathay said something I
couldn't hear and came back to join the class. That was
me, Denver, Trigger, and Cathay, the last two being the
teachers, me and Denver being the students. I know,
you're not supposed to be able to tell which is which, but
believe me, you usually know.

That's when the chase started. This woman wouldn't
take no for an answer, and she followed us wherever we
went. She was about as awkward an animal as you could
imagine, and I certainly wasn't feeling sorry for her after
the way she had talked to Cathay who is my friend. Every
time she slipped and landed on her behind, we all had a
good laugh.

For a while. After an hour, she started to seem a little
frightening. I had never seen anyone so determined.

The reason she kept slipping was that she was chasing
us through Beatnik Bayou which is Trigger's home. Trigger herself describes it as "twelve acres of mud, mosquitoes, and moonshine." Some of her visitors had been
less poetic but more colorful. I don't know what an acre

is, but the bayou is fairly large. Trigger makes the moon-shine in a copper and aluminum still in in the middle of a cane-brake. The mosquitoes don't bite, but they buzz a lot. The mud is just plain old Mississippi mud, suitable for beating your feet. Most people see the place and hate it instantly, but it suits me fine.

Pretty soon the woman was covered in mud. She had three things working against her. One was her ankle-length maternity gown, which covered all of her except for face, feet, and bulging belly and breasts. She kept step-ping on the long skirt and going down. After a while, I winced every time she did that.

Another handicap was her tummy which made her walk with her weight back on her heels. That's not the best way to go through mud, and every so often she sat down real hard, proving it.

Her third problem was the Birthgirdle pelvic bone which must have just been installed. It was one of those which sets the legs far apart and is hinged in the middle so when the baby comes it opens out and gives more room. She needed it because she was tall and thin, the sort of build that might have died in childbirth back when such things were a problem. But it made her waddle like a duck.

"Quack, quack," Denver said with an attempt at a smile. We both looked back at the woman, still follow-ing, still waddling. She went down and struggled to her feet. Denver wasn't smiling when she met my eyes. She muttered something.

"What's that?" I said.

"She's unnerving," Denver repeated. "I wonder what the hell she wants?"

"Something pretty powerful."

Cathay and Trigger were a few paces ahead of us, and I saw Trigger glance back. She spoke to Cathay. I don't think I was supposed to hear it, but I did. I've got good ears.

"This is starting to upset the kids."

"I know," he said, wiping his brow with the back of his hand. All four of us watched her as she toiled her way up the far side of the last rise. Only her head and shoulders were visible.

"Damn. I thought she'd give up pretty soon." He groaned, but then his face became expressionless.

"There's no help for it. We'll have to have a confrontation."

"I thought you already did," Trigger said, lifting an eyebrow.

"Yeah. Well, it wasn't enough, apparently. Come on, people. This is part of your lives, too." He meant me and Denver, and when he said that we knew this was supposed to be a "learning experience." Cathay can turn the strangest things into learning experiences. He started back toward the shallow stream we had just waded across, and the three of us followed him.

If I sounded hard on Cathay, I really shouldn't have been. Actually, he was one damn fine teacher. He was able to take those old saws about learning by doing, seeing is believing, one-on-one instruction, integration of life experiences—all the conventional wisdom of the educational establishment—and make it work better than any teacher I'd ever seen. I knew he was a counterfeit child. I had known that since I first met him, when I was seven, but it hadn't started to matter until lately. And that was just the natural cynicism of my age group, as Trigger kept pointing out in that smug way of hers.

Okay, so he was really forty-eight years old. Physically he was just my age, which was almost thirteen: a short, slightly chubby kid with curly blonde hair and an androgynous face, just starting to grow a little fuzz around his balls. When he turned to face that huge, threatening woman and stood facing her calmly, I was moved.

I was also fascinated. Mentally, I settled back on my haunches to watch and wait and observe. I was sure I'd be learning something about "life" real soon now. Class was in session.

When she saw us coming back, the woman hesitated. She picked her footing carefully as she came down the slight rise to stand at the edge of the water, then waited for a moment to see if Cathay was going to join her. He wasn't. She made an awful face, lifted her skirt up around her waist, and waded in.

The water lapped around her thighs. She nearly fell over when she tried to dodge some dangling Spanish moss. Her lace dress was festooned with twigs and leaves and smeared with mud.

"Why don't you turn around?" Trigger yelled, standing beside me and Denver and shaking her fist. "It's not going to do you any good."

"I'll be the judge of that," she yelled back. Her voice was harsh and ugly, and what had probably been a sweet face was now set in a scowl. An alligator was swimming up to look her over. She swung at it wth her fist, nearly losing her balance. "Get out of here, you slimy lizard!" she screamed. The reptile recalled urgent business on the other side of the swamp and hurried out of her way.

She clambered ashore and stood ankle-deep in ooze, breathing hard. She was a mess, and beneath her anger I could now see fear. Her lips trembled for a moment. I wished she would sit down; just looking at her exhausted me.

"You've got to help me," she said simply.

"Believe me, if I could, I would," Cathay said.

"Then tell me somebody who can."

"I told you, if the Educational Exchange can't help you, I certainly can't. Those few people I know who are available for a contract are listed on the exchange."

"But none of them are available any sooner than three years."

"I know. It's the shortage."

"Then help me," she said miserably. "Help me."

Cathay slowly rubbed his eyes with a thumb and forefinger, then squared his shoulders and put his hands on his hips.

"I'll go over it once more. Somebody gave you my name and said I was available for a primary stage teaching contract. I—"

"He did! He said you'd—"

"I never heard of this person," Cathay said, raising his voice. "Judging from what you're putting me through, he gave you my name from the Teacher's Association listings just to get you off his back. I guess I could do something like that, but frankly I don't think I have the right to subject another teacher to the sort of abuse you've heaped on me." He paused, and for once she didn't say anything.

"Right," he said, finally. "I'm truly sorry that the man you contracted for your child's education went to Pluto instead. From what you told me, what he did was legal, which is not to say ethical." He grimaced at the thought of a teacher who would run out on an ethical obligation.

"All I can say is you should have had the contract analyzed, you should have had a stand-by contract drawn up *three years ago* . . . oh, hell. What's the use? That doesn't do you any good. You have my sympathy, I hope you believe that."

"Then help me," she whispered, and the last word turned into a sob. She began to cry quietly. Her shoulders shook and tears leaked from her eyes, but she never looked away from Cathay.

"There's nothing I can do."

"You have to."

"Once more. I have obligations of my own. In another month, when I've fulfilled my contract with Argus' mother," he gestured toward me, "I'll be regressing to seven again. Don't you understand? I've already got an intermediate contract. The child will be seven in a few months. I contracted for her education four years ago. There's no way I can back out of that, legally or morally."

Her face was twisting again, filling with hate.

"Why not?" she rasped. "Why the hell not? He ran out on *my* contract. Why the hell should I be the only one to suffer? Why me, huh? Listen to me, you shitsucking little son of a blowout. You're all I've got left. After you, there's nothing but the public educator. Or trying to raise him all by myself, all alone, with no guidance. You want to be responsible for that? What the hell kind of start in life does that give him?"

She went on like that for a good ten minutes, getting more illogical and abusive with every sentence. I'd vacillated between a sort of queasy sympathy for her—she *was* in a hell of a mess, even though she had no one to blame but herself—and outright hostility. Just then she scared me. I couldn't look into those tortured eyes without cringing. My gaze wandered down to her fat belly, and the glass eye of the wombscope set into her navel. I didn't need to look into it to know she was due, and overdue. She'd been having the labor postponed while she tried to line up a teacher. Not that it made much sense; the kid's education didn't start until his sixth month. But it was a measure of her desperation and of her illogical thinking under stress.

Cathay stood there and took it until she broke into tears again. I saw her differently this time, maybe a little more like Cathay was seeing her. I was sorry for her, but the tears failed to move me. I saw that she could devour us all if we didn't harden ourselves to her. When it came right down to it, she was the one who had to pay for her carelessness. She was trying her best to get someone else to shoulder the blame, but Cathay wasn't going to do it.

"I didn't want to do this," Cathay said. He looked back at us. "Trigger?"

Trigger stepped forward and folded her arms across her chest.

"Okay," she said. "Listen, I didn't get your name, and I don't really want to know it. But whoever you are, you're on my property, in my house. I'm ordering you to leave here, and I further enjoin you never to come back."

"I won't go," she said stubbornly, looking down at her feet. "I'm not leaving till he promises to help me."

"My next step is to call the police," Trigger reminded her.

"I'm not leaving."

Trigger looked at Cathay and shrugged helplessly. I think they were both realizing that this particular life experience was getting a little too raw.

Cathay thought it over for a moment, eye to eye with the pregnant woman. Then he reached down and scooped up a handful of mud. He looked at it, hefting it experimentally, then threw it at her. It struck her on the left shoulder with a wet plop and began to ooze down.

"Go," he said. "Get out of here."

"I'm not leaving," she said.

He threw another handful. It hit her face, and she gasped and sputtered.

"Go," he said, reaching for more mud. This time he hit her on the leg, but by now Trigger had joined him, and the woman was being pelted.

Before I quite knew what was happening, I was scooping mud from the ground and throwing it. Denver was too. I was breathing hard, and I wasn't sure why.

When she finally turned and fled from us, I noticed that my jaw muscles were tight as steel. It took me a long time to relax them, and when I did, my front teeth were sore.

There are two structures on Beatnik Bayou. One is an old, rotting bait shop and lunch counter called the Sugar Shack, complete with a rusty gas pump out front, a battered Grapette machine on the porch, and a sign advertising Rainbow Bread on the screen door. There's a gray Dodge pickup sitting on concrete blocks to one side of the building, near a pile of rusted auto parts overgrown with weeds. The truck has no wheels. Beside it is a Toyota sedan with no windows or engine. A dirt road runs in front of the shack, going down to the dock. In the other direction the road curves around a cypress tree laden with moss—

—and runs into the wall. A bit of a jolt. But though twelve acres is large for a privately-owned disneyland, it's not big enough to sustain the illusion of really being there. "There," in this case, is supposed to be Louisiana in 1951, old style. Trigger is fascinated by the twentieth century which she defines as 1903 to 1987.

But most of the time it works. You can seldom see the walls because trees are in the way. Anyway, I soak up the atmosphere of the place not so much with my eyes but with my nose and ears and skin. Like the smell of rotting wood, the sound of a frog hitting the water or the hum of the compressor in the soft drink machine, the silver wiggle of a dozen minnows as I scoop them from the metal tanks in back of the shack, the feel of sun-heated wood as I sit on the pier fishing for alligator gar.

It takes a lot of power to operate the "sun," so we get a lot of foggy days and long nights. That helps the illusion too. I would challenge anyone to go for a walk in the bayou night with the crickets chirping and the bullfrogs booming and not think they were back on Old Earth. Except for the Lunar gravity of course.

Trigger inherited money. Even with that and a teacher's salary, the bayou is an expensive place to maintain. It used to be a more conventional environment, but she discovered early that the swamp took less upkeep, and she likes the sleazy atmosphere anyway. She put in the bait shop, bought the automotive mockups from artists, and got it listed with the Lunar Tourist Bureau as an authentic period reconstruction. They'd die if they knew the truth about the Toyota, but I certainly won't tell them.

The only other structure is definitely not from Louisiana of any year. It's a teepee sitting on a slight rise, just out of sight of the Sugar Shack. Cheyenne, I think. We spend most of our time there when we're on the bayou.

That's where we went after the episode with the pregnant woman. The floor is hard-packed clay, and there's a fire always burning in the center. There's lots of pillows scattered around and two big waterbeds.

We tried to talk about the incident. I think Denver was more upset than the rest of us, but from the tense way Cathay sat while Trigger massaged his back I knew he was bothered too. His voice was troubled.

I admitted I had been scared, but there was more to it than that, and I was far from ready to talk about it. Trigger and Cathay sensed it, and let it go for the time being. Trigger got the pipe and stuffed it with dexeplant leaves.

It's a long-stemmed pipe. She got it lit, then leaned back with the stem in her teeth and the bowl held between her toes. She exhaled, sweet, honey-colored smoke. As the day ended outside, she passed the pipe around. It tasted good and calmed me wonderfully. It made it easy to fall asleep.

But I didn't sleep. Not quite. Maybe I was too far into puberty for the drug in the plant to act as a tranquilizer anymore. Or maybe I was too emotionally stimulated. Denver fell asleep quickly enough.

Cathay and Trigger didn't. They made love on the other side of the teepee, did it in such a slow, dreamy way that I knew the drug was affecting them. Though Cathay is in his forties and Trigger is over a hundred, both have the bodies of thirteen-year-olds and the metabolism that goes with the territory.

They didn't actually finish making love; they sort of tapered off, like we used to do before orgasms became a factor. I found that made me happy, lying on my side and watching them through slitted eyes.

They talked for a while. The harder I strained to hear them, the sleepier I got. Somewhere in there I lost the battle to stay awake.

I became aware of a warm body close to me. It was still dark, the only light coming from the embers of the fire.

"Sorry, Argus," Cathay said. "I didn't mean to wake you."

"It's okay. Put your arms around me?" He did, and I squirmed until my back fit snugly against him. For a long time I just enjoyed it. I didn't think about anything, unless it was his warm breath on my neck, or his penis slowly hardening against my back. If you can call that thinking.

How many nights had we slept like this in the last seven years? Too many to count. We knew each other every way possible. A year ago he had been female, and before that both of us had been. Now we were both male, and that was nice too. One part of me thought it didn't really matter which sex we were, but another part was wondering what it would be like to be female and know Cathay as a male. We hadn't tried that yet.

The thought of it made me shiver with anticipation. It had been too long since I'd had a vagina. I wanted Cathay between my legs, like Trigger had had him a short time while before.

"I love you," I mumbled.

He kissed my ear. "I love you too, silly. But how *much* do you love me?"

"What do you mean?"

I felt him shift around to prop his head up on one hand. His fingers unwound a tight curl in my hair.

"I mean, will you still love me when I'm no taller than your knee?"

I shook my head, suddenly feeling cold. "I don't want to talk about that."

"I know that very well," he said. "But I can't let you forget it. It's not something that'll go away."

I turned onto my back and looked up at him. There was a faint smile on his face as he toyed with my lips and hair with his gentle fingertips but his eyes were concerned. Cathay can't hide much from me anymore.

"It has to happen," he emphasized, showing no mercy. "For the reasons you heard me tell the woman. I'm committed to going back to age seven. There's another child waiting for me. She's a lot like you."

"Don't do it," I said, feeling miserable. I felt a tear in the corner of my eye, and Cathay brushed it away.

I was thankful that he didn't point out how unfair I was being. We both knew it; he accepted that and went on as best he could.

"You remember our talk about sex? About two years ago, I think it was. Not too long after you first told me you love me."

"I remember. I remember it all."

He kissed me. "Still, I have to bring it up. Maybe it'll help. You know we agreed that it didn't matter what sex either of us was. Then I pointed out that you'd be growing up, while I'd become a child again. That we'd grow further apart sexually."

I nodded, knowing that if I spoke I'd start to sob.

"And we agreed that our love was deeper than that. That we didn't need sex to make it work. It *can* work."

This was true. Cathay was close to all his former students. They were adults now and came to see him often. It was just to be close, to talk and hug. Lately sex had entered it again, but they all understood that would be over soon.

"I don't think I have that perspective," I said carefully. "They know in a few years you'll mature again. I know it too, but it still feels like. . . ."

"Like what?"

"Like you're abandoning me. I'm sorry, that's just how it feels."

He sighed and pulled me close to him. He hugged me fiercely for a while, and it felt so good.

"Listen," he said finally. "I guess there's no avoiding this, I could tell you that you'll get over it—you will—but it won't do any good. I had this same problem with every child I've taught."

"You did?" I hadn't known that, and it made me feel a little better.

"I did. I don't blame you for it. I feel it myself. I feel a pull to stay with you. But it wouldn't work, Argus. I love my work, or I wouldn't be doing it. There are hard times like right now. But after a few months you'll feel better."

"Maybe I will." I was far from sure of it, but it seemed important to agree with him and get the conversation ended.

"In the meantime," he said, "we still have a few weeks together. I think we should make the most of them." And he did, his hands roaming over my body. He did all the work, letting me relax and try to get myself straightened out.

So I folded my arms under my head and reclined, trying to think of nothing but the warm circle of his mouth.

But eventually I began to feel I should be doing some

thing for him, and knew what was wrong. He thought he was giving me what I wanted by making love to me in the way he had done since we grew older together. But there was another way, and I realized I didn't so much want him to stay thirteen. What I really wanted was to go back with him, to be seven again.

I touched his head and he looked up, then we embraced again face to face. We began to move against each other as we had done since we first met, the mindless, innocent friction from a time when it had less to do with sex than with simply feeling good.

But the body is insistent and can't be fooled. Soon our movements were frantic, and then a feeling of wetness between us told me as surely as entropy that we could never go back.

On my way home the signs of change were all around me.

You grow a little, let out the arms and legs of your pressure suit until you finally have to get a new one. People stop thinking of you as a cute little kid and start talking about you being a fine young person. Always with that smile, like it's a joke that you're not supposed to get.

People treat you differently as you grow up. At first you hardly interact at all with adults, except your own mother and the mothers of your friends. You live in a kid's world, and adults are hardly even obstacles because they get out of your way when you run down the corridors. You go all sorts of places for free; people want you around to make them happy because there are so few kids and just about everybody would like to have more than just the one. You hardly even notice the people smiling at you all the time.

But it's not like that at all when you're thirteen. Now there was the hesitation, just a fraction of a second before they gave me a child's privileges. Not that I blamed anybody. I was nearly as tall as a lot of the adults I met.

But now I had begun to notice the adults, to watch them. Especially when they didn't know they were being watched. I saw that a lot of them spent a lot of time frowning. Occasionally, I would see real pain on a face. Then he or she would look at me and smile. I could see that wouldn't be happening forever. Sooner or later I'd cross some invisible line, and the pain would stay in those faces, and I'd have to try to understand it. I'd be an adult, and I wasn't sure I wanted to be.

It was because of this new preoccupation with faces that I noticed the woman sitting across from me on the Archimedes train. I planned to be a writer, so I tended to see everything in terms of stories and characters. I watched her and tried to make a story about her.

She was attractive: physically mid-twenties, straight black hair and brownish skin, round face without elaborate surgery or startling features except her dark brown eyes. She wore a simple thigh-length robe of thin white material that flowed like water when she moved. She had one elbow on the back of her seat, absently chewing a knuckle as she looked out the window.

There didn't seem to be a story in her face. She was in an unguarded moment, but I saw no pain, no big concerns or fears. It's possible I just missed it. I was new at the game, and I didn't know much about what was important to adults. But I kept trying.

Then she turned to look at me, and she didn't smile.

I mean, she smiled, but it didn't say isn't-he-cute. It was the sort of smile that made me wish I'd worn some clothes. Since I'd learned what erections are for, I no longer wished to have them in public places.

I crossed my legs. She moved to sit beside me. She held up her palm and I touched it. She was facing me with one leg drawn up under her and her arm resting on the seat behind me.

"I'm Trilby," she said.

"Hi. I'm Argus." I found myself trying to lower my voice.

"I was sitting over there watching you watch me."

"You were?"

"In the glass," she explained.

"Oh." I looked, and sure enough, from where she had been sitting she could appear to be looking at the landscape while actually studying my reflection. "I didn't mean to be rude."

She laughed and put her hand on my shoulder, then moved it. "What about me?" she said. "I was being sneaky about it; you weren't. Anyhow, don't fret. I don't mind." I shifted again, and she glanced down. "And don't worry about that either. It happens."

I still felt nervous but she was able to put me at ease.

We talked for the rest of the ride, and I have no memory of what we talked about. The range of subjects must have been quite narrow, as I'm sure she never made reference to my age, my schooling, her profession—or just why she had started a conversation with a thirteen-year-old on a public train.

None of that mattered. I was willing to talk about anything. If I wondered about her reasons, I assumed she actually was in her twenties and not that far from her own childhood.

"Are you in a hurry?" she asked at one point, giving her head a little toss.

"Me? No. I'm on my way to see—" No, no, not your mother. "—a friend. She can wait. She expects me when I get there." That sounded better.

"Can I buy you a drink?" One eyebrow raised, a small motion with the hand. Her gestures were economical, but seemed to say more than her words. I mentally revised her age upward a few years. Maybe quite a few.

This was timed to the train arriving at Archimedes; we got up and I quickly accepted.

"Good. I know a nice place."

The bartender gave me that smile and was about to give me the customary free one on the house toward my legal limit of two. But Trilby changed all that.

"Two Irish whiskeys, please. On the rocks." She said it firmly, raising her voice a little, and a complex thing happened between her and the bartender. She gave him a look; his eyebrow twitched and he glanced at me, seemed to understand something. His whole attitude toward me changed.

I had the feeling something had gone over my head, but didn't have time to worry about it. I never had time to worry when Trilby was around. The drinks arrived, and we sipped them.

"I wonder why they still call it Irish?" she said.

We launched into a discussion of the Invaders, or Ireland, or Occupied Earth. I'm not sure. It was inconsequential, and the real conversation was going on eye to eye. Mostly it was her saying wordless things to me, and me nodding agreement with my tongue hanging out.

We ended up at the public baths down the corridor. Her nipples were shaped like pink valentine hearts. Other than that, her body was unremarkable, though wonderfully firm beneath the softness. She was so unlike Trigger and Denver and Cathay. So unlike me. I catalogued the differences as I sat behind her in the big pool and massaged her soapy shoulders.

On the way to the tanning room she stopped beside one of the private alcoves and just stood there, waiting, looking at me. My legs walked me into the room and she followed me. My hands pressed against her back, and my mouth opened when she kissed me. She lowered me to the soft floor and took me.

What was so different about it?

I pondered that during the long walk from the slide terminus to my home. Trilby and I had made love for the better part of an hour. It was nothing fancy, nothing I had not already tried with Trigger and Denver. I had thought she would have some fantastic new tricks to show me, but that had not been the case.

Yet she had not been like Trigger or Denver. Her body responded in a different way, moved in directions I was not used to. I did my best. When I left her, I knew she was happy, and yet felt she expected more.

I found that I was very interested in giving her more.

I was in love again.

With my hand on the doorplate, I suddenly knew that she had already forgotten me. It was silly to assume anything else. I had been a pleasant diversion, an interesting novelty.

I hadn't asked for her name, her address, or call number. Why not? Maybe I already knew she would not care to hear from me again.

I hit the plate with the heel of my hand and brooded during the elevator ride to the surface.

My home is unusual. Of course, it belongs to Darcy, my mother. She was there now, putting the finishing touches on a diorama. She glanced up at me, smiled, and offered her cheek for a kiss.

"I'll be through in a moment," she said. "I want to finish this before the light fails."

We live in a large bubble on the surface. Part of it is partitioned into rooms without ceilings, but the bulk forms Darcy's studio. The bubble is transparent. It screens out the ultraviolet light so we don't get burned.

It's an uncommon way to live, but it suits us. From our vantage point at the south side of a small valley only three similar bubbles can be seen. It would be impossible for an outsider to guess that a city teemed just below the surface.

Growing up, I never gave a thought to agoraphobia, but it's common among Lunarians. I felt sorry for those not fortunate enough to grow up with a view.

Darcy likes it for the light. She's an artist and particular about light. She works two weeks on and two off, resting during the night. I grew up to that schedule, leaving her alone while she put in marathon sessions with her airbrushes, coming home to spend two weeks with her when the sun didn't shine.

That had changed a bit when I reached my tenth birthday. We had lived alone before then, Darcy cutting her work schedule drastically until I was four, gradually picking it up as I attained more independence. She did it so she could devote all her time to me. Then one day she sat me down and told me two men were moving in. It was only later that I realized how Darcy had altered her lifestyle to raise me properly. She is a serial polyandrist, especially attracted to fierce-faced, uncompromising, maverick male artists whose work doesn't sell and who are usually a little hungry. She likes the hunger, and the determination they all have not to pander to public tastes. She usually keeps three or four of them around, feeding them and giving them a place to work. She demands little of them other than that they clean up after themselves.

I had to step over the latest of these household pets to get to the kitchen. He was sound asleep, snoring loudly, his hands stained yellow and red and green. I'd never seen him before.

Darcy came up behind me while I was making a snack, hugged me, then pulled up a chair and sat down. The sun would be out another half hour or so, but there wasn't time to start another painting.

"How have you been? You didn't call for three days."

"Didn't I? I'm sorry. We've been staying on the bayou."

She wrinkled her nose. Darcy had seen the bayou. Once.

"*That* place. I wish I knew why—"

"Darcy. Let's not get into that again. Okay?"

"Done." · She spread her paint-stained hands and waved them in a circle as if erasing something, and that was it. Darcy is good that way. "I've got a new roommate."

"I nearly stumbled over him."

She ran one hand through her hair and gave me a lopsided grin. "He'll shape up. His name's Thogra."

"Thogra," I said, making a face. "Listen, if he's housebroken, and stays out of my way, we'll—" But I couldn't go on. We were both laughing and I was about to choke on a bite that went down wrong. Darcy knows what I think of her choice in bedmates.

"What about . . . what's his name? The armpit man. The guy who kept getting arrested for body odor."

She stuck her tongue out at me."

"You know he cleaned up months ago."

"Hah! It's those months *before* he discovered water that I remember. All my friends wondering where we were raising sheep, the flowers losing petals when he walked by, the—"

"Abil didn't come back," Darcy said, quietly.

I stopped laughing. I'd known he'd been away a few weeks, but that happens. I raised one eyebrow.

"Yeah. Well, you know he sold a few things. And he had some offers. But I keep expecting him to at least stop by to pick up his bedroll."

I didn't say anything. Darcy's loves follow a pattern that she is quite aware of, but it's still tough when one breaks up. Her men would often speak with contempt of the sort of commercial art that kept me and Darcy eating and paying the oxygen bills. Then one of three things would happen. They would get nowhere and leave as poor as they had arrived, contempt intact. A few made it on their own terms, forcing the art world to accept their peculiar visions. Often Darcy was able to stay on good terms with these; she was on a drop-in-and-make-love basis with half the artists in Luna.

But the most common departure was when the artist decided he was tired of poverty. With just a slight lowering of standards they were all quite capable of making a living. Then it became intolerable to live with the woman they had ridiculed. Darcy usually kicked them out quickly with a minimum of pain. They were no longer hungry, no longer fierce enough to suit her. But it always hurt.

Darcy changed the subject.

"I made an appointment at the medico for your Change," she said. "You're to be there next Monday in the morning."

A series of quick, vivid impressions raced through my mind. Trilby. Breasts tipped with hearts. The way it had felt when my penis entered her, and the warm exhaustion after the semen had left my body.

"I've changed my mind about that," I said, crossing my legs. "I'm not ready for another Change. Maybe in a few months."

She just sat there with her mouth open.

"Changed your *mind?* Last time I talked to you, you were all set to change your *sex.* In fact, you had to talk me into giving permission."

"I remember," I said, feeling uneasy about it. "I just changed my mind, that's all."

"But Argus. This just isn't fair. I sat up two nights convincing myself how nice it would be to have my daughter back again. It's been a long time. Don't you think you—"

"It's really not your decision, mother."

She looked like she was going to get angry, then her eyes narrowed. "There must be a reason. You've met somebody. Right?"

But I didn't want to talk about that. I had told her the first time I made love, and about every new person I'd gone to bed with since. But I didn't want to share this with her.

So I told her about the incident earlier that day on the bayou. I told her about the pregnant woman, and about the thing Cathay had done.

Darcy frowned more and more. When I got to the part about the mud, there were ridges all over her forehead.

"I don't like that," she said.

"I don't really like it, either. But I didn't see what else we could do."

"I just don't think it was handled well. I think I should call Cathay and talk to him about it."

"I wish you wouldn't," I didn't say anything more, and she studied my face for a long, uncomfortable time. She and Cathay had differed before about how I should be raised.

"This shouldn't be ignored."

"Please, Darcy. He'll only be my teacher for another month. Let it go, okay?"

After a while she nodded and looked away from me. "You're growing more every day," she said sadly. I didn't know why she said that, but was glad she was dropping the subject. To tell the truth, I didn't want to think about the woman anymore. But I was going to have to think about her, and very soon.

I had intended to spend the week at home, but Trigger called the next morning to say that Mardi Gras '56 was being presented again, and it was starting in a few hours. She'd made reservations for the four of us.

Trigger had seen the presentation before, but I hadn't, and neither had Denver. I told her I'd come, went in to tell Darcy, found her still asleep. She often slept for two days after a Lunar Day of working. I left her a note and hurried to catch the train.

It's called the Cultural Heritage Museum, and though they pay for it with their taxes, most Lunarians never go there. They find the exhibits disturbing. I understand that lately, however, with the rise of the Free Earth Party, it's become more popular with people searching for their roots.

Once they presented London Town 1903, and I got to see what Earth museums had been like by touring the replica British Museum. The CHM isn't like that at all. Only a very few art treasures, artifacts, and historical curiosities were brought to Luna in the days before the Invasion. As a result, all the tangible relics of Earth's past were destroyed.

On the other hand, the Lunar computer system had a capacity that was virtually limitless even then; *everything* was recorded and stored. Every book, painting, tax receipt, statistic, photograph, government report, corporate record, film, and tape existed in the memory banks. Just as the disneylands are populated with animals cloned from cells stored in the Genetic Library, the CHM is filled with cunning copies made from the old records of the way things were.

I met the others at the Sugar Shack where Denver was trying to talk Trigger into taking Tuesday along with us.

Tuesday is the hippopotamus that lives on the bayou, in cheerful defiance of any sense of authenticity. Denver had her on a chain, and she stood placidly watching us, blinking her piggy little eyes.

Denver was tickled at the idea of going to Mardi Gras with a hippo named Tuesday, but Trigger pointed out that the museum officials would never let us into New Orleans with the beast. Denver finally conceded and shooed her back into the swamp. The four of us went down the road and out of the bayou, boarded the central sidewalk, and soon arrived in the city center.

There are twenty-five theaters in the CHM. Usually about half of them are operating while the others are being prepared for a showing. Mardi Gras '56 is a ten-year-old show, and generally opens twice a year for a two week run. It's one of the more popular environments.

We went to the orientation room and listened to the lecture on how to behave, then were given our costumes. That's the part I like the least. Up until about the beginning of the twenty-first century, clothing was designed with two main purposes in mind: modesty and torture. If it didn't hurt, it needed redesigning. It's no wonder they killed each other all the time. Anybody would, with high gravity and hard shoes mutilating their feet.

"We'll be beatniks," Trigger said, looking over the racks of period clothing. "They were more informal, and it's accurate enough to get by. There are beatniks in the French Quarter."

Informality was fine with us. The girls didn't need bras, and we could choose between leather sandals and canvas sneakers for our feet. I can't say I cared much for something called Levis though. They were scratchy and pinched my balls. But after visiting Victorian England— I had been female at the time, and what those people made girls wear would shock most Lunarians silly—anything was an improvement.

Entry to the holotorium was through the restrooms at the back of a nightclub that fronted on Bourbon Street. Boys to the left, girls to the right. I think they did that to impress you right away that you were going back into the past when people did things in strange ways. There was a third restroom, actually, but it was only a false door with the word "colored" on it. It was impossible to sort *that* out anymore.

I like the music of 1956 New Orleans. There are many varieties, all sounding similar for modern ears with their simple rhythms and blends of wind, string, and percussion. The generic term is jazz, and the particular kind of jazz that afternoon in the tiny, smoke-filled basement was called dixieland. It's dominated by two instruments called a clarinet and a trumpet, each improvising a simple melody while the rest of the band makes as much racket as it can.

We had a brief difference of opinion. Cathay and Trigger wanted me and Denver to stay with them, presumably so they could use any opportunity to show off their superior knowledge—translation: "educate" us. After all, they were teachers. Denver didn't seem to mind, but I wanted to be alone.

I solved the problem by walking out onto the street, reasoning that they could follow me if they wished. They didn't, and I was free to explore on my own.

Going to a holotorium show isn't like the sensies, where you sit in a chair and the action comes to you. And it's not like a disneyland, where everything is real and you just poke around. You have to be careful not to ruin the illusion.

The majority of the set, most of the props, and all of the actors are holograms. Any real people you meet are costumed visitors like yourself. What they did in the case of New Orleans was to lay out a grid of streets and surface them as they had actually been. Then they put up two-meter walls where the buildings would be and concealed them behind holos of old buildings. A few of the doors in these buildings were real, and if you went in you would find the interiors authentic down to the last detail. Most just concealed empty blocks.

You don't go there to play childish tricks with holos, that's contrary to the whole spirit of the place. You find yourself being careful not to shatter the illusion. You don't talk to people unless you're sure they're real, and you don't touch things until you've studied them carefully. No holo can stand up to a close scrutiny, so you can separate the real from the illusion if you try.

The stage was a large one. They had reproduced the French Quarter—or *Vieux Carre*—from the Mississippi

River to Rampart Street, and from Canal Street to a point about six blocks east. Standing on Canal and looking across, the city seemed to teem with life for many kilometers in the distance, though I knew there was a wall right down the yellow line in the middle.

New Orleans '56 begins at noon on Shrove Tuesday and carries on far into the night. We had arrived in late afternoon with the sun starting to cast long shadows over the endless parades. I wanted to see the place before it got dark.

I went down Canal for a few blocks, looking into the "windows." There was an old flat movie theater with a marquee announcing *From Here to Eternity,* winner of something called an Oscar. I saw that it was a real place and thought about going in, but I'm afraid those old #2-D movies leave me flat, no matter how good Trigger says they are.

So instead I walked the streets, observing, thinking about writing a story set in old New Orleans.

That's why I hadn't wanted to stay and listen to the music with the others. Music is not something you can really put into a story, beyond a bare description of what it sounds like, who is playing it, and where it is being heard. In the same way, going to the flat movie would not have been very productive.

But the streets, the streets! There was something to study.

The pattern was the same as old London, but all the details had changed. The roads were filled with horseless carriages, great square metal boxes that must have been the most inefficient means of transport ever devised. Nothing was truly straight nor very clean. To walk the streets was to risk broken toes or cuts on the soles of the feet. No wonder they wore thick shoes.

I knew what the red and green lights were for, and the lines painted on the road. But what about the rows of timing devices on each side of the street? What was the red metal object that a dog was urinating on? What did the honking of the car horns signify? Why were wires suspended overhead on wooden poles? I ignored the Mardi Gras festivities and spent a pleasant hour looking for the answers to these and many other questions.

What a challenge to write of this time, to make the story a slice of life where these outlandish things seemed normal and reasonable. I visualized one of the inhabitants of New Orleans transplanted to Archimedes and tried to picture her confusion.

Then I saw Trilby and forgot about New Orleans.

She was behind the wheel of a 1955 Ford station wagon. I know this because when she motioned for me to join her, slid over on the seat, and let me drive, there was a gold plaque on the bulkhead just below the forward viewport.

"How do you run this thing?" I asked, flustered and trying not to show it. Something was wrong. Maybe I'd known it all along and was only now admitting it.

"You press that pedal to go and that one to stop. But mostly it controls itself." The car proved her right by accelerating into the stream of holographic traffic. I put my hands on the wheel, found that I could guide the car within limits. As long as I wasn't going to hit anything it let me be the boss.

"What brings you here?" I asked, trying for a light voice.

"I went by your home," she said. "Your mother told me where you were."

"I don't recall telling you where I live."

She shrugged, not seeming too happy. "It's not hard to find out."

"I . . . I mean, you didn't. . . ." I wasn't sure if I wanted to say it, but decided I'd better go on. "We didn't meet by accident, did we?"

"No."

"And you're my new teacher."

She sighed. "That's an oversimplification. I *want* to be *one* of your new teachers. Cathay recommended me to your mother, and when I talked to her, she was interested. I was just going to get a look at you on the train, but when I saw you looking at me . . . well, I thought I'd give you something to remember me by."

"Thanks."

She looked away. "Darcy told me today that it might have been a mistake. I guess I judged you wrong."

"It's nice to hear that you can make a mistake."

"I guess I don't understand."

"I don't like to feel predictable. I don't like to be toyed

with. Maybe it hurts my dignity. Maybe I get enough of that from Trigger and Cathay. All the 'lessons.' "

"I see it now," she sighed. "It's a common enough reaction, in bright children, they—"

"Don't say that."

"I'm sorry, but I must. There's no use hiding from you that my business is to know people, and especially children. That means the phases they go through, including the phase when they like to imagine they don't go through phases. I didn't recognise it in you, so I made a mistake."

I sighed. "What does it matter anyway? Darcy likes you. That means you'll be my new teacher, doesn't it?"

"It does not. Not with me anyway. I'm one of the first big choices you get to make with no adult interference."

"I don't get it."

"That's because you've never been interested enough to find out what's ahead of you in your education. At the risk of offending you again, I'll say it's a common response in people your age. You're only a month from graduating away from Cathay, ready to start more goal-oriented aspects of learning, and you haven't bothered to find out what that will entail. Did you ever stop to think what's between you and becoming a writer?"

"I'm a writer already," I said, getting angry for the first time. Before that, I'd been feeling hurt more than anything. "I can use the language, and I watch people. Maybe I don't have much experience yet, but I'll get it with or without you. I don't even *have* to have teachers at *all* anymore. At least I know that much."

"You're right, of course. But you've known your mother intended to pay for your advanced education. Didn't you ever wonder what it would be like?"

"Why should I? Did you ever think that I'm not interested because it just doesn't seem important? I mean, who's asked me what I felt about any of this up to now? What kind of stake do I have in it? Everyone seems to know what's best for me. Why should I be consulted?"

"Because you're nearly an adult now. My job, if you hire me, will be to ease the transition. When you've made it, you'll know, and you won't need me anymore. This isn't primary phase. Your teacher's job back then was to work with your mother to teach you the basic ways of getting along with people and society, and to cram your little head with all the skills a seven-year-old can learn. They taught you language, dexterity, reasoning, responsibility, hygiene, and not to go in an airlock without your suit. They took an ego-centered infant and turned him into a moral being. It's a tough job; so little, and you could have been a sociopath.

"Then they handed you to Cathay. You didn't mind. He showed up one day, just another playmate your own age. You were happy and trusting. He guided you very gently, letting your natural curiosity do most of the work. He discovered your creative abilities before you had any inkling of them, and he saw to it that you had interesting things to think about, to react to, to experience.

"But lately you've been a problem for him. Not your fault, nor his, but you no longer want anyone to guide you. You want to do it on your own. You have vague feelings of being manipulated."

"Which is not surprising," I put in. "I *am* being manipulated."

"That's true, so far as it goes. But what would you have Cathay do? Leave everything to chance?"

"That's beside the point. We're talking about my feelings now, and what I feel is you were dishonest with me. You made me feel like a fool. I thought what happened was . . . was spontaneous, you know? Like a fairy tale."

She gave me a funny smile. "What an odd way to put it. What I intended to do was allow you to live out a wet dream."

I guess the easy way she admitted that threw me off my stride. I should have told her there was no real difference. Both fairy tales and wet dreams were visions of impossibly convenient worlds, worlds where things go the way you want them to go. But I didn't say anything.

"I realize now that it was the wrong way to approach you. Frankly, I thought you'd enjoy it. Wait, let me change that. I thought you'd enjoy it even *after* you knew. I submit that you *did* enjoy it while it was happening."

I once again said nothing because it was the simple truth. But it wasn't the point.

She waited, watching me as I steered the old car through traffic. Then she sighed and looked out the viewport again.

"Well, it's up to you. As I said, things won't be

planned for you anymore. You'll have to decide if you want me to be your teacher."

"Just what is it you teach?" I asked.

"Sex is part of it."

I started to say something, but was stopped by the novel idea that someone thought she could—or *needed* to —teach me about sex. I mean, what was there to learn?

I hardly noticed it when the car stopped on its own, was shaken out of my musings only when a man in blue stuck his head in the window beside me. There was a woman behind him, dressed the same way. I realized they were wearing 1956 police uniforms.

"Are you Argus-Darcy-Meric?" the man asked.

"Yeah. Who are you?"

"My name is Jordan. I'm sorry, but you'll have to come with me. A complaint has been filed against you. You are under arrest."

Arrest. To take into custody by legal authority. Or, to stop suddenly.

Being arrested contains both meanings, it seems to me. You're in custody, and your life comes to a temporary halt. Whatever you were doing is interrupted, and suddenly only one thing is important.

I wasn't too worried until I realized what that one thing must be. After all, everyone gets arrested. You can't avoid it in a society of laws. Filing a complaint against someone is the best way of keeping a situation from turning violent. I had been arrested three times before, been found guilty twice. Once I had filed a complaint myself and had it sustained.

But this time promised to be different. I doubted I was being hauled in for some petty violation I had not even been aware of. No, this had to be the pregnant woman, and the mud. I had a while to think about that as I sat in the bare-walled holding cell, time to get really worried. We had physically attacked her, there was no doubt about that.

I was finally summoned to the examination chamber. It was larger than the ones I had been in before. Those occasions had involved just two people. This room had five wedge-shaped glass booths, each with a chair inside, arranged so that we faced each other in a circle. I was shown into the only empty one and I looked around at Denver, Cathay, Trigger, . . . and the woman.

It's quiet in the booths. You are very much alone.

I saw Denver's mother come in and sit behind her daughter, outside the booth. Turning around, I saw Darcy. To my surprise, Trilby was with her.

"Hello, Argus." The Central Computer's voice filled the tiny booth, mellow as usual but without the reassuring resonance.

"Hello, CC," I tried to keep it light, but of course the CC was not fooled.

"I'm sorry to see you in so much trouble."

"Is it real bad?"

"The charge certainly is, there's no sense denying that. I can't comment on the testimony or on your chances. But you know you're facing a possible mandatory death penalty with automatic reprieve."

I was aware of it. I also knew it was rarely enforced against someone my age. But what about Cathay and Trigger?

I've never cared for that term "reprieve." It somehow sounds like they aren't going to kill you, but they are. Very, very dead. The catch is that they then grow a clone from a cell of your body, force it quickly to maturity, and play your recorded memories back into it. So someone very like you will go on, but *you* will be dead. In my case, the last recording had been taken three years ago. I was facing the loss of almost a quarter of my life. If it was found necessary to kill me, the new Argus—*not* me, but someone with my memories and my name—would start over at age ten. He would be watched closely, be given special guidance to insure he didn't grow into the socio-path I had become.

The CC launched into the legally-required explanation of what was going on: my rights, the procedures, the charges, the possible penalties, what would happen if a determination led the CC to believe the offense might be a capital one.

"Whew!" the CC breathed, lapsing back into the informal speech it knew I preferred. "Now that we have that out of the way, I can tell you that, from the preliminary reports, I think you're going to be okay."

"You're not just saying that?" I was sincerely frightened. The enormity of it had now had time to sink in.

"You know me better than that."

The testimony began. The complainant went first, and I learned her name was Tiona. The first round was free-form; we could say anything we wanted to, and she had some pretty nasty things to say about all four of us.

The CC went around the circle asking each of us what had happened. I thought Cathay told it most accurately, except for myself. During the course of the statements both Cathay and Trigger filed counter-complaints. The CC noted them. They would be tried simultaneously.

There was a short pause, then the CC spoke in its "official" voice.

"In the matters of Argus and Denver: testimony fails to establish premeditation, but neither deny the physical description of the incident, and a finding of Assault is returned. Mitigating factors of age and consequent inability to combat the mob aspect of the situation are entered, with the following result: the charge is reduced to Willful Deprivation of Dignity.

"In the case of Tiona versus Argus: guilty.

"In the case of Tiona versus Denver: guilty.

"Do either of you have anything to say before sentence is entered?"

I thought about it. "I'm sorry," I said. "It upset me quite a bit, what happened. I won't do it again."

"I'm not sorry," Denver said. "She asked for it. I'm sorry for her, but I'm not sorry for what I did."

"Comments are noted," the CC said. "You are each fined the sum of three hundred Marks, collection deferred until you reach employable age, sum to be taken at the rate of ten percent of your earnings until paid, half going to Tiona, half to the State. Final entry of sentence shall be delayed until a further determination of matters still before the court is made."

"You got off easy," the CC said, speaking only to me. "But stick around. Things could still change, and you might not have to pay the fine after all."

It was a bit of a wrench, getting a sentence, then sympathy from the same machine. I had to guard against feeling that the CC was on my side. It wasn't, not really. It's absolutely impartial, so far as I can tell. Yet it is so vast an intelligence that it makes a different personality for each citizen it deals with. The part that had just talked to me was really on my side, but was powerless to affect what the judgmental part of it did.

"I don't get it," I said. "What happens now?"

"Well, I've been rashomoned again. That means you all told your stories from your own viewpoints. We haven't reached deeply enough into the truth. Now I'm going to have to wire you all and take another round."

As it spoke, I saw the probes come up behind everyone's chairs: little golden snakes with plugs on the end. I felt one behind me search through my hair until it found the terminal. It plugged in.

There are two levels to wired testimony. Darcy and Trilby and Denver's mother had to leave the room for the first part, when we all told our stories without our censors working. The transcript bears me out when I say I didn't tell any lies in the first round, unlike Tiona, who told a lot of them. But it doesn't sound like the same story, nevertheless. I told all sorts of things I never would have said without being wired: fears, selfish, formless desires, infantile motivations. It's embarrassing, and I'm glad I don't recall any of it. I'm even happier that only Tiona and I, as interested parties, can see my testimony. I only wish I was the only one.

The second phase is the disconnection of the subconscious. I told the story a third time, in terms as bloodless as the stage directions of a holovision script.

Then the terminals withdrew from us and I suffered a moment of disorientation. I knew where I was, where I had been, and yet I felt like I had been told about it rather than lived it. But that passed quickly. I stretched.

"Is everyone ready to go on?" the CC asked politely. We all said that we were.

"Very well. In the matters of Tiona versus Argus and Denver: the guilty judgment remains in force in both cases, but both fines are rescinded in view of provocation, lessened liability due to immaturity, and lack of signs of continuing sociopathic behavior. In place of the fines, Denver and Argus are to report weekly for evaluation and education in moral principles until such time as a determination can be made, duration of such sessions to be no less than four weeks.

"In the matter of Tiona versus Trigger: Trigger is guilty of an Assault. Tempering this judgment is her motive, which was the recognition of Cathay's strategy in dealing with Tiona and her belief that he was doing the right thing. This court notes that he was doing the *merciful* thing; right is another matter. There can be no doubt that a physical assault occurred. It cannot be condoned, no matter what the motive. For bad judgment, then, this court fines Trigger ten percent of her earnings for a period of ten years, all of it to be paid to the injured party, Tiona."

Tiona did not look smug. She must have known by then that things were not going her way. I was beginning to understand it too.

"In the matter of Tiona versus Cathay," the CC went on, "Cathay is guilty of an Assault. His motive has been determined to be the avoidance of just such a situation as he now finds himself in, and the knowledge that Tiona would suffer greatly if he brought her to court. He attempted to bring the confrontation to an end with a minimum of pain for Tiona, never dreaming that she would show the bad judgment to bring the matter to court. She did, and now he finds himself convicted of Assault. In view of his motives, mercy will temper this court's decision. He is ordered to pay the same fine as his colleague, Trigger.

"Now to the central matter, that of Trigger and Cathay versus Tiona." I saw her sink a little lower in her chair.

"You are found to be guilty by reason of insanity of the following charges: harassment, trespassing, verbal assault, and four counts of infringement.

"Your offense was in attempting to make others shoulder the blame for your own misjudgments and misfortunes. The court is sympathetic to your plight, realizes that the fault for your situation was not entirely your own. This does not excuse your behavior, however.

"Cathay attempted to do you a favor, supposing that your aberrant state of mind would not last long enough for the filing of charges, that when you were alone and thought it over you would realize how badly you had wronged him and that a court would find in his favor.

"The State holds you responsible for the maintenance of your own mind, does not care what opinions you hold or what evaluations you make of reality so long as they do not infringe on the rights of other citizens. You are free to think Cathay responsible for your troubles, even if this opinion is irrational, but when you assault him with this opinion the State must take notice and make a judgment as to the worth of the opinion.

"This court is appointed to make that judgment of right and wrong and finds no basis in fact for your contentions.

"This court finds you to be insane.

"Judgment is as follows:

"Subject to the approval of the wronged parties, you are given the choice of death with reprieve or submission to a course of treatment to remove your sociopathic attitudes.

"Argus, do you demand her death?"

"Huh?" That was a big surprise to me, and not one that I liked. But the decision gave me no trouble.

"No, I don't demand anything. I thought I was out of this, and I feel just rotten about the whole thing. Would you really have killed her if I asked you to?"

"I can't answer that, because you didn't. It's not likely that I would have, mostly because of your age." It went on to ask the other four, and I suspect that Tiona would have been pushing up daisies if Cathay had wanted it that way, but he didn't. Neither did Trigger or Denver.

"Very well. How do you choose, Tiona?"

She answered in a very small voice that she would be grateful for the chance to go on living. Then she thanked each of us. It was excruciatingly painful for me; my empathy was working overtime, and I was trying to imagine what it would feel like to have society's appointed representative declare me insane.

The rest of it was clearing up details. Tiona was fined heavily, both in court costs and taxes, and in funds payable to Cathay and Trigger. Their fines were absorbed in her larger ones, with the result that she would be paying them for many years. Her child was in cold storage; the CC ruled that he should stay there until Tiona was declared sane, as she was now unfit to mother him. It occurred to me that if she had considered suspending his animation while she found a new primary teacher, we all could have avoided the trial.

Tiona hurried away when the doors came open behind us. Darcy hugged me while Trilby stayed in the background, then I went over to join the others, expecting a celebration.

But Trigger and Cathay were not elated. In fact, you

would have thought they'd just lost the judgment. They congratulated me and Denver, then hurried away. I looked at Darcy, and she wasn't smiling either.

"I don't get it," I confessed. "Why is everyone so glum?"

"They still have to face the Teacher's Association," Darcy said.

"I still don't get it. They won."

"It's not just a matter of winning or losing with the TA," Trilby said. "You forget, they were judged guilty of Assault. To make it even worse, in fact as bad as it can be, you and Denver were there when it happened. They were the cause of you two joining in the assault. I'm afraid the TA will frown on that."

"But if the CC thought they shouldn't be punished, why should the TA think otherwise? Isn't the CC smarter than people?"

Trilby grimaced, "I wish I could answer that. I wish I was even sure how I feel about it."

She found me the next day shortly after the Teacher's Association announced its decision. I didn't really want to be found, but the bayou is not so big that one can really hide there, so I hadn't tried. I was sitting on the grass on the highest hill in Beatnik Bayou, which was also the driest place.

She beached the canoe and came up the hill slowly, giving me plenty of time to warn her off if I really wanted to be alone. What the hell. I'd have to talk to her soon enough.

For a long time she just sat there. She rested her elbows on her knees and stared down at the quiet waters just like I'd been doing all afternoon.

"How's he taking it?" I said, at last.

"I don't know. He's back there if you want to talk to him. He'd probably like to talk to you."

"At least Trigger got off okay." As soon as I'd said it, it sounded hollow.

"Three years' probation isn't anything to laugh about. She'll have to close this place down for a while. Put it in mothballs."

"Mothballs." I saw Tuesday the hippo, wallowing in the deep mud across the water. Tuesday in suspended animation? I thought of Tiona's little baby, waiting in a bottle until his mother became sane again. I remembered the happy years slogging around in the bayou mud, and saw the waters frozen, icicles mixed with Spanish moss in the tree limbs. "I guess it'll cost quite a bit to start it up again in three years, won't it?" I had only hazy ideas of money. So far, it had never been important to me.

Trilby glanced at me, eyes narrowed. She shrugged.

"Most likely, Trigger will have to sell the place. There's a buyer who wants to expand it and turn it into a golf course."

"Golf course," I echoed, feeling numb. Manicured greens, pretty water hazards, sand traps, flags whipping in the breeze. Sterile. I suddenly felt like crying, but for some reason I didn't do it.

"You can't come back here, Argus. Nothing stays the same. Change is something you have to get used to."

"Cathay will too." And just how much change should a person be expected to take? With a shock, I realized that now Cathay would be doing what I had wanted him to do. He'd be growing up with me, getting older instead of being regressed to grow up with another child. And it was suddenly just too much. It hadn't been my fault that this was happening to him, but having wished for it and having it come true made it feel like it was. The tears came, and they didn't stop for a long time.

Trilby left me alone, and I was grateful for that.

She was still there when I got myself under control. I didn't care one way or the other. I felt empty, with a burning in the back of my throat. Nobody had told me life was going to be like this.

"What . . . what about the child Cathay contracted to teach?" I asked, finally, feeling I should say something. "What happens to her?"

"The TA takes responsibility," Trilby said. "They'll find someone. For Trigger's child, too."

I looked at her. She was stretched out, both elbows behind her to prop her up. Her valentine nipples crinkled as I watched.

She glanced at me, smiled with one corner of her mouth. I felt a little better. She was awfully pretty.

"I guess he can . . . well, can't he still teach older kids?"

"I suppose he can," Trilby said with a shrug. "I don'
know if he'll want to. I know Cathay. He's not going t
take this well."

"Is there anything I could do?"

"Not really. Talk to him. Show sympathy, but not to
much. You'll have to figure it out. See if he wants to b
with you."

It was too confusing. How was I supposed to know
what he needed? He hadn't come to see me. But Trilby
had.

So there was one uncomplicated thing in my life righ
then, one thing I could do where I wouldn't have to think
I rolled over and got on top of Trilby and started to kis
her. She responded with a lazy eroticism I found irresist
ible. She *did* know some tricks I'd never heard of.

"How was that?" I said, much later.

That smile again. I got the feeling that I constantly
amused her, and somehow I didn't mind it. Maybe it wa
the fact that she made no bones about her being the adul
and me being the child. That was the way it would b
with us. I would have to grow up to her; she would not g
back and imitate me.

"Are you looking for a grade?" she asked. "Like the
twentieth century?" She got to her feet and stretched.

"All right. I'll be honest. You get an *A* for effort, bu
any thirteen-year-old would. You can't help it. In tech
nique, maybe a low *C*. Not that I expected any more, fo
the same reason."

"So you want to teach me to do better? That's you
job?"

"Only if you hire me. And sex is such a small part of it
Listen, Argus. I'm not going to be your mother. Darcy
does that okay. I won't be your playmate, either, like
Cathay was. I won't be teaching you moral lessons.
You're getting tired of that, anyway."

It was true. Cathay had never really been my contemporary, though he tried his best to look it and act it. But
the illusion had started to wear thin, and I guess it had to.
I was no longer able to ignore the contradictions, I was
too sophisticated and cynical for him to hide his lessons
in everyday activities.

It bothered me in the same way the CC did. The CC

could befriend me one minute and sentence me to death the next. I wanted more than that, and Trilby seemed to be offering it.

"I won't be teaching you science or skills either," she was saying. "You'll have tutors for that, when you decide just what you want to do."

"Just what *is* it you do, then?"

"You know, I've never been able to find a good way of describing that. I won't be around all the time like Cathay was. You'll come to me when you want to, maybe when you have a problem. I'll be sympathetic and do what I can, but mostly I'll just point out that you have to make all the hard choices. If you've been stupid I'll tell you so, but I won't be surprised or disappointed if you go on being stupid in the same way. You can use me as a role model if you want to, but I don't insist on it. But I promise I'll always tell you things straight, as I see them. I won't try to slip things in painlessly. It's time for pain. Think of Cathay as a professional child. I'm not putting him down. He turned you into a civilized being, and when he got you you were hardly that. It's because of him that you're capable of caring about his situation now, that you have loyalties to feel divided about. And he's good enough at it to know how you'll choose."

"Choose? What do you mean?"

"I can't tell you that." She spread her hands and grinned. "See how helpful I can be?"

She was confusing me again. Why can't things be simpler?

"Then if Cathay's a professional child, you're a professional adult?"

"You could think of it like that. It's not really analogous."

"I guess I still don't know what Darcy would be paying you for."

"We'll make love a lot. How's that? Simple enough for you?" She brushed dirt from her back and frowned at the ground. "But not on dirt anymore. I don't care for dirt."

I looked around too. The place *was* messy. Not pretty at all. I wondered how I could have liked it so much. Suddenly I wanted to get out, to go to a clean, dry place.

"Come on," I said, getting up. "I want to try some of those things again."

"Does this mean I have a job?"

"Yeah. I guess it does."

Cathay was sitting on the porch of the Sugar Shack, a line of brown beer bottles perched along the edge. He smiled at us as we approached him. He was stinking drunk.

It's strange. We'd been drunk many times together, the four of us. It's great fun. But when only one person is drunk, it's a little disgusting. Not that I blamed him. But when you're drinking together all the jokes make sense. When you drink alone, you just make a sloppy nuisance of yourself.

Trilby and I sat on either side of him. He wanted to sing. He pressed bottles on both of us, and I sipped mine and tried to get into the spirit of it. But pretty soon he was crying, and I felt awful. And I admit that it wasn't entirely in sympathy. I felt helpless because there was so little I could do, and a bit resentful of some of the promises he had me make. I would have come to see him anyway. He didn't have to blubber on my shoulder and beg me not to abandon him.

So he cried on me and on Trilby, then just sat between us looking glum. I tried to console him.

"Cathay, it's not the end of the world. Trilby says you'll still be able to teach older kids. My age and up. The TA just said you couldn't handle younger ones."

He mumbled something.

"It shouldn't be that different," I said, not knowing when to shut up.

"Maybe you're right," he said.

"Sure I am." I was unconsciously falling into that false heartiness people use to cheer up drunks. He heard it immediately.

"What the hell do you know about it? You think you . . . damn it, what do you know? You know what kind of person it takes to do my job? A little bit of a misfit, that's what. Somebody who doesn't want to grow up any more than you do. We're *both* cowards, Argus. You don't know it, but *I* do. *I* do. So what the hell am I going to do? Huh? Why don't you go away. You got what you wanted, didn't you?"

"Take it easy, Cathay," Trilby soothed, hugging him close to her. "Take it easy."

He was immediately contrite and began to cry quietly. He said how sorry he was, over and over, and he was sincere. He said he hadn't meant it, it just came out, it was cruel.

And so forth.

I was cold all over.

We put him to bed in the shack, then started down the road.

We'll have to watch him the next few days," Trilby said. "He'll get over this, but it'll be rough."

"Right," I said.

I took a look at the shack before we went around the false bend in the road. For one moment I saw Beatnik Bayou as a perfect illusion, a window through time. Then we went around the tree and it all fell apart. It had never mattered before.

But it was such a sloppy place. I'd never realized how ugly the Sugar Shack was.

I never saw it again. Cathay came to live with us for a few months, tried his hand at art. Darcy told me privately that he was hopeless. He moved out, and I saw him frequently after that, always saying hello.

But he was depressing to be around, and he knew it. Besides, he admitted that I represented things he was trying to forget. So we never really talked much.

Sometimes I play golf in the old bayou. It's only two holes, but there's talk of expanding it.

They did a good job on the renovation.

WINDOW

Bob Leman

The discovery of a "window" to an alternative world . . . the site quickly being sealed off by the government as Top Secret . . . experts being called in to study the inhabitants of this other world: all this sounds routine in science fiction. But this story presents some startling surprises. The people seen through the window are evidently completely human, a loving family in a world resembling our Victorian era; and there's a beautiful young woman with whom one observer falls in love. Can he go through the window physically? Can he win her love? Or are there further surprises awaiting him? (Of course there are.)

Bob Leman has been selling stories at an increasing rate since 1967, and has won the admiration of readers and his fellow writers. He lives in Bethel Park, Pennsylvania.

"WE DON'T KNOW WHAT THE HELL'S GOING ON out there," they told Gilson in Washington. "It may be pretty big. The nut in charge tried to keep it under wraps, but the army was furnishing routine security, and the commanding officer tipped us off. A screwball project. Apparently been funded for years without anyone paying much attention. Extrasensory perception, for God's sake. And maybe they've found something. The security colonel thinks so, anyway. Find out about it."

The Nut-in-Charge was a rumpled professor of psychology named Krantz. He and the colonel met Gilson at the airport, and they set off directly for the site in an army sedan. The colonel began talking immediately.

"You've got something mighty queer here, Gilson," he said. "I never saw anything like it, and neither did anybody else. Krantz here is as mystified as anybody. And it's his baby. We're just security. Not that they've needed any, up to now. Not even any need for secrecy, except to keep the public from laughing its head off. The setup we've got here is—"

"Dr. Krantz," Gilson said, "you'd better give me a complete rundown on the situation here. So far, I haven't any information at all."

Krantz was occupied with the lighting of a cigar. He blew a cloud of foul smoke, and through it he said, "We're missing one prefab building, one POBEC computer, some medical machinery, and one, uh, researcher named Culvergast."

"Explain 'missing,'" Gilson said.

248

"Gone. Disappeared. A building and everything in it. Just not there any more. But we do have something in exchange."

"And what's that?"

"I think you'd better wait and see for yourself," Krantz said. "We'll be there in a few minutes." They were passing through the farther reaches of the metropolitan area, a series of decayed small towns. The highway wound down the valley beside the river, and the towns lay stretched along it, none of them more than a block or two wide, their side streets rising steeply toward the first ridge. In one of these moribund communities they left the highway and went bouncing up the hillside on a crooked road whose surface changed from cobblestones to slag after the houses had been left behind. Beyond the crest of the ridge the road began to drop as steeply as it had risen, and after a quarter of a mile they turned into a lane whose entrance would have been missed by anyone not watching for it. They were in a forest now; it was second growth, but the logging had been done so long ago that it might almost have been a virgin stand, lofty, silent, and somewhat gloomy on this gray day.

"Pretty," Gilson said. "How does a project like this come to be way out here, anyhow?"

"The place was available," the colonel said. "Has been since World War Two. They set it up for some work on proximity fuses. Shut it down in '48. Was vacant until the professor took it over."

"Culvergast is a little bit eccentric," Krantz said. "He wouldn't work at the university—too many people, he said. When I heard this place was available, I put in for it, and got it—along with the colonel, here. Culvergast has been happy with the setup, but I guess he bothers the colonel a little."

"He's a certifiable loony," the colonel said, "and his little helpers are worse."

"Well, what the devil was he doing?" Gilson asked.

Before Krantz could answer, the driver braked at a chain-link gate that stood across the lane. It was fastened with a loop of heavy logging chain and manned by armed soldiers. One of them, machine pistol in hand, peered into the car. "Everything O.K., sir?" he said.

"O.K. with waffles, Sergeant," the colonel said. It was evidently a password. The noncom unlocked the enormous padlock that secured the chain. "Pretty primitive," the colonel said as they bumped through the gateway, "but it'll do until we get proper stuff in. We've got men with dogs patrolling the fence." He looked at Gilson. "We're just about there. Get a load of this, now."

It was a house. It stood in the center of the clearing in an island of sunshine, white, gleaming, and incongruous. All around was the dark loom of the forest under a sunless sky, but somehow sunlight lay on the house, sparkling in its polished windows and making brilliant the colors of massed flowers in carefully tended beds, reflecting from the pristine whiteness of its siding out into the gray, littered clearing with its congeries of derelict buildings.

"You couldn't have picked a better time," the colonel said. "Shining there, cloudy here."

Gilson was not listening. He had climbed from the car and was staring in fascination. "Jesus," he said. "Like a goddamn Victorian postcard."

Lacy scrollwork foamed over the rambling wooden mansion, running riot at the eaves of the steep roof, climbing elaborately up towers and turrets, embellishing deep oriels and outlining a long, airy veranda. Tall windows showed by their spacing that the rooms were many and large. It seemed to be a new house, or perhaps just newly painted and supremely well-kept. A driveway of fine white gravel led under a high porte-cochère.

"How about that?" the colonel said. "Look like your grandpa's house?"

As a matter of fact, it did: like his grandfather's house enlarged and perfected and seen through a lens of romantic nostalgia, his grandfather's house groomed and pampered as the old farmhouse never had been. He said, "And you got this in exchange for a prefab, did you?"

"Just like that one," the colonel said, pointing to one of the seedy buildings. "Of course we could use the prefab."

"What does that mean?"

"Watch," the colonel said. He picked up a small rock and tossed it in the direction of the house. The rock rose, topped its arc, and began to fall. Suddenly it was not there.

"Here," Gilson said. "Let me try that."

He threw the rock like a baseball, a high, hard one. It disappeared about fifty feet from the house. As he stared

at the point of its disappearance, Gilson became aware
that the smooth green of the lawn ended exactly below.
Where the grass ended, there began the weeds and rocks
that made up the floor of the clearing. The line of separation was absolutely straight, running at an angle across
the lawn. Near the driveway it turned ninety degrees, and
sliced off lawn, driveway and shrubbery with the same
precise straightness.

"It's perfectly square," Krantz said. "About a hundred
feet to a side. Probably a cube, actually. We know the
top's about ninety feet in the air. I'd guess there are
about ten feet of it underground."

"It?" Gilson said. " 'It'? What's 'it'?"

"Name it and you can have it," Krantz said. "A three-
dimensional television receiver a hundred feet to a side,
maybe. A cubical crystal ball. Who knows?"

"The rocks we threw. They didn't hit the house. Where
did the rocks go?"

"Ah. Where, indeed? Answer that and perhaps you answer all."

Gilson took a deep breath. "All right. I've seen it. Now
tell me about it. From the beginning."

Krantz was silent for a moment; then, in a dry lecturer's
voice he said, "Five days ago, June thirteenth, at eleven
thirty a.m., give or take three minutes, Private Ellis
Mulvihill, on duty at the gate, heard what he later described as 'an explosion that was quiet, like.' He entered
the enclosure, locked the gate behind him, and ran up
here to the clearing. He was staggered—'shook-up' was
his expression—to see, instead of Culvergast's broken-
down prefab, that house, there. I gather that he stood
gulping and blinking for a time, trying to come to terms
with what his eyes told him. Then he ran over there to the
guardhouse and called the colonel. Who called me. We
came out here and found that a quarter of an acre of
land and a building with a man in it had disappeared and
been replaced by this, as neat as a peg in a pegboard."

"You think the prefab went where the rocks did," Gilson said. It was a statement.

"Why, we're not even absolutely sure it's gone. What
we're seeing can't actually be where we're seeing it. It
rains on that house when it's sunny here, and right now
you can see the sunlight on it, on a day like this. It's a
window."

"A window on what?"

"Well—that looks like a new house, doesn't it? When were they building houses like that?"

"Eighteen seventy or eighty, something like—oh."

"Yes," Krantz said. "I think we're looking at the past."

"Oh, for God's sake," Gilson said.

"I know how you feel. And I may be wrong. But I have to say it looks very much that way. I want you to hear what Reeves says about it. He's been here from the beginning. A graduate student, assisting here. Reeves!"

A very tall, very thin young man unfolded himself from a crouched position over an odd-looking machine that stood near the line between grass and rubble and ambled over to the three men. Reeves was an enthusiast. "Oh, it's the past, all right," he said. "Sometime in the eighties. My girl got some books on costume from the library, and the clothes check out for that decade. And the decorations on the horses' harnesses are a clue, too. I got that from—"

"Wait a minute," Gilson said. "*Clothes?* You mean there are people in there?"

"Oh, sure," Reeves said. "A fine little family. Mamma, poppa, little girl, little boy, old granny or auntie. A dog. Good people."

"How can you tell that?"

"I've been watching them for five days, you know? They're having—*were* having—fine weather there—or then, or whatever you'd say. They're nice to each other, they *like* each other. Good people. You'll see."

"When?"

"Well, they'll be eating dinner now. They usually come out after dinner. In an hour, maybe."

"I'll wait," Gilson said. "And while we wait, you will please tell me some more."

Krantz assumed his lecturing voice again. "As to the nature of it, nothing. We have a window, which we believe to open into the past. We can see into it, so we know that light passes through; but it passes in only one direction, as evidenced by the fact that the people over there are wholly unaware of us. Nothing else goes through. You saw what happened to the rocks. We've shoved poles through the interface there—there's no resistance at all—but anything that goes through is gone, God knows where. Whatever you put through stays there. Your pole is cut off clean. Fascinating. But wherever it is, it's not where the house is. That interface isn't between us and the past; it's between us and—someplace else. I think our window here is just an incidental side-effect, a—a twisting of time that resulted from whatever tensions exist along that interface."

Gilson sighed. "Krantz," he said, "what am I going to tell the secretary? You've lucked into what may be the biggest thing that ever happened, and you've kept it bottled up for five days. We wouldn't know about it now if it weren't for the colonel's report. Five days wasted. Who knows how long this thing will last? The whole goddamn scientific establishment ought to be here—should have been from day one. This needs the whole works. At this point the place should be a beehive. And what do I find? You and a graduate student throwing rocks and poking with sticks. And a girlfriend looking up the dates of costumes. It's damn near criminal."

Krantz did not look abashed. "I thought you'd say that," he said. "But look at it this way. Like it or not, this thing wasn't produced by technology or science. It was pure psi. If we can reconstruct Culvergast's work, we may be able to find out what happened; we may be able to repeat the phenomenon. But I don't like what's going to happen after you've called in your experimenters, Gilson. They'll measure and test and conjecture and theorize, and never once will they accept for a moment the real basis of what's happened. The day they arrive, I'll be out. And damnit, Gilson, this is *mine*."

"Not any more," Gilson said. "It's too big."

"It's not as though we weren't doing some hard experiments of our own," Krantz said. "Reeves, tell him about your batting machine."

"Yes, *sir*," Reeves said. "You see, Mr. Gilson, what the professor said wasn't absolutely the whole truth, you know? Sometimes something *can* get through the window. We saw it on the first day. There was a temperature inversion over in the valley, and the stink from the chemical plant had been accumulating for about a week. It broke up that day, and the wind blew the gunk through the notch and right over here. A really rotten stench. We were watching our people over there, and all of a sudden they began to sniff and wrinkle their noses and make disgusted faces. We figured it had to be the chemical stink. We pushed a pole out right away, but the end just disappeared, as usual. The professor suggested that maybe there was a pulse, or something of the sort, in the interface, that it exists only intermittently. We cobbled up a gadget to test the idea. Come and have a look at it."

It was a horizontal flywheel with a paddle attached to its rim, like an extended cleat. As the wheel spun, the paddle swept around a table. There was a hopper hanging above, and at intervals something dropped from the hopper onto the table, where it was immediately banged by the paddle and sent flying. Gilson peered into the hopper and raised an interrogatory eyebrow. "Ice cubes," Reeves said. "Colored orange for visibility. That thing shoots an ice cube at the interface once a second. Somebody is always on duty with a stopwatch. We've established that every fifteen hours and twenty minutes the thing is open for five seconds. Five ice cubes go through and drop on the lawn in there. The rest of the time they just vanish at the interface."

"Ice cubes. Why ice cubes?"

"They melt and disappear. We can't be littering up the past with artifacts from our day. God knows what the effect might be. Then, too, they're cheap, and we're shooting a lot of them."

"Science," Gilson said heavily. "I can't wait to hear what they're going to say in Washington."

"Sneer all you like," Krantz said. "The house is there, the interface is there. We've by God turned up some kind of time travel. And Culvergast the screwball did it, not a physicist or an engineer."

"Now that you bring it up," Gilson said, "just what *was* your man Culvergast up to?"

"Good question. What he was doing was—well, not to put too fine a point upon it, he was trying to discover spells."

"Spells?"

"The kind you cast. Magic words. Don't look disgusted yet. It makes sense, in a way. We were funded to look into telekinesis—the manipulation of matter by the mind. It's obvious that telekinesis, if it could be applied with precision, would be a marvelous weapon. Culvergast's hypothesis was that there are in fact people who perform feats of telekinesis, and although they never seem to know or be able to explain how they do it, they nevertheless perform a specific mental action that enables them to tap some source of energy that apparently exists all around us, and to some degree to focus and direct that energy. Culvergast proposed to discover the common factor in their mental processes.

"He ran a lot of putative telekinesists through here, and he reported that he had found a pattern, a sort of mnemonic device functioning at the very bottom of, or below, the verbal level. In one of his people he found it as a set of musical notes, in several as gibberish of various sorts, and in one, he said, as mathematics at the primary arithmetic level. He was feeding all this into the computer, trying to eliminate simple noise and the personal idiosyncrasies of the subjects, trying to lay bare the actual, effective essence. He then proposed to organize this essence into *words;* words that would so shape the mental currents of a speaker of standard American English that they would channel and manipulate the telekinetic power at the will of the speaker. Magic words, you might say. Spells.

"He was evidently further along than I suspected. I think he must have arrived at some words, tried them out, and made an attempt at telekinesis—some small thing, like causing an ashtray to rise off his desk and float in the air, perhaps. And it worked, but what he got wasn't a dainty little ashtray-lifting force; he had opened the gate wide, and some kind of terrible power came through. It's pure conjecture, of course, but it must have been something like that to have had an effect like *this.*"

Gilson had listened in silence. He said, "I won't say you're crazy, because I can see that house and I'm watching what's happening to those ice cubes. How it happened isn't my problem, anyhow. My problem is what I'll recommend to the secretary that we do with it now that we've got it. One thing's sure, Krantz: this isn't going to be your private playpen much longer."

There was a yelp of pure pain from Reeves. "They can't *do* that," he said. "This is ours, it's the professor's. Look at it, look at that house. Do you want a bunch of damn engineers messing around with *that?*"

Gilson could understand how Reeves felt. The house was drenched now with the light of a red sunset; it seemed to glow from within with a deep, rosy blush. But, Gilson reflected, the sunset wasn't really necessary; sentiment and the universal, unacknowledged yearning for a simple,

cleaner time would lend rosiness enough. He was quite
aware that the surge of longing and nostalgia he felt was
nostalgia for something he had never actually experienced, that the way of life the house epitomized for him
was in fact his own creation, built from patches of novels
and films; nonetheless he found himself hungry for that
life, yearning for that time. It was a gentle and secure
time, he thought, a time when the pace was unhurried and
the air was clean; a time when there was grace and style,
when young men in striped blazers and boater hats might
pay decorous court to young ladies in long white dresses,
whiling away the long drowsy afternoons of summer in
peaceable conversations on shady porches. There would
be jolly bicycle tours over shade-dappled roads that
twisted among the hills to arrive at cool glens where swift
little streams ran; there would be long sweet buggy rides
behind somnolent patient horses under a great white
moon, lover whispering urgently to lover while nightbirds
sang. There would be excursions down the broad clean
river, boats gentle on the current, floating toward the
sound from across the water of a brass band playing at
the landing.

Yes, thought Gilson, and there would probably be an
old geezer with a trunkful of adjectives around somewhere, carrying on about how much better things had
been a hundred years before. If he didn't watch himself
he'd be helping Krantz and Reeves try to keep things hidden. Young Reeves—oddly, for someone his age—seemed
to be hopelessly mired in this bogus nostalgia. His description of the family in the house had been simple doting.
Oh, it was definitely time that the cold-eyed boys were
called in. High time.

"They ought to be coming out any minute, now,"
Reeves was saying. "Wait till you see Martha."

"Martha," Gilson said.

"The little girl. She's a doll."

Gilson looked at him. Reeves reddened and said, "Well,
I sort of gave them names. The children. Martha and
Pete. And the dog's Alfie. They kind of look like those
names, you know?" Gilson did not answer, and Reeves
reddened further. "Well, you can see for yourself. Here
they come."

A fine little family, as Reeves had said. After watching
them for half an hour, Gilson was ready to concede that

they were indeed most engaging, as perfect in their way as their house. They were just what it took to complete the picture, to make an authentic Victorian genre painting. Mama and Papa were good-looking and still in love, the children were healthy and merry and content with their world. Or so it seemed to him as he watched them in the darkening evening, imagining the comfortable, affectionate conversation of the parents as they sat on the porch swing, almost hearing the squeals of the children and the barking of the dog as they raced about the lawn. It was almost dark now; a mellow light of oil lamps glowed in the windows, and fireflies winked over the lawn. There was an arc of fire as the father tossed his cigar butt over the railing and rose to his feet. Then there followed a pretty little pantomime, as he called the children, who duly protested, were duly permitted a few more minutes, and then were firmly commanded. They moved reluctantly to the porch and were shooed inside, and the dog, having delayed to give a shrub a final wetting, came scrambling up to join them. The children and the dog entered the house, then the mother and father. The door closed, and there was only the soft light from the windows.

Reeves exhaled a long breath. "Isn't that something," he said. "That's the way to live, you know? If a person could just say to hell with all this crap we live in today and go back there and live like that. . . . And Martha, you saw Martha. An angel, right? Man, what I'd give to—"

Gilson interrupted him: "When does the next batch of ice cubes go through?"

"—be able to—Uh, yeah. Let's see. The last penetration was at 3:15, just before you got here. Next one will be at 6:35 in the morning, if the pattern holds. And it has, so far."

"I want to see that. But right now I've got to do some telephoning. Colonel!"

Gilson did not sleep that night, nor, apparently, did Krantz and Reeves. When he arrived at the clearing at five a.m. they were still there, unshaven and red-eyed, drinking coffee from thermos bottles. It was cloudy again, and the clearing was in total darkness except for a pale light from beyond the interface, where a sunny day was on the verge of breaking.

"Anything new?" Gilson said.

"I think that's my question," Krantz said. "What's going to happen?"

"Just about what you expected, I'm afraid. I think that by evening this place is going to be a real hive. And by tomorrow night you'll be lucky if you can find a place to stand. I imagine Bannon's been on the phone since I called him at midnight, rounding up the scientists. And they'll round up the technicians. Who'll bring their machines. And the army's going to beef up the security. How about some of that coffee?"

"Help yourself. You bring bad news, Gilson."

"Sorry," Gilson said, "but there it is."

"Goddam!" Reeves said loudly. "Oh, goddamn!" He seemed to be about to burst into tears. "That'll be the end for me, you know? They won't even let me in. A damn graduate student? In *psychology*? I won't get near the place. Oh, damn it to hell!" he glared at Gilson in rage and despair.

The sun had risen, bringing gray light to the clearing and brilliance to the house across the interface. There was no sound but the regular bang of the ice cube machine. The three men stared quietly at the house. Gilson drank his coffee.

"There's Martha," Reeves said. "Up there." A small face had appeared between the curtains of a second-floor window, and bright blue eyes were surveying the morning. "She does that every day," Reeves said. "Sits there and watches the birds and squirrels until I guess they call her for breakfast." They stood and watched the little girl, who was looking at something that lay beyond the scope of their window on her world, something that would have been to their rear had the worlds been the same. Gilson almost found himself turning around to see what it was that she stared at. Reeves apparently had the same impulse. "What's she looking at, do you think?" he said. "It's not necessarily forest, like now. I think this was logged out earlier. Maybe a meadow? Cattle or horses on it? Man, what I'd give to be there and see what it is."

Krantz looked at his watch, "We'd better go over there. Just a few minutes, now."

They moved to where the machine was monotonously batting ice cubes into the interface. A soldier with a stop-watch sat beside it, behind a table bearing a formidable chronometer and a sheaf of charts. He said, "Two minutes, Dr. Krantz."

Krantz said to Gilson, "Just keep your eye on the ice cubes. You can't miss it when it happens." Gilson watched the machine, mildly amused by the rhythm of its homely sounds: *plink*—a cube drops; *whuff*—the paddle sweeps around; *bang*—paddle strikes ice cube. And then a flat trajectory to the interface, where the small orange missile abruptly vanishes. A second later, another. Then another.

"Five seconds," the soldier called. "Four. Three. Two. One. *Now.*"

His timing was off by a second; the ice cube disappeared like its predecessors. But the next one continued its flight and dropped onto the lawn, where it lay glistening. It was really a fact, then, thought Gilson. Time travel for ice cubes.

Suddenly behind him there was an incomprehensible shout from Krantz and another from Reeves, and then a loud, clear, and anguished, "Reeves, *no!*" from Krantz. Gilson heard a thud of running feet and caught a flash of swift movement at the edge of his vision. He whirled in time to see Reeves' gangling figure hurtle past, plunge through the interface, and land sprawling on the lawn. Krantz said, violently, *"Fool!"* An ice cube shot through and landed near Reeves. The machine banged again; an ice cube flew out and vanished. The five seconds of accessibility were over.

Reeves raised his head and stared for a moment at the grass on which he lay. He shifted his gaze to the house. He rose slowly to his feet, wearing a bemused expression. A grin came slowly over his face, then, and the men watching from the other side could almost read his thoughts: Well, I'll be damned. I made it. I'm really here.

Krantz was babbling uncontrollably. "We're still here, Gilson, we're still here, we still exist, everything seems the same. Maybe he didn't change things much, maybe the future is fixed and he didn't change anything at all. I was afraid of this, of something like this. Ever since you came out here, he's been—"

Gilson did not hear him. He was staring with shock and disbelief at the child in the window, trying to comprehend what he saw and did not believe he was seeing. Her behavior was wrong, it was very, very wrong. A man had materialized on her lawn, suddenly, out of thin air, on a sunny morning, and she had evinced no surprise or amazement or fear. Instead she had smiled—instantly, spontaneously, a smile that broadened and broadened until it seemed to split the lower half of her face, a smile that showed too many teeth, a smile fixed and incongruous and terrible below her bright blue eyes. Gilson felt his stomach knot; he realized that he was dreadfully afraid.

The face abruptly disappeared from the window; a few seconds later the front door flew open and the little girl rushed through the doorway, making for Reeves with furious speed, moving in a curious, scuttling run. When she was a few feet away, she leaped at him, with the agility and eye-dazzling quickness of a flea. Reeves' eyes had just begun to take on a puzzled look when the powerful little teeth tore out his throat.

She dropped away from him and sprang back. A geyser of bright blood erupted from the ragged hole in his neck. He looked at it in stupefaction for a long moment, then brought up his hands to cover the wound; the blood boiled through his fingers and ran down his forearms. He sank gently to his knees, staring at the little girl with wide astonishment. He rocked, shivered, and pitched forward on his face.

She watched with eyes as cold as a reptile's, the terrible smile still on her face. She was naked, and it seemed to Gilson that there was something wrong with her torso, as well as with her mouth. She turned and appeared to shout toward the house.

In a moment they all came rushing out, mother, father, little boy, and granny, all naked, all undergoing that hideous transformation of the mouth. Without pause or diminution of speed they scuttled to the body, crouched around it, and frenziedly tore off its clothes. Then, squatting on the lawn in the morning sunshine, the fine little family began horribly to feed.

Krantz's babbling had changed its tenor: "Holy Mary, Mother of God, pray for us. . . ." The soldier with the stopwatch was noisily sick. Someone emptied a clip of a machine pistol into the interface, and the colonel cursed luridly. When Gilson could no longer bear to watch the grisly feast, he looked away and found himself staring at the dog, which sat happily on the porch, thumping its tail.

"By God, it just can't be!" Krantz burst out. "It would be in the histories, in the newspapers, if there'd been people like that here. My God, something like that couldn't be forgotten!"

"Oh, don't talk like a fool!" Gilson said angrily. "That's not the past. I don't know what it is, but it's not the past. Can't be. It's—I don't know—someplace else. Some other —dimension? Universe? One of those theories. Alternate worlds, worlds of If, probability worlds, whatever you call 'em. They're in the present time, all right, that filth over there. Culvergast's damn spell holed through to one of those parallels. Got to be something like that. And, my God, what the *hell* was its history to produce *those*? They're not human, Krantz, no way human, whatever they look like. 'Jolly bicycle tours.' How wrong can you be?"

It ended at last. The family lay on the grass with distended bellies, covered with blood and grease, their eyelids heavy in repletion. The two little ones fell asleep. The large male appeared to be deep in thought. After a time he rose, gathered up Reeves' clothes, and examined them carefully. Then he woke the small female and apparently questioned her at some length. She gestured, pointed, and pantomimed Reeves' headlong arrival. He stared thoughtfully at the place where Reeves had materialized, and for a moment it seemed to Gilson that the pitiless eyes were glaring directly into his. He turned, walked slowly and reflectively to the house, and went inside.

It was silent in the clearing except for the thump of the machine. Krantz began to weep, and the colonel to swear in a monotone. The soldiers seemed dazed. And we're all afraid, Gilson thought. Scared to death.

On the lawn they were enacting a grotesque parody of making things tidy after a picnic. The small ones had brought a basket and, under the meticulous supervision of the adult females, went about gathering up the debris of their feeding. One of them tossed a bone to the dog, and the timekeeper vomited again. When the lawn was once again immaculate, they carried off the basket to the rear, and the adults returned to the house. A moment later the male emerged, now dressed in a white linen suit. He carried a book.

"A Bible," said Krantz in amazement. "It's a Bible."

"Not a Bible," Gilson said. "There's no way those— things could have Bibles. Something else. Got to be."

It looked like a Bible; its binding was limp black

leather, and when the male began to leaf through it, evidently in search of a particular passage, they could see that the paper was the thin, tough paper Bibles are printed on. He found his page and began, as it appeared to Gilson, to read aloud in a declamatory manner, mouthing the words.

"What the hell do you suppose he's up to?" Gilson said. He was still speaking when the window ceased to exist.

House and lawn and white-suited declaimer vanished. Gilson caught a swift glimpse of trees across the clearing, hidden until now by the window, and of a broad pit between him and the trees. Then he was knocked off his feet by a blast of wind, and the air was full of dust and flying trash and the wind's howl. The wind stopped, as suddenly as it had come, and there was a patter of falling small objects that had momentarily been wind-borne. The site of the house was entirely obscured by an eddying cloud of dust.

The dust settled slowly. Where the window had been there was a great hole in the ground, a perfectly square hole a hundred feet across and perhaps ten feet deep, its bottom as flat as a table. Gilson's glimpse of it before the wind had rushed in to fill the vacuum had shown the sides to be as smooth and straight as if sliced through cheese with a sharp knife; but now small-landslides were occurring all around the perimeter, as topsoil and gravel caved and slid to the bottom, and the edges were becoming ragged and irregular.

Gilson and Krantz slowly rose to their feet. "And that seems to be that," Gilson said. "It was here and now it's gone. But where's the prefab? Where's Culvergast?"

"God knows," Krantz said. He was not being irreverent. "But I think he's gone for good. And at least he's not where those things are."

"What are they, do you think?"

"As you said, certainly not human. Less human than a spider or an oyster. But, Gilson, the way they look and dress, that house—"

"If there's an infinite number of possible worlds, then every possible sort of world will exist."

Krantz looked doubtful. "Yes, well, perhaps. We don't know anything, do we?" He was silent for a moment. "Those things were pretty frightening, Gilson. It didn't take even a fraction of a second for her to react to

Reeves. She knew instantly that he was alien, and she moved instantly to destroy him. And that's a baby one. I think maybe we can feel safer with the window gone."

"Amen to that. What do you think happened to it?"

"It's obvious, isn't it? They know how to *use* the energies Culvergast was blundering around with. The book— it has to be a book of spells. They must have a science of it—tried-and-true stuff, part of their received wisdom. That thing used the book like a routine everyday tool. After it got over the excitement of its big feed, it didn't need more than twenty minutes to figure out how Reeves got there, and what to do about it. It just got its book of spells, picked the one it needed (I'd like to see the index of that book) and said the words. Poof! Window gone and Culvergast stranded, God knows where."

"It's possible, I guess. Hell, maybe even likely. You're right, we don't really know a thing about all this."

Krantz suddenly looked frightened. "Gilson, what if— look. If it was that easy for him to cancel out the window, if he has that kind of control of telekinetic power, what's to prevent him from getting a window on *us?* Maybe they're watching us now, the way we were watching them. They know we're here, now. What kind of ideas might they get? Maybe they need meat. Maybe they—my God."

"No," Gilson said. "Impossible. It was pure, blind chance that located the window in that world. Culvergast had no more idea what he was doing than a chimp at a computer console does. If the Possible-Worlds Theory is the explanation of this thing, then the world he hit is one of an infinite number. Even if the things over there do know how to make these windows, the odds are infinite against their finding us. That is to say, it's impossible."

"Yes, yes, of course," Krantz said, gratefully. "Of course. They could try forever and never find us. Even if they wanted to." He thought for a moment. "And I think they do want to. It was pure reflex, their destroying Reeves, as involuntary as a knee jerk, by the look of it. Now that they know we're here, they'll have to try to get at us; if I've sized them up right, it wouldn't be possible for them to do anything else."

Gilson remembered the eyes. "I wouldn't be a bit surprised," he said. "But now we both better—"

"Dr. Krantz!" someone screamed. *"Dr. Krantz!"* There was absolute terror in the voice.

The two men spun around. The soldier with the stop-watch was pointing with a trembling hand. As they looked, something white materialized in the air above the rim of the pit and sailed out and downward to land beside a similar object already lying on the ground. Another came; then another, and another. Five in all, scattered over an area perhaps a yard square.

"It's bones!" Krantz said. "Oh, my God, Gilson, it's bones!" His voice shuddered on the edge of hysteria. Gilson said, "Stop it, now. Stop it! Come on!" They ran to the spot. The soldier was already there, squatting, his face made strange by nausea and terror. "That one," he said, pointing. "That one there. That's the one they threw to the dog. You can see the teeth marks. Oh, Jesus. It's the one they threw to the dog."

They've already made a window, then, Gilson thought. They must know a lot about these matters, to have done it so quickly. And they're watching us now. But why the bones? To warn us off? Or just a test? But if a test, then still why the bones? Why not a pebble—or an ice cube? To gauge our reactions, perhaps. To see what we'll do.

And what *will* we do? How do we protect ourselves against *this*? If it is in the nature of these creatures to co-operate among themselves, the fine little family will no doubt lose no time in spreading the word over their whole world, so that one of these days we'll find that a million million of them have leaped simultaneously through such windows all over the earth, suddenly materializing like a cloud of huge, carnivorous locusts, swarming in to feed with that insensate voracity of theirs until they have left the planet a desert of bones. Is there any protection against that?

Krantz had been thinking along the same track. He said, shakily, "We're in a spot, Gilson, but we've got one little thing on our side. We know when the damn thing opens up, we've got it timed exactly. Washington will have to go all out, warn the whole world, do it through the U.N. or something. We know right down to the second when the window can be penetrated. We set up a warning system, every community on earth blows a whistle or rings a bell when it's time. Bell rings, everybody grabs a weapon and stands ready. If the things haven't come in five seconds, bell rings again, and everybody goes about his business until time for the next opening. It could work,

Gilson, but we've got to work fast. In fifteen hours and, uh, a couple of minutes it'll be open again."

Fifteen hours and a couple of minutes, Gilson thought, then five seconds of awful vulnerability, and then fifteen hours and twenty minutes of safety before terror arrives again. And so on for—how long? Presumably until the things come, which might be never (who knew how their minds worked?), or until Culvergast's accident could be duplicated, which, again, might be never. He questioned whether human beings could exist under those conditions without going mad; it was doubtful if the psyche could cohere when its sole foreseeable future was an interminable roller coaster down into long valleys of terror and suspense and thence violently up to brief peaks of relief. Will a mind continue to function when its only alternatives are ghastly death or unbearable tension endlessly protracted? Is there any way, Gilson asked himself, that the race can live with the knowledge that it has no assured future beyond the next fifteen hours and twenty minutes?

And then he saw, hopelessly and with despair, that it was not fifteen hours and twenty minutes, that it was not even one hour, that it was no time at all. The window was not, it seemed, intermittent. Materializing out of the air was a confusion of bones and rent clothing, a flurry of contemptuously flung garbage that clattered to the ground and lay there in an untidy heap, noisome and foreboding.

TELL US A STORY

Zenna Henderson

Zenna Henderson began her series of stories about The People in 1952, and has continued them to the present. They are all warm, moving stories about people from another planet who have crash-landed on Earth and must make new lives here; though they have psi powers, the tasks of readjustment are still difficult. The series has been enormously popular, and two books (so far) have resulted: *Pilgrimage: The Book of the People* and *The People: No Different Flesh*. Here is her latest story about them—a long one, and certainly one of the best.

Zenna Henderson, who has spent most of her life as a schoolteacher in Arizona and elsewhere, began writing science fiction and fantasy a year before she inaugurated the "People" series, and most of her stories have been about other subjects. (Two collections of these have been published: *The Anything Box* and *Holding Wonder*.) Nonetheless, the "People" stories have been primarily important in establishing her great popularity.

"TELL US A STORY, NATHAN." LUCAS' VOICE was hardly more than a whisper at Nathan's elbow in the darkness of the loft. "Tell about the plow again."

"Oh, yes!" Adina's voice came on a long, indrawn breath from the far corner. "And the cradle. The cradle in the tree."

The loft wasn't very big and it was crowded with things waiting for use again when the seasons swung. So there was hardly room on the floor for the quilts laid over heaps of straw that had long ago lost their crinkle and resilience. Lucas and Nathan were side by side, and Adina, behind bundles, was out of sight against the far wall where she had to roll off the bed before she tried to sit up—because of the pitch of the roof.

"Again?" Nathan mock-protested, pleased. "I've already told it a dozen times."

"It's better'n a story," said Adina. " 'Cause it's true, isn't it, Nathan?"

"Sometimes I get to thinking and I kinda wonder." Lucas' voice came, hoarsely cautious. He coughed tentatively a couple of times, but it wasn't very winter yet and a couple of times was enough.

"Wonder!" Adina's voice came indignantly, followed by a *whack* as she forgot to roll before sitting up.

"Shhh! Shhhh!" The cabin was so quiet that breathing was too loud, but there was no sound of grown-ups turning to wake, and so the children breathed again.

"Oh," Lucas' voice came a little louder. "They don't ever wake up. They're too tired."

"No matter," Adina's voice snapped. "You don't believe——"

"I didn't say that!" protested Lucas. "I only wonder sometimes!" There was a scrabble as Lucas sat up and leaned forward in the darkness. "Don't *you?*"

"But it's true, isn't it, Nathan?" Adina's half-whispering voice wanted comfort.

"It's true," said Nathan, "But sometimes I wonder, too——"

"Yeah!" said Lucas. "What if he told Father——"

"I had to go after Kelly Cow." Nathan's voice slid smoothly into the silence, into the well-worn grooves of the story. "Now we know where she goes when she runs away, but last spring I had to hunt for her and got all tore up in the thicket by the river. Course, I know now to go around the thicket instead of through. I found her footprints in the mud on our side of the thicket and followed them through. And Kelly Cow was browsing right along the edge of the field."

Nathan drew a deep breath of mingled pleasure and wonder. "And the plow was plowing—straight as a string, all the length of the field and back again. With no horse pulling! And nobody following! I—I wondered what made it work. I was kinda scared, but I followed it clear down the field, and it just went along with a kind of crunching, sussing sound coming from it. I don't mean it was making any noise by itself. The sound was just the furrow opening up as the plow cut through. I stood in front of it and watched it come. I was watching it so hard that I mighty near got Plowed my own self."

"Plowed your own self!" Lucas echoed, with a giggle.

"And then the baby cried," said Adina. The rustle of her pleased settling down under her covers filled the little pause.

"Made me jump," said Nathan. "To hear a baby crying out there. I hadn't seen anyone around and I couldn't figure where it was—the baby. I looked and looked along the field and under the trees—not moving much, just looking. I didn't know—but I was looking too low. It was up in a tree! There was a cradle hanging from a limb by a couple of ropes. Just like *Rockaby baby up in a tree top* —and a baby was crying in it. It was clear across the field from me, but I could see its little fists waving while it cried. And then the cradle began to rock."

Adina sang softly, *"When the wind blows, the cradle will rock—"*

"Only there wasn't any wind," said Nathan. "It just started to rock. And not a leaf moving except when the cradle touched it. But the baby kept crying. So—so a lady came out of another tree and went over and got the baby from the cradle, and *then*—and *then* she walked on the ground! She just slid through the air and stopped by the cradle to take the baby out—on her way down to the ground."

"And a father came," Lucas prompted.

"A father came and threw the baby up in the air and laughed. And the baby laughed, too, waving its hands and kind of bouncing around up there. And it didn't come down! Its father went up and got it. Then he hugged the mother with one arm and carried the baby with the other. They went away through the trees. I waited to be sure they were gone. Then, all at once, a little brown basket came down out of the other tree and went away after them."

Nathan's voice died; then he said. "It was a black walnut tree, and the basket was full of green leaves. That seemed crazy to me until Adina reminded me later."

"For the dye pot," said Adina, complacently, in the dark. "To dye brown."

There was a sudden rustle as Nathan sat up on his pallet. "I just remembered," he said. "The baby's dress was pink—real pink—like—like the little wild roses on the edge of the thicket—when they're only part open."

"Like a rose?" Adina was unbelieving. "Like a rose!" She was wistful. "I wish we could make pretty colors."

"Well," said Nathan, "Kelly Cow was going back toward the river. So I went after her. The plow was still going back and forth and back and forth. A lot of birds would fly up from the furrows at the far end, when it came; then, after the plow turned back, they all settled down again. I watched the plow go down the last row and run off the field and make a kind of curlicue at the end of the field, as if—as if it'd been writing something all over the field and was just finishing it. Then it got up in the air and went off through the trees after the people." Nathan sighed.

"It was a good field. No stumps. No stones. There was a pile of stumps near the thicket. The roots were all long and spidery looking. None of them were cut off. They reminded me a little bit of a bunch of radishes pulled up and dropped in a pile.

"And that's all." There was an empty feeling after Nathan's voice stopped. There had to be more—

"But you've gone back a lot of times," said Lucas. "Kelly Cow keeps running away."

"Yes," said Nathan. "They have a real good stand of corn. That's all I ever see any more—the corn."

The silence lengthened and lengthened until it became slow breathing sleep.

Nathan was hunting for Kelly Cow again. He shivered and groped in the ankle-deep snow for a more secure footing. No matter what they did to keep her home, short of locking her in the barn, she always managed to get away. And always headed for the farm beyond the thicket. Nathan started on, miserable with the cold and wanting supper. He bumped carelessly against a snow-laden bush, which immediately flipped and slapped him with a handful of snow. He sank down to sit on the ground—and sat where a hollow under the snow sprawled him sideways. He lay there, twisted, with difficult tears forcing themselves out of his eyes. Then he scrambled to his knees, alert and startled.

Someone was standing, half-concealed, behind a screen of bare bushes.

"Oh, hello," said Nathan, backhanding his eyes. "I didn't hear you coming."

"Hello." The voice was soft and friendly—with just a hint of accent about it. "Are you hurt?"

"No," said Nathan, getting slowly to his feet, stiff with cold and shyness. "I'm just cold. That Kelly Cow—"

"Here." The figure moved into plain sight. "Here is warmness." Ungloved girl hands offered something to Nathan.

Automatically, he took the thing, his hand sagging a bit under the slight weight, and warmness flowed from it into his hands and began to creep slowly into his coldness.

"What is it?" he asked, looking more closely at the dark, irregular chunk in his hands.

"It is warmness. We use it in the time of cold when we do not want to shield. It is small. It will last small."

"Thank you," said Nathan. "It feels good." He pressed the warmness against his cold cheek and felt the hurting warmth of returning circulation in his ear. "I'm going to die of that Kelly Cow yet," he said, wishing he had a warmness for each cold foot. "I can't figure why she keeps coming over here anyway."

The person's face turned pink. "I think that perhaps we —we call her to our loneliness. And we pet her. And give her things to eat, though—" thoughtfully— "she didn't care for the rabbit bone."

"Cows don't eat meat," Nathan scoffed. "Well, I hafta be getting home or the dark will catch me." He looked around for the cow.

"She is over on the other side of the small trees," said the person. "Why do you always come for Kelly Cow? If she doesn't want to stay, why do you want her to?"

Nathan was startled. "Don't you know anything about cows?" he asked. "Who are you anyway?"

. "I'm Eliada," said the girl. "But what about Kelly Cow?"

"We need her milk," said Nathan patiently. How could anyone not know about *cows?* "We drink her milk and use it for bread-and-milk and mush, and, if she's giving enough, we can make butter and cheese—a little, anyway. Sometimes it's the only food we have, between crops."

"Oh," Eliada was thoughtful. Then she smiled. "Like our multibeasts. I had a multiyouny, but—" Her face tightened and she struggled with something in her throat until she could add: "We had to leave it, when we left. It liked to have its ears rubbed. It was Mahco." Her eyes were very bright and her voice broke.

Nathan was embarrassed before her emotion. "Yeah, I know," he said, tossing the warmness from one hand to the other. "I had to leave my dog. He was too old to travel all that way afoot and Papa said he couldn't ride. Jimmy said he'd take good care of him." His face stilled for a breath-length. "I had to leave Jimmy, too—my best friend."

"Now," said Eliada, her face serene again. "Here is Kelly Cow. May I taste the—the milk of Kelly Cow?"

Nathan had jumped at the nudge of Kelly Cow's nose

against his back. He whirled and gathered up the raggedy old rope end as though the cow were going to take off at a dead run. Then he dropped it and half grinned at Eliada. "But how?" he asked. "What'll you drink out of?"

"Oh, yes, a container." Eliada looked around as though containers grew magically on trees; then she squatted down and, drawing a double handful of snow toward her, molded it rapidly into a bowl shape. A piece of the rim crumbled out as the two looked at it. With an embarrassed glance at Nathan, Eliada cupped her hands around the container and closed her eyes in concentration. The bowl melted immediately into a puddle of clear water than began to dull into ice.

"Oops!" she said, smiling up at Nathan. "That was for metal."

She quickly formed another bowl from the snow. Again she cupped it. Again she concentrated. And the surface of the bowl flowed upon itself, then solidified into ice. Eliada grasped it with both hands and lifted firmly. The bowl came away with an audible snap at its base.

"There. A container. If milk isn't too warm and we don't use a slow time."

Nathan closed his mouth and shrugged. He didn't know everything about everything. And the two of them waded through the loose snow to Kelly Cow, who, perversely, was wandering slowly homeward again.

"Here," said Nathan, holding out the warmness. "I need both hands."

"Do you have a place in your clothes to put it?" she asked.

"Sure, I've got a pocket," said Nathan, half smiling at her odd way of talking. You meet all kinds of strangers in a wilderness. He slipped the small chunk into his shirt pocket. "Now give me that snow thing."

Squatting awkwardly without a milking stool, he managed to half fill the snow cup. He handed it to Eliada. She took it and lifted it to her mouth. She hesitated and smiled at him apologetically. "There have been so many things lately that—" she shuddered a little, then tilted her head and the bowl and drank.

"It's good!" Eliada lowered the cup, a little mustache of milk foam at the corners of her mouth.

"Kelly Cow gives good milk," said Nathan. "But I gotta go now. It's settin' in to snow all night." He wound the short frazzled end of the old rope around his hand, but something about Eliada kept him from starting. She was standing, staring down at the snow cup. Without moving her head, her eyes lifted to Nathan. The tip of her tongue wiped away the milk smudges on her lip. "We are hungry," she said. "We are very hungry."

"Hungry?" Nathan asked. "How come? You had a good corn crop—"

"If that is all you have to eat, it does not last until the year turns." Eliada's finger tightened on the bowl. "We are trying different barks now. But they are bitter!" Her voice broke. "And we are hungry!"

"Well, my golly! I don't have—" Nathan fumbled for words.

"You have Kelly Cow." Eliada's eyes were shut as she forced the words out. "And it has milk—"

"Yeah, but we have to eat, too!" Nathan defended.

Eliada drooped from crown to snow, the bowl slipping from her hand and plopping wetly at her feet.

"All right! All right!" he said gruffly. "I'll give you some of the milk." Visions of milkless cornmeal mush streaked through his mind and, even milkless, made him hungry. "I guess a cup of cold—milk—"

Eliada was suddenly close to him, pinching a fold of his coat between her finger and thumb.

"You know, too!" She cried softly. "Who feeds the hungry feeds two."

Nathan twisted away and thumped the heel of his hand against Kelly Cow's shoulder. "What you going to put it in?" he asked. "But not all of it! Papa would tan my hide if I brought Kelly Cow home dry!"

"I will go," said Eliada eagerly. "I will go quickly. We have a container." She whirled and fled over the snow, swiftly, lightly, as though the snow was no hindrance to her feet—as though she flew through the deepening snowfall.

She was back, panting, with her container, its odd misshapenness bending her wrists downward.

Nathan looked at it dubiously. "Where'd you get that thing?" he asked. "If it's that heavy empty, how you going to carry it full?"

"I will carry it," she said, her eyes shining. "It is made of—of what was left after—after—" She hugged it to her with both arms. "It is not beautiful. We have not had much time for beauty yet. Besides, there is no metaller among us now. But it is loved. It is from Home."

"Yeah—well—home," said Nathan, reaching for the container. "Mama has her little trunk. We couldn't bring much, either."

He took the container and squatted again by Kelly Cow and began milking. White foam backed away from the far edge and the stream of milk rang musically against the metal.

"Almost a song," said Eliada. "Can you hear it?" She paced her words to the rhythm of the milking. "Praise—praise—food—food—Sing—sing. Oh, let us sing our praise for food!"

Her words caught Nathan's fancy and he tried it. "Praise—God—from—whom—all—blessing—" Then he slipped sideways and almost spilled the milk, righted himself and ended up triumphantly, though the rhythm was a little muffled because of the level of the milk rising. "Praise Father, Son, and Holy Ghost!" Then he looked a little dismayed at the amount of the milk in the container —and a little dubiously at depleted Kelly Cow. Eliada caught his uncertainty.

"You have given us too much?" she asked.

"Naw, guess not. Can't put it back anyway. If I'm gonna catch it, another cup or two won't change things. Think you can carry it?" He lifted the awkward, slopping basin up to her hands.

"Oh, yes!" Her eyes were shining. "I will make it less heavy. This good gift of food you have given us. But the best gift is—well, I knew it was the same everywhere, but to hear you sing to Them—" softly she echoed, "Praise Father, Son and Holy Ghost—Though you named them other—that is the best gift you have given. Thank you."

Nathan wound the tattered rope around his hand again, shy to hear her speak so freely of such things. "You're welcome. Now you got something to go on your mush."

"Mush?"

"Well, porridge."

"Porridge?"

"Gollee! You *must* be foreigners! Look, have you got any corn left?"

"Yes." She shuddered a little. "But, now, our stomachs—"

"Well, grind some up to make meal, but not as fine as

flour—here—" he said to her not-knowing look—"about this coarse." He held out his hand and the grainy snow began settling on his old green mitten. "See? About that big. And cook it with water and a little salt." He watched her comprehending nods at each step of the directions. "Stir it good or you'll get lumps. Then put it in a dish and pour milk on it. If you've got any sweetening, put that on, too." His stomach suddenly spoke to him out of its hunger.

"Gotta go." He dragged at Kelly Cow. "I'm late now, and the snow——"

He looked back from the far side of the thicket and saw only the flick of Eliada's skirt disappearing among the trees. He became conscious of the warmness against his chest and caught his breath to call out. But, eying the distance, he turned and trudged off with Kelly Cow, the warmness in his cold, free hand.

"You're late." Mama was brisk about the table and didn't look at Nathan. "Strain the milk into the crock. Supper's almost ready. Adina, you help him."

Adina stretched the strainer cloth tight across the top of the heavy crock and watched carefully as Nathan poured the milk, to make sure that the cheese cloth didn't slip.

"Is that all?" she asked, her clear voice loud in the evening silence.

"Shush!" Nathan elbowed her sharply.

"Mama!" came her outraged squawk.

"Nathan." Papa's voice was heavy with weariness.

"Yes, sir," said Nathan.

"Is something wrong with the milk tonight?"

"No, sir," said Nathan. "There's nothing wrong with it."

"Is so!" said Adina.

"Is not!" retorted Nathan. "There's nothing *wrong* with the milk. There just isn't as much as usual."

"Oh, dear!" Mama came over to see. "You didn't throw rocks at her, again and scare her so that—"

"Rocks scare Kelly Cow—ha!" Adina said pertly, then wilted at Papa's glance.

"Wolves might!" Lucas' eyes were big. "Was it wolves, Nathan?"

"No," said Nathan, shortly. "I gave some of the milk away."

"Give it away? Who on earth could you meet way out

here—?" Mama was anxious to know. Who out here in all this loneliness—?

"The people on the place where Kelly Cow always goes. You know, the other side of the thicket. That old man that won't ever talk—only this was a girl from there. We talked." Nathan was getting more and more uncomfortable. "She said they were hungry."

"This was a good year," said Papa slowly.

"But I guess they had only corn—and maybe rabbits. She said they were trying different barks to find something they could eat."

"Bark?" cried Lucas. "Like the deer do?"

"They must be very slack, not to have laid in provisions for the winter," said Papa.

"I don't know," said Nathan, holding the snow bowl tightly in his mind. "Only she tasted the milk and told me they were hungry. I didn't mean to milk so much for them, but—"

"Well," Papa said ponderously. "No matter, for one time. But remember, family must come first."

"Yes, sir," said Nathan. He had a sudden notion. "She—she gave me something—" He reached into his pocket for the warmness and, with a pang, held it out to Papa on the palm of his hand.

"A rock," said Papa, not taking it. "Not much good for supper. Maybe that's why she gave it to you."

Nathan smiled and put the warmness back into his pocket. "Yes, sir," he said, and the room swept back happily into supper activity. Papa was in a good mood.

"*We* called them other?" Adina was shocked. "How could they be anything but Father-Son-and-Holy-Ghost? Maybe they're bad people!"

"Adina!" Nathan's voice came sternly through the dark of the loft. "If you don't shut up, I won't *ever* tell you about the baby again."

A rustling plop signified Adina's lying down again.

"People don't all talk the same language. All the languages have a different name for God."

"But," Adina was shaken, "I thought God was always God!"

"He is!" said Nathan. "But—"

"If you keep fighting about God," said Lucas, "you won't never get to finish what happened."

Silence came in the loft. Then there was a sound of turning on the rustling, unsoft pallets. Nathan's voice came again.

"Then I told her how to make corn-meal mush—"

"Mush! She didn't even know that!" Adina was horrified.

"No," said Nathan shortly, resenting the criticism. "They're foreigners. So I told her how and she went away. I forgot to give her back the warmness, and that's why we've still got it."

"It isn't very warm now," said Lucas, coughing as he squeezed it in his hands. "Bet Adina wore it out before I ever got it."

"Did not," said Adina, too tired to get mad.

"Eliada said it wouldn't stay warm very long. It's little." Silence grew again in the loft and became very drowsy. Nathan's voice came sleepily.

"She said she'd make that bowl thing less heavy to carry it home." Silence and heavy breathing were his only answer. Then, sharply awake, Nathan's voice came again. "But she didn't leave any tracks! Not even in the snow!"

The weather closed in that night and snow fell on snow and storm followed storm, seemingly endlessly. During those days in the dusky one room that flickered with firelight, the children worked at the lessons set for them by their mother. Lucas struggled with his alphabet and numbers and his name—and the cough that shook his thin body.

Adina sounded out the stories in Mama's old Primary reading book that had to be read at the table because it was so fragile and so apart—and so precious. Nathan rather guiltily used part of his time to re-read David and Goliath in the Old Testament part of the Bible. He could have read it with his eyes shut, but he read it again, because it belonged to a time and place like this—shut in, sheltered. The shadowy room swirling with warmth and cold as the fire leaped and sank and the drafts billowed the hanging clothes hanging on pegs against the wall.

Finally, he set aside the Bible and the pleasant containment of the old story, and got out the box of carefully hoarded pieces of newspapers they had salvaged from wherever they happened to be found. Some made no sense at all when you tried to read what there was of them, but some were exciting and engrossing—and seldom complete. But something to read, words to learn.

It was a warm, contained sort of time, with no world except the house. Its outside corners shrieked in the wind, but its inside corners were sheltering, though chilly. Outside was lightless tumult. Inside at one or two places beneath the roof, there was the companionable sound of dripping water—the hurried *plik, plik, plik* intermingling with the deeper, slower *plunk-a, plunk-a.*

Papa rocked in his big chair that he had made after they got here. He looked long into the fire or at the dark ceiling, thinking whatever thoughts came to a wilderness farmer in off season. Or he worked on the horses' harness. Or sat with the Bible on his knees, drowsing, his chair slowing—rousing, his chair picking up tempo.

Mama never lacked for something to do, but even she arrived at a time when she could sit for long, resting moments, her current task on her lap, with no urgency about it.

There were no days or nights. Time was kept only by the checking of the stock in the small barn behind the house, and the coming of bedtime and rising and the diminishing of the woodpile beside the fireplace.

At some point in this timelessness, Nathan glanced up from his reading—*bride wore white mousseline de sois*—as if someone had called him. No one in the room was even looking at him, and so he bent to his work again. Again the call came, sharply, urgently, with not a sound—not a word. He got up uneasily and went to the fireplace. The woodbox had been refilled recently. The fire was about its secret munching and crunching of the old wood from clearing the land. Even the *plunk-a, plunk-a,* was the same.

"I think I'll go check the stock," he said, trying to sound like Papa.

"Little early for that," said Papa, glancing up.

"I need to stretch my legs," Nathan said, reaching for his coat. He lighted the small lantern with a splinter blazed from the fire, and turned to the door. Lucas was ahead of him, coughing in his hurry, hacking at the frozen lumps at the bottom of the door with the crowbar.

"Don't let go of the rope," said Mama, anxious because of the wilderness out of doors.

The call caught Nathan as he opened the door, and he

stumbled a little on the uneven floor. What was it? What was urging him? Not *out*, he realized, just—just *listen*. No —he wrestled with the problem as he wrestled with closing the door. No—not *listen*. It was *there's need!* Who called?

He got the door shut and clung firmly to the rope stretched from house to barn, while he caught his balance against the howling fury of the wind and the knifing of the snow against the exposed parts of his face. He hugged the lantern to him, under his coat, to keep it from being blown out—and away.

It seemed like a hundred miles and a hundred years before he half stumbled, half fell into the barn. The animals swung drowsy faces to look at him, their eyes catching, with unexpected brightness, what little light came from the lantern that flared smokily, then settled to its small glow.

The snow had housed the animals completely against the wind. Their own bodies had warmed the place and melted some of the snow that had sifted in at the top of the rough walls. The moisture had run down the logs to freeze smoothly again near the floor. The water trough was partly frozen, and Nathan hacked at the thin ice with his heel.

There's need! It was words now, that came so shocking loud inside his head that Nathan whirled, his elbow going up defensively. No one was in the half-light of the chilly stillness except the huddled animals who rippled across with small movement. Then they swung about to stare at the wall opposite the door. Nathan went to the wall and rested his hands against it, his eyes fanning a scared look over the rough logs.

There's need! There's need! The soundless words sobbed into the silence.

"El—" His voice wouldn't work. He tried again. "Eliada?"

Nathan! Nathan! Relief cried in every syllable.

"You can't get in that way," Nathan called foolishly to the rough wall and the quiet stock. "The door is around two corners from you."

The animals blinked their eyes and came apart from their concerted staring, and swung slowly away from each other, unpatterned. There was a thud on the door, and

Nathan moved to it quickly, pushing out against the frantic pushing in, and Eliada fell into the barn.

"Nathan! Nathan!" she cried from the floor, reaching blindly.

Nathan knelt and reached a hand to help her up. His fingertips rapped and his fingers bent and slid away with no touch of Eliada.

"Oh!" She drew a sobbing breath. "I'm shielding." Then she reached out for Nathan's hand and clung. "Oh, Nathan," she cried as he pulled her, shivering, to her feet. She sagged and almost fell before he caught and held her. "We're dying! There is nothing to eat! Not anything! And no small creatures in the forest because of the—the falling whiteness."

"Snow," said Nathan, wondering that his face was slowly warming to a tingle and that water on the walls was sliding liquidly down to the floor.

"You don't have a coat." he said blankly.

"A—a coat?" Eliada sank down on a hump of hay near the wall. "Oh—oh. No—no coat. I can warm without, and my— Oh, but, Nathan! You don't understand? We are being Called. We are—dying of—of hunger! There is *nothing*. Oh, Nathan, to have nothing! To put out your hand and there is nothing to fill it. To swallow nothing and hurt and hurt—!" She curled herself down on the hay and cried.

Nathan looked around at the dim animals, their eyes taking turns at catching the light as their jaws crunched, wondering what on earth he could do.

"Come on," he said. "Come to the house. We'll tell Mama and Papa. How—how many people? I mean, how big a family do you have?" He helped Eliada up from the hay.

"We are only six—now," she said, a great sorrow filling the room. "All the others—all those I could see from my slip—went in flicks of brightness—back to the Presence. But what was left—we finally found each other, and we are six. But soon our bodies will not be able to contain us —unless we can find food—" She sagged down against his holding hand.

"We can share," said Nathan. "But for how long—" He used two hands trying to hold the weight.

"Only until the—the snow goes," she said. "We found

roots to eat and food even inside the hard round black things under the trees—"

"Walnuts," said Nathan. "Why didn't you gather them last fall? Not much meat for a lot of work but—"

"But we didn't know!" cried Eliada. "We don't know this new world! We came so far—And now to die—" Her eyes closed and she floated, slowly down—not quite to the floor and hovered there in a small unconscious heap. Nathan grabbed clumsily for her, rapping his knuckles against her shoulder. And she slid slowly—inches above the barn floor—away from him to bump softly against Kelly Cow's winter shaggy legs. Kelly Cow backed up a step, and went on chewing her cud, her eyes large and luminous in the half dark.

Nathan snatched the lantern and turned to the door. He felt cold flooding back all round him. Then he turned from the door and reached for Eliada. Then turned back—panic squeezed his breath. He crouched on the floor beside Eliada and closed his eyes as tightly as he could, fighting against running and screaming and—

A sudden blast of cold air on his back whirled him around. Papa was leaning back against the push of the door, getting it shut.

"What's keeping you?" Papa asked, thumping snow off his boots. "Your mother—" He broke off as Nathan's shift to hide Eliada pushed her out between them. She straightened out as she floated, and her hair spilled darkly bright, longer than the distance to the floor.

"It's—it's Eliada," Nathan said, his eyes intent on Papa's face as he gathered the inert body into his arms. "The girl I gave the milk to. She came for help. They're starving in this storm."

"She'll freeze in this storm if you stay out here," said Papa. "Give her to me."

Nathan stood up, lifting Eliada with him. He looked at his father, his eyes wide with wonder. "She is less heavy —like she said she'd make the milk."

"You're wasting time," said Papa and took Eliada. His arms jerked upward at the lack of expected weight. Nathan caught the limpness of a trailing hand and kept Eliada from leaving Papa's grasp. Papa took a firmer hold, one arm over and one under, turning Eliada so her face pressed against his shoulder.

"The door," he said, and Nathan slipped around him and opened the door to the blast of the storm.

After endlessly struggling with wind and the stinging slap of driven snow, Nathan, clinging to the stretched rope with one hand and the darkened lantern with the other, stopped to gasp for breath. Papa stopped close behind him, pushing Eliada against him to provide some small, brief shelter. Nathan felt a movement against his back and felt Eliada say something. He turned and groped to touch her to—to warn her?

"Cold," said Eliada, stirring. "Cold."

And the howl and shove of the storm slowly muted. The sting and slap of the snow-laden wind swirled, hesitated, and was stilled. And slowly, slowly warmth wrapped them about. Slowly? It was all in the space of a started in-breathing and an astonished out-breathing.

Nathan clung to the rope, trying to see Papa. It was too dark. Papa muttered something and pushed Eliada against Nathan's back. Nathan stumbled on toward the house, his troubled face seeking for the wind and snow that should be punishing him.

Then he saw the lighted doorway ahead, with Mama anxiously peering out, a quilt clutched around her for warmth. As they moved into the lightened darkness of the doorway, Nathan glanced up. He saw the snow driving, swirling down, but it never reached them. It curved and slid away as if—as if there were something between them and the night. Then Eliada stirred again, lifting her pale face to look up. And, with a doubled roar and chill, the storm smote them again.

Then they were in and the door was shut and the unbelievable warmth and comfort of the house enveloped them.

"It is so good." Eliada looked up from the bowl of bread-and-milk—hard crusts of bread broken into a bowl of milk—hot milk, this time, because of the cold.

"Best not eat anything else now," said Mama, who glowed with having a guest to feed. "What with being hungry so long—"

"Else?" said Eliada, her eyes widening. "More to eat than this?" She lifted a white spoonful. "At the same eating? In *this* world?"

"Eggs," said Mama, her worried look sliding to Papa.

"From our hens. Before the storm began, they were laying pretty good—"

"Eggs?" Eliada slid back into some place in her head that she seemed to have to go to often, for some reason.

"Oh, eggs!" Her eyes shone again. "The bird ones were so small. But they all went away when the cold came. Did your birds not go away?" She asked Lucas who had followed her like a clumsy, quilt-wrapped shadow ever since she had come in. He leaned on the table opposite her, his eyes feeding even more hungrily than her mouth did.

"Yes," he said hoarsely, "The birds went away, but our hens—" He wrapped his arms tightly around himself and coughed until he gagged. He sat swiping at the cough-driven tears with the worn quilt over his arm, and sniffed and shook with the cold that shook anyone if they left the reach of the fireplace. Everyone except Eliada.

Eliada looked around at the rest of the family, her cheeks becoming faintly pink. "You are all cold," she said. "I'm sorry. I forgot you are not my People." She broke off, then turned to Papa. "I am not strong enough or skilled enough in that Persuasion, since it is not my gift, but if you have a metal—something—I can make it give heat for you for a while."

Papa looked at her, his eyes too deep in shadows to show any glint. Nathan rushed into the moment of silence. "Like the little one she gave me. You know, you thought it was a rock, but it was metal and it was warm."

Before Papa could say anything, Lucas darted for the door, shedding his outer layer as he went, and got there at the same moment as Adina, and both snatched up the heavy metal crowbar that, at this season, was the tool for breaking the ice from the door when the drifts froze too hard to kick aside. It was a short, stout metal bar, bent into a hook at one end and flattened to a stubbly blade at the other.

Together, the two children wrestled the bar back to Eliada.

"Yes," she smiled. "Put it with the fire."

"Aw, heating it in the fire's no good. The pots get cold right away when you take them off." Lucas was disappointed.

"Do what she says," said Adina, tugging at the bar. "Give it to me and I'll—"

The two, tugging against each other, managed to plop

the bar into the front of the ashes. It raised a small grimy snow from the feathery ashes.

"It is better in front," said Eliada. "In the fire, the warmness would go up the opening to outside. It is odd—" Her cheeks pinked-up and she moved to the fireplace.

Eliada knelt in front of the bar, little fluffs of ashes stirring around her as she knelt. She made a quick sign with one hand; then she reached a finger to touch the end of the bar. She glanced back at the absorbed faces. "I'm not practiced," she said. "I must touch first."

There was a brief silence during which the sound of the wind filled the house as completely as though it were empty of life. Then Eliada lifted her finger from the bar and sat back sideways, but still looking at the bar. She lifted herself a little to pull her dress free from where it had twisted under her, and sat again.

Slowly, wonderfully, warmth began. And flowed into the chilly room like a warming stream, loosening muscles that were unconsciously tightened against the cold, making cheeks and ears start to tingle.

Eliada came to her feet. "I cannot make it more than warm," she said. "Some can make it glow dull red, but—"

"Gollee!" Adina's eyes were wide. "That's magic! Where did you learn that?"

"At Home," said Eliada. She seemed suddenly unsteady and held tightly to the edge of the table with white fingertips. "Before our Crossing. Before we fell here—" Then she straightened and managed a smile. "But we learn here also," she said. "We have learned to make mush from corn—"

"Mush!" Lucas' scorn was large again. "How to make mush!"

"It fed us," said Eliada. "And the bar—it warms you. Why is one more wonderful than the other?"

Nathan shook his head. Maybe so. But to compare something like making mush to this miracle—and yet— he shook his head again.

"Feeding," said Papa suddenly. "Your people. They're still hungry?"

"Yes," Eliada's face sobered. "They were so hungered that I was the only one who could come. The others are in protective sleep until I come with food. And, if I could not find food, or if I should be Called while I am away, they will sleep until their Calling."

"Oh," said Mama, clutching the side of her apron. "We'll have to——" Her eyes went to Papa, but he was going back to his rocking chair, hitching it to an angle to put the fireplace out of his sight. "Well," said Mama, hesitantly. Then she smiled and turned to Eliada, her face alight with the pleasure of being able to share.

"And these?" Eliada touched one finger to the rosy brown curve of an egg.

"Eggs," said Lucas, torn between scorn for her ignorance and his fascination with her.

"So big!" said Eliada. "The bird one, so small! So small to hold all that feathers and singing! Do your—do your hens sing, too?"

"They might call it singing," said Nathan smiling. "On warm summer days, all lazy in the sun——" Tears bit suddenly at the back of his eyes at the remote memory.

"We can let you have these," said Mother. "When they are gone, there will be others." She gathered them, with a practiced outspreading of her fingers, lifting them from the bowl. "But how—they'll break——"

"I can carry them," assured Eliada. And Mama, hesitating for a moment, put them down on the table. One egg began a slow, flopping roll to the edge, but Eliada looked at it, and it reversed itself and hid itself in the middle of the small cluster.

"And to eat them?" Eliada's cheeks were less white now, and her eyes were losing their hooded look of suffering.

"If you were hungry enough, raw would do," said Nathan with a grimace. "But, cooked—? You have fire to cook with?"

"We have to cook with," said Eliada, her eyes going to the bar on the hearth.

"But how can you carry all this by yourself?" Nathan shivered. Even Eliada's magic didn't operate very well on the far side of the room. Eliada's eyes were on the little heaps of food, as if her eyes were still hungry. Then her smile, fed and comfortable, said, "I can carry it. We —we can carry much. I will show you."

She folded the rough piece of canvas Nathan had found up in the loft up around the food; then, stepping back a little from the table, she looked at the lumpy package. It suddenly quivered through, then lifted a little from the table and slid toward Eliada. She took hold of one loose corner of the canvas and moved over to the door. The bundle followed her, obedient to the tug of her fingertips.

Eliada smiled, her eyes touching each person, like a warm hand. "And, see? One whole hand left to carry the container of milk!" The lard can, with its tightly fitted cover, lifted up at a gesture of her hand and hung itself on her fingers.

"How are you going to get home?" asked Adina, anxiously. "It's so cold and dark."

"I can always find home," said Eliada, smiling at her. "And I can shield against the storm." Her glance gathered them together again, her eyes glowing in the twilight of the room. "Truly the Presence, the Name and the Power are here with you. From your little, you have given us abundance. Even here—so far from Home. So the Old Ones assured us, but—but—" Nathan felt her spasm of grief and sorrow, and then she smiled a little. "It is so much easier to doubt than to believe."

She glanced at the fireplace where the heavy length of the crowbar sent out almost visible waves of warmth. "It will cool," she reminded. "A day or two days. Or, if gratitude counts, maybe many more days." She made a farewell sign with her hand. "Dwell comforted in the Presence." And then she was gone, the door stubbing back on the chunks of ice and snow that had fallen against the threshhold.

There was a silence, broken only by the vast rush of the wind. Surely not so loudly now that warmth was in the room.

Then Papa moved to the fireplace and kicked thoughtfully at the crowbar. "I'm not sure I want to be warmed by this warmth," he said, his voice rolling deep through the unaccustomed length of his sentence. "It may be of evil. This will take some thinking out."

"Papa," Nathan's voice was urgent. "It can't be evil. She knew Father, Son and Holy Ghost, only she said they called them something else. Other languages—"

"And yet," said Papa. "The Devil can quote Scriptures for his purposes. This will take some thinking out." And he sat again in his chair, the Bible on his lap again, his eyes deep-shadowed by his heavy brows, and stared into the almost visible warmth of the bar.

"Too easy," he muttered. "By the sweat of thy brow——"

The storm cleared from the skies and the crackling cold came. It lay heavily on the land, so heavily that it crushed every vestige of color from everything so that, in a black and white world, Nathan's red cap was like a sudden shout.

He had walked over the crispness of the frozen world to the thicket where even Kelly Cow had sense enough not to venture this day. He stood on the other side of the thicket, his hands in his pockets, his shoulders hunched against the cold, and looked across the smooth, stumpless, sunless field beyond, wondering how those people were doing.

Then he heard a clear call and the sound of laughter, and shrank back, startled, into the shadow of the thicket.

A streak of color shot across the smoothness of the field, dark hair streaming free, bright blue clothes an exclamation point against the white. Eliada? It seemed of a size.

Then came the others, staying in a little cluster, a small child piggy-back on one of them. Brightly, laughingly, they followed Eliada, skimming the snow as if——

Nathan clutched a limb for something solid to hang on to. Eliada swung by him, close enough for him almost to touch. And was gone before he could blink. But she couldn't have! No one—— Then the cluster swirled past, the laughing child clinging to the hair of the laughing man. Then they were all at the far side of the field again.

"They can't!" Nathan whispered indignantly. "They can't skate with no skates on. And without moving their feet! They can't."

And a thin, sweet memory stabbed back to him from Back Home. A red sled, and a very high hill, and the delightful terror of letting go at the top—and collecting your breath again at the bottom. But you had to have a hill—and a sled——

He looked across the flatness of the field. The people had stopped now and were clustered together. Then one slid away from the others, and Eliada was skimming the snow, back across the field. Toward him? He shrank farther back in the thicket, suddenly afraid.

Eliada came slower and slower and stopped. "Nathan?" she called. "Nathan?"

Nathan crunched snow to face her. "Yeah," he said.

"Oh, Nathan!" Eliada took his two hands and pulled him out of the thicket. "I sensed you as we went by! But I wasn't sure, so I came— Isn't it a beautiful day?" She whirled lightly around Nathan, making him feel heavy-footed and as awkward as a hub. Then she shot away from him—not even *touching*—but, yes, because, as she turned, a skiff of snow sprayed briefly—and again when she returned to him and stopped, laughing and panting.

"You're all right now?" he asked. "You have plenty to eat?" Her glowing face told him how unnecessary was the question.

"Oh, Nathan!" she laughed. "It would be all funny, if we hadn't so nearly been Called because of hunger."

"What happened?" Nathan hunched and shivered. Standing still, the cold flowed into you fast.

"Oh, I forgot," said Eliada. "Here, I'll extend."

And a motion came between Nathan and the cold, a motion that circled him completely and closed him into warmth with Eliada.

"How do you do that!" he asked, unhappily.

Eliada's face sobered. "Does it offend you?" she asked. "It is more comfortable, merely."

Nathan rubbed his nose, which had started to tingle.

"What was funny?" he asked.

Eliada's face brightened. "After we ate your food— and, Nathan, nothing, not even the festival foods we had to leave behind on The Home, ever tasted so good. We cried for its goodness as we ate. And laughed because we cried. But the food didn't last very long. And we thought to sleep again to our Calling rather than to take food again from your family. But one morning I received a directive to go dig in the little hill behind the house. Such a silly thing to do! But a directive! So two of us went. I could hardly lift the digging thing, but Roth was stronger. He has no sight because of the Crossing, but he is strong. So we tried to dig—and blocks fell away and there was a door! and we opened it—and food! Food!"

"The root cellar," said Nathan. "The people before you put the food by for the winter. How come they didn't tell you before they left?"

Eliada's face saddened. "There was only one, and he did not leave. He was Called the day we arrived. One of the Life slips shattered and his body was too broken to hold him more. So he was Called. With my brother. It was his slip that shattered." She tightened her lips and a tear slid from the corner of one eye. "How joyfully he went Otherside, but how lonely for us who are still this side."

"Your brother—" Nathan swallowed with an effort that didn't get rid of the heavy lump choking him. "My— my—" He watched his toe kick against a skeletal bush until he could stop his lips.

"It's too bad you didn't get the directive before you got that hungry," he said, still not looking at her. "Whatever a directive is."

"A directive?" asked Eliada. "But surely—I mean, maybe you have another name for it. For when the Power says to you, *Do,* unless you are too far separated from the Presence, you *do* for that is what must be done, when it must be done."

"No," said Nathan. "At least, I don't know. Still think it could have passed the word—"

"We sometimes wonder," said Eliada, "But we never question. If the directive had come sooner, I would not have gone to you. And I would not now be saying, how can I help loose you from the burden you bear of sorrow and—and evil, Nathan? Evil?"

Nathan turned his face away, biting his lip to hold his face straight. Eliada moved to where she could see his face again. "And evil? Oh, Nathan!"

"My father killed my brother!" Nathan's voice grated his throat with its suppressed intensity. "I hate him!"

"Killed?" Eliada touched Nathan's arm. "You mean, sent him ahead of his time, back into the Presence? Oh, surely not! Not really so?"

"The same as—" Nathan raked a violent fist across his face because of the wetness.

"But—but his own son—" Eliada's face was troubled. "Oh, Nathan, tell me!"

"My father." The words were bitter in his tight mouth. "He decided it was an evil power you used to heat up the crowbar. He raked it out of the fireplace with a stick and shoved it out the door into the dark. He said you had no right to warm us better than he could, and that at least we know why wood makes us warm. Lucas—" his voice died and he gulped. "Lucas cried and grabbed my father's arm, trying to keep him from throwing the warm away, but my father back-handed him clear across the room and did anyway. And Lucas coughed and coughed and wouldn't put the quilt around him again. He sort of settled down, only crying and coughing and shivering, and he wouldn't go over by the fire.

"Then all at once he had the door open and was out in all that wind and storm, trying to find the crowbar in the puddle of water it had melted in the snow. By the time we got him back inside, he was sopping wet, with ice sliding out of his hair when I lifted him.

"And he died. He only lasted a day. My father killed him."

And Nathan cried into the crook of his elbow and into the vast warm comfortingness that flowed from Eliada.

"Nathan," Eliada said finally. "We cannot know if Lucas was truly Called or if he was sent ahead, but you must not hate. It is an evil you must not take for a burden. It will eat your heart and cloud your mind and, worst of all, it will separate you from the Presence."

"But Lucas is dead." Nathan's voice was dull.

"He is back in the Presence," said Eliada. "He is healed of the body that was so frail and so often with pain."

Nathan shook his heavy hanging head. "Words—all kinds of words. But Lucas is dead and my father killed him."

He surged away from Eliada and felt a sudden tightness against his forehead. It released suddenly, flooding him with the crisp, cold air. He blinked at the sun as he ran clumsily. The sun? The sun was still shining?

Spring came slowly. Then, one day, it seemed as if every drop of water tied up in every snowflake let go all at once. For days the house perched on a rise that was usually hardly noticeable but that it held it above the rising waters. Then the waters began to move, coursing down to the river. The river came up to meet the house and nibbled away at the rise, slowly, slowly, with the whole world a-swim.

Then the torrents began. They ripped across the field Nathan and his father had worked so hard to clear, gouging out gullies and wiping out almost every trace of last year's furrows.

Then the barn went, hardly splashing, as it slid into the greedy waters, just after Nathan and his father had led Kelly Cow and the other stock up the hill behind the barn and left them there with three raggedly wet chickens. The rest of the flock was gone.

Water gathered around the house closer and lapped at the bottom course of logs. The whole family watched from the small window and the door—watched the waters quiver and lift towards the house. Once, the sun came out suddenly and they were in the middle of a glittering sea of brightness. They had to squint their eyes against the glory. Then it was gray and miserable again.

Adina's breath was a warm tickle on Nathan's ear. "It's gone, Nathan! It's gone!" And hot tears started down her scalded-looking cheeks.

"What's gone?" Nathan whispered.

"Where," she gulped. "Where we buried Lucas. Under the little tree. The tree's gone. The grave's gone. Lucas is gone!" Nathan held her while she shook with crying. He lifted his head as Mama came heavily across the floor. She sat down on the bed, then lay back, her feet still on the floor. One bent arm covered her eyes and she said, in a tight, small voice. "Lucas is gone. And I have to carry this other one to be born and be killed—"

Father turned from the window, but he didn't go to Mama.

"I didn't kill him," he said, his voice tired of making the same words over and over. "I didn't kill him. Before that evil creature—"

"She isn't evil." Nathan's voice was loud and defiant in the room. "She wanted to warm us—"

"With evil," said Father. "With evil."

"Is everything you don't understand evil?" asked Nathan. "Do you know what makes the sun shine? But you let it warm you anyway."

"God—" said Father.

"God," said Nathan. "God made her, too. And taught her how to warm the crowbar."

"The devil," said Father. He turned back to the window, hunched inside the body that suddenly looked too big for him, that skunched down on Father, bending and stooping, trying to fit.

Then suddenly, briefly, the whole cabin lifted a little and settled again. There was a dark wetness along the long cracks of the rough floor.

"Good," said Mama into the startled silence. "Take it all. Take it all." And she turned her face away from all of them.

But the waters had taken all they were to take and they shrank away from every rise, compressing down into all the low places. There was one spot in the front yard that held a puddle of water for a long time, and it glittered like a watching eye until long after everything else had dried up.

Nathan and his father now faced the task of clearing more land to replace that scoured-out, washed-away deeply gullied part of the farm. Everything around shouted and hummed and smelled of spring and new life and abundant blossoming, but Nathan had no part in the singing, springing, upsurge of delight that was on the land. He was a dark, plodding figure, bowed and unresponsive in the sunlight.

The tree shuddered under every blow of Father's ax. The brightness of the sky hurt Nathan's eyes, and his neck ached from looking up at the shaken branches. Every move that he made was awkward and aching because of the tight hampering of the darkness inside him. He squatted down against a bank of earth and pulled his knees up to his chest, trying to ease the endless aching.

A sharp *crack* from the tree snatched his eyes upward. The tree was twisting—turning unnaturally—splitting!

Something in Nathan cried out, rejoicing—*Now he'll die, too! Now he'll die, too!* But even before the thought formed itself in his mind, he was surging forward on his hands and knees, scrambling to get to his feet.

"Papa!" he yelled. "Papa!"

Papa looked up, dropped his ax and stood for one long, stunned moment before turning to run—to run in exactly the wrong direction. The splintering tree twisted again and seemed to explode. Papa's cry and Nathan's cry were drowned in the crash.

"Papa!" Nathan groped frantically among the branches. "Papa! Papa!"

Then he found Papa's face. And his hands groped to slide under Papa's shoulders. He cried out as he fell forward over Papa's chest. There was nothing under Papa's shoulders! His head and neck and part of his shoulders were pushed out across the bank of the ragged gully. The weight of the splintery heaping of the tree across his legs and body was all that kept him from slithering backwards down into the rock-jumbled gully behind and below him.

"Papa!" Nathan whispered urgently. He touched the quiet face, his hand wincing away, almost immediately, from the intimacy of the touch.

The face twisted to pain, and the eyes opened, unfocusing beyond Nathan's left shoulder. Then the eyes focused with a vast effort.

"Get it off!" The whisper jerked with the painful effort. "Get it off!" The eyes rolled shut and the head rolled to press against Nathan's startled hand.

"But, Papa!" The words were so loud they splintered the silence. "But, Papa!" he whispered. Then he turned to the twisted mountain of limbs behind him. He scrambled over and grabbed one piece of the splintered trunk. But it was shredded to another piece that peeled from another piece that rocked the edge of the gully, spilling more dirt and rocks from under Papa's shoulder.

Nathan let go hurriedly and could see even that little movement of release flow jerkily through the whole scrambled length of the trunk. And it pushed two more pebbles from under Papa's shoulders.

Nathan slumped down to his knees and slid sideways, his hands grabbing each other and his arms going up to hide his scared face.

"What can I do? What can I do? Oh, God, help me—!"

He jerked around, lifting himself on his knees. *Nathan! Nathan!* Calling him? Not Mama—not Adina!

"Eliada!" he called. "Eliada! Come help! I need—"

There's need? Eliada's call came clearly to him.

"Yes!" he called. "There's need! Come help! I can't—!"

For a long, tight pause Nathan listened to all the busy small sounds of the world of growth. Then a rustle in the trees just back of the jagged half-stump snatched his attention. The branches shuddered and parted, and an anxious-looking Eliada threw herself over the fallen tree to Nathan.

"Oh, Nathan!" She caught her eyes checking Nathan

rapidly. "There was a directive—so strong! So strong! You have need?"

"Papa," gulped Nathan. "The tree fell on him. I can't move him—"

"Tree?" Eliada's eyes widened. "The broken one? But your papa—"

"Can you help?" Nathan scrambled back to the branches. "Papa is caught under the tree. I can't lift it. Can you help?"

Eliada crouched beside him. "Let me—let me—" She took a deep breath and sat back on her heels, her hand on Papa's arm, her hair swaying forward over her intent face.

"I cannot lift the tree from him," she said from behind the curtain of her hair. "He would fall to the rocks. I cannot lift him and the tree at one time. It is two different Persuasions—animate and inanimate. If he would not waken—but he would—"

"You gotta help!" cried Nathan. "We can't let him—"

"So you must take from under him the rocks and dirt—" as though Nathan hadn't spoken. "And I will hold him until you have freed him—" She backed away and huddled herself over the edge of the slope down in the gully. "You have digging things?"

"Yes, but—" he turned hopelessly to Papa and then to Eliada.

"He will hurt when he wakens." Eliada sighed without opening her eyes. "While he is not awake—"

Nathan stumbled over to the clutter of tools under the near tree. He brought back the shovel and the crowbar. Sweat streaked his face, and dust streaked the sweat as Nathan labored. He hacked away at the bank under Papa with the bar, scrabbled at it with his bare hands and whacked with the edge of the shovel.

Slowly, slowly, the bank crumbled. And Nathan stubbornly refused to look up at Papa, wondering why he believed Eliada could "hold" Papa, but believing desperately.

He had stopped to drag his muddy sleeve across his face again, when Papa cried out and moved, sending dirt cascading down on Nathan.

"Don't move!" Nathan cried. "Papa, don't move! I'm getting you out. Stay still!"

Desperately, he pried at the rounded rock that stuck

out of the bank. With a sudden jolt, the rock came loose —and Nathan barely stumbled out of the way of the smothery cascade of the dissolving bank.

The dust cleared slowly and Nathan looked up. There, above him, pressed still up against the splintered tree, lay Papa. Up there! In the air! With nothing between him and Nathan except—nothing! And Papa's terrified face peered down at Nathan.

Then Papa screamed hoarsely and, with one hand, groped blindly at the emptiness under and around him. Then both hands waved frantically. They found the splintery tree above him and clung to it with desperate strength.

"I cannot move him," said Eliada past the still circling of her arms. "He is holding so strong. If I move him, the tree will go with him."

"Papa!" yelled Nathan. "Let go! Let go!"

But Papa paid no attention, only fumbled with one foot, trying to find a holding place with it.

"I cannot sleep him," said Eliada, her voice unsteady. "I am not strong enough enough to all at the same time. And, until his hands open—"

Nathan stood, fists clenched at his ribs, staring up at Papa. Then he wet his lips with his tongue. "When I holler," he said, "Let him fall—a little ways. Can you do that?"

"Yes," said Eliada. "When you holler—a little fall—"

"Papa!" yelled Nathan. "The tree's going! You're falling! You're falling!"

And Papa fell about a foot. He screamed once before his eyes rolled and his hands relaxed to let his arms dangle below him.

There was an ominous splinter above him and the tree began to sag. Eliada cried out, "Back, Nathan! Quick!" And Nathan, stumbling backward, caught his feet on the rough ground and fell heavily, feeling the scrunching under his doubled knees. He heard a cry from Eliada and twisted, to see Papa jerking away from the falling tree. For a moment Papa hovered in the dusty air above the up-puff from the broken wood landing. Then, as Nathan watched, Papa drifted over Nathan's head. A something hit Nathan's hand, and his other hand smeared it to a wet, red streak as Papa slanted slowly down to the uneven floor of the gully.

Nathan scrambled on hands and knees over to him. "He's bleeding somewhere," he said, glancing up at Eliada.

And she wasn't there.

Nathan never could remember how he got up out of the gully and to Eliada. She was lying quietly, her face turned to the sky, her eyes closed, her mouth a little open, and blood running darkly down from her forehead where a flying stub of a branch had hit her.

Nathan afterwards remembered that day as something that had no meaning in his ordinary life. And yet, in itself, that day was a whole lifetime that fitted together like a jeweled watch. All those impossibilities fitting so neatly together to make the only possible possibility.

Eliada was unconscious only briefly. Then she cried out, her hand going to her head. She lifted dizzily on her elbow and peered about in the bright sunlight. "Lytha? 'Chell? Oh, Simon, look again! Did we come this far to be Called?" The desolation in her voice called Nathan from halfway back down the gully back up to her in a hurried scramble.

"I had to go see. It's a big cut on Papa's leg," he said. "I tore his shirt and wrapped it up, but something white—" He reached out a startled hand and touched Eliada's forehead. "Oh, Eliada!"

Her wide, blind-looking eyes turned to him, then she surged across the space between them. She clung to him so tightly that he had no breath. "Oh, David, David! I thought you crashed! Oh, David!"

"I'm Nathan," he said, prying her fingers gently loose so she could lie down again. "You're hurt—your head—" He touched it again, his eyes anxious on her face.

Eliada's eyes slowly cleared and focused on Nathan. The patient sorrow that resolutely came back over her face made Nathan want to cry.

"Yes," said Eliada, touching her head, then looking at her fingers. She closed her eyes for a moment, then she sat up, leaned forward and wiped her forehead with the under part of the hem of her skirt. "But it is not bleeding now. Your Papa—"

Weakly, as though from far off, he heard Papa's voice. "Nathan! You all right? Nathan!"

Nathan turned from Eliada and scrambled down the unsure footing of the slope of the gully.

"Papa! You all right?" and dropped to his knees by him.

"Don't know," said Papa. "Help me up."

And Nathan sagged under the weight of Papa's hands as he pulled himself to a sitting position. Papa got his arm around Nathan's shoulder and the two of them strained to lift him to his feet. They had only started upward when Papa cried out and slid down Nathan to the ground again. Nathan straightened him out, moving the rocks that kept him from lying flat, then he looked up at Eliada who was drifting down the slope.

"What are we going to do?" he asked hopelessly. "Papa's hurt."

"I have a need for water," said Eliada. "And perhaps your Papa has, too. Is there water?"

Nathan hurried over to where they had put their water pail and the tools. He lifted the lard bucket that sloshed heavily with water and looked back toward where Papa and Eliada were.

Maybe he ought to go get Mama. Maybe somebody else could help them better. Maybe if he just left—he grinned unhappily. With Mama in the family way? And who else to help? Just to walk off from Papa and Eliada? That was kid thinking. *I can't ever be a kid again!* Nathan swung the pail and hurried back.

"It is good." Eliada's eyes were large and luminous on Nathan. Then she smiled a small smile. "Always you are feeding the hungry and giving the cup of water." The smile faded and the eyes closed. "And always, I receive. It is hard always to receive."

"You saved Papa," said Nathan, uneasily looking up the slope.

"For you to hate—" Eliada's eyes opened again.

"I don't hate him," said Nathan, startled that it was so. "Not any more. He is—is Papa." He moved over to look at his father. Papa opened his eyes briefly to dull slits and closed them again as if forever. "Papa?"

"We must move him," said Eliada, wearily, drifting up to her feet, leaning for a moment on some unseen support. "I cannot lift him. I am not now strong enough. But I can make him less heavy for you. Lift him."

Nathan knelt on one knee and slid his hands under Papa, lifting him at knees and shoulders. For a moment, the sheer size of Papa made it awkward; then he had stumbled to his feet and was walking slowly toward the house, leaning back from the less-heavy load. It suddenly seemed as if he were carrying Lucas, for under the whiskered, grown-up face, he could trace in the features—as of Lucas—the other long-ago boy who became Papa. Who maybe was as unhappy and hurting now as Lucas had been—a tenderness welled up inside him and he felt his eyes get wet.

"Na—than! Din—ner!" Nathan's head jerked up at the far, thin cry. "Na—than!" Adina's voice came across the scarred wreckage of the field in the long, familiar calling chant. "Din—ner!"

"It's Adina," said Nathan. "Time to eat. Are you coming? Can you come?"

"Yes," said Eliada. "I can come. If I may hold—" She reached out and took Papa's hand where it drooped down, and Nathan started on, carrying the too-light Papa. Feeling a tug, he looked back to see Eliada, trailing like a limp scarf after him, holding fast to Papa's hand.

Adina came running to meet them.

"Is that Eliada? Oh, Eliada!" Then they got close enough for her to see, and her happy call fell silent and her two hands clasped over her open mouth. Her eyes looked again at Nathan, sagging to a stop under the bulk of Papa. And Papa, white and dead-looking, with blood dripping down over one shoe. And Eliada, a pool of limpness at Nathan's feet. And her eyes filled with frightened tears.

"Oh, Nathan! What's the matter with Papa? And Eliada? There's just us kids, because Mama can't— Oh, Nathan! What are we going to do? What are we going to do?"

Papa was lying on the bed, damply clean, his cream-colored night shirt pulled smoothly and decently down to the folded-back quilt covering him to the waist. His eyes were open and wary, watching as Eliada's hair shook itself in a swirly cloud until it was dry and smoothed itself decorously down against her head, only to lift again into exuberant curls and waves.

"Oh, it is good to be clean again," she said. "Pain is twice as much when there is dirt and confusion—and blood!" Her finger touched her head where the flesh had closed itself to a thin, red line.

"You sure get well fast," said Adina, engrossed in curling a strand of Eliada's hair around her hand and letting it spring free.

"It was small," said Eliada, smiling at her. Then she went over to the bed and melted down upon herself until she was eye to level eye with Papa, straight across.

"But yours is not small," she said. "Your bone is broken. And there is a—a—the flesh is torn to show the bone. It will be long for it to get well after it is put right again. Do you have those whose gift is to put right?"

Papa looked at her for a long moment, then he said, "Doctors. None closer than the county seat. Six days' horseback."

"Then—" Eliada's face pinked a little. "Then will you let us help you? My People? We can make your leg more right so it will get well and be straight, but I cannot do it alone. Will you let us?"

"Evil," said Papa, but slowly, not so quickly sure any more.

"Evil," said Eliada, thoughtfully, twisting her hand in her hair. "I am not sure I know this evil you know so well—"

"Badness," said Nathan. "Disobeying God. Sometimes it seems good, but only to lead you astray. Thou shalt not—"

"Oh," said Eliada after searching somewhere inside herself. "Separation. Oh, but we would do nothing to separate anyone from the Presence!" She was astonished. "We want to help you, but not if you feel it would separate—"

Papa looked at Eliada for a sharp, short moment. Then he turned his face away. "No," he said. "Get thee behind me, Satan."

Eliada toiled to her feet wearily, her face drawn and unhappy, one foot caught in her skirt. Adina, with a sharp little cry rushed to hinder by trying to help. Nathan lifted Eliada free of her skirts' tangle and of Adina.

"I'm sorry," he said. "Papa sees so much evil—"

"It's because Lucas is dead," said Mama. "That's why he won't let you help. He was so sure that Lucas died because of—of you, that he can't let you help him now, because, if he gets well— And Lucas is dead."

Eliada's head turned alertly. "Roth is here," she said, moving to the door. "We had hoped—"

The tall man who had skated so happily with the small child on his shoulders—so long, oh, so long ago—moved into sight at the door.

"But you said he was blind," said Nathan.

"Yes," said Eliada. "But he has learned to move freely in many places. And there is Moorma—"

A shy, smiling face peered from behind Roth's right leg. Then dodged away, only to peek again from behind his left leg. Nathan felt a smile crack through his tired face, and looked at Eliada. She was smiling, too, as Moorma disappeared again. Adina's giggle was smothered behind quick hands and even Mama's face lightened.

"Moorma is like that," said Eliada. "Smiles come with her always, but she is shy with new people. She sees for Roth, when Roth requires it." She went to the door and put her hand into Roth's reaching hand.

"We will help—when you will accept it," she said. "Take comfort in the Presence." And the three of them were gone.

Adina ran out of the door after them crying, "Goodbye! Goodbye!"

She came back into the cabin with a happy little skip. "They're flying," she said. "I knew they would! And Moorma—Moorma's doing it best—holding onto Roth!"

Nathan straightened his weary back by the bed, which had been pulled to the middle of the room, and looked across it at Mama. Mama, her hand holding the wet, folded cloth on Papa's briefly quiet forehead, looked across it at Nathan. Adina wept quietly in the far corner in her shadowy refuge behind hanging clothes.

"He isn't getting better," said Nathan.

"No," said Mama. "He is getting worse. The poultice isn't doing any good at all. The infection is spreading. And we can't keep the splint straight, the way he tosses—"

Papa jerked away from Mama's hand. "Hell's fires! Hot! Warm warm warm warm—Lucas—!"

Then his eyes opened to look into Nathan's, too close for comfort, at the edge of the bed. "It hurts!" His voice was thin and young and painfully surprised. The shadowy little boy again looked through the thicket of pain and whiskers and age. Then his eyes closed and his body twisted as he cried out in a ragged shaken voice.

And Adina wailed from her corner.

Mama straightened up, her hand pressing the swell of her side. She smoothed her hair back with both hands, her eyes shut, her chin tightly lifted. Then she shrugged herself wearily, twisting to ease her own aching.

"Go get them," she said. "He can die if he wants to, but not like this. Not to kill us all with him. Go get Eliada and that man—"

"And Moorma!" Adina was prancing at Mama's elbow. "Get Moorma!"

"Get them all," said Mama. "He can talk about evil, but by their fruits ye shall know them—"

Nathan heard the last words fade as he pounded across the front yard. *Why, it's daylight,* he thought, astonished. *The sun is shining!*

Halfway across the ruined field, he faltered and stumbled. They were coming! All of them! Fast! Don't ask how they come. Don't think of how they come! *A band of angels, coming—*

Three grown-ups and Eliada and the little girl and a cradle—the cradle—tell me a story—

"We have waited," said Eliada, taking Nathan's hand to hurry him back to the cabin. "Each day we have been renewing our strength through the Power, and we have waited. We can help! Oh, truly, Nathan, we can help!"

Mama and Nathan hunched under the tree across the flat from the cabin. Adina had slipped sideways across Mama's lap, and slept, her hands still tightly interlaced under her chin.

Eliada had told them when they were banished from the cabin: "If you have a way of coming into the Presence—to speak the Name—"

"We can pray," he told her.

"Pray," she said. "Help us with your prayers."

And the family had prayed—aloud and silently—until the words blurred and Adina could only remember *Now I lay me.* Now Mama's head was leaning back against the tree trunk, her eyes closed, her breath coming quietly.

Nathan looked around. *It is a good country,* he thought. *Everything about it is good—now. If only we could—could be more like the country. Open—busy—growing—* His head drooped with his heavy eyes. *With singing and wings and how big the snowflakes are—the stars—and* he slept.

He woke, too warm in the late afternoon sun, his neck aching, his mouth dry. He straightened his neck cautiously with the pressure of one hand—and his whole body throbbed with alarm before he knew it was Eliada. She was sitting quietly in the pool of her skirts, her hands loosely clasped in her lap.

She smiled and said quietly, "He is sleeping."

Mama woke to the strange voice.

"We have done what we could—the Power helping," said Eliada. "His leg—" she faltered. "It was bad. We got it straight again, and secured, and have started it back from the—the—"

"Infection," supplied Mama. "The infection—" She was getting awkwardly to her feet, leaving Adina fisting weary eyes.

"Yes, the infection." Eliada drifted up to her feet. "It will be long, but it will get well. Already we are planning a Rejoice for when he walks again—our first Rejoice since—"

"Moorma—where's Moorma?" Adina grabbed at Mama's skirt and hugged a handful of it tightly to her face before Mama broke away to hurry stiffly toward the cabin.

"She is waiting for you," Eliada said, smiling. "She found a—a play people of yours. It looks like a little girl—"

"My doll!" cried Adina. "Where did she find it? I lost it—"

"It's in the green growth by the animals' house. She would not touch it until you came—but she is singing to it."

"Moorma!" called Adina. "Moorma!" as she ran toward the lean-to, make shift barn.

Eliada and Nathan went toward the cabin to meet Mama. Her face was smoother and younger. "He's sleeping," she said. And the breath she took seemed to push away all the burdens she had been carrying.

"Before he slept," said Eliada. "He was much troubled because of—of the fields. That, we think we know. And the—the crops. That we do not know. We must know to put it right so that his rest will not be broken by worry."

Mama turned to Nathan. He felt suddenly grown up.

"Our field was practically ruined by the floods," he said. "We were trying to clear another field to get ready to plant. The crops are what we grow—" he half smiled at Eliada. "And we grow things besides corn, too. If we are too late with the planting, we'll have nothing to eat when winter comes.

"Oh! We know crops!" said Eliada happily. "We know growing and harvesting! At Home—at Home!—"

"Roth—" she called. "Marilla—Dor—"

They came sedately, quickly across the yard to meet Mama and Nathan halfway. Marilla held the baby with the wild-rose-pink dress against her shoulder, and Dor's arm across her back steadied her in case of roughness.

The two groups looked at each other. Then smiled. Then they were strangers no more.

"Roth," said Eliada eagerly. "The crops are the things—" She and the men—Nathan grew up some more —huddled under the tree to plan.

Marilla and Mama, who was now holding the baby and smiling—went back toward the cabin, talking supper and baths for a weary, hungry family.

There was never a happier made field in all the world, Nathan thought in the days that followed. Laughter and foolishness and fun—except when Papa came to watch the world, helped by Roth and Dor. Slowly out into the thin shadows near the field he would come, not knowing that even his one good leg never took all his weight. Then, settled cautiously in his big chair, sometimes with Mama sitting near him, he watched the effort and the sweating, the blister-raising labor that went with clearing and leveling the field.

Papa was satisfied when the men individually came to the shade to drink great, dribbling drinks of the spring water and to splash their sweating faces and heads with coolness, then pause briefly to catch their breaths. Papa could accept this, Nathan knew, because—by the sweat of your brows thou shalt—whatever you had to do to get things to eat. Papa distrusted anything that was too easy. But he could accept the neighborly help in time of need. He felt bound to do the same for those who had a need.

The making of the field was a long, hot, hard job— when Papa was watching. But, oh! when Papa had been helped back into the cabin! It was still hard and hot and heavy—but not blister-making. And Nathan had learned to laugh and he laughed often—with surprise and pleasure and astonishment—and just sheer enjoyment. And his ribs never quite broke—it only felt that way. They weren't used to laughter movements.

He saw, one day, the reason why the roots around Eliada's field looked like radishes. They had been pulled up, bodily, like radishes.

"Together like that, at the Home," said Eliada as they watched Marilla, Dor and Roth, hovering in a handholding circle above the last big tree to be uprooted. "Making the Circle. Remembering, 'We are gathered in Thy Name,' then the Power arrives to be used. That's the way they sealed the ships, on the Home, before we left—"

Nathan turned, thoughtfully, away from her struggle with tears, to watch the tree. It lurched and creaked and lifted, rocks and dirt jolting off in chunks from its roots as it rose. It shook the roots free and drifted over to the edge of the field. And the three workers drifted down to a far shade, thinly, wearily still against the ground.

"But you didn't pull up the ships," said Nathan, wondering if he was just helping Eliada make up a story. But the stories she told—

"No," said Eliada. "But I watched while the Old Ones finished our craft. The outside of it was made in pieces, you know, as the cabin is made of individual logs. So, to finish it, they made the Circle and—and the whole outside of the craft wrinkled and flowed and stilled and became one, a shell for all the craft." Eliada was sadly-happy, back on the Home.

A shout across the field brought them to their feet.

"The last one!" shouted Roth. "Oh, rejoice—rejoice!" And the three grown-ups shot across the field, tumbling and soaring, diving and twisting like young wild things set free, up and up!

And Eliada was gone, romping in the air over the field, joining in the song that lifted brightly, clearly. Nathan heard the high, thin piping of Moorma's voice, as she lifted jerkily, uncertainly, up from the edge of the field, to be gathered in by the others and tossed, with laughter and delighted shrieking, from one to another of the laughing, singing group.

Adina came through the underbrush and stood by Nathan, watching with longing, as Nathan was.

"I wish I could," she said, lifting her arms and rising on

her tiptoes. Then she sighed and lowered her arms. "Well, anyway, the baby can't yet. I'll go play with her."

When she was safely gone on her way back to the shade where the baby lay in the cradle, Nathan lifted his arms and came, clumsily, to tiptoe. He gave a longing little hop. Then hunkered down on a fallen log, hunched over his soundless, welling cry—*Oh, if only I could! If only I could!*

Then the plows came! Theirs and Papa's, snicking past the idle, astonished horses, slicing through the field, each with one of the workers hovering as an attendant, who at the first click of a rock, whisked it out of the way, arching through the air, to the rock pile filling in one of the gashes across the land.

Then, the first plowing done, came the rippling of the land as though it were a quilt on a bed, shaking across, filling hollows and smoothing humps, until the whole field lay smooth and dark and ready.

Papa watched some of the furrowing. And some of the planting. And said, heavily pleased, to Mama one evening, "Many hands make light work."

And Mama's eyes crinkled at Nathan as she snipped off her sewing thread with her front teeth and snapped another knot in her sewing thread and bent again to a wild-rosebud-pink ruffle for Adina's new Sunday dress.

"Tell us a story, Eliada," said Adina, softly, in the darkness of the loft. Because, in and out of the hours and days and the long evenings, Eliada had told Adina and Nathan much of the Home. She sighed for the lostness of the Home. They sighed for the wonder of her stories.

"Story!" Moorma's voice was high and clear. "Story!"

"Shh!" said Adina. "Don't wake Papa and Mama!"

"Don't wake Papa and Mama." Moorma's voice was as light as a breath.

Eliada and Moorma were staying the night at the cabin because their folks had gone somewhere, at sunset, their eyes excited and hopeful, their attention long gone ahead of their last goodbyes.

"Tell us a story, Eliada," Nathan repeated from his far, alone corner. "About the Crossing again." *If only Lucas could hear her! Oh, if only!*

"—so when we found the Home would be destroyed we made ships to take us away. There were three in our valley and we were assigned to one of them. And my cousin was filled with sorrow—"

"Because her love had to go in another ship—" Adina's voice mourned for them.

"Yes," said Eliada. "And then, at the last moment, Evalee was Called, so she left the ship—"

"Called?" asked Adina, knowing the answer—

"Called back to the Presence," said Eliada. "Her days totaled. Always, at Home, we were Called before we went back into the Presence. So we had time for our farewells and to put things in order and to give our families and friends the personal things we want them to have. And, most important, time to cleanse ourselves of anything that might make it hard to return to the Presence that sent us forth." Eliada sighed deeply. "At Home—at Home— there was time. We could go quietly Otherside, loving hands holding ours, back into the Presence, and have our castasides put in some shadowy place among the growing things, in the cool, growing soil—but—but here —we were so snatched—"

"So snatched—" Moorma parroted in her light, now-yawning, voice.

"Tell about the moon," said Nathan, to turn Eliada's thoughts.

"The moon—" Eliada's voice crinkled a little in the darkness. "When we first saw the moon, we hoped it was our new Home, because we knew we could not go as far as another sun. But when we skimmed just above its sur-face for all those miles and saw it all dead and dry and pocked with holes and not a blade of green and with only a thin slice of shadow far on the horizon, we were *afraid* it would be our new Home!"

"Then we swept to the other side, and saw—"

"Our world!" cried Adina, softly. "Our world!"

"Our world," said Eliada. "All clouds and blue and. wonderful! We sang! Oh, how we sang for journey's end and the loveliness offered us—" Her voice broke abruptly.

"But you had forgotten—" reminded Nathan.

"We had forgotten," sighed Eliada. "For so many years there had been no need to know how to move the ships, or take them into other atmospheres; so we had forgotten. During all the journey, the motivers had sought back through all of us and our memories of our Befores, to find the skills they needed, but they were not wise enough. They knew too little. They could do so few of the things that should have been done. Our ship was alone now. All the others had other parts of the sky to search. They were too far for us to work together to get the knowledge we needed before—"

"Before the air—" prompted Adina.

"Before the air," said Eliada. "Like a finger of flame pulled along our ship. By then we were all in our life slips —each all alone—to leave the craft before we died of the heating. Then we moved our slips—or our parents moved us, if we were not of an age to have the skill. And, out there all alone in the empty dark, I saw the ship glow brighter and brighter and—and flow apart and drip down and down—" A sob broke the story.

"Don't tell any more," said Nathan, groping through the multitude of new pictures tonight's story fanned out in his mind. "We shouldn't ask you. It makes you—"

"But telling it helps to end the pain," said Eliada. "I cannot change what happened, but I can change the way I remember it.

"I saw the life slips around me dart down through the air like needles of light, and I got caught up in trying to remember how to move mine—how to bring mine down safely—"

Silence filled the loft, and the wind spoke softly to one corner of the cabin.

"It was so wonderful to find we could breathe unshielded right from the beginning. And that there was land, and trees and the food and water were friendly to us. And some of us had landed close together—"

"We put into the new soil the castasides of those who were Called by the time we landed. My brother. Moorma's parents. Roth's wife and little boy. But not—" hope glowed. "Not my parents. Not Roth's daughter. Not Moorma's older brother. So perhaps somewhere, they are still alive—maybe half the world away—wondering if we are still alive. But maybe—"

In the silence, the even breathing from Adina's corner told that she and Moorma were sleeping.

Eliada lifted onto one elbow and spoke to the darkness where Nathan was. "That's where they have gone, Roth, Marilla and Dor. Roth thinks he has been hearing the

Questing of the People. Somewhere, not too far away. If they can find—maybe it will be—"

She lay back with a sigh. "It is hard to wait. But—weeping endureth for a night, but joy cometh in the morning. That was in the book we read to comfort the one who lived in our cabin before he was Called from his broken body. To find a book that has the thoughts—the words—and even—" her voice was hardly a whisper—"even our Brother— Truly, though I take the wings of the morning—"

The wind spoke softly again. Moorma murmured in her corner. And the quiet breathing of sleep was the only sound in the loft.

"Tell us a story, Daddy," said Little Lucas. "Tell about those People and the happy field."

"Isn't very happy now," said Nat, roughly, pretending disinterest. " 's where the lumber yard is."

"Lumber yards are happy!" Dena protested. "They smell of forest and they build houses—"

"When it was the happy field," said Nathan, leaning back in Papa's big old chair, about the only thing left from the old cabin. "Ours was the only cabin for ten miles or so, except where—those People lived.

"That's where the school is now!" cried Dena, perching on one of the rockers, clinging to Nathan's arm. "At the end of Koomatka road."

"Koomatka!" scoffed Nat. "Crazy Indian names!"

"It isn't Indian," said Nathan automatically, his eyes far and seeking. "On their Home, the People had a fruit call Koomatka. It tasted like music sounds and was for special holidays—They sang—they had songs for every—"

"Tasted like music—" The children snuggled down into themselves on the floor with quick, happy looks at each other. It had worked! Daddy was started on a People story!

"—and they came back the next day, so happy they could hardly land in our front yard. And they had brought three more of the People with them—starving—broken—raggedy. They had never found a settling place since their Landing. And Mama cried while she helped Marilla bathe and care for them. They had come to our place because two of the new People were Eliada's parents. They had to let her know—and Mama could help. Eliada couldn't help. All she could do was hover— *half the time* above *the bed*—so close they had to keep pushing her out of the way. Finally they told me to take her out under the big tree across the yard. So I did. And I held onto her there until she suddenly—like fainting—was asleep across my lap.

"The other one they found was Moorma's brother— Perez. He had cared for the others and defended them and starved so they could eat and was strong until they got him to our place, and then he collapsed—"

"But they got well!" Little Lucas was anxious—as always—clambering up to lean hard against Nathan's arm.

"They got well." Nathan nodded, his arm tight about Little Lucas' fragile shoulders, wondering that Lucas was in the face of his child as he had been in Papa's face— Papa—

"Papa was pleased at how well the field did," said Nathan. "He even thanked the People for helping him." The children settled back around him, used to sudden changes in Daddy's stories, after Daddy thought.

"Besides the field, we had our kitchen garden, and it grew more than enough to feed us—and them too, if they had needed it. But—"

The long, old sorrow was as piercing as when it was new. No, it couldn't be—or how could you live?

"But they went away," prompted Dena.

"They went away," said Nathan. "Perez—his gift was communications—had spent an hour every day, sending out their Questing call. He changed the hour every day in case someone was listening at a different time. And he finally got an answer.

" '*A Group!*' Perez could hardly speak. '*A lot of families! So many! So many of our old Group! And they're coming! They have a craft!*' he laughed, half crying. '*A little cobbled-together, busted-up thing!*' they said. '*But they're coming as soon as the dark of the moon, so no one—*' "

"And they went away—" Little Lucas' voice was sad.

"In an airship!" cried Nat, his eyes big with his crowding dreams.

"And left the cradle for when Gramma's little baby came." Dena looked at the cradle by the fireplace, with

Adina's play-person, tattered and fragile, still in it. "And the baby was *my* Uncle Luke!" she said triumphantly.

"And mine, too!" hastened Little Lucas. "And I'm named after him!"

"Daddy." Dena leaned against his knees, her eyes intent on his face. "Were you sorry when they went?"

"Sorry—" Even this long after, he hadn't been able to change much the way he 'remembered it.' He could never forget the quick smother of Eliada's embrace. And his stiffness that could not relax quickly enough to close his arms around her. There had been a quick, smooth swirl of her hair across his face. And she was gone. Up into the dark yawning of that door that waited, treetop high above the yard. Then the whisperings came—but not through his ears. All the thankings and rememberings and then the final—*Rest secure in the Presence through the Name and the Power.*

And they were gone—somewhere far. Somewhere west. But—scant comfort—still in this world.

"Don't cry, Daddy," said Dena, patting his cheek.

"Men don't cry!" scoffed Nat.

No, men don't cry—but boys do. Face-down in the darkness in the grass behind the big tree, wetting huddling sleeves through with hot tears—crying for a magic that was gone and could never come again.

"Yes, I was very sorry," said Nathan. But—

Nathan looked around the good room, felt the blessed warmth of Miriam, busy in the kitchen, and the wholeness of his life. The tightness inside him began to loosen, as it always finally did.

"We'll hug you happy," said Dena. And the three children clustered and climbed on the chair and on his lap— even Nat, who sometimes now was too old to hug people happy.

So—life widens. All kinds of loves come. Others come into the circle to complete it. And someday—maybe Otherside—but someday Eliada would be there again, sitting in the pool of her skirts, her hands lightly folded in her lap, her luminous eyes smiling and her soft voice saying:

"Tell us a story, Nathan. Tell us all the wonderful story of after we left—"

LE CROIX (THE CROSS)

Barry Malzberg

As its title indicates, this is a story about
religion . . . or at least religious experiences as perceived by its protagonist. A
rigid future bureaucracy that has discovered a method of apparent time travel al-
lows one man to experience brief periods
in the lives of historical religious leaders;
they think it's a safe, non-political field of
study, but people who are totally caught up
in one system of belief can be quite blind
to the power of different, even antiquated,
viewpoints. Barry Malzberg has made of
this situation a typically intense, subtle and
often hilariously funny story that says much
more than it seems to say.

Malzberg's writing has been controversial
ever since he started writing fifteen years
ago; he has been praised as an original
thinker and stylist, condemned as a "hack"
who didn't even care about plots. (This
story has a plot.) In 1973, he won the first
John W. Campbell Memorial Award for his
novel *Beyond Apollo*.

DEPERSONALIZATION TAKES OVER. AS USUAL, he does not quite feel himself, which is for the best; the man that he knows could hardly manage these embarrassing circumstances. Adaptability, that is the key; swim in the fast waters. There is no other way that he, let alone I, could get through. *"Pardonnez tout ils,"* he says, feeling himself twirling upon the crucifix in the absent Roman breezes, a sensation not unlike flight, *"mais ils ne comprendre pas que ils fait."*

Oh my, is that awful. He wishes that he could do better than that. Still, there is no one around, strictly speaking, to criticize and besides, he is merely following impulse which is the purpose of the program. Do what you will. *"Ah pere,* this is a bitch," he mutters.

The thief on his left, an utterly untrustworthy type, murmurs foreign curses, not in French, to the other thief; and the man, losing patience with his companions who certainly *look* as culpable as all hell, stares below. Casting his glance far down he can see the onlookers, not so many as one would think, far less than the texts would indicate but certainly enough (fair is fair and simple Mark had made an effort to get it right) to cast lots over his vestments. They should be starting that stuff just about now.

Ah, well. This too shall pass. He considers the sky, noting with interest that the formation of clouds against the dazzling sunlight must yield the aspect of stigmata.

314

For everything a natural, logical explanation. It is a rational world back here after all. If a little on the monolithic side.

"I wonder how long this is going to go on," he says to make conversation. "It does seem to be taking a bloody long time."

"Long time?" the thief on the left says. "Until we die, that's how long, and not an instant sooner. It's easier," the thief says confidentially, "if you breathe in tight little gasps. Less pain. You're kind of grabbing for the air."

"Am I? Really?"

"Leave him alone," the other thief says. "Don't talk to him. Why give him advice?"

"Just trying to help a mate on the stations, that's all."

"Help *yourself*," the second thief grumbles. "That's the only possibility. If I had looked out for myself I wouldn't be in this mess."

"I quite agree," I say. "That's exactly my condition, *exactly*."

"Ah, stuff it, mate," the thief says.

It is really impossible to deal with these people. The texts imbue them with sentimental focus but truly they are swine. I can grasp Pilate's dilemma. Thinking of Pilate leads into another channel, but before I can truly consider the man's problems a pain of particular dimension slashes through me and there I am, there I am, suspended from the great croix groaning, all the syllables of thought trapped within.

"Ah," I murmur, "ah," he murmurs, *"ah monsieurs, c'est le plus,"* but it is not, to be sure, it is not *le plus* at all. Do not be too quick to judge.

It goes on, in fact, for an unsatisfactorily extended and quite spiritually laden period of time. The lot-casting goes quickly and there is little to divert on the hillside; one can only take so much of that silly woman weeping before it loses all emotional impact. It becomes a long and screaming difficulty, a passage broken only by the careless deaths of the thieves who surrender in babble and finally, not an instant too soon, the man's brain bursts . . . but there is time, crucifixion being what it is, for slow diminution beyond that. Lessening color; black and grey. If there is one thing to be said about this process, it is exceedingly generous. One will be spared nothing.

Of course I had pointed out that I did not *want* to be spared anything. "Give me Jesus," I had asked and co-operating in their patient way they had given me Jesus. There is neither irony nor restraint to the process, which is exactly the way that it should be.

Even to the insult of the thieves abusing me.

Alive to the tenor of the strange and difficult times, I found myself moved to consider the question of religious knowledge versus fanaticism. Hard choices have to be made even in pursuit of self-indulgence. Both were dangerous to the technocratic state of 2219, of course, but of the two religion was considered the more risky because fanaticism could well be turned to the advantage of the institutions. (Then there were the countervailing arguments of course that they were partners, but these I chose to dismiss.) Sexuality was another pursuit possibly inimical to the state but it held no interest for me; the general Privacy and Social Taboo acts of the previous century had been taken very seriously by my subdivision and I inherited neither genetic nor socially-derived interest in sex for its own non-procreative sake.

Religion interested me more than fanaticism for a permanent program, but fanaticism was not without its temptations. "Religion after all imposes a certain rigor," I was instructed. "There is some kind of a rationalizing force and also the need to assimilate text. Then too there is the reliance upon another, higher power. One cannot fulfill ultimately narcissistic tendencies. On the other hand, fanaticism dwells wholly within the poles of self. You can destroy the systems, find immortality, lead a crushing revolt, discover immortality within the crevices. It is not to be neglected; it is also purgative and satisfying and removes much of that indecision and social alienation of which you have complained. No fanatic is truly lonely or at least he has learned to cherish his loneliness."

"I think I'd rather have the religious program," I said after due consideration. "The lives of the prophets, the question of the validity of the text, the matters of the passion attract me."

"You will find," they pointed out, "that much of the religious experience is misrepresented. It leads only to an increasing doubt for many, and most of the major religious figures were severely maladjusted. You would be surprised at how many were psychotics whose madness was retrospectively falsified by others for their own purpose."

"Still," I said, "there are levels of feeling worth investigating."

"That, of course, is your decision," they said, relenting. They were nothing if not cooperative; under the promulgated and revised acts of 2202, severely liberalizing board procedures, there have been many improvements of this illusory sort. "If you wish to pursue religion we will do nothing to stop you. It is your inheritance and our decree. We can only warn you that there is apt to be disappointment.

"Disappointment!" I said, allowing some affect for the first time to bloom perilously forth. "I am not interested in disappointment. This is of no concern to me whatsoever; what I am interested in is the truth. After all, and was it not said that it is the truth which will make ye—"

"Never in this lifetime," they cut me off, sadly, sadly, and sent me on my way with a proper program, a schedule of appointments with the technicians, the necessary literature to explain the effects that all of this would have upon my personal landscape, inevitable changes, the rules of dysfunction, little instances of psychotic break but all of it to be contained within the larger pattern. By the time I exit from the transverse I have used up the literature, and so I dispose of it, tearing it into wide strips, throwing the strips into the empty, sparkling air above the passage lanes, watching them catch the little filters of light for the moment before they flutter soundlessly to the metallic, glittering earth of this most unspeakable time.

I find myself at one point of the way the Grand Lubavitcher Rabbi of Bruck Linn administering counsel to all who would seek it. The Lubavitcher Sect of the Judaic religion was, I understand, a twenty- or twenty-first reconstitution of the older, stricter European forms which was composed of refugees who fled to Bruck Linn in the wake of one of the numerous purges of that crime. Now defunct, the Judaicists are, as I understand it, a sect characterized by a long history of ritual persecution from which they flourished, or at least the surviving remnants flourished, but then again the persecution might have been the most important part of the ritual. At this remove in time it is hard to tell. The hypnotics, as the literature and procedures have made utterly clear, work upon personal projections and do not claim historical accuracy, as historical accuracy exists for the historicists, if anyone, and often enough not for them. Times being what they are.

It is, in any case, interesting to be the Lubavitcher Rabbi in Bruck Linn, regardless of the origins of the sect or even of its historical reality; in frock coat and heavy beard I sit behind a desk in cramped quarters surrounded by murmuring advisors and render judgments one by one upon members of the congregation as they appear before me. Penalty for compelled intercourse during a period of uncleanliness is three months of abstention swiftly dealt out and despite explanations that the young bride had pleaded for comfort. The Book of Daniel, reinterpreted, does not signal the resumption of Holocaust within the coming month; the congregant is sent away relieved. Two rabbis appear with Talmudic dispute; one says that Zephaniah meant that all pagans and not all things were to be consumed utterly off the face of the Earth, but the other says that the edict of Zephaniah was literal and that one cannot subdivide "pagans" from "all things". I return to the text for clarification, remind them that Zephaniah no less than Second Isaiah or the sullen Ecclesiastes spoke in doubled perversities and advise that the literal interpretation would have made this conference unnecessary, therefore metaphor must apply. My advisors nod in approval at this and there are small claps of admiration. Bemused, the two rabbis leave. A woman asks for a ruling on *mikvah* for a pre-menstrual daughter who is nonetheless now fifteen years old, and I reserve decision. A conservative rabbi from Yawk comes to give humble request that I give a statement to the congregation for one of the minor festivals, and I decline pointing out that for the Lubavitcher fallen members of the Judaicists are more reprehensible than those who have never arrived. Once again my advisors applaud. There is a momentary break in the consultations and I am left to pace the study alone while advisors and questioners withdraw to give me time for contemplation.

It is interesting to be the Lubavitcher, although somewhat puzzling. One of the elements of which I was not aware was that in addition to the grander passions, the

greater personages, I would also find myself enacting a
number of smaller roles, the interstices of the religious
life, as it were, and exactly as it was pointed out to me
there is a great deal of rigor. Emotion does not seem to
be part of this rabbi's persona; the question of Talmudic
interpretation seems to be quite far from the thrashings of
Calvary. Still, the indoctrinative techniques have done
their job; I am able to make my way through these roles
even as the others, on the basis of encoded knowledge;
and although the superficialities I babble seem meaningless to me, they seem to please those who surround. I
adjust my cuffs with a feeling of grandeur; Bruck Linn
may not be all of the glistening spaces of Rome but it is a
not inconsiderable part of the history, and within it I
seem to wield a great deal of power. "Rabbi," an advisor
says opening the door, "I am temerarious to interrupt
your musings, but we have reached a crisis and your intervention is requested at this time."

"What crisis?" I say. "You know I must be allowed to
meditate."

"Yes," he says. "Yes, we respect your meditations. It
is wrong to impose. I should not—" and some edge of
agony within his voice, some bleating aspect of his fact
touches me even as he is about to withdraw. I come from
behind the desk saying, "What then, what?" and he says,
"Rabbi, it was wrong to bother you, we should protect,
we will respect," and now I am really concerned, from
large hat to pointed shoe he is trembling and I push past
him into the dense and smoky air of the vestibule where
congregants, advisors, women and children are gathered.
As they see me their faces one by one register intent and
then they are pleading, their voices inchoate but massed.
Save us, Rabbi, they are saying, *save us,* and I do not
know what is going on here, an awkward position for a
Talmudic judge to occupy, but I simply do not know; I
push my way through the clinging throng pushing them
aside, *Oh my God, Rabbi,* they are saying, *Oh my God,*
and I go through the outer doors, look down the street and
see the massed armaments, see the troops eight abreast
moving in great columns toward the building, behind them
the great engines of destruction, and in the sky, noise,
the holocaust, Rabbi, someone says, *the holocaust has
come, they will kill us,* and I feel disbelief. How can this
be happening? There was no purge in Bruck Linn to the

best of my recollection; there have never been any great purges on this part of the continent. Nevertheless here they are and behind me I can hear the children screaming. It is all that I can do to spread my arms and, toward them, toward the massed congregants and advisors behind, cry, "Stay calm, this is not happening; it is an aspect of the imagination, some misdirection of the machinery." Surely it must be that, some flaws in the fabric of my perceptions being fed through the machines and creating history out of context, and yet the thunder and smell of the armies is great in the air and I realize that they are heading directly toward this place, that they have from the beginning, and that there is nothing I can do to stop them.

"Be calm, be calm," I cry, "you are imagining this, indeed you are all imagining," but the words do not help, and as I look at the people, as they look at me, as the sounds of Holocaust overwhelm, I seem to fall through the situation leaving them to a worse fate—or perhaps it is a better, but it is only I who have exited, leaving the rest, these fragments of my imagination, to shore themselves against their ruins, and not a moment too soon, too soon.

Otherwise, life such as it is proceeds as always. I spend a portion of the time on the hypnotics and in the machinery, but there are commitments otherwise: to eat, to sleep, to participate in the minimal but always bizarre social activities of the complex; even, on occasion to copulate, which I accomplish in methodical fashion. The construction, I have been reminded, is only a portion of my life; responsibilities do not cease on its account. I maintain my cubicle, convey the usual depositions from level to level, busy myself in the perpetuation of microcosm. Only at odd times do I find myself thinking of the nature of the hypnotic experiences I have had, and then I try to push these recollections away. They are extremely painful and this subtext, as it were, is difficult to integrate into the outer span of my life. In due course I am assured that the fusion will be made, but in the meantime there is no way to hasten it. "You have changed, Harold," Edna says to me. Edna is my current companion. She is not named Edna, nor I Harold, but these are the names that they have assigned for our contemporary interaction, and Harold is as good as any; it is a name by which I would

as soon be known. *Harold in Galilee. And I have spoken
his name and it is Harold.* She leans toward me confidentially. "You are not the same person that you were."

"That is a common illusion provided by the treatments," I say. "I am exactly the same person. Nothing is
any different than it was."

"Yes it is," she murmurs. "You may not realize how
withdrawn and distracted you have become." She is a
rather pretty woman and there are times, during our
more or less mechanical transactions, when I have felt
real surges of feeling for her, but they have only been incidental to the main purpose. In truth I can have no feeling for anyone but myself; I was told this a long time ago.
She puts a hand on me intensely. "What are they doing to
you?"

"Nothing," I say quite truthfully. "They are merely
providing a means. Everything that is done I am doing
myself; this is the principle of the treatment."

"You are deluded," she says and loops an arm around
me, drags me into stinging but pleasurable embrace. Forehead to forehead we lay nestled amidst the bedclothes; I
feel the tentative touch of her fingers. "Now," she says,
moving her hand against me. "Do it now."

I push against her embrace. "No. It is impossible."

"Why?"

"During the treatments——"

"Nonsense," she says, "you are avoiding me. You are
avoiding yourself. The treatments are anaesthetic, don't
you see that? They are forcing you to avoid the terms of
your life and you cannot do that." Her grasp is more insistent, at the beginning of pain. "Come on," she says.
Insistent woman. Against myself, I feel a slow gathering.

"No," I mutter against her cheekbone, "it is impossible. I will not do it now."

"Fool."

"The chemicals. I am awash in chemicals; I remain in
a sustaining dose all the time. I would upset all of the
delicate balances——"

"You understand nothing," she says, but in an inversion of mood turns from me anyway, scurrying to a far
point. "Have it as you will. Do you want me to leave?"

"Of course not."

"*Of course not.* You are so accommodating. Do you
want me to entertain you then?"

"Whatever you will."

"You have changed utterly. You are not the same. These treatments have rendered you cataleptic. I had hopes for you, Harold; I want you to know that. I thought that there were elements of ~~genuine~~ perception, real thought. How was I to know that all of the time you merely wanted to escape into your fantasies?"

"What did you want me to do?" I say casually. "Overthrow the mentors?"

She shrugs. "Why not?" she says. "It would be something to keep us occupied."

"I'd rather overthrow myself."

"You know, Harold," she says and there is a clear, steady light of implication in her eye, "it is not impossible for me to like you; we could really come to understand one another, work together to deal with this crazy situation, but there is this one overwhelming problem, and do you know what that is?"

"Yes I do," I say wearily because this has happened before. "I surely do."

"Don't deprive me of the satisfaction," she says. "Harold, you are a fool."

"Well," I say shrugging, "in these perilous and difficult times, this madly technocratic age of 2219, when we have so become merely the machinery of our institutions, where any search for individuality must be accomplished by moving within rather than without, taking all of this into consideration and what with one thing being like every other thing in this increasingly homogeneous world, tell me, aren't we all?"

"Not like you," she says. "Harold, even in these perilous and difficult times, not like you at all."

On the great and empty desert he takes himself to see the form of Satan, manifest in the guise of an itinerant, wandering amidst the sands. Moving with an odd, off-center gait, rolling on limping leg, Satan seems eager for the encounter, and he is ready for it too, ready at last to wrestle the old, damned angel and be done with it, but Satan is taking his time—the cunning of the creature—and seems even reluctant to make the encounter. Perhaps he is merely being taunted. Once again he thinks of the odd discrepancy of persona; he is unable in this particular role to work within the first person but is instead a

detached observer seeing all of it at a near and yet
far remove, imprisoned within the perception, yet not
able to effect it. An interesting phenomenon, perhaps he
has some fear that to become the persona would be blas-
phemous. He must discuss this with the technicians sometime. Then again, maybe not. Maybe he will not discuss
it with the technicians; it is none of their damned business, any of it, and besides, he has all that he can do to
concentrate upon Satan, who in garb of bright hues and
dull now comes upon him. "Are you prepared?" Satan
says to him. "Are you prepared for the undertaking?"

He looks down at his sandals embedded in the dense
and settled sands. "I am ready for the encounter," he says.

"Do you know the consequences?" Satan says. He has a
curiously ingratiating voice, a warm and personal manner, an offhand ease which immediately grants a feeling
of confidence, but then again this was to be expected.
What belies the manner, however, is the face, the riven
and broken features, the darting aspect of the eyes, the
small crevices in which torment and desert sweat seem to
lurk and which compel attention beyond the body which
has been broken by the perpetration of many seeming
injustices. Satan extends his arm. "Very well, then," Satan
says, "let us wrestle."

"Non disputandum," he says. "I understood that first
we were to talk and only after that to struggle."

"Latin is no protection here," Satan says firmly. "All
tongues pay homage to me."

"Mais non," he says in his abominable French,
"voulez-vous je me porte bien."

"Nor does humor exist in these dark spaces," Satan
says. "From walking up and down upon the earth and to
and fro I have learned the emptiness of present laughter.
Come," he says, leaning forward, his arm extended, "let
us wrestle now."

He reaches for that gnarled limb, then brings his hands
back. The sun is pitiless overhead but like a painting; he
does not feel the heat. His only physical sensation is of
the dry and terrible odor seeping from his antagonist.
"No," he says. *"Mais non, mon frere.* Not until we have
had the opportunity to speak."

"There is nothing to speak about. There are no
sophistries in this emptiness, merely contention."

Do not argue with Satan. He had been warned of this,

had known it as his journey toward the darkness had begun, that there was no way in which the ancient and terrible enemy could be engaged with dialectic and yet, *non disputandum,* he has failed again. Not to do it. Not to try argument; it is time to wrestle and it might as well be done. He seizes the wrist and slowly he and the devil lock.

Coming to grips with that old antagonist it is to the man as if he has found not an enemy but only some long-removed aspect of himself, as if indeed, just as in sex or dreams, he is in the act of completing himself with this engagement. The stolidity of the form, the interlocking of limbs, gives him not a sense of horror, as he might have imagined, but rather comfort. It must have been this way. Their hands fit smoothly together. "Do you see?" Satan says winking and coming to close quarters. "You know that it must always have been meant this way. Touch me, my friend, touch me and find grace," and slowly, evenly, Satan begins to drag him forward.

He understands, he understands what is happening to him: Satan in another of his guises would seduce him with warmth when it is really a mask for evil. He should be fighting against the ancient and terrible enemy with renewed zeal for recognizing this, but it is hard, it is hard to do so when Satan is looking at him with such compassion, when the mesh of their bodies is so perfect. Never has he felt anyone has understood him this well; his secret and most terrible agonies seem to flutter, one by one, birdlike, across the features of the antagonist, and he could if he would sob out all of his agonies knowing that Satan could understand. Who ever would as well? It must have been the same for him. I do not believe, he wants to cry to the devil; I believe none of it; I am taken by strange, shrieking visions and messages in the night; I feel that I must take upon the host of Heaven, and yet these dreams which leave me empty and sick are, I know, madness. I hear the voice of God speaking unto me saying I am the Father, I am the incompleteness which you will fill and know that this must be madness, and yet I cannot deny that voice, can deny no aspect of it, which is what set me here upon the desert, but I am filled with fear, filled with loathing and trembling. . . . he wants to cry all of this out to Satan, but he will not, he will not, and slowly he finds himself being drawn to the ground.

"Comfort," Satan says in the most confiding and compassionate of whispers, covering him now with his gnarled body so that the sun itself is obscured, all landscape dwindled to the small perception of shifting colors, "comfort: I understand, I am your dearest and closest friend. Who can ever understand you as I? Who would possibly know your anguish. Easy, be easeful," Satan says, and he begins to feel the pressure come across his chest. "So easy," Satan murmurs, "it will be so easy, for only I understand; we can dwell together," and breath begins to desert him. The devil is draining his respiration.

Understanding that, he understands much else: the nature of the engagement, the quality of deception, exactly what has been done to him. Just as Satan was the most beautiful and best-loved of all the angels, so in turn he would be Satan's bride in the act of death. It is the kiss that will convey the darkness, and seeing this, he has a flickering moment of transcendence: he thinks he knows now how he might be able to deal with this. Knowing the devil's meaning will enable him to contest, and yet it would be so easy—inevitable is the word—necessary— to yield to his antagonist and let it be done, let the old, cold, bold intruder have his will, thy will be done, and Satan's too, and the yielding is so close to him now he can feel himself leaning against the network of his being, the empty space where desire might have rested, in the interstices the lunge toward annihilation—*mais non,* he says, *mais non, je renonce, I will not do it!*—and forces himself against the figure, understanding finally the nature of this contest, what it must accomplish, in what mood it must be done and wearily, wearily, carrying all of consequence upon him he begins the first and final of all his contests with the devil.

It is a madly technocratic age, a madly technocratic age, and yet it is not cruel; the devices of our existence, we have been assured, exist only in order to perpetrate our being. Take away the technology and the planet would kill us; take away the institutions and the technology would collapse. There is no way in which we can continue to be supported without the technology and the institutions, and furthermore they are essentially benign. They are essentially benign. This is not rationalization or an attempt to conceal from myself and others the dreadful aspects of our mortality, the engines of our condition grinding us slowly away . . . no, this is a fixed and rational judgment which comes from a true assessment of this life.

It is true that a hundred years ago, in the decades of the great slaughters and even beyond, the institutions were characterized by vengeance, pusillanimity, murder and fear, but no more. In 2160 the oligarchy was finally toppled, the reordering began, and by 2189, the very year in which I was born, the slaughter was already glimpsed within a historical context. I was nurtured by a reasonable state in a reasonable fashion; if I needed love, I found it; sustenance was there in more forms than the purely physical. I grew within the bounds of the state; indeed, I matured to a full and reasonable compassion. Aware of the limits which were imposed, I did not resent them nor find them stifling.

There was space; there has been space for a long time now. Standing on the high parapet of the dormer, looking out on Inter-valley Six and the web of connecting arteries beneath the veil of dust, I can see the small lights of the many friendly cities nodding and winking in the darkness, the penetrating cast of light creating small spokes of fire moving upward in the night. Toward the west the great thrust of South Harvest rears its bulk and spires, lending geometry to a landscape which would otherwise be endless, and I find reassurance in that presence just as I find reassurance in the act of being on the parapet itself. There was a time, and it was not so terribly long ago, that they would not have allowed residents to stand out on the parapet alone; the threat of suicide was constant, but in the last years the statistics have become increasingly favorable, and it is now within the means of all of us, if only we will to come out in the night for some air.

Edna is beside me. For once we are not talking; our relationship has become almost endlessly convoluted now, filled with despair, rationalization and dialogue, but in simple awe of the vision she too has stopped talking and it is comfortable, almost companionable standing with her thus, our hands touching lightly, smelling the strange little breezes of our technology. A long time ago people went out in pairs to places like this and had a kind of emotional connection by the solitude and the vision, but now emotions are resolved for more sensible arenas such as the hypnotics. Nevertheless, it is pleasant to stand with her thus. It would almost be possible for me at this moment to conceive some genuine attachment to her, except that I know better; it is not the union but its absence which tantalizes me at this moment, the knowledge that there is no connection which will ever mean as much to us as this landscape. The sensation is unbearably poignant although it does not match in poignance other moments I have had under the hypnotics. At length she turns toward me, her touch more tentative in the uneven light and says, "It hurts me too. It hurts all of us."

"I wasn't really thinking about pain."

"Nevertheless," she says. "Nevertheless. Pain is the constant for all of us. Some can bear it and others cannot. Some can face this on their own terms and others need artificial means of sustentation. There is nothing to be done about this."

"I don't *need* artificial means," I way. "I have elected—"

"Surely," she says. "Surely."

And they are not artificial, I want to add; the experiences under the hypnotics are as real, as personally viable, as much the blocks of personality formulation as anything which this confused and dim woman can offer, as anything which has passed between us. But that would only lead to another of our arguments and I feel empty of that need now. Deep below we can hear the uneven cries of the simulacrum animals let out at last for the nighttime zoo, the intermingled roars of tigers.

"Has it made any difference?" she says. "Any of it?"

"Any of what? I don't understand."

"The treatments. Your treatments."

Tantalizingly, I find myself on the verge of a comment which will anneal everything, but it slips away from me as is so often the case, and I say, "Of course they have made a difference."

"What have you gained?"

"*Pardonne? Pardonnez moi?*"

"Don't be obscure on me," she says. "That will get you nowhere. Tell me the truth."

I shrug. My habit of lapsing into weak French under stress is an old disability; nonetheless I find it difficult to handle. Most have been more understanding than Edna. "I don't know," I say. "I think so."

"I know. It's done nothing at all."

"Let's go inside now," I say. "It's beginning to chill here."

"You are exactly the same as you were. Only more withdrawn, more stupid. These treatments are supposed to heal?"

"No. Merely broaden. Healing comes from within."

"Broaden! You understand less than ever."

I put a hand to my face, feel the little webbing where years from now deep lines will be. "Let's go inside," I say again. "There's nothing more—"

"Why don't you face the truth? These treatments are not meant to help you; they are meant to make you more stupid so that you won't cause any trouble—"

I move away from her. "It doesn't matter," I say. "None of it matters. It is of no substance whatsoever. Why do you care for it to be otherwise?"

There is nothing for her to do but to follow me into the funnel. She would argue in position but my withdrawal has offered the most devastating answer of all: I simply do not care. The attitude is not simulated: on the most basic level I refuse to interact.

"You are a fool," she says, crowding against me for the plunge. "You do not understand what they are doing to you. You simply don't care."

"Quite right," I say. "Quite right. Absolutely. Not at all. That is the point now, isn't it?"

The light ceases and we plunge.

I am in an ashram surrounded by incense and the dull outlines of those who must be my followers. Clumped in the darkness they listen to me chant. It is a mantra which I appear to be singing in a high, cracked chant; it resembles the chanting of the Lubavitchers of Bruck Linn, although far more regularized in the vocal line, and limited in sound. *Om* or *ay* or *eeh*, the sounds are interchangeable and I am quite willing to accept the flow of it, not rationalize, not attempt to control those sounds but rather to let them issue according to my mood. It is peaceful and I am deeply locked within myself; the soft breathing of my followers lending resonance to the syllables which indeed seem to assume a more profound meaning, but at a certain point there is a commotion and the sound of doors crashing and then in the strophes of light I can see that the room has been invaded by what appear to be numerous members of the opposition. They are wearing their dull attack uniforms, even this if nothing else is perceptible in the light and from the glint of weaponry I can see that this is very serious. They move with an awful tread into the room, half a dozen of them, and then the portable incandescence is turned on and we are pinned there in frieze.

I know that it is going to be very bad; the acts of 2013 specifically proscribed exactly what is going on here and yet five years later the pogroms have dwindled to harassment, random isolated incursions. I did not think that in this abandoned church in the burned-out core of the devastated city they would ever move upon me, and yet it seems now that my luck has suddenly, convulsively run out, as I always knew that it would. Surely in some corner of the heart I must have known this; the *om* must have always been informed by doom; and yet it is one thing to consider demolition in a corner of the heart and another, quite another, to live it. *Ahbdul,* one of them says pointing, his finger enormous, dazzling, and as I lift my eyes to it I feel myself subsiding in the wickers of light, *Ahbdul, you are in violation of the codes and you have brought woe to all.*

In a moment, in one moment, they will plunge toward me. I know how it goes then, what will happen; they will strike at me with their weapons and bring me to a most painful position; they will obliterate consciousness and cause bloodstains; not of the least importance they will humiliate me before my small congregation, which has already witnessed enough humiliation—thank you very much—otherwise why would they have gathered here?— and yet I can tolerate all of that, I suppose. I have dreamed worse, not to say suffered many privations and indignities before opening this small, illegal sub-unit. In fact, none of this concerns me; what does, I must admit, is the fear that I will show weakness before my congregation. To be humiliated is one thing, but to show fear, beg for mercy, is quite another; I would hardly be able to deal with it. A religious man must put up a stiff front. A religious man whose cult is based upon the regular, monotonic articulation of ancient chants to seek for inner serenity can hardly be seen quivering and shrieking in front of those who have come for tranquility. If tranquility is all that I have to offer, I cannot give them pain.

Thinking this, I resolve to be brave and draw myself to full stature or what there is left of it after all these years of controlled diet and deliberate physical mutilation. "You will not prevail," I say. "You cannot prevail against the force of the om," and with a signal I indicate to my congregation that I wish to resume the chant, humiliate them by my own transcendence, but they do not attend. Indeed they do not attend at all, so eager do so many of them appear to search out any means of exit open to them. A small alley has been left open by the massed opposition leading to one of the doors, and in their unseemly haste to clear the hall they ignore me. Religious disposition, it would seem, is a function of boredom: give people something really necessary to face in their lives and religion can be ignored, all except for the fanatics who consider religion itself important, of course; but they are disaster-ridden. Like flies these little insights buzz about, gnawing and striking small pieces of psychic flesh while the hall is emptied, the opposition standing there looking at me bleakly, but I find as usual that this insight does me no good whatsoever. It can, indeed, be said merely to magnify my sense of helplessness.

"Gentlemen," I say, raising a hand, "this is a futile business. Join me in a chant." I kneel, my forehead near the floor, and begin to mumble, hoping that the intensity of this commitment will strike shame within them, convince them that they are dealing with someone so dangerously self-absorbed that all of their attacks would be futile, but even as I commence the syllables I am pulled to my feet by a man in a uniform which I do not recognize, obviously a late-comer to the room. He stares at me from a puffy, heart-shaped face and then raises his hand, strikes me skillfully across first one cheek and then the other. The collision of flesh is enormous; I feel as if I am spattering within. "Fool," he says, "why have you done this?"

"Why do you care? Why are you asking?"

He hits me again. No progression of the sacred blocks of personality; the levels of eminent reason have prepared me for this kind of pain. I realize that I am crying. "Give me a response," he says. "Don't withdraw, don't protest, don't argue; it will lead only to more blows and eventually the same results. Simply answer questions and it will go much easier for both of us. Knowing all of the penalties, knowing of the responsibilities for your acts and what would happen to you if you were discovered, why did you nonetheless persist? Didn't you understand? Didn't you know what danger you brought not only upon yourself but the fools you seduced? Now they too will have to pay."

He is choleric with rage, this man; his face seems to have inflatêd with blood and reason as he stands there and I begin to comprehend that he is suffering from more than situational stress. Looking at him I want to accentuate that sudden feeling of bonding, but there is every emotion but sympathy in that ruined face and suddenly he hits me again convulsively; this the most painful blow yet because it was not expected. I fall before him and begin to weep. It is not proper context for a martyr, but I never wanted it to be this way; I never imagined that there would be such blood in sacrifice. He puts one strong hand under an arm, drags me grunting to my feet, positions me in front of him as if I were a statue.

"Do you know what we're going to have to do now?" he says. "We're going to have to make an example of you, that's all, we're going to have to kill you. Why did you put us into this position?"

"I am not able to believe that you will do that," I say. I am struggling for tranquility. "You wouldn't kill me, not here in the temple—"

"This is not a temple. It is a dirty cluttered room and you are an old fool who imagines it to be a church—"

"Om," I say. The word comes; I did not calculate. *"Om. Eeeh. Ay."*

"You would fight the state regardless. If the state believed in *om* you would cry for freedom of choice. If the state were stateless you would wish to form institutions within. There is no hope for you people, none at all; you would be aberrants in any culture at any time and you cannot understand this. You want to be isolated, persecuted, to die. It has nothing to do with religion."

"Eeh. Ay. Oooh. Ahh. Om."

"Enough," he says, "enough of this," and signals to the others at the rear; they come forward slowly, reluctantly, but with gathering speed at the approach, perhaps catching a whiff of death which comes from the syllables. "You wish a public death, you wish a martyrdom; then you will have it. Reports will be issued to all of the provinces.

Icons will be constructed. Dispatches will even glorify. You will achieve everything that you were unable in life. But this will do you no good whatsoever."

The fear is tightly controlled now. Truly, the syllables work. I would not have granted them such efficacy and yet what I have advised my congregants all of this time turns out to be true. They paste over the sickness with the sweet contaminations of courage, grant purchase upon terror, make it possible for the most ignorant and cowardly of men, which must be myself, to face annihilation with constant grace. *"Om,"* I say. *"Eeh.* If it were to be done, then it must be done quickly."

"Ah," he says, "it is impossible. Nothing will be gained from this and yet you still will not face the truth. It would be so much easier if at least you would give up your bankrupt purchase, if you would understand that you are dying for no reason whatsoever and that it could have been no other way; it would make matters so much easier—"

"Ah," I say. "Oh."

"Ah, shit," the man with the heart-shaped face says and gives a signal to one of the supporters, who closes upon me, a small man in uniform with a highly calibered weapon and puts its cold surfaces against my temple. His hand shakes, imperceptibly to the vision, but I can feel that quiver against the ridged veins. It is remarkable how I have gained in courage and detachment; just a few moments ago it would have seemed impossible. Yet here I am, apparently, prepared to face what I feared the most with implacable ardor. "Now." the man says. "Do it now."

There is a pause. *Om* resonates through me; it will be that with which I will die, carrying me directly to the outermost curved part of the universe. I close my eyes, waiting for transport, but it does not come, and after a while I understand that it will not. Therefore I open my eyes, reasonable passage seeming to have been denied me. The positions are the same except that the leader has moved away some paces and the man carrying the gun has closed his eyes.

"Shoot him, you fool," the leader says. "Why haven't you shot him?"

"I am having difficulty—"

"Kill him, you bastard."

There is another long pause. I flutter my eyes. *Om* has

receded. "I can't," the man with the gun says at last. "I can't put him down, just like that. This isn't what I was prepared to do. You didn't say that it would be this way. You promised—"

"Ah, shit," the heart-shaped man says again and comes toward us, breaks the connection with a swipe of his hand, knocking the gun arm down and the supporter goes scuttling away squealing. The leader looks at me with hatred, red-tinted veins alight. "You think you've proven something," he says. "Well, you've proven absolutely nothing. Weakness is weakness. I will have to do it myself."

I shrug. It is all that I can do to maintain my demeanor considering the exigencies but I have done it. Will; everything is will. *"Om,"* I murmur.

"Om," he says, *"om* yourself," and goes to the supporter; the supporter hands him the gun silently; the leader takes it in his left hand, flexes fingers, then puts it against my "temple." "All right," he says, "it could have been easier but instead it will be more complex. That does not matter, all that matters is consummation."

"Consummate," I say. *"Om."*

"I don't want to do this," he says with the most immense kindness. "I hope you understand. It's nothing personal; I have little against you; it's just a matter of assignment, of social roles." Unlike the others he seems to need to prepare himself for assassination through a massive act of disconnection. "Nothing personal," he says mildly, "I really don't want to."

I shrug. "I don't wait to die, particularly," I say. "Still, I seem able to face it." And this is the absolute truth. Calm percolates from the center of the corpus to the very brain stem; I seem awash in dispassion. Perhaps it is the knowledge that this is all a figment, that it is a dream and I will not die but awake again only to sterile enclosure and the busy hands of technicians. "Do it," I say. "Do it." Is this the secret of all the martyrs? That at the end, past flesh and panic, they knew when they would awaken and to what? Probably. On the other hand, maybe not. Like everything else it is difficult and complex. Still, it can be met with a reasonable amount of dignity, which is all that we can ask.

"Indeed," he says sadly, "indeed," and fires the gun into my temple killing me instantly and precipitating in one jagged bolt the great religious riots and revivals of the early twenties. And not one moment too soon, Allah and the rest of them be praised.

Systematically I face examination in the cold room. It is a necessary part of the procedure. "The only hint of depersonalization other than at the end of the last segment," I say calmly, "has been during the Jesus episodes. I seem unable to occupy it within the first person but feel a profound disassociative reaction in which I am witnessing him as if from the outside, without controlling the actions."

The counselor nods. "Highly charged emotional material obviously," he says. "Disassociative reaction is common in such cases. At some point in your life you must have had a Jesus fixation."

"Not so," I say. "In fact I did not know who he was until I was introduced through the texts."

"Then it must have hit some responsive chord. I wouldn't be unduly concerned about this. As you integrate into the persona it will fall away and you will begin to actively participate."

"I feel no emotional reaction to the material at all. I mean, no more than to any of the others. It's inexplicable to me."

"I tell you," the counselor says with a touch of irritation, "that is of no concern. The process is self-reinforcing. What we are concerned about is your overall reactions, the gross medical signs, the question of organic balances. The psychic reactions will take care of themselves."

I look past him at the walls of the room which contain schematic portraits of the intervalley network. Interspersed are various documents certifying the authenticity of his observer's role. The absence of anything more abstract disturbs me; previously it never occurred to me how deprived our institutions seem to be of artistic effect, but now it does; the hypnotics must be working. There is a clear hunger within me for something more than a schematic response to our condition. "Are you listening to me?" he says. "Did you hear my question."

"I heard it."

"I am going to administer a gross verbal reaction test now, if you will pay attention."

"I assure you that is not necessary," I say. "I am in excellent contact."

"That is a judgment which we will make."

"Must you?"

"I'm afraid so," the counselor says. "We wish to guard against exactly that which you manifest, which strikes me as a rather hostile, detached response. We do not encourage this kind of side-effect, you see; we consider it a negative aspect of the treatment."

"I'm sorry to hear that."

"It is often necessary to terminate treatment in the face of such reactions, so I would take this very seriously."

"Why do you do this to us?" I say. I look at his bland, pleasant face, masked by the institutional sheen but nonetheless concealing, I am convinced, as passionate and confused a person as I might be, perhaps a little *more* passionate and confused since he has not had, after all, the benefit of the treatments. "Why can we simply not go through this on our own terms, take what we can take, miss the rest of it? Why must we be *monitored?*"

"The procedures—"

"Don't tell me of procedures," I say, leaning forward with a sudden intensity, aware that I am twitching at the joints and extremities in a new fashion, emotionally moved as rarely has been the case. Definitely the treatments are affecting me. "The real reason is that you're afraid that unless we're controlled we might really be changed, that we might begin to react in fashions that you couldn't predict, that we wouldn't be studying *religion* and *fanaticism* any more but would actually become religious fanatics and what would you do with us then?"

"Confine you," my confessor says flatly, "for your own protection. Which is exactly what we want to avoid by the process of what you call monitoring, which is merely certifying that you are in condition to continue the treatments without damage to yourself."

"Or to the state."

"Of course to the state. I work for it, you live within it; why should we not have the interests of the state at heart? The state need not be perceived as the enemy by you people, you know."

"I never perceived—"

"You can't make the state the repository of all your difficulties, the rationalizing force for your inadequacies.

The state is a positive force in all of your lives and you have more personal freedom than any citizenry at any time in the history of the world."

"I never said that it wasn't—"

"In fact," the counselor says, rising, his face suffused now with what might be passion but then on the other hand might only be the consequence of improper diet, highly spiced intake, the slow closure of arteries, "we can get damned sick of you people and your attitudes. I'm no less human because I have a bureaucratic job, I want you to know; I have the same problems that you do. The only difference is that I'm trying to apply myself toward constructive purposes, whereas all you want to do is to tear things down." He wipes a hand across his streaming features, shrugs, sits again. "Sorry to overreact," he says. "It's just that a good deal of frustration builds up and it has to be expressed. This isn't easy for any of us, you know. We're not functionaries; we're people just as you are."

There seems nothing with which I can disagree. I consider certain religious virtues which would have to do with the absorption of provocation without malice and remain quietly in my chair, thinking of this and that and many other things having to do with the monitoring conducted by these institutions and what it might suggest about the nature of the interrelation, but thought more and more is repulsive to me; what I concentrate upon, what seems to matter is feeling, and it is feeling which I will cultivate. "Some questions," the counselor says in a more amiable tone. "Just a series of questions which I would like you to answer as briefly and straightforwardly as possible."

"Certainly," I say, echoing his calm. *"Trés bonne, merci. Maintenant et pourquoi."*

"Pourquoi?" he says with a glint in his eye and asks me how often I masturbate.

He looks at the man who has come from the tomb. Little sign of his entrapment is upon him; he looks merely as one might who had been in deep sleep for a couple of days. He touches him once gently upon the cheek to assure the pulse of light, then backs away. The crowd murmurs with awe. This is no small feat; here he has clearly outdone the loaves and the fishes. They will hardly be able to dismiss this one; it will cause great difficulty when the reports hit Rome. "How are you?" he says to Lazarus. "Have you been merely sleeping or did you perceive the darkness? What brings you back from those regions?"

Documentary sources indicate no speech from the risen man, of course. But documentary sources are notoriously undependable, and, besides, this is a free reconstruction as he has been so often advised. Perhaps Lazarus will have something to say after all; his eyes bulge with reason and his tongue seems about to burst forward with the liquid syllables of discovery. But only an incoherent babble emerges; the man says nothing.

He moves in closer, still holding the grip. "Were you sleeping?" he says, "or did you perceive?"

"*Ah,*" Lazarus says. "*Eeeh. Om.*"

He shrugs and dropping his hand moves away. If a miracle is to succeed, it must do so on its own terms; one must have a detached, almost airy attitude toward the miracles because at the slightest hint of uncertainty or effort they will dissipate. "Very well," he says, "be on your way. Return to your life."

The disciples surround him, all but Judas, of course, who as usual is somewhere in the city, probably making arrangements for betrayal. There is nothing to be done; he must suffer Judas exactly as Judas must suffer him, it is the condition of their pact. Peter puts a heavy hand on his shoulder. "What if the man cannot move, master?" he says, always practical. "What if he is unable to complete the journey from the grave."

"He will be able to."

Indeed Lazarus seems to have adopted a stiff gait which takes him slowly toward the crowd. The crowd is surprisingly sparse after all; it is not the throng indicated by scriptures, but instead might be only forty or fifty, many of whom are itinerants drawn to the scene in their wanderings. Scriptural sources were often only a foundation for the received knowledge, of course; the scribes had their own problems, their own needs to fill and retrospective falsification was part of their mission . . . still, he thinks, it is often embarrassing to see how hollow that rock is upon which the church was built. Oh well. "I think we had better leave now," Peter says.

"Oh?"

"Indeed," this man of practicality says. "It will make more of an impression, I think; it will lend more of an air of mystery and have greater lasting effect than if you were to stay around. A certain detachment must be cultivated."

"We will surround you, Master," little Mark says, "and leave together hiding your aspect from the populace. In this way you will seem to be attended at all times by a shield." He beckons to Luke, John, the others. "Come," Peter says, "nothing can be served by staying here longer. It would be best to move on."

He does admire the practicality, the disciples simply acting within the situation to bring the maximum interest, and yet reluctance tugs at him. He is really interested in Lazarus. He would like to see what happens next: will the man leave the area of the tomb or will he simply return to it? The rock has merely been pulled aside, the dark opening gapes; Lazarus could simply return to that comfort if he desired, and perhaps he does. Or perhaps not; it is hard to evaluate the responses of an individual toward death. The man is now shielded from view by the crowd which seems to be touching him, checking for the more obvious aspects of mortality. "Let us wait a moment," he says. "This is very interesting. Let's see what is happening here."

"It would not serve, Master," Peter says.

"It is not a matter of serving, merely one of observation. I am responsible for this man, after all; it is only reasonable that I would take an interest in his condition."

"No," Luke says. He scuttles over, a thin man with bulging, curiously piercing eyes. No wonder he wrote the most elaborate of the gospels—dictated, that is to say, all of the disciples being fundamentally illiterate. "That will not serve. It is important that we leave at once, Master."

"Why?"

"The mood of the crowd is uncertain; it could turn ugly at any time. There can be much contretemps over miracles, and the superstitious are turned toward fear. The very hills are filled with great portents—"

"Enough," Peter says. "You have a tendency for hyperbole, Luke; there is no danger here. But it would be better, from many standpoints if we were to leave; an air of mystery would serve best—"

"Oh, all right," I say. *"Je renouncée."* It is, after all,

best to adopt a pose of dignity and to give in to the wishes of the disciples, all of whom at least intermittently take this matter more seriously than I . . . they are, after all, in a position of greater vulnerability. I cast one last look at Lazarus, who is now leaning back against the suspended door of the tomb, elbows balanced precariously on stones, trying to assume an easeful posture for the group almost obscuring him. How exactly is one to cultivate a *je ne sais quoi* about death? It is something to consider; of course I will have ample time to consider the issue myself, but Lazarus could hardly yield much information on the subject. The man is speechless, highly inarticulate; one would have hoped that for a miracle such as this that I could have aroused someone less stupid, but nothing to be done. All of existence is tied together in one tapestry, take it all or leave it, no parts. Surrounded by my muttering disciples I walk toward the west, kicking up little stones and puffs of dust with my sandals.

It is disappointing, quite a letdown really, and I would like to discuss this, but not a one of them would want to hear it. I know that they already have sufficient difficulties having given up their lives for the duration of this mission and it would be an embarrassment for them to hear that I too do not quite know what I am doing. Or perhaps I do. It is hard to tell. In the distance I hear a vague collision of stone. I would not be surprised if Lazarus had gone back into the tomb. Of the tapestry of existence *je ne sais pas.*

As I copulate with Edna, images of martyrdom tumble through my mind, a stricken figure on the cross, stigmata ripped like lightning through the exposed sky, and it is all that I can do under the circumstances to perform, but thy will be done, the will must transcend, and so I force myself into a smaller and smaller corner of her, squeezing out the images with little birdcalls and carrying her whimpers through me. She coils and uncoils like a springy steel object and at long last obtains sexual release; I do so myself by reflex and then fall from her grunting. It is quite mechanical, but in a highly technological culture sexual union could only be such; otherwise it would be quite threatening to the apparatus of the state, or so, at least, I have deduced. She lies beside me, her face closed to all feeling, her fingers clawed around my wrist. I groan deep in my throat and compose for sleep, but it is apparent then that there will be no sleep because suddenly she is moving against me and then sitting upright in the bed, staring. Hands clasped behind my head, elbows jutting at an angle of eighty-five degrees I regard her bleakly. "I can't talk now," I say. "Please, if you must say something, let it be later. There's nothing right now."

"You mean you have to face your treatments in the morning and you need your rest so that you can be alert for the drugs. That's all you think about now, those treatments. Where are you living? Here or there? Come on, tell me."

"I don't want to talk, I told you."

"You've changed," she said. "They've destroyed you. You aren't what you used to be."

There comes a time in every relationship when one has approached terminus, when the expenditure of pain is not worth the pleasure input, where one can feel the raw edges of difference collide through the dissolved flesh of care. Looking at Edna I see that we have reached that point, that there is not much left, and that it will be impossible for me to see her again. This will be the end. After she leaves this time there will be no recurrence. It is this, more than anything else, which enables me to turn from her with equanimity, to confront the bold and staring face of the wall. "Goodnight," I say. "We won't talk about this any more."

"You can't avoid this. You can run from me but not from what has happened. You're not living here any more; you're living in the spaces of your own consciousness. Don't you realize that? You've turned inside; you've shut it out! These aren't experiences that you're having; they're dreams, and all of this is taking place inside you. I hate to see it happen; you're better than this; together we could have helped one another, worked to understand what our lives were, maybe even made progress—"

Too late. I stand. "You'd better leave now, Edna."

Arms folded across her little breasts, she juts her chin at me. "That won't solve anything at all. Getting rid of me won't change it."

"The only truth is the truth we create—within ourselves."

"I don't believe that. That's what they tell us, that's how you got started on these treatments, but it isn't so. There's an objective truth and it's outside of this and you're going to have to face it sooner or later. You're just going to have to realize—"

I look at her with enormous dispassion and my expression must be a blade which falls heavily across her rhetoric, chopping it, silencing her. At length, and when I know that she is ready to receive the necessary question, I pose it as calmly and flatly as I have ever done and its resonance fills the room, my heart, her eyes until there is nothing else but her flight, and at last that peace which I have promised myself.

"Why?" I say.

At Bruck Linn they do not start the pogrom after all, but instead seize me roughly and hurl me into detention. It seems that it was only this in which they were interested; they entered in such massive numbers only to make sure that they could scour the area for me if I were not at my appointed place. In detention I am given spartan but pleasant quarters within what appears to be their headquarters, and a plate of condiments on which to nibble, as well as the five sacred books of the Penteteuch, which, since they know I am a religious man, they have obviously given for the purposes of recreation. I look through them idly, munching on a piece of cake, but as always find the dead and sterile phrases insufficient on their own to provoke reaction, and it is almost with relief that I see them come into the room, obviously to explain themselves and advise what will happen next. It is high time. There are two of them, both splendidly uniformed, but one is apparently in the role of secretary; unspeaking, he sits in a corner with a recording device. The other has a blunt face and surprisingly expressive eyes. I would not have thought that they were permitted large wet blue eyes like this.

"You are giving us much difficulty," he says directly, sitting. "Too much and so we have had to arrange this rather dramatic interview. Our pardon for the melodrama but it could not, you see, be spared; we needed to seize and detain as quickly as possible, and we could not take a chance on riots."

"Certainly," I say rather grandly. "I am a world figure. My abduction would not be easy."

"It is not only that."

"But that in itself would be enough."

"No matter," he says. He looks at me intently. "We're going to have to abort the treatments," he says. "You are becoming obsessive."

"What?"

"It has leached out into your personal life and you are beginning to combine treatments and objective reality in a dangerous fashion. Therefore under the contract we are exercising our option to cut them off."

"I have no understanding of this," I say. "Treatments? I am the Lubavitcher Rabbi of Bruck Linn and I have been torn from the heart of my congregation in broad daylight by fascists who will tell me this? This is unspeakable. You speak madness."

"I am afraid," he says, and those expressive eyes are linked to mine, "that you are displaying precisely those symptoms which have made this necessary. You are not the Lubavitcher Rabbi, let alone of Brooklyn. You are Harold Thwaite of the twenty-third century; the Lubavitchers are a defunct, forgotten sect, and you are imagining all of this. You have reconceived your life; the partitions have broken; and we are therefore, for your own good, ceasing the treatments and placing you in temporary detention."

"This is an outrage," I say. "This is impossible. Pogrom? Pogroms I can understand, I can deal with them. But this madness is beyond me."

The uniformed man leans toward me and with the gentlest of fingers strokes my cheek. "It will go easier if you cooperate, Harold," he says. "I know how difficult this must be for you, the shock—"

"My followers will not be easy to deal with. You will have to cut them down with rifle fire. I am sure that you can do this, but the cost in blood and bodies will be very high, and in the long run you will not win. You will find a terrible outcome. We are God's chosen; we and only the Lubavitchers carry forth his living presence in this century, and you cannot tamper with that presence lacking the most serious consequences—"

And I see to my amazement and to my dismay that the interrogator, the one who has come to intimidate and defile, this man in the hard and terrible uniform of the state, appears to be weeping.

I part the Red Sea with a flourish of the cane but the fools nonetheless refuse to cross. "What is wrong with them?" I say to Aaron. "It's perfectly safe." I move further into the abyss between the waves and turn, but the throng remains on the shore staring with bleak expressions. Only Aaron is beside me. "I'm afraid they don't trust the evidence of sight," he says, "and also they don't trust you either; they feel that this is merely a scheme to lead them astray and as soon as they step over, the waters will close upon them."

"That is ridiculous," I say to him. "Would I take them this far, do so much, walk with the guidance of the Lord to betray the Children of Israel?"

Aaron shrugs, a bucolic sort. "What can I tell you?" he says. "There's no accounting for interpretation."

At the first great hammer to the temple it comes to me that they were all the time as serious as I. More serious, in fact. I was willing to trust the outcome of my rebellion to a higher power, whereas they, solid businessmen to the end, decided to make sure that the matter rested in their own hands.

Nevertheless, it hurts. I never knew that there was so much pain in it until they put me down at the mosque and oh my oh my oh my oh my no passion is worth any of the real blood streaming.

"You see now," the counselor says to me, "that you are clearly in need of help. There is no shame in it; there is precedent for this; it has all happened before. We know exactly how to treat the condition, so if you will merely lie quietly and cooperate, we should have you on your way before long. The fact that you are back in focus now, for instance, is a very promising sign. Just a few hours ago we despaired of this, but you are responding nicely."

I rear up on my elbows. "Let me out of here," I say. "I demand to be let out of here. You have no right to detain me in this fashion; I have a mission to perform, and I assure you that you will suffer greatly for what you have done. This is serious business; it is not to be trifled with.

Detention will not solve your problems; you are in grave difficulty."

"I urge you to be calm."

"I am perfectly calm." I note that I appear to be lashed to the table by several painless but well contrived restraints, which pass across my torso, digging in only when I flail. It is a painless but humiliating business and I subside, grumbling. "Very well," I said. "You will find what happens when you adopt such measures, and that judgment will sit upon you throughout eternity."

The counselor sighs. He murmurs something about many of them at the beginning not being reasonable, and I do not remind him that this is exactly as Joseph had warned.

Tormented by the anguish on the Magdalene's face, the tears which leak unbidden down her cheeks, he says, "It is all right. The past does not matter; all that matters is what happens in the timeless present, the eternal future." He lifts a hand, strokes her cheeks, feeling its intensity; it is of a different sort from the more generalized tenderness he has felt through his earlier travels. "Come," he said. "You can join me."

She puts her hand against his. "You don't understand," she says. "This is not what I want."

"What?"

"Talk of paradise, of your father, of salvation; I don't understand any of it. I don't know what you think they want."

"I know what they want."

"You don't know anything," she says. "You are a kind man but of these people you know nothing." She smooths her garments with a free hand. "To them you are merely a diversion, an entertaining element in their lives, someone who amuses them, whereas you think in passionate terms. You will be deeply hurt."

"Of course."

"No," she says, "not in the way you think. Martyrdom will not hurt you; that is, after all, what you seek. It will be something else." Something else, he thinks. *Something else, I think.*

She is an attractive woman not without elements of sympathy, but staring at her I remember that she was, until very recently, a prostitute who committed perhaps even darker acts, and that it is an insolent thing which she, of all people, is doing in granting her Saviour such rebuke. "Come," I say to her. I should note that we have been having this dialogue by a river bank, the muddy waters of the river arching over the concealed stones, the little subterranean animals of the river whisking their way somewhere toward the north, the stunted trees of this time holding clumps of birds which eye us mournfully. "It is time to get back to the town."

"Why?"

"Because if we remain out here talking like this much longer some will misconceive. They will not understand why we have been gone so long."

"You are a strange, strange man."

"I am not a man. I am—"

"I would not take all of this so seriously," she says, and reaches toward me, a seductive impact in the brush of her hand, seductive clatter in her breath, and oh my Father it is a strange feeling indeed to see what passes between us then, and with halt and stuttering breath I hurl myself upright, thrust her away, and run toward Galilee. Behind me, it cannot be the sound of her laughter which trails. It cannot, it cannot.

"Fools," I say, my fingers hurtling through the sacred, impenetrable text, looking for the proper citation. "Can't you understand that you are living at the end of time? The chronologies of the Book of Daniel clearly indicate that the seven beasts emerge from the seven gates in the year 2222, the numbers aligned; it is this generation which will see the gathering of the light." They stare at me with interest but without conviction. "You had better attend," I say. "You have little time, little enough time to repent, and it will go easier for you if you do at the outset."

One of the congregants raises his hand and steps toward me. "Rabbi," he says, "you are suffering from a terrible misapprehension—"

"So are you all," I say with finality, "but misapprehension can itself become a kind of knowledge."

"This is not Bruck Linn and the Book of Daniel has nothing to do with what is happening."

"Fool," I say, lunging against my restraining cords,

"you may conceive of a pogrom, but that cannot alter the truth. All of your murders will not stop the progress of apocalypse for a single moment."

"There is no apocalypse, rabbi," the congregant says, "and you are not a rabbi."

I scream with rage, lunging against the restraints once again and they back away with terror on their solemn faces. I grip Penteteuch firmly and hurl it at them, the pages opening like a bird's wing in flight, but it misses, spatters against an opposing wall, falls in spatters of light. "I have my duties," I say, "my obligations. You had better let me go out and deliver the summons to the world; keeping me here will not keep back the truth. It cannot be masked, and I assure you that it will go better for you if you cooperate."

"You are sick, rabbi," he says very gently. "You are a sick man. Thankfully you are getting the treatment that you so desperately need and you will be better."

"The great snake," I point out, "the great snake which lies coiled in guard of the gates is slowly rising; he is shaking off the sleep of ten thousand years—"

"To throw a holy book—"

"No books are holy. At the end of time, awaiting the pitiless and terrible judgment even the sacred texts fall away. All that is left is judgment, mercy, the high winds rising—"

"If you will relax, rabbi—"

"I want to walk to and fro upon the earth and up and down upon it!" I scream. "From all of these wanderings I will come to a fuller knowledge, crouching then at the end of time with the old antagonist to cast lots over the vestments of the saved and the damned alike, bargaining for their garments out of a better world—"

"If you will only be quiet—"

"The snake is quiet too," I say, "quiet and waiting for the time of judgment, but let me tell you that the silence which you will demand is the silence of the void—"

And so on and so forth, *je ne sais pas.* It is wearying to recount all of those admonitions which continue to rave through the spaces of the room at this time. If there is one thing to say about a Talmudic authority in heat, it is that once launched upon a point he can hardly pause; pauses would form interstices where the golem itself might worm. And of the golem, of course, little more need be said.

"Will you yield?" Satan says to me, putting me into an untenable position upon the sands. His face looms near mine like a lover's; he might be about to implant the most sustained and ominous of kisses. "Yield and it will go easier with you."

"No," I say, "never. I will not yield." The French has fled, likewise the depersonalization. I feel at one with the persona, which is a very good sign, surely a sign that I am moving closer to the accomplishment of my great mission. "You may torture me; you may bring all of your strength to bear; it is possible that you will bend and break me, but you will never hear renunciation." I grab purchase with my ankles, manage to open up a little bit of space, which of course I do not share with my ancient antagonist, and then with a sly wrench drag him toward me, defy his sense of balance and send him tumbling beside. He gasps, the exhalation of breath full as dead flowers in my face, and it is possible for me now to hurl myself all the way over him, pressing him into the sands. Gasping, he attempts to fling me, but as I collapse on top of him my knee strikes his horned and shaven head, administering a stunning blow and from the opening I see leaching the delicate, discolored blood of Satan. His eyes flutter to attention and then astonishment as I close upon him and my strength is legion. "Do you see?" I say to him. "Do you see now what you have done? You cannot win against the force of light," and I prepare myself to deliver the blow of vanquishment. Open to all touch he lies beneath me; his mouth opens.

"Stop!" he says weakly, and to my surprise I do so. There is no hurry, after all; he is completely within my power. "That's better," he says. His respiration is florid. "Stop this nonsense at once. Help me arise."

"No," I say, "absolutely not."

"You don't understand, you fool. This dispute was supposed to be purely dialectical; there was no need to raise arms—"

Ah, the cunning of Satan! Defeated on his own terms he would shift to others, but I have been warned against this too, I have been fully prepared for all the flounderings of the ancient enemy; there is nothing that he can do now to dissuade me, and so I laugh at him, secure in my own power and say, "Dialectical! No, it was a struggle unto the death; those were clearly the terms and you know that as well as I."

"No," he says, twitching his head. "No, absolutely not, you never saw this right. There was never the matter of murder; don't you realize that? We aren't antagonists at all! We are two aspects of the overwhelming one; our search was for fusion in these spaces, and that is what we are now prepared to do." His head sinks down; he is clearly exhausted. Still he continues muttering. "You fool," he says. "There is no way that one of us can vanquish the other. To kill either is to kill the self."

Sophistry! Sophistry! I am so sick of it; I intimate a life, a dark passageway through to the end lit only by the flickering and evil little candles of half-knowledge and witticism, casting ugly pictures on the stones, and the image enrages me; I cannot bear the thought of a life which will contain little more than small alterations of language or perception to make it bearable, reconsideration of a constant rather than changing the unbearable constant itself, but this is to what I have been condemned. Not only Satan, but I will have to live by rhetoric; there will be nothing else.

But at least, this first time on the desert, rhetoric will not have to prevail. Perhaps for the only time in my life I will have the opportunity to undertake the one purposive act, an act of circumstance rather than intellection.

And so, without wishing to withhold that moment any longer, I wheel fiercely upon Satan. "I've had enough of this shit," I say. "I've got to deal with it; I cannot go on like this forever; there has to be a time for confrontation." The words seem a bit confused, but my action is not; I plunge a foot into his face. It yields in a splatter of bone, and in that sudden rearrangement I look upon his truest form.

"Well," says Satan through flopping jaw. "Well, well." He puts a claw to a slipped cheekbone, "Well, I'll be damned."

"Oh, yes," I say, "but you don't have to take all of us with you."

His eyes, surprisingly mild, radiate, of all things, compassion. "You don't understand," he says. He falls to his knees like a great, stricken bird. "You don't understand anything at all."

"I do enough."

"I'm not here by choice," Satan murmurs. "I'm here because you *want* me. Do you think that this is easy? Being thrown out of Heaven and walking up and down the spaces of the earth, and to and fro upon it, and the plagues and the cattle and the boils? I've just been so *busy*, but it was you who brought me into being, or again——" Satan says, drawing up his knees to a less anguished posture, fluttering on the desert floor, "——is this merely rationalization? I am very good at sophistry, you know, but this isn't easy; there's a great deal of genuine *pain* in it. I have feelings too."

I stand, considering him. What he is saying is very complex and doubtless I should attend to it more closely (I sense that it would save me the most atrocious difficulty later on if only I would) but there is a low sense of accomplishment in having dealt with this assignment so effectively, and I do not want to lose it so easily. It may be one of the least equivocal moments in a life riven, as we all know, with conflicts. "I'm dying," Satan says. "Won't you at least reach out a hand to comfort me?"

The appeal is grotesque and yet I am moved. He is, after all, a creature of circumstance no less than any of us. I kneel beside him, trying not to show my revulsion at the smell of leaking mortality from him. Satan extends a hand. "Hold me," he says. "Hold me; you owe me at least that. You called me into being; you have to take responsibility for my vanquishment. Or are you denying complicity?

"No," I say, "I can hardly do that." I extend my hand. His claw, my fingers, interlock.

"You see," Satan says gratefully, "you *know* at least that you're implicated. There may be some hope in that for all of us and now if you will permit me, I believe that I am going to die."

Grey and greenish blood spills from his mouth, his nasal passages, eyes and ears. It vaults into the desert and as I stare fascinated, he dies with quick muffled sighs not unlike the sounds of love. It is an enormous and dignified accomplishment not noted in all the Scripture, and I am held by the spectacle for more than a few moments.

But as his claw slips away, as touch is abandoned,

I have a vision and in that vision I see what I should have known before going through all of this. I see what might have saved me all of this passage, which is to say that knowing he is dead there is a consequent wrench in my own corpus indicating an echoing, smaller death, and as I realize that he has told me the truth, that the divestment of Satan has resulted only in my own reduction, I stand in the desert stunned, knowing that none of this—and I am here to testify, gentlemen, I am here to testify!—is going to be as simple as I thought.

"Even the minor prophets have problems," I point out in the mosque. "The fact that I am not famous and that many of my judgments are vague does not mean that they are not deeply felt or that I will not suffer the fate of Isaiah. Jeremiah, Zephaniah, had their problems. Ezekiel had a limp and was tormented by self-hatred. Hosea had blood visions too."

They look at me bleakly, those fifteen. This is what my flock has dwindled into, and I should be grateful to have them, what with all of the efforts to discredit and those many threats of violence made toward those who would yet remain with me. They are quite stupid, the intelligent ones long since having responded to the pressure, but they are all I have, and I am grateful, I suppose, to have them. "Attend," I say. "The institutions cannot remain in this condition. Their oppression is already the source of its own decay; they panic, they can no longer control the uprising. The inheritors of these institutions are stupid; they do not know why they work or how, but just mechanically reiterate the processes for their own fulfillment, massacre to protect themselves, oppress because oppression is all they know of the machinery. But their time is limited; the wind is rising and the revolution will be heard," and so on and so forth, the usual rhetorical turns and flourishes done so skillfully that they occupy only the most fleeting part of my attention. Actually I am looking at the door. It is the door which I consider; from the left enter three men in the dress of the sect, but I have never seen them before and by some furtive, heightened expressions of their eyes I know that they have not come here on a merciful business.

They consult with one another against the wall and it is all that I can do to continue speaking. I must not show a lapse of rhetoric, I must not let them know that I suspect them, because all that I hold is the prospect of my inattention, but as my customary prose rolls and thunders I am already considering the way out of here. My alternatives are very limited. The windows are barred, the walls are blank behind me, the only exits are at the edge of the hall and what has happened to the guards? Did they not screen this group? Are they not supposed to protect me, or are they all part of the plot? "Be strong, be brave," I am telling my followers, but I do not feel strong or brave myself; I feel instead utterly perplexed and filled with a fear which is very close to self-loathing. Their conference concluded, the men scatter, one going for a seat in the center, the other two parting and sliding against the walls. They fumble inside their clothing; I am sure they have firearms.

I am sure that the assassins, on my trail for so very long, have at last stalked me to this point; but I am in a very unique and difficult position because, if I show any fear whatsoever, if I react to their presence, they will doubtless slay me in the mosque, causing the most unusual consternation to my followers assembled; but on the other hand, if I proceed through the speech and toward an orderly dismissal, all that will happen is that I will make the slaying more convenient and allow for less witnesses, to say nothing of giving them an easier escape. Anything I do, in short, is calculated to work against me, and yet I am a man who has always believed in dignity, the dignity of position, that is to say, taking a stand, following it through whatever the implications; and so I continue, my rhetoric perhaps a shade florid now, my sentences not as routinely parsed as I would wish but it is no go, no go at all; they have a different method, I see, as the seated one arises and moves briskly toward me. "This is not right," I say as he comes up to me, takes me by an elbow. "You could at least have let me finish; if I was willing to take this through, then you could have gone along with me." The congregants murmur.

"You'd better come with me, Harold," he says. "You need help."

"Take your hands off me."

"I'm afraid I'd best not do that," he says gently, gesturing toward the two in the back who begin to come toward me solemnly. "You see, what we have to do is to jolt you out of these little fugues, these essays in martyr-dom, and it would be best if you cooperated; the more you cooperate, the quicker you see that it becomes evident that you are accepting reality, and therefore the more quickly you will be back to yourself. Come," he says, giving me a hearty little tug, "let's just bounce out of here now," and the others flank me fore and aft and quite forcefully I am propelled from the rostrum. To my sur-prise my congregants do not express dismay, nor are there scenes of riot or dislocation as I might have expected; on the contrary they look at me with bleak, passive interest, as I am shoved toward the door. It is almost, I think, as if they had expected me to come exactly to this state and they are glad that I am being taken off in this fashion.

"Can't you see," I say gesticulating to them, "can't you see what is happening here? They don't want you to know the truth, they don't want you to accept the truth of your lives; that's why they're taking me away from here, be-cause I was helping you to face the truth."

"Come on, Harold," they murmur taking me away. "All of this has its place, but after a while it's just best to cooperate; just go along," and now they have me through the doors, not a single one of my congregants making the slightest attempt to fracture their progress. I shake a fist at them.

"For God's sake," I say, "don't any of you care, don't you know what's going on here?" and so on and so forth, the sounds of my rhetoric filling my ears, if hardly all the world, and outside I am plunged repeatedly into the brackish waters of Galilee, which to no one's surprise at all (or at least not to mine) hardly lend absolution.

"You'd better destroy them," I say in a conversational tone, settling myself more comfortably underneath the gourd. "They're a rotten bunch of people as you will note. Not a one of them has but a thought of their own pleas-ure, to say nothing of the sexual perversity."

"I may not," he says reasonably. He is always reason-able, which is a good thing if one is engaged in highly in-ternalized dialogues. What would I do if he were to lose patience and scream? I could hardly deal with it. "After all, it's pretty drastic, and besides that, without life there is no possibility of repentance."

"Don't start that again," I say. "You sent me all of

these miles, through heat and water, fire and pain to warn them of doom, and you would put both of us in a pretty ridiculous position, wouldn't you, if you didn't follow through? They'd never take me seriously again."

"You let *me* decide that, Jonah," he says, and there is no arguing with him when he gets into one of these moods, no possibility of argument whatsoever when he becomes stubborn, and so I say, "We'll see about this in the morning," much as if I were controlling the situation rather than he, which is not quite true of course, and slip into a thick doze populated with the images of sea and flying fish, but at the bottom of the sleep is pain, and when I bolt from it it is with terrible pain through the base of being, my head in anguish, my head as if it were carved open, and looking upward I see that the gourd which he had so kindly spread for me has shrivelled overnight, and I am now being assaulted by a monotonous eastern sun. "Art thou very angry?" he says companionably, lapsing into archaicism as is his wont.

"Of course I am very angry," I say, "You have allowed my gourd to die. And besides I want to know when you're going to get rid of these people. Looking down from this elevation I can see very distinctly that the city is still standing."

"Ah," he says as I scratch at my head, trying to clobber the sun away, "thou takest pity upon the gourd which was born in a night and died in a night; why should I not take pity upon forty thousand people who cannot discern their right hand from their left to say nothing of much cattle?"

"Sophistry," I say, "merely sophistry."

"Unfortunately," he says, "there is no room for your reply," and smites me wildly upon the head, causing me to stumble into the ground, Gomorrah still upright, and I am afflicted (and not for the first time I might add) with a perception of the absolute perversity of this creature who dwelleth within me. At all times.

The thieves have died, but I am still alive to the pain of the sun when I feel the nails slide free and I plunge a hundred feet into the arms of the soldiers. They cushion my fall, lave my body with strong liquids, murmur to me until slowly I come over the sill of consciousness to stare at them. Leaning over me is a face which looks familiar.

"Forgive them," I say weakly, "forgive them, they know not what they do."

"They know what they do."

"*Jamais,*" I say and to clarify, "never."

"You have not been crucified," he says. "You'd better accept that."

"Then this must be hell," I say, "and I still in it."

He slaps me across the face, a dull blow with much resonance. "You're just not being reasonable," he says. "You are not a reasonable man."

"Help me up there, then," I say. "It is not sufficient. Help me up there and crucify me again."

"Harold—"

"*Jesu,*" I say admonishingly and close my eyes waiting for ascent and the perfect striations of the nails through the wrist: vaulting, stigmata.

The face looking at me is Edna's, but this is strange because Edna will not be born for several centuries yet, and what is even stranger than that is the fact that despite this I recognize her. How can this be? Nevertheless, one must learn to cope with dislocations of this sort if one is to be a satisfactory martyr. "They asked me to come here and speak to you," she says. "I don't know why I'm here. I don't think it will be of any use whatsoever. But I will talk to you. You have got to stop this nonsense now, do you hear me?"

"You could help by getting me out of here," I say, plucking at my clothing. "My appearance is disgusting and it is hardly possible for me to do the work when I am confined to a place like this. Or at least you could have them hurry and order up the crucifixion. Get it over with. There's no reason to go on this way; it's absolutely futile."

"That's what they want me to talk to you about. They seem to think that this is something that can be reasoned with. I keep on telling them that this is ridiculous; you're too far gone but they say to try so I will. They're as stupid as you. All of you are stupid; you've let the process take over and you don't even understand it. Face reality, Harold, and get out of this or it is going to go very badly—"

"*Jesu,*" I remind her.

"Do you see?" she says to someone in the distance.

"It's absolutely hopeless. Nothing can come of this. I told you that it was a waste."

"Try," the voice says. "You have to try."

She leans toward me. Her face is sharp, her eyes glow fluorescent in the intensity. "Listen, Harold," she says. "You are not *Jesu* or anyone else—any of your religious figures. This is 2219 and you have been undergoing an administered hypnotic procedure enabling you to live through certain of your religious obsessions, but as is very rarely the case with others you have failed to come back all of the way at one point, and now they say you're in blocked transition or something. They're quite able to help you and to reverse the chemotherapeutic process, but in order to begin you have to accept these facts, that we are telling you the truth, that they are trying to help you. That isn't too much, is it? I mean, that isn't too much of an admission for you to make; and in return look at the wonderful life you'll have. Everything will be just as it was before, and you can remember how you loved it that way."

"Let me out of here," I say. "Where are my robes? Where are my disciples? Where are the sacred scrolls and the voice of the Lord? You cannot take all of this away; you will be dealt with very harshly."

"There are no sacred scrolls or followers. All of those people died a long time ago. This is your last chance, Harold; you'd better take it. Who knows what the alternative might be? Who knows what these people might be capable of doing?"

"Magdalene," I say reasonably, "simply because you're a whore does not mean that you always speak the truth. That is a sentimental fallacy."

Her face congests and she spits. I leave it rest there. A celebration. A stigmata.

Conveyed rapidly toward Calvary I get a quick glimpse of the sun appearing in strobes of light as they drive me with heavy kicks toward the goal. The yoke is easy at this time and burdens light; it is a speedy journey that I have made from the court to this place and it will be an easier one yet that I will make to Heaven. A few strokes of the hammer, some pain at the outset: blood, unconsciousness, ascension. Nothing will be easier than this, I think; the getting to this condition has far outweighed in difficulty this final stage. Struggling with the sacred texts has been boring, the miracles sheer propaganda; now at least I will find some consummative task worthy of my talents.

"Faster," they shout, "faster!" and I trot to their urging. *Vite, vite, vite* to that great mountain where I will show them at last that passion has as legitimate a place in this world as any of their policies and procedures and will last; I will convince them as I have already convinced myself a hell of a lot longer. *Brava passione! Brava!*

So they yank me from the restraints and toss me into the center of the huge room to meet the actors. There they all are, there they are: congregants, disciples, Romans, pagans, troopers, all of the paraphernalia and armament of my mission. Edna and the Magdalene are somewhere, but concealed; I have to take their presence on faith. I have had to take everything on faith, and at the end it destroys me; this is my lesson.

"Enough of this!" they cry. Or at least one of them says this; it is very difficult to be sure. The shout must come from an individual but then again it would appear to be a collective shout; they all feel this way. "This is your last chance, your very last chance to cooperate before it becomes very difficult."

"I don't know——"

"*Ne rien,*" they cry. A great clout strikes, knocking me to the floor. It hurts like hell. *Attende bien,* I could have expected nothing less; I have waited for it so very long. Still, one tries to go on. I scramble for purchase, hurl myself upright. My capacity to absorb pain, oh happy surprise, seems limitless after all.

"Listen!" they say, not without a certain sympathy. "Listen, this is very serious business; it cannot go on; the matter of the treatments themselves is at sake. The treatment process is complex and expensive and there are complications, great difficulties——"

I confront them reasonably. I am a reasonable man. I always have been. "I will see you with my Father in Heaven," I say. "That is where I will see you and not a bloody moment sooner."

"Don't you understand? Don't you realize what you are doing? The penalties can be enormous. This must stay controlled; otherwise——"

"Otherwise," I say. "Otherwise you will lose your world and it is well worth losing. I have considered this. I have given it a great deal of thought. Martyrdom is not a posture, not at all; martyrdom springs from the heart. I am absolutely serious; it did not begin that way but that is the way it has ended. I will not yield. I will not apologize. I will not be moved. Thy will be done, *pater noster,* and besides, once you get going you can't just turn it off, if you have any respect, if you have any respect at all."

There is a sound like that of engines. They close upon me. I know exactly what they have in mind but am nonetheless relieved.

It would have had to be this way. "I will not yield," I say to them quietly. "I will not apologize. I will not be moved. This isn't folklore, you know; this is real pain and history."

They tear me apart.

I think of Satan now and am glad that we were able to have that little conversation in the desert the second time, to really get to know one another and to establish a relationship. He was quite right, of course, the old best-loved angel, and I wish I'd had the grace to acknowledge it at the time. We wanted him; we called him into it. It was better to have him outside than in that split and riven part of the self. Oh how I would like to embrace him now.

They leave me on the Cross for forty days and forty nights. On the forty-first the jackals from the south finally gnaw the wood to ash and it collapses. I am carried off, what is left of me, in their jaws and on to further adventures I cannot mention in bowels and partitions of the Earth.

MARTIAN WALKABOUT

F. Gwynplaine MacIntyre

Here's a very different science fiction story about religion . . . in this case that of the Australian aborigines. A native Australian of the future who has failed in his walkabout becomes a member of the space program and goes to Mars—where he leaves the crew to re-attempt his walkabout there, having been called by a voice from the Dreamtime. His experiences are fascinating and wondrous.

(It's only in the latter sense that this story has any plot-similarity to Stanley G. Weinbaum's classic "A Martian Odyssey," whose title it seemingly parodies.)

You may wonder why a man with the name F. Gwynplaine MacIntyre would write a story about native Australian religion. Answer: MacIntyre was born in Scotland but was raised in the Australian outback. He currently spends his time commuting between his home in Wales and his publishers in New York, a procedure which is exhausting to say the least. Somewhere in there, he finds time to edit *Orion*, a new combination sf magazine and parapsychology journal.

There are two edges to reality, son of my son, each as different from the other as night is from day. There is the Wakingworld, and then there is the Dreamtime. In the Dreamtime all times and all places are one, my child, and every corner of the universe touches every other. And remember, my child, that when the Dreamtime commands, then you must obey. For it is in the Dreamtime that we will dance among the stars. . . .

When Kundekundeka was five, his grandfather Ramijirring told him legends of the Dreamtime and beyond. On a summer night, while the tribe gathered in the ritual of *corroboree,* while the moon glistened mystically over the waters of the distant billabong, and while the silver airships of the Men-with-White-Skins drifted overhead, Ramijirring spoke.

He told of Kunapipi, the feathered she-serpent of the far-distant Dreamtime, who created men from the grass and women from the sand and bade them multiply across the desert outback. He told of Jangardbla, the red-haired warrior who slew a hundred enemies with his strong left hand, and who conquered the beast-men of Looritcha and he told of the people *Wandjina,* who came from the stars and went back to them, in the days of our grandfathers' grandfathers, and who wore lightning in their hair. All this was many rains ago, in the Big Walktime when the coolibah groves breathed magic, and the Bunyip sang, and the enchanted *Miruru* spirits rode the high wind. But then the Men-with-White-Skins came, and brought their guns and horses and fences, and said this place Woombalooru was now part of some land called Australia, and on that day the magic left Woombalooru forever.

When Kundekundeka was nine, his grandfather Ramijirring taught him how to play the wooden drum and the tree-flute, and then when Kundekundeka had mastered these his grandfather taught him to play the most beautiful instrument of all; the didjeridoo. Ten feet long and as thick as a man's arm it was, but Kundekundeka never forgot how it sang silver notes when his grandfather breathed life into it:

OOdaOOdaOOdadadaOOROOdadaOOROOdaah ... !

When Kundekundeka was twelve, the time came to prepare for his entry into manhood. His grandfather Ramijirring taught him how to use the woomera and the spear and the knife. He taught him how to stalk game, how to bring down the giant red *gang'garu* with one throw of the curved-stick boonang, and how to make the boonang fly back to his hand if he missed. And he taught him how to use the bull-roarer, the flat stick on a thong that could sing to the spirits and let them know that the hunting was good.

"Always remember, son of my son," Ramijirring would say, "that you are a member of the tribe Woombalooru, the most noble of nations. And we the tribe Woombalooru are the favoured ones, for we are watched over by the spirits who dwell in mighty Oolooru, the Stone-from-the-Sky. Sacred is Oolooru above all else."

Oftentimes, on a steaming summer night while the men of the tribe did their snake-dance to the throb of the didjeridoo, young Kundekundeka could see Oolooru towering on the desert horizon. He asked his aged grandfather why the Woombalooru spent their days wandering, instead of living peacefully in the shade of Oolooru.

"Many rains ago," the old man whispered in the light of the flickering fire, "mighty Oolooru fell out of the heavens, fell between the stars and landed in this place. Oolooru Stone-from-Sky is the sacred place of our tribe Woombalooru.

"Nowadays no man among us goes there, but in my day Oolooru was home. Shall I tell you what the place was like, child? Rock and sand and little else but if you can climb the rocky peaks of Oolooru as I did once, aye, and reach the very centre of the crest you shall find the Valley of Oolooru. And there grow trees and birds and grasses, and the waters are sweet. In the Valley of Oolooru, son of my son, far away from mortal eyes."

Kundekundeka was silent, and for a moment he sat and listened to the throb of the didjeridoo:

OOdaOOdaOOdadadaOOROOdadaOOROOdaah . . . !

"But why have we wandered from Oolooru, grandfather? Why may we never see the Valley of Oolooru?"

"Because the Men-with-White-Skins came with their jeeps and their trucks," said Ramijirring, "with their dollars and their sunglasses and their Coca-Cola stands and their Polaroid cameras and they chased us away from our homeland Oolooru." The old man's eyes moistened as he spoke. "They call the place Ayers Rock now, I think."

Kundekundeka was silent, and in the stillness of night the didjeridoo played more loudly.

When Kundekundeka was fourteen he became a man. Two Woombalooru tribesmen held him down while the tribe Doctor Man performed the circumcision with a Wilkinson Sword razor blade. Kundekundeka was determined not to cry out during the ordeal, lest he shame the spirits of mighty Oolooru. But the pain was too great and he screamed. Afterwards, he crept alone to a place where none could see him behold Oolooru on the twilight horizon. "I have been unworthy, Oolooru," he whispered to the towering monolith. "but I shall make it up to you, in the time of walkabout."

And the huge sandstone form heard him, and turned from orange to purple and back again, to show that it understood.

The day of walkabout arrived, and Kundekundeka and each of the other young males stood proud and erect as the elders addressed them. Each youth stood, some naked and some with loincloth and one in Levi dungarees, and took the weapon of his choosing. Kundekundeka chose the knife, and took a bull-roarer as well so the spirits would know if his hunting was good.

He struck out towards the south with two other lads. After three miles he left them and began travelling east, towards Oolooru Stone-from-the-Sky.

In the distance he suddenly heard a didjeridoo playing, mocking him with its notes, and he froze: was this a good omen or bad? He squinted into the eastern sky towards Oolooru, and at that instant the angry red monolith turned a friendly shade of yellow as the sun climbed over its peak.

A good omen. Kundekundeka gripped the knife in his teeth and broke into a run towards the peak. Towards the Valley of Oolooru, where the waters were sweet. And if the Valley was there, then he, Kundekundeka, was going to find it.

"Ayers Rock," said the tour guide, "one single massive sandstone, the largest rock to be found anywhere on Earth. Over a thousand feet high, friends, and five miles round at the base. Why, it covers more ground than the city of London!"

A fat lady held up her hand. "But aren't there aborigines living here? I thought they were living on the peak of the rock."

"Not quite, mum," said the tour guide as flashcubes popped. "Years ago the abos lived here, yes, but they're gone. When we get a bit farther on you'll see paintings on the rock, aboriginal paintings where they mix the paint with blood. Some sort of mumbo-jumbo ritual, I'll be bound. Every so often some abo would try to freshen up the paintings with a bit of his own blood supply, and we had to chase them away."

A skinny man with absolutely no hair spoke up. "Why is this place so sacred to the aborigines, anyway?"

"The abos believe the rock fell out of the sky many years ago and landed here. All I can say is I'm glad I wasn't standing there when it happened."

In the shadows of the trees Kundekundeka watched. It was late afternoon by now; he wanted to reach the Valley of Oolooru before moonrise. Kundekundeka edged warily towards the superhighway that ran between him and Oolooru; he had never seen asphalt before and was sure it would feel horribly alien.

His foot touched the road, and at that instant he heard the distant drone of a didjeridoo: *OOdaOOda*. Kundekundeka jumped back as if he'd been stabbed. Overhead, mighty Oolooru suddenly turned bright magenta.

It was too late to turn back. There were no white men

in sight now. Kundekundeka took a deep breath, stuck his knife between powerful jaws and raced across the roadway towards the sandstone monolith. A mighty leap, black fingers scrabbling for a grip, and then he was up. He, Kundekundeka, son of the Woombalooru, had returned to the home of his people!

OOdaOOdaOOdadadaOOROOdadaOOROOdaah . . . !

He climbed. Even in the afternoon that was turning to evening it was blistering hot, and the sweat rolled off Kundekundeka in rivulets. At last he came to a flat place three hundred feet up, and rested for a time. He was still gasping for breath when he heard footsteps behind him.

The old man was white, but the sun had made him nearly as bronze as Kundekundeka. The wary youth was too exhausted to stand as the white man came over.

"You speak English, fella?"

Kundekundeka remained silent.

"Not to worry mate; I'm dinkum. My name's Lofty. You get lost or something?"

Kundekundeka sat up with an effort. His knife was lying on the ground beside his hand and he wondered how to pick it up without provoking an attack. These white men had guns . . .

Lofty took a step towards him, saw the youth tense, and stayed where he was. "Look, cobber, I live on this rock. Government pays me, y'know. If you're lost I can help you get home but if you're huntin' budgeree you'll have to do it someplace else. So what's it to be?"

Off in the distance a whine, a thrum of gathering power. Kundekundeka looked and saw some strange sort of flying machine coming towards him, parallel to the wall of Oolooru. He reached for the knife and gripped it hard.

"That's just the whirlybird, mate. You want a ride back down? Be somethin' to tell your brothers and sisters about, over the . . ."

Kundekundeka broke into a run, slipping past the man Lofty and on up the slope toward the crest. A bit of scrub here, some shrubbery there springing up from the sandstone; he used whatever cover he could find on his rush to reach the Valley of Oolooru. Helter-skelter he ran, with the sweat pouring out of his flesh and the blood vessels pounding in his eardrums . . .

OOdaOOdaOOdadadaOOROOdadaOOROOdaah . . . !

A shadow dropped out of the sky, hovering over him like some winged carrion-eater, and Kundekundeka looked up and saw the flying machine. He screeched in dismay and ran faster, ducked beneath an overhang where the flying machine could not follow, and raced upwards toward the crest of Oolooru while the didjeridoo went mad inside his brain . . .

OOdaOOdaOOROOdada . . . !

Another hundred feet, another hundred feet. He risked a glance backwards and saw the white man Lofty puffing along right behind him. "Hi! Stop there, you! We won't hurt you, sonny, but you've got to get off this bloomin' rock!"

"Oolooru!" gasped Kundekundeka as he ran. A face flashed past him, red and blue it was with much yellow, and even as he ran Kundekundeka recognised it: the face of the *Wandjina*, the sky-beings, painted on the edge of the rock one night centuries past. He was getting close to the Valley of Oolooru!

OOdaOOdaOOROOdada . . . !

The flying machine rushed down upon him. Kundekundeka turned and dodged, and then in the last fading glow of desert twilight he scrambled to the top of the crest and looked down to see what lay beyond.

The Valley of Oolooru!

The flying machine was right over him now, and the boy scrambled away, slipping into the undergrowth and towards the lush green valley that beckoned beneath him. Another few steps, another few steps, *OOdaOOda*, and then on the very edge of the mystic valley white fingers gripped him and white hands pinioned his arms, and then they were dragging him up the hillside towards the flying machine.

"Oolooru!" sobbed Kundekundeka, but the valley was gone.

"Crazy abos," grunted Lofty. "Always tryin' to do their mumbo-jumbo on the bleedin' rock. Hi, Charlie, this darkie's a right wild 'un."

The last thing Kundekundeka saw as they dragged him away was the sky full of stars, and suddenly for no reason at all he remembered his grandfather's tales of the *Wandjina*, who came from the stars and went back to them, in the days beyond the Dreamtime. For a long moment he wondered which of those tiny lights in the sky was the *Wandjina* homeland, and then suddenly nothing mattered anymore.

OOdaOOdaOOdadadaOOROOdadaOOROOdaah . . . !

"You want to *what?*" screeched Arnstein. After ten years in the Service he'd have sworn that nothing could surprise him anymore, but right now he was getting the surprise of his career.

"I want to stay behind," repeated the brown-skinned crewman. "Here on Mars, with just a spear and a knife. The ship can get back to Earth without me, and there'll be another ship coming for me in three months' time."

"You're crazy," said the commander. "I'd have booted you out of the Service long since if you weren't the best astrogator I've ever seen. What's this walkabout nonsense, anyway?"

Johnny Kundekundeka Longfellow, which was the name they'd saddled him with when he'd joined the Service, drew himself up to full height. "The walkabout is one of the sacred rituals of Woombalooru. It is one man's attempt to triumph over a hostile environment. When a boy becomes a man he sets out alone in the desert. If he comes back alive he has proven worthy of manhood. If not, well . . ."

Arnstein grunted. "And you figured you'd wait until you got to Mars to walkabout, hey?"

"No, sir; I did my walkabout on Earth, but I failed and was brought home by the white men in disgrace. I could not face my Woombalooru brothers and went to live among the white men."

Arnstein switched on the ventilator so he could light his pipe. Outside the porthole he could see a team of surveyors returning to the ship, faces masked by breathing apparatus, bodies glowing an eerie red in the light of the far-off volcano Olympus Mons on the Martian horizon. "I still don't see why you're so eager to commit suicide," he said.

"Sir, are you familiar with the ways of Woombalooru? Our most sacred possession is the Dreamtime, the other side of reality that we journey to in sleep. We hold our dreams and our nightmares to be of vital importance."

Commander Arnstein sucked hard on his pipe. "So?"

"Most dreams, commander, are omens of a sort: warnings or predictions of some major event. So says Woombalooru lore. But last night, sir, last night breathing Martian air through Terran converters, I had a dream that took the form of a *command*." Arnstein was silent and Kundekundeka continued. "The dream commanded me to do walkabout again, to succeed where before I had failed. I *must* do walkabout on Mars."

"Do people in your tribe who flunk walkabout first time generally get a second chance?" Arnstein wanted to know.

"Never, sir. It has never been done. But neither has a son of Woombalooru trod the Martian sands before. Last night the Dreamtime told me that I must not fail my second walkabout because there will be no hope of rescue; after this ship leaves without me tomorrow I'll be alone on this planet until the next expedition lands in three months."

"Let me get this straight," said the commander. The surveying team was aboard by now; he'd better end this discussion fast if he didn't want to miss chow. "You want me to dump you butt-naked on Mars with no supplies and no chance of rescue? And you're doing this because a *dream* told you to?"

Kundekundeka nodded. "It sounds foolish to you, I know. But when the Dreamtime commands, the Woombalooru obey. I do not believe I would receive a dream of this nature unless there were some vital purpose behind it. That is my religion. I could point out characteristics of your own religion that seem just as foolish to . . ."

"Damn it, religion is one thing, but you're talking about *suicide!* Request denied, Longfellow. Dismissed!"

Johnny Kundekundeka Longfellow went to the hatchway and turned. "When the Dreamtime commands, then the Woombalooru obey. This ship leaves tomorrow morning, commander. I will not be on board."

"You'll be on board and at your post if I have to *nail* you to it!" growled Arnstein. "You're the only astrogations man aboard I can trust to get this crate back to Earth, and I'll be damned if I leave you here on Mars and have your death on *my* Service record. Request denied, denied, and denied once again! Dis-*missed!*"

These crazy foreigners, Arnstein thought as he made his way down to mess. Oh well, maybe there'll be pie for dessert . . .

Kundekundeka made one last check of the breathing

apparatus and then fitted the respirator over his mouth and nose. He'd gone through quite a moral struggle and finally decided the oxygen device would not violate the basic strictures of walkabout. In the walkabout on Earth such a device would have been forbidden, of course, but on Earth it would have been unnecessary.

He shrugged himself into the jumpsuit and zipped it up; one more item that was vital to survival in the Martian climate. But from here on it was strictly back-to-nature: no radio, no medical supplies, and he'd have to hunt for his water and food. Provided there *was* life on Mars that qualified as food, of course; so far the expedition hadn't found any. But surely the spirits of the Dreamtime would provide.

He ripped loose the emergency survival kit that was sewn into the jumpsuit's lining and flung it aside, then picked up the survival kit of the Woombalooru: a spear and a knife. He hefted the curved-stick boonang (which the white men insisted on calling a *boomerang*), and wondered if it would return to his hand as it did on Earth. He took it along.

In the silence of his cabin the commander's words came back to him, and for a moment Kundekundeka thought that perhaps Arnstein was right: he *was* committing suicide. But no, that was ridiculous; had not the Dreamtime counseled him wisely all his life? Why should it betray him now?

Silently, as befit a Woombalooru stalker, he slipped along down the passageway to the airlock. MacDonald was on duty and Kundekundeka strode up jovially and waved to the older man.

"Got a little treat here, Mack." Johnny Kundekundeka Longfellow grinned broadly and held up two frosty cans of Foster's Lager that he'd bartered out of the mess officer. "Here, have a drink." He pressed one can into his friend's hand, then held up the other can and winked. "Me, I think I'll enjoy this outside. Sip a little beer and admire the view, eh?"

"Fine by me, Johnny." MacDonald activated the airlock mechano and then stopped. "Hey, what's with the spear, friend?"

"Eh? Oh, just thought I'd get in a little target practice before lights-out." The brown man grinned. "Who knows?

Say, Mack, sing out my name at roll call tomorrow, will you? I'd like to get a little extra sack time."

"Sure thing, Johnny. Just be back before we shove off tomorrow morning," MacDonald opened the can of beer he'd been given and raised it to his lips. "Hey, wouldn't it be funny if you missed the boat and had to wait three whole months for the next one?"

The Martian wind bit hard into his face and Kundekundeka hunched over and turned up the respirator. It suddenly occurred to him that he ought to go back and get a spare power pack just in case the apparatus didn't have enough juice for the whole three months . . . No, on second thought he'd have to take that chance; he was supposed to survive the walkabout on Woombalooru wits, not white men's hardware.

Besides, wasn't it preordained that he *had* to survive? The Dreamtime would never have told him to do walkabout in this unearthly place without some definite reason. And when the Dreamtime speaks to a son of Woombalooru, he *must* obey.

In the low Martian gravity a hundred yards was like nothing, and with long loping strides Kundekundeka had soon left the ship far behind. The next expedition from Earth would be landing a few hundred miles to the north, and of course the Southern Cross that he'd always used as a pathfinding aid on Earth would be useless here even if he could find it (which he couldn't). But the ancient aboriginal instincts were strong in his Woombalooru soul, and in no time Kundekundeka had plotted out a course to the north. Already the ship from Earth was out of sight in the distance behind him . . .

OOdaOOdaOOROOdada . . .

Kundekundeka stopped dead in his tracks and felt the flesh crawl at the back of his neck. The sound of the didjeridoo was unmistakable . . . and it was coming from the east.

OOdadadaOOROOdaah . . . !

As if in a trance he took a step towards the sound, then recovered his senses and turned to the north, then back again to the south. What was wrong? What was he doing out here anyway? The ship! Get back to the ship before they leave without you! This was crazy, sneaking out here like this *OOdaOOda* go north! No, south, damn it!

Noise in my *OOda* east, in the *OOdaOOda* look at *OO-ROOdadaOOROOdada* . . .

The sound was undeniable, cutting into his brain like a knife, throbbing until he thought his eardrums would split. *OOdaOOda.* Kundekundeka turned and ran, pounded hard through the red dust of Mars until he suddenly stopped and cried out:

"Oolooru!"

It was there, rising straight up from the flat Martian desert towards the sky: the single red towering monolith that he knew, that he'd known, that his grandfather Ramijirring had whispered tales of in the flickering firelight of evening . . .

"Oolooru!"

It was the same, it was the exact same hulking silhouette: every crevice and peak was the same, the same shape that he'd known back on Earth. Exactly the same in every possible way except that it was a hundred million miles from where it ought to be . . .

How?

OOdaOOdaOOROOdada . . .

It was too late to go back. It was too late to do anything except heed the summons of the Dreamtime. He felt a suffocating sensation, tore the white man's clothing from his body and let his brown skin breathe free. He gripped his spear in one hand and his knife in the other and stood tall and erect. He, Kundekundeka, son of the tribe Woombalooru, had returned to Oolooru at last!

OOdaOOdaOOROOdada . . .

He tore the respirator from his face and breathed pure desert air, filled his lungs with its tang. Then he flung aside his spear, stuck his knife between powerful jaws and raced towards the sandstone monolith. A mighty leap, black fingers scrabbling for a grip, and then he was up.

OOdaOOdaOOdadadaOOROOdadaOOROOdaah . . . !

He climbed. In the gravity of Mars he practically flew up the hard rock face, bare feet and fingers soaring effortlessly up the sandstone wall, until at last he came to a flat place nine hundred feet up, and rested although he needed no rest. The call of the didjeridoo was louder now, in the back of his brain *OOdaOOda* . . .

Off in the distance a whine, a thrum of gathering power. Kundekundeka looked and saw some strange sort of flying machine coming toward him, some manner of . . . No! The rocket sled from the ship! They'd found out he was missing and now they were coming after him! He reached for the knife and gripped it hard.

OOdaOOdaOOROOdada . . .

The sound jarred him back to his senses. What the hell was he doing here? What was he doing on some Martian mountain, freezing his butt without a jumpsuit, trying to breathe this crazy pink Martian air with no respirator? He should have dropped dead by now!

OOdadadaOOROOdaah . . . !

And if that was a didjeridoo he heard, coming down from the peak of this rock that looked just like Oolooru, if that was a didjeridoo, then who was *playing* it?

OOda! OOda! OOdadada!

Kundekundeka broke into a run, scrambling on up the slope towards the crest. A bit of scrub here, some shrub *. . . shrubs on Mars? No such thing!* on his rush to reach the Valley of Oolooru that he instinctively knew was there, that *had* to be there. Helter-skelter he ran, with the sweat pouring out of his flesh and the blood vessels pounding in his eardrums . . .

OOdaOOdaOOdadadaOOROOdadaOOROOdaah . . . !

A shadow dropped out of the Martian sky, hanging over him like some carrion-eating rocket sled, and Kundekundeka looked up and saw the helicopter (no that's back on Earth) I mean flying machine. He screeched in dismay and ran faster up the sloping rock face towards the crest of Oolooru while the didjeridoo went mad inside his brain . . .

OOdaOOdaOOROOdada . . .
OOdaOOdaOOROOdada . . .

"Oolooru!" gasped Kundekundeka as he ran. The flying machine rushed down upon him, its streamlined hull gleaming in the crimson aurora of its jets. He turned and dodged and in the first dawning glow of Martian sunrise he scrambled to the top of the crest, eleven hundred feet above the surface of the planet, and looked down to see what lay beyond.

OOROOdadaOOROOdada . . .

The ground collapsed beneath him, and Kundekundeka fell, hustling down in a shower of sandstone. Something hard struck his skull and he lay moaning, trying to fathom where he could possibly be.

Child of the Woombalooru, child of the coolibah desert . . .

A cavern . . . light, strange light coming from everywhere at once and from no place in particular. A *fading* light, a light about to die. Kundekundeka sniffed; the air was like Earth air but mustier, and the cavern was warm. The gravity was wrong too; if anything, a little heavier than on Earth. . . .

Child of the Woombalooru, hear me. . . .

Words in his head. Through haggard eyes, Kundekundeka found the source of the light: an altar, an elevation in the centre of the chamber. A withered figure lying calmly on the hard stone surface, wizened fingers outstretched and sightless eyes gazing longingly towards the stars. . .

Kundekundeka, son of the tribe Woombalooru, hear my words . . .

Dazed, confused, the brown man staggered towards the figure on the slab. Body like a man, yet not a man; feet and fingers incredibly old with the life fading out of them. Face like a . . . Kundekundeka knew that face. He'd looked upon it a hundred times in the cavern paintings of his homeland, glimpsed it fleetingly on the rock walls of mighty Oolooru Stone-from-the-Sky. His grandfather Ramijirring had whispered the ancient tales to him, of how the *Wandjina* came from the stars and went back to them, in the days beyond the Dreamtime. And now somehow Kundekundeka knew, knew without asking, that this was the very last of the ancient *Wandjina* that lay silent before him.

Hear my words, Kundekundeka, for my time here is short . . .

Wordless, the brown man huddled in the half-light at the foot of the slab.

We were many once and mighty, my people Wandjina. On a thousand thousand worlds we made our homes, observing life, watching a thousand races flourish. . . . And one such race was your own, my child: the Woombalooru.

"Was it you who summoned me to this place?" Kundekundeka whispered.

Yes. I detected Woombalooru life-strength when first you came to this world. The means by which I planted the dream in your mind, by which I enabled you to survive without oxygen on the high Martian plain, by which

*control the climate in this chamber and made this very
mountain itself assume the likeness of blessed Oolooru in
our eyes . . . these are all quite simple things for a race
as old as mine, although they required an exertion of
so much of my fast-dwindling life-strength that I fear I
can remain but little longer . . .*

"You brought me here . . . Why?"

*For selfish reasons, I fear: I am dying and would look
upon Earth-child life once again.* The words in Kundekundeka's head were growing fainter every moment. *And
now the time approaches when I must depart . . .*

"But wait!" pleaded Kundekundeka. "You have
touched the stars, your mind must contain great wisdom
and knowledge. My people, the people of Earth, are still
taking our first steps into space. And we have famines and
disease and war and hate and madness. Can't you please,
please, tell me how my race can stop these . . ."

"Fool!" cried the withered voice in his mind, fairly
weeping with rage. *Man, man, foolish little mortal man.
Do you think me a god, who can solve your race's troubles with a single cosmic Answer?*

Kundekundeka shivered in coldness and fear. "But
there must be an Answer, a way to end forever death and
poverty and ignorance and . . ."

*Man, man, Earth-child, shall I tell you why my people
Wandjina have travelled to a thousand thousand worlds?
We were searching for that very same Answer! For a million aeons it has eluded us. Perhaps if, instead of looking
outward, to the heavens, we had looked inward, sought
the Answer within ourselves . . .*

Kundekundeka was silent.

But this much have I learned, said the whisper, and
then the words came Kundekundeka heard them not in
his head but in every fibre of his being:

*You must never fail to heed the summons of the
Dreamtime, for of all the creatures of Earth, only the
man-child and woman-child can truly dream. And it is
only the dreamers who can reach out to touch the stars . . .*

Harsh wind, a blast of cold Martian air on his face.
Kundekundeka started in fear and found himself naked
with the air getting colder and more alien every moment.

"Johnny! You in there? Where in . . . Jesus! Get that

blanket in here, will you?" In the thickening haze Johnny Kundekundeka Longfellow made out the features of MacDonald, squinting out from behind a respirator. A blanket was thrown over Kundekundeka from somewhere and without a moment's hesitation MacDonald tore the respirator from his own face and pressed it over the other man's mouth and nose.

Commander Arnstein appeared, mad as hell. "Longfellow, you idiot, I'm going to see you court-martialed for this if it takes from now till . . ."

"With all due respect, commander, shut your trap," growled MacDonald. "Don't you see where we are? A stone chamber, carved out of the rock. Some kind of altar over there. It's an *archaeological find*, man; life on Mars, and Johnny here found it! He'll be a hero once we get back to Earth, and . . ."

Kundekundeka heard no more. Through half-closed eyes he saw a bit of dust on the cold stone slab, a bit of dust that had once been something very like a man and now was whirling away in the shrill Martian wind. And completely exhausted now, Kundekundeka left the World of Waking and journeyed across the edge of reality to the Dreamtime. For it was in the Dreamtime that he would dance among the stars. . . .

SLOW MUSIC

James Tiptree, Jr.

James Tiptree, Jr., is a writer of powerful,
thought-provoking stories, and the present
one is a superb example. Set on a future
Earth that has been visited by mysterious
aliens offering immortality to everyone who
will go away with them, this is the story of
a young man and woman who are apparently the only humans who chose to remain
on Earth. They cannot, by themselves, maintain the technology of the past, but the
world still holds sufficient artifacts and re-
sources to enable them to survive . . . and
to begin to repopulate the planet. Still,
there are debts to be paid to their parents. . . .

"James Tiptree, Jr." is the primary pen-
name of Alice B. Sheldon, a research
psychologist now "retired" to full-time
writing; she has also written several stories
under the name "Raccoona Sheldon." She
has won two Nebula Awards and two Hugo
Awards, for "The Girl Who Was Plugged
In," "Houston, Houston, Do You Read?"
(a double award winner) and "Love Is the
Plan the Plan Is Death."

*Caoilte tossing his burning hair
and Niamh calling "Away, come away;
Empty your heart of its mortal dream.
... We come between man and the deed of his hand,
We come between him and the hope of his heart."*
—W. B. Yeats

LIGHTS CAME ON AS JAKKO WALKED DOWN
the lawn past the house; elegantly concealed spots and
floods which made the night into a great intimate room.
Overhead the big conifers formed a furry nave drooping
toward the black lake below the bluff ahead. This had
been a beloved home, he saw; every luxurious device was
subdued to preserve the beauty of the forested shore. He
walked on a carpet of violets and mosses, in his hand the
map that had guided him here from the city.

It was the stillness before dawn. A long-winged night-
bird swirled in to catch a last moth in the dome of light.
Before him shone a bright spear point. Jakko saw it was
the phosphorescent tip of a mast against the stars. He
went down velvety steps to find a small sailboat floating at
the dock like a silver leaf reflected on a dark mirror.

In silence he stepped on board, touched the mast.

A gossamer sail spread its fan, the mooring parted
soundlessly. The dawn breeze barely filled the sail, but
the craft moved smoothly out, leaving a glassy line of
wake. Jakko half-poised to jump; he knew nothing of such

376

play-toys, he should go back and find another boat. As he did so, the shore lights went out, leaving him in darkness. He turned and saw Regulus rising ahead where the channel must be. Still, this was not the craft for him. He tugged at the tiller and sail, meaning to turn it back.

But the little boat ran smoothly on, and then he noticed the lights of a small computer glowing by the mast. He relaxed; this was no toy, the boat was fully programmed and he could guess what the course must be. He stood examining the sky, a statue-man gliding across reflected night.

The eastern horizon changed, veiled its stars as he neared it. He could see the channel now, a silvery cut straight ahead between dark banks. The boat ran over glittering shallows where something splashed hugely, and headed into the shining lane. As it did so, all silver changed to lead and the stars were gone. Day was coming. A great pearl-coloured blush spread upward before him, developed bands of lavender and rays of coral-gold fire melting to green iridescence overhead. The boat was now gliding on a ribbon of fiery light between black silhouetted banks. Jakko looked back and saw dazzling cloud-cities heaped behind him in the west. The vast imminence of sunrise. He sighed aloud.

He understood that all this demonstration of glory was nothing but the effects of dust and vapour in the thin skin of air around a small planet, whereon he crawled wingless. No vastness brooded; the planet was merely turning with him into the rays of its mediocre primary. His family, everyone, knew that on the River he would encounter the Galaxy itself in glory. Suns beyond count, magnificence to which this was nothing. And yet—and yet to him this was not nothing. It was intimately his, man-sized. He made an ambiguous sound in his throat. He resented the trivialization of this beauty, and he resented being moved by it. So he passed along, idly holding the sail-rope like a man leashing the living wind, his face troubled and very young.

The little craft ran on unerringly, threading the winding sheen of the canal. As the sun rose, Jakko began to hear a faint drone ahead. The sea-surf. He thought of the persons who must have made this voyage before him: the ship's family, savouring their final days of mortality. A happy voyage, a picnic. The thought reminded him that he was hungry; the last groundcar's synthesizer had been faulty.

He tied the rope and searched. The boat had replenished its water, but there was only one food-bar. Jakko lay down in the cushioned well and ate and drank comfortably, while the sky turned turquoise and then cobalt. Presently they emerged into an enormous lagoon and began to run south between low islands. Jakko trailed his hand and tasted brackish salt. When the boat turned east again and made for a seaward opening, he became doubly certain. The craft was programmed for the River, like almost everything else on the world he knew.

Sure enough, the tiny bark ran through an inlet and straight out into the chop beyond a long beach, extruded outriggers, and passed like a cork over the reef-foam onto the deep green swells beyond. Here it pitched once and steadied; Jakko guessed it had thrust down a keel. Then it turned south and began to run along outside the reef, steady as a knifecut with the wind on its quarter. Going Riverward for sure. The nearest River-place was here called Vidalita or Beata, or sometimes Falaz, meaning Illusion. It was far south and inland. Jakko guessed they were making for a landing where a moveway met the sea. He still had time to think, to struggle with the trouble under his mind.

But as the sun turned the boat into a trim white-gold bird flying over green transparency, Jakko's eyes closed and he slept, protected by invisible deflectors from the bow-spray. Once he opened his eyes and saw a painted fish tearing along magically in the standing wave below his head. He smiled and slept again, dreaming of a great wave dying, a wave that was a many-headed beast. His face became sad and his lips moved soundlessly, as if repeating. "No . . . no . . ."

When he woke they were sailing quite close by a long bluff on his right. In the cliff ahead was a big white building or tower, only a little ruined. Suddenly he caught sight of a figure moving on the beach before it. A living human? He jumped up to look. He had not seen a strange human person in many years.

Yes—it was a live person, strangely colored gold and black. He waved wildly.

The person on the beach slowly raised an arm.

Alight with excitement, Jakko switched off the computer and grabbed the rudder and sail. The line of reef-surf seemed open here. He turned the boat shoreward, riding on a big swell. But the wave left him. He veered erratically, and the surf behind broached into the boat, overturning it and throwing him out. He knew how to swim; he surfaced and struck out strongly for the shore, spluttering brine. Presently he was wading out onto the white beach, a short, strongly-built, reddened young male person with pale hair and water-blue eyes.

The stranger was walking hesitantly toward him. Jakko saw it was a thin, dark-skinned girl wearing a curious netted hat. Her body was wrapped in orange silk and she carried heavy gloves in one hand. Three nervous moon-dogs followed her. He began turning water out of his shorts pockets as she came up.

"Your . . . boat," she said in the language of that time. Her voice was low and uncertain.

They both turned to look at the confused place by the reef where the sailboat floated half-submerged.

"I turned it off. The computer." His words came jerkily, too; they were both unused to speech.

"It will come ashore down there." She pointed, still studying him in a wary, preoccupied way. She was much smaller than he. "Why did you turn? Aren't you going to the River?"

"No." He coughed. "Well, yes, in a way. My father wants me to say goodbye. They left while I was travelling."

"You're not . . . ready?"

"No. I don't—" He broke off. "Are you staying alone here?"

"Yes. I'm not going either."

They stood awkwardly in the sea-wind. Jakko noticed that the three moondogs were lined up single file, tiptoeing upwind toward him with their eyes closed, sniffing. They were not, of course, from the moon, but they looked it, being white and oddly shaped.

"It's a treat for them," the girl said. "Something different." Her voice was stronger now. After a pause she added, "You can stay here for awhile if you want. I'll show you but I have to finish my work first."

"Thank you," he remembered to say.

As they climbed steps cut in the bluff Jakko asked, "What are you working at?"

":Oh, everything. Right now it's bees."

"Bees!" he marvelled. "They made what—honey? I thought they were all gone."

"I have a lot of old things." She kept glancing at him intently as they climbed. "Are you quite healthy?"

"Oh yes. Why not? I'm all alpha so far as I know. Everybody is."

"Was," she corrected. "Here are my bee-skeps."

They came around a low wall and stopped by five small wicker huts. A buzzing insect whizzed by Jakko's face, coming from some feathery shrubs. He saw that the bloom-tipped foliage was alive with the golden humming things. Recalling that they could sting, he stepped back.

"You better go around the other way." She pointed. "They might hurt a stranger." She pulled her veil down, hiding her face. Just as he turned away, she added, "I thought you might impregnate me."

He wheeled back, not really able to react because of the distracting bees. "But isn't that terribly complicated?"

"I don't think so. I have the pills." She pulled on her gloves.

"Yes, the pills. I know." He frowned. "But you'd have to stay, I mean one just can't—"

"I know that. I have to do my bees now. We can talk later."

"Of course." He started away and suddenly turned back.

"Look!" He didn't know her name. "You, look!"

"What?" She was a strange little figure, black and orange with huge hands and a big veil-muffled head. "What?"

"I felt it. Just then, desire. Can't you see?"

They both gazed at his wet shorts.

"I guess not," he said finally. "But I felt it, I swear. Sexual desire."

She pushed back her veil, frowning. "It will stay, won't it? Or come back? This isn't a very good place. I mean, the bees. And it's no use without the pills."

"That's so."

He went away then, walking carefully because of the tension around his pubic bone. Like a keel, snug and tight. His whole body felt reorganized. It had been years since he'd felt flashes like that, not since he was fifteen at least. Most people never did. It was variously thought to be because of the River, or from their parents' surviving the Poison Centuries, or because the general alpha strain was so forebrain-dominant. It gave him an archaic, secret pride. Maybe he was a throwback.

He passed under cool archways, and found himself in a green, protected place behind the seaward wall. A garden, he saw, looking round surprised at clumps of large tied-up fruiting plants, peculiar trees with green balls at their tops, disorderly rows of rather unaesthetic greenery. Tentatively he identified tomatoes, peppers, a feathery leaf which he thought had an edible root. A utilitarian planting. His uncle had once amused the family by doing something of the sort, but not on this scale. Jakko shook his head.

In the center of the garden stood a round stone coping with a primitive apparatus on top. He walked over and looked down. Water, a bucket on a rope. Then he saw that there was also an ordinary tap. He opened it and drank, looking at the odd implements leaning on the coping. Earth-tools. He did not really want to think about what the strange woman had said.

A shadow moved by his foot. The largest moondog had come quite close, inhaling dreamily. "Hello," he said to it. Some of these dogs could talk a little. This one opened its eyes wide but said nothing.

He stared about, wiping his mouth, feeling his clothes almost dry now in the hot sun. On three sides the garden was surrounded by arcades; above him the ruined side was a square cracked masonry tower with no roof. A large place, whatever it was. He walked into the shade of the nearest arcade, which turned out to be littered with a myriad of disassembled or partly assembled objects: tools, containers, who knew what. Her "work?" The place felt strange, vibrant and busy. He realised he had entered only empty houses on his year-long journey. This one was alive, lived-in. Messy. It hummed like the bee-skeps. He turned down a cool corridor, looking into rooms piled with more stuff. In one, three white animals he couldn't identify were asleep in a heap of cloth on a bed. They moved their ears at him like big pale shells but did not awaken.

He heard staccato noises and came out into another courtyard where plump birds walked with jerking heads. "Chickens!" he decided, delighted by the irrational variety of this place. He went from there into a large room with windows on the sea, and heard a door close.

It was the woman, or girl, coming to him, holding her hat and gloves. Her hair was a dark curly cap, her head elegantly small; an effect he had always admired. He remembered something to say.

"I'm called Jakko. What's your name?"

"Jakko." She tasted the sound. "Hello, Jakko. I'm Peachthief." She smiled very briefly, entirely changing her face.

"Peachthief." On impulse he moved toward her, holding out his hands. She tucked her bundle under her arm and took both of his. They stood like that a moment, not quite looking at each other. Jakko felt excited. Not sexually, but more as if the air was electrically charged.

"Well." She took her hands away and began unwrapping a leafy wad. "I brought a honeycomb even if it isn't quite ready." She showed him a sticky-looking frame with two dead bees on it. "Come on."

She walked rapidly out into another corridor and entered a shiny room he thought might be a laboratory.

"My food-room," she told him. Again Jakko was amazed. There stood a synthesizer, to be sure, but beside it were shelves full of pots and bags and jars and containers of all descriptions. Unknown implements lay about and there was a fireplace which had been partly sealed up. Bunches of plant-parts hung from racks overhead. He identified some brownish ovoids in a bowl as eggs. From the chickens?

Peachthief was cleaning the honeycomb with a manually-operated knife. "I use the wax for my loom, and for candles. Light."

"What's wrong with the lights?"

"Nothing." She turned around, gesturing emphatically with the knife. "Don't you understand? All these machines, they'll go. They won't run forever. They'll break or wear out or run down. There won't *be* any, any more. Then we'll have to use natural things."

"But that won't be for centuries!" he protested. "Decades, anyhow. They're all still going, they'll last for us."

"For you," she said scornfully. "Not for me. I intend to stay. With my children." She turned her back on him and added in a friendlier voice, "Besides, the old things are aesthetic. I'll show you, when it gets dark."

"But you haven't any children! Have you?" He was purely astonished.

"Not yet." Her back was still turned.

"I'm hungry," he said, and went to work the synthesizer. He made it give him a bar with a hard filler; for some reason he wanted to crunch it in his teeth.

She finished with the honey and turned around. "Have you ever had a natural meal?"

"Oh yes," he said, chewing. "One of my uncles tried that. It was very nice," he added politely.

She looked at him sharply and smiled again, on—off. They went out of the food-room. The afternoon was fading into great gold and orange streamers above the courtyard, coloured like Peachthief's garment.

"You can sleep here." She opened a slatted door. The room was small and bare, with a window on the sea.

"There isn't any bed," he objected.

She opened a chest and took out a big wad of string. "Hang this end on that hook over there."

When she hung up the other end he saw it was a large mesh hammock.

"That's what I sleep in. They're comfortable. Try it."

He climbed in awkwardly. The thing came up around him like a bag. She gave a short sweet laugh as brief as her smile.

"No, you lie on the diagonal. Like this." She tugged his legs, sending a peculiar shudder through him. "That straightens it, see?"

It would probably be all right, he decided, struggling out. Peachthief was pointing to a covered pail.

"That's for your wastes. It goes on the garden, in the end."

He was appalled, but said nothing, letting her lead him out through a room with glass tanks in the walls to a big screened-in porch fronting the ocean. It was badly in need of cleaners. The sky was glorious with opalescent domes and spires, reflections of the sunset behind them, painting amazing colors on the sea.

"This is where I eat."

"What is this place?"

"It was a sea-station last, I think. Station Juliet. They monitored the fish and the ocean traffic, and rescued people and so on."

He was distracted by noticing long convergent dove-blue rays like mysterious paths into the horizon; cloud-shadows cast across the world. Beauty of the dust. Why must it move him so?

"—even a medical section," she was saying. "I really could have babies, I mean in case of trouble."

"You don't mean it." He felt only irritation now. "I don't feel any more desire," he told her.

She shrugged. "I don't, either. We'll talk about it later on."

"Have you always lived here?"

"Oh, no." She began taking pots and dishes out of an insulated case. The three moondogs had joined them silently; she set bowls before them. They lapped, stealing glances at Jakko. They were, he knew, very strong despite their stick-like appearance.

"Let's sit here." She plumped down on one end of the lounge and began biting forcefully into a crusty thing like a slab of drybar. He noticed she had magnificent teeth. Her dark skin set them off beautifully, as it enhanced her eyes. He had never met anyone so different in every way from himself and his family. He vacillated between interest and a vague alarm.

"Try some of the honey." She handed him a container and spoon. It looked quite clean. He tasted it eagerly; honey was much spoken of in antique writings. At first he sensed nothing but a waxy sliding, but then an overpowering sweetness enveloped his tongue, quite unlike the sweets he was used to. It did not die away but seemed to run up his nose and almost into his ears, in a peculiar physical way. An *animal* food. He took some more, gingerly.

"I didn't offer you my bread. It needs some chemical, I don't know what. To make it lighter."

"Don't you have an access terminal?"

"Something's wrong with part of it," she said with her mouth full. "Maybe I don't work it right. We never had a big one like this, my tribe were travelers. They believed in sensory experiences." She nodded, licking her fingers. "They went to the River when I was fourteen."

"That's very young to be alone. My people waited till this year, my eighteenth birthday."

"I wasn't alone. I had two older cousins. But they wanted to take an aircar up north, to the part of the River called Rideout. I stayed here. I mean, we never stopped travelling, we never *lived* anywhere. I wanted to do like the plants, make roots."

"I could look at your program," he offered. "I've seen a lot of different models, I spent nearly a year in cities."

"What I need is a cow. Or a goat."

"Why?"

"For the milk. I need a pair, I guess."

Another animal thing; he winced a little. But it was pleasant, sitting here in the deep blue light beside her, hearing the surf plash quietly below.

"I saw quite a number of horses," he told her. "Don't they use milk?"

"I don't think horses are much good for milk." She sighed in an alert, busy way. He had the impression that her head was tremendously energic, humming with plans and intentions. Suddenly she looked up and began making a high squeaky noise between her front teeth, "Sssswwt! Sssswwwt!"

Startled, he saw a white flying thing swooping above them, and then two more. They whirled so wildly he ducked.

"That's right," she said to them. "Get busy."

"What are they?"

"My bats. They eat mosquitoes and insects." She squeaked again and the biggest bat was suddenly clinging to her hand, licking honey. It had a small, fiercely complicated face.

Jakko relaxed again. This place and its strange inhabitant were giving him remarkable memories for the River, anyway. He noticed a faint glow moving where the dark sky joined the darker sea.

"What's that?"

"Oh, the seatrain. It goes to the River landing."

"Are there people on it?"

"Not any more. Look, I'll show you." She jumped up and was opening a console in the corner, when a sweet computer voice spoke into the air.

"Seatrain Foxtrot Niner calling Station Juliet! Come in, Station Juliet!"

"It hasn't done that for years," Peachthief said. She tripped tumblers. "Seatrain, this is Station Juliet, I hear you. Do you have a problem?"

"Affirmative. Passenger is engaging in nonstandard activities. He-slash-she does not conform to parameters. Request instructions."

Peachthief thought a minute. Then she grinned. "Is your passenger moving on four legs?"

"Affirmative! Affirmative!" Seatrain Foxtrot sounded relieved.

"Supply it with bowls of meat-food and water on the floor and do not interfere with it. Juliet out."

She clicked off, and they watched the far web of lights go by on the horizon, carrying an animal.

"Probably a dog following the smell of people," Peachthief said. "I hope it gets off all right. . . . We're quite a wide genetic spread," she went on in a different voice. "I mean, you're so light, and body-type and all."

"I noticed that."

"It would give good heterosis. Vigour."

She was talking about being impregnated, about the fantasy-child. He felt angry.

"Look, you don't know what you're saying. Don't you realise you'd have to stay and raise it for years? You'd be ethically and morally bound. And the River places are shrinking fast, you must know that. Maybe you'd be too late."

"Yes," she said somberly. "Now it's sucked everybody out it's going. But I still mean to stay."

"But you'd hate it, even if there's still time. My mother hated it, toward the end. She felt she had begun to deteriorate energically, that her life would be lessened. And me—what about me? I mean, I should stay too."

"You'd only have to stay a month. For my ovulation. The male parent isn't ethically bound."

"Yes, but I think that's wrong. My father stayed. He never said he minded it, but he must have."

"You only have to do a month," she said sullenly. "I thought you weren't going on the River right now."

"I'm not. I just don't want to feel bound, I want to travel. To see more of the world, first. After I say goodbye."

She made an angry sound. "You have no insight. You're going, all right. You just don't want to admit it. You're going just like Mungo and Ferrocil."

"Who are they?"

"People who came by. Males, like you. Mungo was last year, I guess. He had an aircar. He said he was going to stay, he talked and talked. But two days later he went right on again. To the River. Ferrocil was earlier, he was walking through. Until he stole my bicycle."

A sudden note of fury in her voice startled him; she seemed to have some peculiar primitive relation to her bicycle, to her *things*.

"Did you want them to impregnate you, too?" Jakko noticed an odd intensity in his own voice as well.

"Oh, I was thinking about it, with Mungo." Suddenly she turned on him, her eyes wide open in the dimness like white-ringed jewels. "Look! Once and for all, I'm not going! I'm alive. I'm a human woman. I am going to stay on this earth and do human things. I'm going to make young ones to carry on the race, even if I have to die here. You can go on out, you—you pitiful shadows!"

Her voice rang in the dark room, jarring him down to his sleeping marrow. He sat silent as though some deep buried bell had tolled.

She was breathing hard. Then she moved, and to his surprise a small live flame sprang up between her cupped hands, making the room a cave.

"That's a candle. That's me. Now go ahead, make fun like Mungo did."

"I'm not making fun," he said, shocked. "It's just that I don't know what to think. Maybe you're right. I really . . . I really don't want to go, in one way," he said haltingly. "I love this earth too. But it's all so fast. Let me . . ."

His voice trailed off.

"Tell me about your family," she said, quietly now.

"Oh, they studied. They tried every access you can imagine. Ancient languages, history, lore. My aunt made poems in English . . . The layers of the earth, the names of body cells and tissues, jewels, everything. Especially stars. They made us memorise star-maps. So we'll know where we are, you know, for awhile. At least the earth-names. My father kept saying, when you go on the River you can't come back and look anything up. All you have is what you remember. Of course you could ask others, but there'll be so much more, so much new . . ."

He fell silent, wondering for the millionth time: Is it possible that I shall go out forever between the stars, in the great streaming company of strange sentiences?

"How many children were in your tribe?" Peachthief was asking.

"Six. I was the youngest."

"The others all went on the River?"

"I don't know. When I came back from the cities the whole family had gone on, but maybe they'll wait a while too. My father left a letter asking me to come and say goodbye, and to bring him anything new I learned. They say you go slowly, you know. If I hurry there'll still be enough of his mind left there to tell him what I saw."

"What did you see? We were at a city once," Peachthief said dreamily. "But I was too young. I don't remember anything but people."

"The people are all gone now. Empty, every one. But everything works, the lights change, the moveways run. I didn't believe everybody was gone until I checked the central control offices. Oh, there were so many wonderful devices." He sighed. "The beauty, the complexity. Fantastic what people made." He sighed again, thinking of the wonderful technology, the creations abandoned, running down. "One strange thing. In the biggest city I saw, old Chio, almost every entertainment-screen had the same tape running."

"What was it?"

"A girl, a young girl with long hair. Almost to her feet, I've never seen such hair. She was laying it out on a sort of table, with her head down. But no sound, I think the audio was broken. Then she poured a liquid all over very slowly. And then she lit it, she set fire to herself. It flamed and exploded and burned her all up. I think it was real." He shuddered. "I could see inside her mouth, her tongue going all black and twisted. It was horrible. Running over and over, everywhere. Stuck."

She made a revolted sound. "So you want to tell that to your father, to his ghost or whatever?"

"Yes. It's all new data, it could be important."

"Oh yes," she said scornfully. Then she grinned at him. "What about me? Am I new data too? A woman who isn't going to the River? A woman who is going to stay here and make babies? Maybe I'm the last."

"That's very important," he said slowly, feeling a deep confusion in his gut. "But I can't believe, I mean, you—"

"*I mean it.*" She spoke with infinite conviction. "I'm going to live here and have babies by you or some other man if you won't stay, and teach them to live on the earth naturally."

Suddenly he believed her. A totally new emotion was rising up in him, carrying with it sunrises and nameless bonds with earth that hurt in a painless way; as though a rusted door was opening within him. Maybe this was what he had been groping for.

"I think—I think maybe I'll help you. Maybe I'll stay with you, for a while at least. Our—our children."

"You'll stay a month?" she asked wonderingly. "Really?"

"No, I mean I could stay longer. To make more and see them and help raise them, like father did. After I come back from saying goodbye I'll really stay."

Her face changed. She bent to him and took his face between her slim dark hands.

"Jakko, listen. If you go to the River you'll never come back. No one ever does. I'll never see you again. We have to do it now, before you go."

"But a month is too long!" he protested. "My father's mind won't be there, I'm already terribly late."

She glared into his eyes a minute and then released him, stepping back with her brief sweet laugh. "Yes, and it's already late for bed. Come on."

She led him back to the room, carrying the candle, and he marvelled anew at the clutter of strange activities she had assembled. "What's that?"

"My weaving-room." Yawning, she reached in and held up a small, rough-looking cloth. "I made this."

It was ugly, he thought; ugly and pathetic. Why make such useless things? But he was too tired to argue.

She left him to cleanse himself perfunctorily by the well in the moonlit courtyard, after showing him another waste-place right in the garden. Other peoples' wastes smelt bad, he noticed sleepily. Maybe that was the cause of all the ancient wars.

In his room he tumbled into his hammock and fell asleep instantly. His dreams that night were chaotic; crowds, storms, jostling and echoing through strange dimensions. His last image was of a great whirlwind that bore in its forehead a jewel that was a sleeping woman, curled like an embryo.

He waked in the pink light of dawn to find her brown face bending over him, smiling impishly. He had the impression she had been watching him, and jumped quickly out of the hammock.

"Lazy," she said. "I've found the sailboat. Hurry up and eat."

She handed him a wooden plate of bright natural fruits and led him out into the sunrise garden.

When they got down to the beach she led him south, and there was the little craft sliding to and fro, overturned in the shallows amid its tangle of sail. The keel was still protruding. They furled the sail in clumsily, and towed it out to deeper water to right it.

"I want this for the children," Peachthief kept repeating excitedly. "They can get fish, too. Oh how they'll love it!"

"Stand your weight on the keel and grab the siderail," Jakko told her, doing the same. He noticed that her silks had come loose from her breasts, which were high and wide-pointed, quite unlike those of his tribe. The sight distracted him, his thighs felt unwieldy, and he missed his handhold as the craft righted itself and ducked him. When he came up he saw Peachthief scrambling aboard like a cat, clinging tight to the mast.

"The sail! Pull the sail up," he shouted, and got another faceful of water. But she had heard him, the sail was trembling open like a great wing, silhouetting her shining dark body. For the first time Jakko noticed the boat's name, on the stern: *Gojack*. He smiled. An omen.

Gojack was starting to move smoothly away, toward the reef.

"The rudder!" he bellowed. "Turn the rudder and come back."

Peachthief moved to the tiller and pulled at it; he could see her strain. But *Gojack* continued to move away from him into the wind, faster and faster toward the surf. He remembered she had been handling the mast where the computer was.

"Stop the computer! Turn it off, turn it off!"

She couldn't possibly hear him. Jakko saw her in frantic activity, wrenching at the tiller, grabbing ropes, trying physically to push down the sail. Then she seemed to notice the computer, but evidently could not decipher it. Meanwhile *Gojack* fled steadily on and out, resuming its interrupted journey to the River. Jakko realised with horror that she would soon be in dangerous water, the surf was thundering on coralheads.

"Jump! Come back, jump off!" He was swimming after them as fast as he could, his progress agonisingly slow. He glimpsed her still wrestling with the boat, screaming something he couldn't hear.

"JUMP!"

And finally she did, but only to try jerking *Gojack* around by its mooring-lines. The boat faltered and jibbed, but then went strongly on, towing the threshing girl.

"Let go! Let go!" A wave broke over his head.

When he could see again he found she had at last let go and was swimming aimlessly, watching *Gojack* crest the surf and wing away. At last she turned back toward shore, and Jakko swam to intercept her. He was gripped by an unknown emotion so strong it discoordinated him. As his feet touched bottom he realised it was rage.

She waded to him, her face contorted by weeping. "The children's boat," she wailed. "I lost the children's boat—"

"You're crazy," he shouted. "There aren't any children."

"I lost it—" She flung herself on his chest, crying. He thumped her back, her sides, repeating furiously, "Crazy! You're insane!"

She wailed louder, squirming against him, small and naked and frail. Suddenly he found himself flinging her down onto the wet sand, falling on top of her with his swollen sex crushed between their bellies. For a moment all was confusion, and then the shock of it sobered him. He raised to look under himself and Peachthief stared too, round-eyed.

"Do you w-want to, now?"

In that instant he wanted nothing more than to thrust himself into her, but a sandy wavelet splashed over them and he was suddenly aware of chafing wet cloth and Peachthief gagging brine. The magic waned. He got awkwardly to his knees.

"I thought you were going to be drowned," he told her, angry again.

"I wanted it so, for—for them . . ." She was still crying softly, looking up desolately at him. He understood she wasn't really meaning just the sailboat. A feeling of inexorable involvement spread through him. This mad little being had created some kind of energy-vortex around her, into which he was being sucked along with animals, vegetables, chickens, crowds of unknown things; only *Gojack* had escaped her.

"I'll find it," she was muttering, wringing out her silks, staring beyond the reef at the tiny dwindling gleam. He looked down at her, so fanatic and so vulnerable, and his inner landscape tilted frighteningly, revealing some ancient-new dimension.

"I'll stay with you," he said hoarsely. He cleared his throat, hearing his voice shake. "I mean I'll really stay, I won't go to the River at all. We'll make them, our babies now."

She stared up at him open mouthed. "But your father! You promised!"

"My father stayed," he said painfully. "It's—it's right, I think."

She came close and grabbed his arms in her small hands.

"Oh, Jakko! But no, listen—*I'll go with you.* We can start a baby as we go, I'm sure of that. Then you can talk to your father and keep your promise and I'll be there to make sure you come back!"

"But you'd be, you'd be pregnant!" he cried in alarm. "You'd be in danger of taking an embryo on the River!"

She laughed proudly. "Can't you get it through your head that I will *not* go on the River? I'll just watch you and pull you out. I'll see you get back here. For a while, anyway," she added soberly. Then she brightened. "Hey, we'll see all kinds of things. Maybe I can find a cow or some goats on the way! Yes, yes! It's a perfect idea."

She faced him, glowing. Tentatively she brought her lips up to his, and they kissed inexpertly, tasting salt. He felt no desire, but only some deep resonance, like a confirmation in the earth. The three moondogs were watching mournfully.

"Now let's eat!" She began towing him toward the cliff-steps. "We can start the pills right now. Oh, I have so much to do! But I'll fix everything, we'll leave tomorrow."

She was like a whirlwind. In the food-room she pounced on a small gold-colored pillbox and opened it to show a mound of glowing green and red capsules.

"The red ones with the male symbol are for you."

She took a green one, and they swallowed solemnly, sharing a water-mug. He noticed that the seal on the box had been broken, and thought of that stranger, Mungo, she had mentioned. How far had her plans gone with him? An unpleasant emotion he had never felt before rose in Jakko's stomach. He sensed that he was heading into more dubious realms of experience than he had quite contemplated, and took his foodbar and walked away through the arcades to cool down.

When he came upon her again she seemed to be incredibly busy, folding and filling and wrapping things, closing windows and tying doors open. Her intense relations with things again . . . He felt obscurely irritated and was pleased to have had a superior idea.

"We need a map," he told her. "Mine was in the boat."

"Oh, great idea. Look in the old control room, it's down those stairs. It's kind of scary." She began putting oil on her loom.

He went down a white ramp that became a tunnel stairway, and came finally through a heavily armoured portal to a circular room deep inside the rock, dimly illumined by portholes sunk in long shafts. From here he could hear the hum of the station energy-source. As his eyes adjusted he made out a bank of sensor screens and one big console standing alone. It seemed to have been smashed open; some kind of sealant had been poured over the works.

He had seen a place like this before; he understood at once that from here had been controlled terrible ancient weapons that flew. Probably they still stood waiting in their hidden holes behind the station. But the master control was long dead. As he approached the console he saw that someone had scratched in the cooling sealant. He could make out only the words, "—WAR NO MORE." Undoubtedly this was a shrine of the very old days.

He found a light-switch that filled the place with cool glare, and began exploring side-alleys. Antique gear, suits, cupboards full of masks and crumbling packets he couldn't identify. Among them was something useful—two cloth containers to carry stuff on one's back, only a little mildewed. But where were the maps?

Finally he found one on the control-room wall, right where he had come in. Someone had updated it with scrawled notations. With a tremor he realised how very old this must be; it dated from before the Rivers had touched earth. He could hardly grasp it.

Studying it he saw that there was indeed a big landing-dock not far south, and from there a moveway ran inland about a hundred kilometers to an airpark. If Peachthief could walk twenty-five kilometers they could make the landing by evening, and if the cars were still running the rest would be quick. All the moveways he'd seen had live cars on them. From the airpark a dotted line ran south-west across mountains to a big red circle with a cross in it, marked "VIDA!" That would be the River. They would just have to hope something on the airpark would fly, otherwise it would be a long climb.

His compass was still on his belt. He memorised the directions and went back upstairs. The courtyard was already saffron under great sunset flags.

Peachthief was squatting by the well, apparently having a conference with her animals. Jakko noticed some more white creatures he hadn't seen before, who seemed to live in an open hutch. They had long pinkish ears and mobile noses. Rabbits, or hares perhaps?

Two of the strange white animals he had seen sleeping were now under a bench, chirruping irritably at Peach-thief.

"My raccoons," she told Jakko. "They're mad because I woke them up too soon." She said something in a high voice Jakko couldn't understand, and the biggest raccoon shook his head up and down in a supercilious way.

"The chickens will be all right," Peachthief said. "Lotor knows how to feed them, to get the eggs. And they can all work the water-lever." The other raccoon nodded crossly, too.

"The rabbits are a terrible problem." Peachthief frowned. "You just haven't much sense, Eusebia," she said fondly, stroking the doe. "I'll have to fix something."

The big raccoon was warbling at her; Jakko thought he caught the word "dog-g-g."

"He wants to know who will settle their disputes with the dogs," Peachthief reported. At this one of the moon-dogs came forward and said thickly, "We go-o." It was the first word Jakko had heard him speak.

"Oh, good!" Peachthief cried. "Well, that's that!" She bounced up and began pouring something from a bucket on a line of plants. The white raccoons ran off silently with a humping gait.

"I'm so glad you're coming, Tycho," she told the dog.

"Especially if I have to come back alone with a baby inside. But they say you're very vigorous, at first anyway."

"You aren't coming back alone," Jakko told her. She smiled a brilliant, noncommittal flash. He noticed she was dressed differently; her body didn't show so much, and she kept her gaze away from him in an almost timid way. But she became very excited when he showed her the backpacks.

"Oh, good. Now we won't have to roll the blankets around our waists. It gets cool at night, you know."

"Does it ever rain?"

"Not this time of year. What we mainly need is lighters and food and water. And a good knife each. Did you find the map?"

He showed it. "Can you walk, I mean really hike if we have to? Do you have shoes?"

"Oh yes. I walk a lot. Especially since Ferrocil stole my bike."

The venom in her tone amused him. The ferocity with which she provisioned her small habitat!

"Men build monuments, women build nests," he quoted from somewhere.

"I don't know what kind of monument Ferrocil built with my bicycle," she said tartly.

"You're a savage," he said, feeling a peculiar ache that came out as a chuckle.

"The race can use some savages. We better eat now and go to sleep so we can start early."

At supper in the sunset-filled porch they scarcely talked. Dreamily Jakko watched the white bats embroidering flight on the air. When he looked down at Peachthief he caught her gazing at him before she quickly lowered her eyes. It came to him that they might eat hundreds, thousands of meals here; maybe all his life. And there could be a child, children, running about. He had never seen small humans younger than himself. It was all too much to take in, unreal. He went back to watching the bats.

That night she accompanied him to his hammock and stood by, shy but stubborn, while he got settled. Then he suddenly felt her hands sliding on his body, towards his groin. At first he thought it was something clinical, but then he realised she meant sex. His blood began to pound.

"May I come in beside you? The hammock is quite strong."

"Yes," he said thickly, reaching for her arm.

But as her weight came in by him she said in a practical voice, "I have to start knotting a small hammock, first thing. Child-size."

It broke his mood.

"Look. I'm sorry, but I've changed my mind. You go on back to yours, we should get sleep now."

"All right." The weight lifted away.

With a peculiar mix of sadness and satisfaction he heard her light footsteps leaving him alone. That night he dreamed strange sensory crescendoes, a tumescent earth and air; a woman who lay with her smiling lips in pale green water, awaiting him, while thin black birds of sunrise stalked to the edge of the sea.

Next morning they ate by candles, and set out as the eastern sky was just turning rose-grey. The ancient white coral roadway was good walking. Peachthief swung right along beside him, her back-pack riding smooth. The moondogs pattered soberly behind.

Jakko found himself absorbed in gazing at the brightening landscape. Jungle-covered hills rose away on their right, the sea lay below on their left, sheened and glittering with the coming sunrise. When a diamond chip of sun broke out of the horizon he almost shouted aloud for the brilliance of it; the palm-trees beyond the road lit up like golden torches, the edges of every frond and stone were startlingly clear and jewel-like. For a moment he wondered if he could have taken some hallucinogen.

They paced on steadily in a dream of growing light and heat. The day-wind came up, and torn white clouds began to blow over them bringing momentary coolnesses. Their walking fell into the rhythm Jakko loved, broken only occasionally by crumbled places in the road. At such spots they would often be surprised to find the moondogs sitting waiting for them, having quietly left the road and circled ahead through the scrub on business of their own. Peachthief kept up sturdily, only once stopping to look back at the far white spark of Station Juliet, almost melted in the shimmering horizon.

"This is as far as I've gone south," she told him.

He drank some water and made her drink too, and they went on. The road began to wind, rising and falling gently.

When he next glanced back the station was gone. The extraordinary luminous clarity of the world was still delighting him.

When noon came he judged they were well over halfway to the landing. They sat down on some rubble under the palms to eat and drink, and Peachthief fed the moondogs. Then she took out the fertility pill-box. They each took theirs in silence, oddly solemn. Then she grinned.

"I'll give you something for dessert."

She unhitched a crooked knife from her belt and went searching around in the rocks, to come back with a big yellow-brown palm nut. Jakko watched her attack it with rather alarming vigor; she husked it and then used a rock to drive the point home.

"Here." She handed it to him. "Drink out of that hole." He felt a sloshing inside; when he lifted it and drank it tasted hairy and gritty and nothing in particular. But sharp, too, like the day. Peachthief was methodically striking the thing around and around its middle. Suddenly it fell apart, revealing vividly white meat. She pried out a piece.

"Eat this. It's full of protein."

The nutmeat was sweet and sharply organic.

"This is a coconut!" he suddenly remembered.

"Yes. I won't starve, coming back."

He refused to argue, but only got up to go on. Peachthief holstered her knife and followed, munching on a coconut piece. They went on so in silence a long time, letting the rhythm carry them. Once when a lizard waddled across the road Peachthief said to the moondog at her heels, "Tycho, you'll have to learn to catch and eat those one day soon." The moondogs all looked dubiously at the lizard but said nothing. Jakko felt shocked and pushed the thought away.

They were now walking with the sun westering slowly to their right. A flight of big orange birds with blue beaks flapped squawking out of a roadside tree, where they were apparently building some structure. Cloud-shadows fled across the world, making blue and bronze reflections in the sea. Jakko still felt his sensory impressions almost painfully keen; a sunray made the surf-line into a chain of diamonds, and the translucent green of the near shallows below them seemed to enchant his eyes. Every vista ached with light, as if to utter some silent meaning.

He was walking in a trance, only aware that the road had been sound and level for some time, when Peachthief uttered a sharp cry.

"My bicycle! There's my bicycle!" She began to run; Jakko saw shiny metal sticking out of a narrow gulch in the roadway. When he came up to her she was pulling a machine out from beside the roadwall.

"The front wheel—Oh, he bent it! He must have been going too fast and wrecked it here. That Ferrocil! But I'll fix it, I'm sure I can fix it at the station. I'll push it back with me on the way home."

While she was mourning her machine Jakko looked around and over the low coping of the roadwall. Sheer cliff down there, with the sun just touching a rocky beach below. Something was stuck among the rocks—a tangle of whitish sticks, cloth, a round thing. Feeling his stomach knot, Jakko stared down at it, unwillingly discovering that the round thing had eye-holes, a U-shaped open mouth, blowing strands of hair. He had never seen a dead body before, nobody had, but he had seen pictures of human bones. Shakenly he realized what this had to be: Ferrocil. He must have been thrown over the coping when he hit that crack. Now he was dead, long dead. He would never go on the River. All that had been in that head was perished, gone forever.

Scarcely knowing what he was doing, Jakko grabbed Peachthief by the shoulders, saying roughly, "Come on! Come on!" When she resisted, confusedly he took her by the arm and began forcibly pulling her away from where she might look down. Her flesh felt burning hot and vibrant, the whole world was blasting colors and sounds and smells at him. Images of dead Ferrocil mingled with the piercing scent of some flowers on the roadway. Suddenly an idea struck him; he stopped.

"Listen. Are you sure those pills aren't hallucinaids? I've only had two and everything feels crazy."

"Three," Peachthief said abstractedly. She took his hand and pressed it on her back. "Do that again, run your hand down my back."

Bewildered, he obeyed. As his hand passed her silk shirt onto her thin shorts he felt her body move under it in a way that made him jerk away.

"Feel? Did you feel it? The lordotic reflex," she said proudly. "Female sexuality. It's starting."

"What do you mean, three?"

"You had three pills. I gave you one that first night, in the honey."

"*What?* But—but—" He struggled to voice the enormity of her violation, pure fury welling up in him. Choking, he lifted his hand and struck her buttocks the hardest blow he could, sending her staggering. It was the first time he had ever struck a person. A moondog growled, but he didn't care.

"Don't you ever—never—play a trick like—" He yanked at her shoulders, meaning to slap her face. His hand clutched a breast instead, he saw her hair blowing like dead Ferrocil's. A frightening sense of mortality combined with pride surged through him, lighting a fire in his loins. The deadness of Ferrocil suddenly seemed violently exciting. He, Jakko, was alive! Ignoring all sanity he flung himself on Peachthief, bearing her down on the road among the flowers. As he struggled to tear open their shorts he was dimly aware that she was helping him. His engorged penis was all reality; he fought past obstructions and then was suddenly, crookedly *in* her, fierce pleasure building. It exploded through him and then had burst out into her vitals, leaving him spent.

Blinking, fighting for clarity, he raised himself up and off her body. She lay wide-legged and dishevelled, sobbing or gasping in a strange way, but smiling too. Revulsion sent a sick taste in his throat.

"There's your baby," he said roughly. He found his canteen and drank. The three moondogs had retreated and were sitting in a row, staring solemnly.

"May I have some, please?" Her voice was very low; she sat up, began fixing her clothes. He passed her the water and they got up.

"It's sundown," she said. "Should we camp here?"

"No!" Savagely he started on, not caring that she had to run to catch up. Was this the way the ancients lived? Whirled by violent passions, indecent, uncaring? His doing sex so close to the poor dead person seemed unbelievable. And the world was still assaulting all his senses; when she stumbled against him he could feel again the thrilling pull of her flesh, and shuddered. They walked in silence awhile; he sensed that she was more tired than he, but he wanted only to get as far away as possible.

"I'm not taking any more of those pills," he broke silence at last.

"But you have to! It takes a month to be sure."

"I don't care."

"But, ohhh——"

He said nothing more. They were walking across a twilit headland now. Suddenly the road turned, and they came out above a great bay.

The waters below were crowded with boats of all kinds, bobbing emptily where they had been abandoned. Some still had lights that made faint jewels in the opalescent air. Somewhere among them must be *Gojack*. The last light from the west gleamed on the rails of a moveway running down to the landing.

"Look, there's the seatrain." Peachthief pointed. "I hope the dog or whatever got ashore . . . I can find a sailboat down there, there's lots."

Jakko shrugged. Then he noticed movement among the shadows of the landing-station and forgot his anger long enough to say, "See there! Is that a live man?"

They peered hard. Presently the figure crossed a light place, and they could see it was a person going slowly among the stalled waycars. He would stop with one awhile and then waver on.

"There's something wrong with him," Peachthief said.

Presently the stranger's shadow merged with a car, and they saw it begin to move. It went slowly at first, and then accelerated out to the center lanes, slid up the gleaming rails and passed beyond them to disappear into the western hills.

"The way's working!" Jakko exclaimed. "We'll camp up here and go over to the way-station in the morning, it's closer."

He was feeling so pleased with the moveway that he talked easily with Peachthief over their foodbar dinner, telling her about the cities and asking her what places her tribe had seen. But when she wanted to put their blankets down together he said no, and took his away to a ledge farther up. The three moondogs lay down by her with their noses on their paws, facing him.

His mood turned to self-disgust again; remorse mingled with queasy surges of half-enjoyable animality. He put his arm over his head to shut out the brilliant moonlight and longed to forget everything, wishing the sky held only cold quiet stars. When he finally slept he didn't dream at all, but woke with ominous tollings in his inner ear. *The Horse is hungry,* deep voices chanted. *The Woman is bad!*

He roused Peachthief before sunrise. They ate and set off overland to the hill station; it was rough going until they stumbled onto an old limerock path. The moondogs ranged wide around them, appearing pleased. When they came out at the station shunt they found it crowded with cars.

The power-pack of the first one was dead. So was the next, and the next. Jakko understood what the stranger at the landing had been doing; looking for a live car. The dead cars here stretched away out of sight up the siding; a miserable sight.

"We should go back to the landing," Peachthief said. "He found a good one there."

Jakko privately agreed, but irrationality smouldered in him. He squinted into the hazy distance.

"I'm going up to the switch end."

"But it's so far, we'll have to come all the way back—"

He only strode off; she followed. It was a long way, round a curve and over a rise, dead cars beside them all the way. They were almost at the main tracks when Jakko saw what he had been hoping for: a slight jolting motion in the line. New cars were still coming in ahead, butting the dead ones.

"Oh, fine!"

They went on down to the newest-arrived car and all climbed in, the moondogs taking up position on the opposite seat. When Jakko began to work the controls that would take them out to the main line, the car bleated an automatic alarm. A voder voice threatened to report him to Central. Despite its protests, Jakko swerved the car across the switches, where it fell silent and began to accelerate smoothly onto the outbound express lane.

"You really do know how to work these things," Peachthief said admiringly.

"You should learn."

"Why? They'll all be dead soon. I know how to bicycle."

He clamped his lips, thinking of Ferrocil's white bones. They fled on silently into the hills, passing a few more station jams. Jakko's perceptions still seemed too sharp, the sensory world too meaning-filled.

Presently they felt hungry, and found that the car's automatics were all working well. They had a protein drink and a pleasantly fruity bar, and Peachthief found bars for the dogs. The track was rising into mountains now; the car whirled smoothly through tunnels and came out in passes, offering wonderful views. Now and then they had glimpses of a great plain far ahead. The familiar knot of sadness gathered inside Jakko, stronger than usual. To think that all this wonderful system would run down and die in a jumble of rust . . . He had a fantasy of himself somehow maintaining it, but the memory of Peachthief's pathetic woven cloth mocked at him. Everything was a mistake, a terrible mistake. He wanted only to leave, to escape to rationality and peace. If she had drugged him he wasn't responsible for what he'd promised. He wasn't bound. Yet the sadness redoubled, wouldn't let him go.

When she got out the pill-box and offered it he shook his head violently. "No!"

"But you *promised*—"

"No. I hate what it does."

She stared at him in silence, swallowing hers defiantly. "Maybe there'll be some other men by the River," she said after a while. "We saw one."

He shrugged and pretended to fall asleep.

Just as he was really drowsing the car's warning alarm trilled and they braked smoothly to a halt.

"Oh, look ahead—the way's gone! What is it?"

"A rock-slide. An avalanche from the mountains, I think."

They got out among other empty cars that were waiting their prescribed pause before returning. Beyond the last one the way ended in an endless tumble of rocks and shale. Jakko made out a faint footpath leading on.

"Well, we walk. Let's get the packs, and some food and water."

While they were back in the car working the synthesizer, Peachthief looked out the window and frowned. After Jakko finished she punched a different code and some brownish lumps rolled into her hand.

"What's that?"

"You'll see." She winked at him.

As they started on the trail a small herd of horses appeared, coming toward them. The two humans politely scrambled up out of their way. The lead horse was a large yellow male. When he came to Peachthief he stopped and thrust his big head up at her.

"Zhu-gar, zhu-gar," he said sloppily. At this all the other horses crowded up and began saying "zhu-ga, zu-cah," in varying degrees of clarity.

"This *I* know," said Peachthief to Jakko. She turned to the yellow stallion. "Take us on your backs around these rocks. Then we'll give you sugar."

"Zhu-gar," insisted the horse, looking mean.

"Yes, sugar. *After* you take us around the rocks to the rails."

The horse rolled his eyes unpleasantly, but he turned back down. There was some commotion, and two mares were pushed forward.

"Riding horseback is done by means of a saddle and bridle," protested Jakko.

"Also this way. Come on." Peachthief vaulted nimbly onto the back of the smaller mare.

Jakko reluctantly struggled onto the fat round back of the other mare. To his horror, as he got himself astride she put up her head and screamed shrilly.

"You'll get sugar too," Peachthief told her. The animal subsided, and they started off along the rocky trail, single file. Jakko had to admit it was much faster than afoot, but he kept sliding backward.

"Hang onto her mane, that hairy place there," Peachthief called back to him, laughing. "I know how to run a few things too, see?"

When the path widened the yellow stallion trotted up alongside Peachthief.

"I thinking," he said importantly.

"Yes, what?"

"I push you down and eat zhugar now."

"All horses think that," Peachthief told him. "No good. It doesn't work."

The yellow horse dropped back, and Jakko heard him making horse-talk with an old gray-roan animal at the rear. Then he shouldered by to Peachthief again and said, "Why no good I push you down?"

"Two reasons," said Peachthief. "First, if you knock me down you'll never get any more sugar. All the humans will know you're bad and they won't ride on you any more. So no more sugar, never again."

"No more hoomans," the big yellow horse said scornfully. "Hoomans finish."

"You're wrong there too. There'll be a lot more humans. I am making them, see?" She patted her stomach.

The trail narrowed again and the yellow horse dropped back. When he could come alongside he sidled by Jakko's mare.

"I think I push you down now."

Peachthief turned around.

"You didn't hear my other reason," she called to him.

The horse grunted evilly.

"The other reason is that my three friends there will bite your stomach open if you try." She pointed up to where the three moondogs had appeared on a rock as if by magic, grinning toothily.

Jakko's mare screamed again even louder, and the gray-roan in back made a haw-haw sound. The yellow horse lifted his tail and trotted forward to the head of the line, extruding manure as he passed Peachthief.

They went on around the great rockslide without further talk. Jakko was becoming increasingly uncomfortable; he would gladly have got off and gone slower on his own two legs. Now and then they broke into a jog-trot, which was so painful he longed to yell to Peachthief to make them stop. But he kept silent. As they rounded some huge boulders he was rewarded by a distant view of the unmistakable towers of an airpark, to their left on the plain below.

At long last the rock-slide ended, quite near a station. They stopped among a line of stalled cars. Jakko slid off gratefully, remembering to say "Thank you" to the mare. Walking proved to be uncomfortable too.

"See if there's a good car before I get off!" Peachthief yelled.

The second one he came to was live. He shouted at her.

Next moment he saw trouble among the horses. The big yellow beast charged in, neighing and kicking. Peachthief came darting out of the melée with the moondogs, and fell into the car beside him, laughing.

"I gave our mares all the sugar," she chuckled. Then she sobered. "I think mares *are* good for milk. I told them to come to the station with me when I come back. If that big bully will let them."

"How will they get in a car?" he asked stupidly.

"Why, I'll be walking, I can't run these things."

"But I'll be with you." He didn't feel convinced.

"What for, if you don't want to make babies? You won't be here."

"Well then, why are you coming with me?"

"I'm looking for a cow," she said scornfully. "Or a goat. Or a man."

They said no more until the car turned into the airpark station. Jakko counted over twenty apparently live ships floating at their towers. Many more hung sagging, and some towers had toppled. The field moveways were obviously dead.

"I think we have to find hats," he told Peachthief.

"Why?"

"So the service alarms won't go off when we walk around. Most places are like that."

"Oh."

In the office by the gates they found a pile of crew-hats laid out, a thoughtful action by the last of the airpark people. A big hand-lettered sign said, ALL SHIPS ON STAND-BY, MANUAL OVERRIDE. READ DIRECTIONS. Under it was a stack of dusty leaflets. They took one, put on their hats, and began to walk toward a pylon base with several ships floating at its tower. They had to duck under and around the web of dead moveways, and when they reached the station base there seemed to be no way in from the ground.

"We'll have to climb onto that moveway."

They found a narrow ladder and went up, helping the moondogs. The moveway portal was open, and they were soon in the normal passenger lounge. It was still lighted.

"Now if the lift only works."

Just as they were making for the lift-shaft they were startled by a voice ringing out.

"Ho! Ho, Roland!"

"That's no voder," Peachthief whispered. "There's a live human here."

They turned back and saw that a strange person was lying half on and half off one of the lounges. As they came close their eyes opened wide: he looked frightful. His thin dirty white hair hung around a horribly creased caved-in face, and what they could see of his neck and arms was all mottled and decayed-looking. His jerkin and pants were frayed and stained and sagged in where flesh should be. Jakko thought of the cloth shreds around dead Ferrocil and shuddered.

The stranger was staring haggardly at them. In a faint voice he said, "When the chevelier Roland died he predicted that his body would be found a spear's throw ahead of all others and facing the enemy . . . If you happen to be real, could you perhaps give me some water?"

"Of course." Jakko unhooked his canteen and tried to hand it over, but the man's hands shook and fumbled so that Jakko had to hold it to his mouth, noticing a foul odor. The stranger sucked thirstily, spilling some. Behind him the moondogs inched closer, sniffing gingerly.

"What's *wrong* with him?" Peachthief whispered as Jakko stood back.

Jakko had been remembering his lessons. "He's just very, very old, I think."

"That's right." The stranger's voice was stronger. He stared at them with curious avidity. "I waited too long. Fibrillation." He put one feeble hand to his chest. "Fibrillating . . . rather a beautiful word, don't you think? My medicine ran out or I lost it. . . . A small hot animal desynchronising in my ribs."

"We'll help you get to the River right away!" Peachthief told him.

"Too late, my lords, too late. Besides, I can't walk and you can't possibly carry me."

"You can sit up, can't you?" Jakko asked. "There have to be some roll-chairs around here, they had them for injured people." He went off to search the lounge office and found one almost at once.

When he brought it back the stranger was staring up at Peachthief, mumbling to himself in an archaic tongue of which Jakko only understood. ". . . *The breast of a grave girl makes a hill against sunrise.*" He tried to heave himself up to the chair but fell back, gasping. They had to lift and drag him in, Peachthief wrinkling her nose.

"Now if the lift only works."

It did. They were soon on the high departure deck, and the fourth portal-berth held a waiting ship. It was a small local ferry. They went through into the windowed main cabin, wheeling the old man, who had collapsed upon himself and was breathing very badly. The moondogs trooped from window to window, looking down. Jakko seated himself in the pilot chair.

"Read me out the instructions," he told Peachthief.

"One, place ship on internal guidance," she read. "Whatever that means. Oh, look, here's a diagram."

"Good."

It proved simple. They went together down the list, sealing the port, disengaging umbilicals, checking vane function, reading off the stand-by pressures in the gas-bags above them, setting the reactor to warm up the drive-motor and provide hot air for operational buoyancy.

While they were waiting, Peachthief asked the old man if he would like to be moved onto a window couch. He nodded urgently. When they got him to it he whispered, "See out!" They propped him up with chair-pillows.

The ready-light was flashing. Jakko moved the controls, and the ship glided smoothly out and up. The computer was showing him wind-speed, altitude, climb, and some-one had marked all the verniers with the words *Course-set*—RIVER. Jakko lined everything up.

"Now it says, put it on automatic," Peachthief read. He did so.

The take-off had excited the old man. He was straining to look down, muttering incomprehensibly. Jakko caught, *"The cool green hills of Earth . . .* Crap!" Suddenly he sang out loudly, *"There's a hell of a good universe next door—let's go!"* And fell back exhausted.

Peachthief stood over him worriedly. "I wish I could at least clean him up, but he's so weak."

The old man's eyes opened.

"Nothing shall be whole and sound that has not been rent; for love hath built his mansion in the place of excrement." He began to sing crackedly, "Take me to the River, the bee-yew-tiful River, and wash all my sins a-away! . . . You think I'm crazy, girl, don't you?" he went on conversationally. "Never heard of William Yeats. Very high bit-rate, Yeats."

"I think I understand a little," Jakko told him. "One of my aunts did English Literature."

"Did literature, eh?" The stranger wheezed, snorted. "And you two—going on the River to spend eternity to-gether as energy matrices or something equally impressive and sexless . . . *Forever wilt thou love and she be fair."*

He grunted. "Always mistrusted Keats. No balls. He'd be right at home."

"We're not going on the River," Peachthief said. "At least, I'm not. I'm going to stay and make children."

The old man's ruined mouth fell open, he gazed up at her wildly.

"No!" he breathed. "Is it true? Have I stumbled on the lover and mother of man, the last?"

Peachthief nodded solemnly.

"What is your name, Oh Queen?"

"Peachthief."

"My god. Somebody still knows of Blake." He smiled tremulously, and his eyelids suddenly slid downward; he was asleep.

"He's breathing better. Let's explore."

The small ship held little but cargo-space at the rear. When they came to the food-synthesizer cubby Jakko saw Peachthief pocket something.

"What's that?"

"A little spoon. It'll be just right for a child." She didn't look at him.

Back in the main cabin the sunset was flooding the earth below with level roseate light. They were crossing huge, coldly pock-marked meadows, the airship whispering along in silence except when a jet whistled briefly now and then for a course correction.

"Look—cows! Those must be cows," Peachthief exclaimed. "See the shadows."

Jakko made out small tan specks that were animals, with grotesque horned shadows stretching away.

"I'll have to find them when I come back. What *is* this place?"

"A big deathyard, I think. Where they put dead bodies. I never saw one this size. In some cities they had buildings just for dead people. Won't all that poison the cows?"

"Oh no, it makes good grass, I believe. The dogs will help me find them. Won't you, Tycho?" she asked the biggest moondog, who was looking down beside them.

On the eastern side of the cabin the full moon was rising into view. The old man's eyes opened, looking at it.

"More water, if you please," he croaked.

Peachthief gave him some, and then got him to swallow broth from the synthesizer. He seemed stronger, smiling at her with his mouthful of rotted teeth.

"Tell me, girl. If you're going to stay and make chil dren, why are you going to the River?"

"He's going because he promised to talk to his fathe and I'm going along to see he comes back. And make th baby. Only now he won't take any more pills, I have t try to find another man."

"Ah yes, the pills. We used to call them Wake-ups. . . They were necessary, after the population-chemicals go around. Maybe they still are, for women. But I think it' mostly in the head. Why won't you take any more, boy What's wrong with the old Adam?"

Peachthief started to answer but Jakko cut her off. " can speak for myself. They upset me. They made me d bad, uncontrolled things, and feel, agh—" He broke off with a grimace.

"You seem curiously feisty, for one who values his calm above the continuance of the race."

"It's the pills, I tell you. They're—they're dehumanis ing."

"Dee-humanising," the old man mocked. "And what do you know of humanity, young one? . . . That's what I went to find, that's why I stayed so long among the old, old things from before the River came. I wanted to bring the knowledge of what humanity really was . . . I wanted to bring it all. It's simple, boy. *They died.*" He drew a rasping breath. "Every one of them died. They lived knowing that nothing but loss and suffering and extinction lay ahead. And they cared, terribly. . . . Oh, they made myths, but not many really believed them. *Death* was be hind everything, waiting everywhere. Aging and death. No escape . . . Some of them went crazy, they fought and killed and enslaved each other by the millions, as if they could gain more life. Some of them gave up their precious lives for each other. They loved—and had to watch the ones they loved age and die. And in their pain and de spair they built, they struggled, some of them sang. But above all, boy, they copulated! Fornicated, fucked, made love!"

He fell back, coughing, glaring at Jakko. Then, seeing that they scarcely understood his antique words, he went on more clearly. "Did sex, do you understand? Made children. It was their only weapon, you see. To send something of themselves into the future beyond their own deaths. Death was the engine of their lives, death fueled

eir sexuality. Death drove them at each other's throats
nd into each other's arms. Dying, they triumphed. . . .
'hat was human life. And now that mighty engine is long
:illed, and you call this polite parade of immortal lem-
nings humanity? . . . Even the faintest warmth of that
nmemorial holocaust makes you flinch away?"

He collapsed, gasping horribly; spittle ran down his
hin. One slit of eye still raked them.

Jakko stood silent, shaken by resonances from the old
nan's words, remembering dead Ferrocil, feeling some
leep conduit of reality reaching for him out of the long-
one past. Peachthief's hand fell on his shoulder, sending
. shudder through him. Slowly his own hand seemed to
ift by itself and cover hers, holding her to him. They
vatched the old man so for a long moment. His face
lowly composed, he spoke in a soft dry tone.

"I don't trust that River, you know. . . . You think
vou're going to remain yourselves, don't you? Communi-
:ate with each other and with the essences of beings from
ther stars? . . . The latest news from Betelgeuse." He
:huckled raspingly.

"That's the last thing people say when they're going,"
Jakko replied. "Everyone learns that. You float out, able
:o talk with real other beings. Free to move."

"Yes. What could better match our dreams?" He
:huckled again. "I wonder . . . could that be the lure, just
:he input end of some cosmic sausage-machine . . ."

"What's that?" asked Peachthief.

"An old machine that ground different meats together
until they came out as one substance . . . Maybe you'll
find yourselves gradually mixed and minced and blended
into some, some energic plasma . . . and then maybe
squirted out again to impose the terrible gift of consciousness on some innocent race of crocodiles, or poached
eggs. . . . And so it begins all over again. Another random engine of the universe, giving and taking oblivi-
ously . . ." He coughed, no longer looking at them, and
began to murmur in the archaic tongue, "Ah, when the
ghost begins to quicken, confusion of the death-bed over,
is it sent . . . Out naked on the roads as the books say,
and stricken with the injustice of the stars for punishment? The injustice of the stars . . ." He fell silent, and
then whispered faintly, "Yet I too long to go."

"You will," Peachthief told him strongly.

"How . . . much longer?"

"We'll be there by dawn," Jakko said. "We'll carry you. I swear."

"A great gift," he said weakly. "But I fear . . . I shall give you a better." He mumbled on, a word Jakko didn't know; it sounded like "afrodisiack."

He seemed to lapse into sleep then. Peachthief went and got a damp, fragrant cloth from the clean-up and wiped his face gently. He opened one eye and grinned up at her.

"Madame Tasselass," he rasped. "Madame Tasselass, are you really going to save us?"

She smiled down, nodding her head determinedly, Yes. He closed his eyes, looking more peaceful.

The ship was now fleeing through full moonlight, the cabin was so lit with azure and silver that they didn't think to turn on lights. Now and again the luminous mists of a low cloud veiled the windows and vanished again. Just as Jakko was about to propose eating, the old man took several gulping breaths and opened his eyes. His intestines made a bubbling sound.

Peachthief looked at him sharply and picked up one of his wrists. Then she frowned and bent over him, opening his filthy jerkin. She laid her ear to his chest, staring up at Jakko.

"He's not breathing, there's no heartbeat!" She groped inside his jerkin as if she could locate life, two tears rolling down her cheeks.

"He's *dead*—Ohhh!" She groped deeper, then suddenly straightened up and gingerly clutched the cloth at the old man's crotch.

"What?"

"He's a woman!" She gave a sob and wheeled around to clutch Jakko, putting her forehead in his neck. "We n-never even knew her name . . ."

Jakko held her, looking at the dead man-woman, thinking, she never knew mine either. At that moment the airship jolted, and gave a noise like a cable grinding or slipping before it flew smoothly on again.

Jakko had never in his life distrusted machinery, but now a sudden terror contracted his guts. This thing could fall! They could be made dead like Ferrocil, like this stranger, like the myriads in the deathyards below. Echoes of the old voice ranting about death boomed in his head, he had a sudden vision of Peachthief grown old and dying like that. After the Rivers went, dying alone. His eyes filled, and a deep turmoil erupted under his mind. He hugged Peachthief tighter. Suddenly he knew in a dreamlike way exactly what was about to happen. Only this time there was no frenzy; his body felt like warm living rock.

He stroked Peachthief to quiet her sobs, and led her over to the moonlit couch on the far side of the cabin. She was still sniffling, hugging him hard. He ran his hands firmly down her back, caressing her buttocks, feeling her body respond.

"Give me that pill," he said to her. "Now."

Looking at him huge-eyed in the blue moonlight, she pulled out the little box. He took out his and swallowed it deliberately, willing her to understand.

"Take off your clothes." He began stripping off his jerkin, proud of the hot, steady power in his sex. When she stripped and he saw again the glistening black bush at the base of her slim belly, and the silver-edged curves of her body, urgency took him, but still in a magical calm.

"Lie down."

"Wait a minute—" She was out of his hands like a fish, running across the cabin to where the dead body lay in darkness. Jakko saw she was trying to close the dead eyes that still gleamed from the shadows. He could wait; he had never imagined his body could feel like this. She laid the cloth over the stranger's face and came back to him, half-shyly holding out her arms, sinking down spread-legged on the shining couch before him. The moonlight was so brilliant he could see the pink colour of her sexual parts.

He came onto her gently, controlledly, breathing in an exciting animal odor from her flesh. This time his penis entered easily, an intense feeling of all-rightness.

But a moment later the fires of terror, pity and defiance deep within him burst up into a flame of passionate brilliance in his coupled groin. The small body under his seemed no longer vulnerable but appetitive. He clutched, mouthed, drove deep into her, exulting. Death didn't die alone, he thought obscurely as the ancient patterns lurking in his vitals awoke. Death flew with them and flowed by beneath, but he asserted life upon the body of the woman, caught up in a great crescendo of unknown sensation, until a culminant spasm of almost painful pleasure rolled through him into her, relieving him from head to feet.

When he could talk, he thought to ask her, "Did you—" he didn't know the word. "Did it sort of explode you, like me?"

"Well, no." Her lips were by his ear. "Female sexuality is a little different. Maybe I'll show you, later. . . . But I think it was good, for the baby."

He felt only a tiny irritation at her words, and let himself drift into sleep with his face in her warm-smelling hair. Dimly the understanding came to him that the great beast of his dreams, the race itself maybe, had roused and used them. So be it.

A cold thing pushing into his ear awakened him, and a hoarse voice said "Ffoo-ood!" It was the moondogs.

"Oh my, I forgot to feed them!" Peachthief struggled nimbly out from under him.

Jakko found he was ravenous too. The cabin was dark now, as the moon rose overhead. Peachthief located the switches, and made a soft light on their side of the cabin. They ate and drank heartily, looking down at the moonlit world. The deathyards were gone from below them now, they were flying over dark wooded foothills. When they lay down to sleep again they could feel the cabin slightly angle upward as the ship rose higher.

He was roused in the night by her body moving against him. She seemed to be rubbing his crotch.

"Give me your hand," she whispered in a panting voice. She began to make his hands do things to her, sometimes touching him too, her body arching and writhing, sleek with sweat. He found himself abruptly tumescent again, excited and pleased in a confused way. "Now, now!" she commanded, and he entered her, finding her interior violently alive. She seemed to be half-fighting him, this time without the terror. He pressed in against her shuddering convulsions. "Yes—Oh, yes!" she gasped, and a series of paroxysms swept through her, carrying him with her to explosive peace.

He held himself on and in her until her body and breathing calmed to relaxation, and they slipped naturally apart. It came to him that this sex activity seemed to have more possibilities, as a thing to do, than he had realised. His family had imparted to him nothing of all this. Perhaps they didn't know it. Or perhaps it was too alien to their calm philosophy.

"How do you know about all this?" he asked Peachthief sleepily.

"One of my aunts did literature, too," She chuckled in the darkness. "Different literature, I guess."

They slept almost as movelessly as the body flying with them on the other couch a world away.

A series of noisy bumpings wakened them. The windows were filled with pink mist flying by. The airship seemed to be sliding into a berth. Jakko looked down and saw shrubs and grass close below; it was a ground-berth on a hillside.

The computer panel lit up: RESET PROGRAM FOR BASE.

"No," said Jakko. "We'll need it going back." Peachthief looked at him in a new, companionable way; he sensed that she believed him now. He turned all the drive controls to stand-by while she worked the food synthesizer. Presently he heard the hiss of the deflating lift-bags, and went to where she was standing by the dead stranger.

"We'll take her, her body, out before we go back," Peachthief said. "Maybe the River will touch her somehow."

Jakko doubted it, but ate and drank his breakfast protein in silence.

When they went to use the wash-and-waste cubby he found he didn't want to clean all the residues of their contact off himself. Peachthief seemed to feel the same way; she washed only her face and hands. He looked at her slender, silk-clad belly. Was a child, his child, starting there? Desire flicked him again, but he remembered he had work to do. His promise to his father; get on with it. Sooner done, sooner back here.

"I love you," he said experimentally, and found the strange words had a startling trueness.

She smiled brilliantly at him, not just off-on. "I love you, too, I think."

The floor-portal light was on. They pulled it up and uncovered a step-way leading to the ground. The moondogs poured down. They followed, coming out into a blowing world of rosy mists. Clouds were streaming around them, the air was all in motion up the hillside toward the crest some distance ahead of the shipberth. The ground here was uneven and covered with short soft grass, as though animals had cropped it.

"All winds blow to the River," Jakko quoted.

They set off up the hill, followed by the moondogs, who stalked uneasily with pricked ears. Probably they didn't like not being able to smell what was ahead, Jakko thought. Peachthief was holding his hand very firmly as they went, as if determined to keep him out of any danger.

As they walked up onto the flat crest of the hilltop the mists suddenly cleared, and they found themselves looking down into a great shallow glittering sunlit valley. They both halted involuntarily to stare at the fantastic sight.

Before them lay a huge midden heap, kilometers of things upon things upon things, almost filling the valley floor. Objects of every description lay heaped there; Jakko could make out clothing, books, toys, jewelry, a myriad artifacts and implements abandoned. These must be, he realized, the last things people had taken with them when they went on the River. In an outer ring not too far below them were tents, ground and air-cars, even wagons. Everything shone clean and gleaming as if the influence of the River had kept off decay.

He noticed that the nearest ring of encampments intersected other, apparently older and larger rings. There seemed to be no center to the pile.

"The River has moved, or shrunk," he said.

"Both, I think." Peachthief pointed to the right. "Look, there's an old war-place."

A big grass-covered mound dominated the hillcrest beside them. Jakko saw it had metal-rimmed slits in its sides. He remembered history: how there were still rulers of people when the River's tendrils first touched earth. Some of the rulers had tried to keep their subjects from the going-out places, posting guards around them and even putting killing-devices in the ground. But the guards had gone themselves out on the River, or the River had swelled and taken them. And the people had driven beasts across the mined ground and surged after them into the stream of immortal life. In the end the rulers had gone too, or died out. Looking more carefully, Jakko could see that the green hill-slopes were torn and pocked, as though ancient explosions had craters everywhere.

Suddenly he remembered that he had to find his father in all this vast confusion.

"Where's the River now? My father's mind should reach there still, if I'm not too late."

"See that glittery slick look in the air down there? I'm sure that's a danger-place."

Down to their right, fairly close to the rim, was a strangely bright place. As he stared it became clearer: a great column of slightly golden or shining air. He scanned about, but saw nothing else like it all across the valley.

"If that's the only focus left, it's going away fast."

She nodded and then swallowed, her small face suddenly grim. She meant to live on here and die without the River, Jakko could see that. But he would be with her; he resolved it with all his heart. He squeezed her hand hard.

"If you have to talk to your father, we better walk around up here on the rim where it's safe," Peachthief said.

"No-oo," spoke up a moondog from behind them. The two humans turned and saw the three sitting in a row on the crest, staring slit-eyed at the valley.

"All right," Peachthief said. "You wait here. We'll be back soon."

She gripped Jakko's hand even tighter, and they started walking past the old war-mound, past the remains of ancient vehicles, past an antique pylon that leaned crazily. There were faint little trails in the short grass. Another war-mound loomed ahead; when they passed around it they found themselves suddenly among a small herd of white animals with long necks and no horns. The animals went on grazing quietly as the humans walked by. Jakko thought they might be mutated deer.

"Oh, look!" Peachthief let go his hand. "That's milk— see, her baby is sucking!"

Jakko saw that one of the animals had a knobby bag between its hind legs. A small one half-knelt down beside it, with its head up nuzzling the bag. A mother and her young.

Peachthief was walking cautiously toward them, making gentle greeting sounds. The mother-animal looked at her calmly, evidently tame. The baby went on sucking, rolling its eyes. Peachthief reached them, petted the mother, and then bent down under to feel the bag. The animal side-stepped a pace, but stayed still. When Peach-thief straightened up she was licking her hand.

"That's good milk! And they're just the right size, we can take them on the airship! On the way-cars, even." She was beaming, glowing. Jakko felt an odd warm con-striction in his chest. The intensity with which she fur-nished her little world, her future nest! *Their* nest . . .

"Come with us, come on," Peachthief was urging. She had her belt around the creature's neck to lead it. It came equably, the young one following in awkward galloping lunges.

"That baby is a male. Oh, this is *perfect*," Peachthief exclaimed. "Here, hold her a minute while I look at that one."

She handed Jakko the end of the belt and ran off. The beast eyed him levelly. Suddenly it drew its upper lip back and shot spittle at his face. He ducked, yelling for Peach-thief to come back.

"I have to find my father first!"

"All right" she said, returning. "Oh, look at that!"

Downslope from them was an apparition—one of the white animals, but partly transparent, ghostly-thin. It drifted vaguely, putting his head down now and then, but did not eat.

"It must have got partly caught in the River, it's half gone. Oh, Jakko, you can see how dangerous it is! I'm afraid, I'm afraid it'll catch you."

"It won't. I'll be very careful."

"I'm so afraid." But she let him lead her on, towing the animal alongside. As they passed the ghost-creature Peachthief called to it, "You can't live like that. You bet-ter go on out. Shoo, shoo!"

It turned and moved slowly out across the piles of litter, toward the shining place in the air.

They were coming closer to it now, stepping over more and more abandoned things. Peachthief looked sharply at everything; once she stooped to pick up a beautiful fleecy white square and stuff it in her pack. The hillcrest was merging with a long grassy slope, comparatively free of debris, that ran out toward the airy glittering column. They turned down it.

The River-focus became more and more awesome as they approached. They could trace it towering up and up now, twisting gently as it passed beyond the sky. A tendril of the immaterial stream of sidereal sentience that had embraced earth, a pathway to immortal life. The air inside looked no longer golden, but pale silver-gilt, like a great shaft of moonlight coming down through the morning sun. Objects at its base appeared very clear but shimmering, as if seen through cool crystal water.

Off to one side were tents. Jakko suddenly recognised one, and quickened his steps. Peachthief pulled back on his arm.

"Jakko, be careful!"

They slowed to a stop a hundred yards from the tenuous fringes of the River's effect. It was very still. Jakko peered intently. In the verges of the shimmer a staff was standing upright. From it hung a scarf of green and yellow silk.

"Look—that's my father's sign!"

"Oh Jakko, you *can't* go in there."

At the familiar-coloured sign all the memories of his life with his family had come flooding back on Jakko. The gentle rationality, the solemn sense of preparation for going out from earth forever. Two different realities strove briefly within him. They had loved him, he realised that now. Especially his father . . . But not as he loved Peachthief, his awakened spirit shouted silently. I am of earth! Let the stars take care of their own. His resolve took deeper hold and won.

Gently he released himself from her grip.

"You wait here. Don't worry, it takes a long while for the change, you know that. Hours, days. I'll only be a minute, I'll come right back."

"Ohhh, it's crazy."

But she let him go and stood holding to the milk-animal while he went down the ridge and picked his way out across the midden-heap toward the staff. As he neared it he could feel the air change around him, becoming alive and yet more still.

"Father! Paul! It's Jakko, your son. Can you still hear me?"

Nothing answered him. He took a step or two past the staff, repeating his call.

A resonant susurrus came in his head, as if unearthly reaches had opened to him. From infinity he heard without hearing his father's quiet voice.

You came.

A sense of calm welcome.

"The cities are all empty, father. All the people have gone, everywhere."

Come.

"No!" He swallowed, fending off memory, fending off the lure of strangeness. "I think it's sad. It's wrong. I've found a woman. We're going to stay and make children."

The River is leaving, Jakko my son.

It was as if a star had called his name, but he said stubbornly, "I don't care. I'm staying with her. Goodbye, father. Goodbye."

Grave regret touched him, and from beyond a host of silent voices murmured down the sky: *Come! Come away.*

"No!" he shouted, or tried to shout, but he could not still the rapt voices. And suddenly, gazing up, he felt the reality of the River, the overwhelming opening of the door to life everlasting among the stars. All his mortal fears, all his most secret dread of the waiting maw of death, all slid out of him and fell away, leaving him almost unbearably light and calmly joyful. He knew that he was being touched, that he could float out upon that immortal stream forever. But even as the longing took him, his human mind remembered that this was the start of the first stage, for which the River was called Beata. He thought of the ghost-animal that had lingered too long. He must leave now, and quickly. With enormous effort he took one step backward, but could not turn.

"Jakko! Jakko! Come back!"

Someone was calling, screaming his name. He did turn then, and saw her on the little ridge. Nearby, yet so far. The ordinary sun of earth was brilliant on her and the two white beasts.

"Jakko! Jakko!" Her arms were outstretched, she was running toward him.

It was as if the whole beautiful earth was crying to him, calling to him to come back and take up the burden of life and death. He did not want it. But she must not come here, he knew that without remembering why. He began uncertainly to stumble toward her, seeing her now as his beloved woman, again as an unknown creature uttering strange cries.

"Lady Death," he muttered, not realising he had ceased to move. She ran faster, tripped, almost fell in the heaps of stuff. The wrongness of her coming here roused him again; he took a few more steps, feeling his head clear a little.

"*Jakko!*" She reached him, clutched him, dragging him bodily forward from the verge.

At her touch the reality of his human life came back to him, his heart pounded human blood, all stars fled away. He started to run clumsily, half-carrying her with him up to the safety of the ridge. Finally they sank down gasping beside the animals, holding and kissing each other, their eyes wet.

"I thought you were lost, I thought I'd lost you," Peachthief sobbed.

"You saved me."

"H-here," she said. "We b-better have some food." She rummaged in her pack, nodding firmly as if the simple human act could defend against unearthly powers. Jakko discovered that he was quite hungry.

They ate and drank peacefully in the soft, flower-studded grass, while the white animals grazed around them. Peachthief studied the huge strewn valley floor, frowing as she munched.

"So many good useful things here. I'll come back some day, when the River's gone, and look around."

"I thought you only wanted natural things," he teased her.

"Some of these things will last. Look." She picked up a small implement. "It's an awl, for punching and sewing leather. You could make children's sandals."

Many of the people who came here must have lived quite simply, Jakko thought. It was true that there could be useful tools. And metal. Books, too. Directions for making things. He lay back dreamily, seeing a vision of himself in the far future, an accomplished artisan, teaching his children skills. It seemed deeply good.

"Oh, my milk-beast!" Peachthief broke in on his reverie. "Oh, no! You mustn't!" She jumped up.

Jakko sat up and saw that the white mother-animal had strayed quite far down the grassy ridge. Peachthief trotted down after her, calling, "Come here! Stop!"

Perversely, the animal moved away, snatching mouthfuls of grass. Peachthief ran faster. The animal threw up its head and paced down off the ridge, among the litter-piles.

"No! Oh, my milk! Come back here, come."

She went down after it, trying to move quietly and call more calmly.

Jakko had got up, alarmed.

"Come back! Don't go down there!"

"The babies' milk," she wailed at him, and made a dash at the beast. But she missed and it drifted away just out of reach before her.

To his horror Jakko saw that the glittering column of the River had changed shape slightly, eddying out a veil of shimmering light close ahead of the beast.

"Turn back! Let it go!" he shouted, and began to run with all his might. "Peachthief— Come back!"

But she would not turn, and his pounding legs could not catch up. The white beast was in the shimmer now; he saw it bound up onto a great sun-and-moonlit heap of stuff. Peachthief's dark form went flying after it, uncaring, and the creature leapt away again. He saw her follow, and bitter fear grabbed at his heart. The very strength of her human life is betraying her to death, he thought; I have to get her physically, I will pull her out. He forced his legs faster, faster yet, not noticing that the air had changed around him too.

She disappeared momentarily in a veil of glittering air, and then reappeared, still following the beast. Thankfully he saw her pause and stoop to pick something up. She was only walking now, he could catch her. But his own body was moving sluggishly, it took all his will to keep his legs thrusting him ahead.

"Peachthief! Love, come back!"

His voice seemed muffled in the silvery air. Dismayed, he realised that he too had slowed to a walk and she was veiled again from his sight.

When he struggled through the radiance he saw her, moving very slowly after the wandering white beast. Her face was turned up, unearthly light was on her beauty. He knew she was feeling the rapture, the call of immortal life was on her. On him, too; he found he was barely stumbling forward, a terrible serenity flooding his heart. They must be passing into the very focus of the River, where it ran strongest.

"Love—" Mortal grief fought the invading transcendence. Ahead of him the girl faded slowly into the glimmering veils, still following her last earthly desire. He saw that humanity, all that he had loved of the glorious earth, was disappearing forever from reality. Why had it awakened, only to be lost? Spectral voices were near him, but he did not want spectres. An agonising lament for human life welled up in him, a last pang that he would carry with him through eternity. But its urgency fell away. Life incorporeal, immortal, was on him now; it had him as it had her. His flesh, his body was beginning to attenuate, to dematerialise out into the great current of sentience that flowed on its mysterious purposes among the stars.

Still the essence of his earthly self moved slowly after hers into the closing mists of infinity, carrying upon the River a configuration that had been a man striving forever after a loved dark girl, who followed a ghostly white milch-deer.

THE SCIENCE FICTION YEAR

Charles N. Brown

THE USUAL PREDICTION OF DISASTER IN THE science fiction publishing industry did not, as usual, prove true in 1980. Despite the worsening recession and cries of anguish by various publishers, over 1,000 sf and fantasy books (both new and reprint) appeared in North America during 1980—nearly three books per day! Prices per book increased again. By the end of this year, the average sf paperback reached $2.25 and the average hardcover hit $12.95. Lead titles were even higher. The average paperback will probably sell for $2.50 by the end of 1981. Various publishers are experimenting with trade paperbacks priced in the $6 to $8 range as an alternative to hardcover sf publishing. Ace Books has been doing the most, but Avon, Del Rey and other paperback houses have also published some. A number of trade publishers have done simultaneous hardcover and oversize paperback editions. Two major science fiction anthologies were published this way in 1980—*The Arbor House Treasury of Modern Science Fiction* and *The Arbor House Treasury of Great Science Fiction Short Novels*. Libraries apparently still demand hardcover books, but the quality of the bindings has gotten so bad, it would be easier to buy paperbacks and set up a special bindery.

The bloom seems to be off the science fiction field as far as general publishing goes. The annual American Booksellers convention, held this past year in Chicago, featured very little science fiction for the upcoming year although Frank Herbert, Stephen R. Donaldson and Stephen King all had popular autographing sessions.

Harlan Ellison and Ben Bova won a major plagiarism lawsuit against ABC-TV and Paramount Pictures. The court agreed that the TV show *Robot Cop* was taken from their 1970 short story "Brillo" and awarded them $292,-500. A.E. van Vogt settled out of court for $50,000 from Twentieth Century Fox after pointing out similarities between *Alien* and his 1939 story "Discord in Scarlet."

The huge advances sf authors were getting a year ago have almost disappeared. Frank Herbert was still able to demand a record-breaking advance, but only for a multiple-book contract. F. Paul Wilson, winner of last year's Prometheus Award, got $50,000 for a fantasy novel which sold first to the movies. Robert Silverberg's $75,000 advance for paperback rights to *Lord Valentine's Castle* was actually a disappointment and a major loss to the hardcover publishers, who had paid $127,500 for the original rights. Very few, if any, of the large-advance books earned enough to justify further payments. Two sf novels, *The Number of the Beast* by Robert A. Heinlein and *Firestarter* by Stephen King, reached the national yearly bestseller lists. *The Wounded Land* by Stephen R. Donaldson, the new sequel to "The Chronicles of Thomas Covenant the Unbeliever," and *The Magic Labyrinth* by Philip José Farmer, the final (finally!) book in the "Riverworld" series, sold about 30,000 copies each. *Mockingbird* by Walter Tevis and *The Snow Queen* by Joan D. Vinge also sold well.

"Because of an inaccuracy in the cover copy . . ." Bantam Books recalled the first American edition of *The Snail on the Slope* by Arkady and Boris Strugatsky, two leading Russian sf writers. The book became an instant collector's item.

RCA sold Random House, Inc., which also includes Knopf, Pantheon and Ballantine, to Newhouse Publications for $70 million. Although Random House was profitable, it was not, according to RCA, profitable enough for them to bother with.

Baronet Books folded without publishing the second volume of a graphic edition of *The Stars My Destination* by Alfred Bester even though they had over eight hundred advance orders.

Phantasia Press started a new trend in sf publishing by

printing limited signed first editions of various new trade books: *The Magic Labyrinth* by Philip José Farmer, *The Ringworld Engineers* by Larry Niven, *Firestarter* by Stephen King and *The Humanoid Touch* by Jack Williamson. All sold out. Various trade publishers decided to get into this lucrative market (all of the books sell for $30 or more). Harper & Row did a special edition of *Lord Valentine's Castle* by Robert Silverberg, and Putnam has announced a special 1981 edition of the new Frank Herbert novel, *God-Emperor of Dune*.

For those interested in hardcover collecting, Gregg Press continued to provide outstanding bargains in limited library editions of top-notch science fiction. They had excellent reprints of work by Frank Herbert, Philip José Farmer and Fritz Leiber in 1980. The Science Fiction Book Club also provided outstanding values including cheap hardcover first editions of many mass market paperbacks.

Tor Books, a new science fiction paperback line to be distributed by Pinnacle Books, was launched by Thomas J. Doherty, former publisher of Ace Books. James P. Baen, former senior editor of Ace, will edit the new line.

Simon & Schuster and Pocket Books have combined their science fiction titles as "Timescape Books." They've pushed it with a lot of publicity.

1980 was both a good and a disappointing year for novels—good because there were fine books by new and not-so-new writers; disappointing because a number of famous authors turned out pedestrian or just plain bad books.

Timescape by Gregory Benford (Simon & Schuster), a near future novel with excellent characterization, was my favorite science fiction novel of the year with *Wild Seed* by Octavia E. Butler (Doubleday), which takes place entirely in the past, a close second. Stephen King is an intensely visual writer and I could see nearly every scene in *Firestarter* (Viking). *Mockingbird* by Walter Tevis (Doubleday) is a tender and loving story about the near extinction of the human race. *Serpent's Reach* by C.J. Cherryh (DAW) was the best sf book about aliens in a long time.

The top fantasy book of the year is harder to pick. *The Shadow of the Torturer* by Gene Wolfe (Simon & Schuster) was the best stylistic fantasy but *The Vampire*

Tapestry by Suzy McKee Charnas (Simon & Schuster) is possibly the outstanding vampire novel of all time. Unlike most sequels, *The Northern Girl* by Elizabeth A. Lynn (Berkley/Putnam), the final book in her "Chronicles of Tornor" trilogy, is even better than the award-winning first volume, *Watchtower*. *Ariosto* by Chelsea Quinn Yarbro (Pocket) is a fine alternative world fantasy, and *Shadow Land* by Peter Straub (Coward, McCann) is a brilliant present-day horror novel.

The biggest thrill for a reviewer is to discover a new or unknown writer. There were some fine first novels in 1980. *Sundiver* by David Brin (Bantam) and *The Gates of Heaven* by Paul Preuss (Bantam) were both "hard science" stories from completely unknown writers. Hilbert Schenck has been writing short fiction for several years; *Wave Rider* (Pocket), a connected series of stories comprising his first book, is terrific. *Hawk of May* by Gillian Bradshaw (Simon & Schuster), the first volume in an Arthurian trilogy, is an excellent fantasy. *The Orphan* by Robert Stallman (Pocket), the first volume in a science fiction trilogy, is very successful. The author finished all three books before his untimely death on August 6, 1980, of cancer. He was fifty.

The Snow Queen by Joan D. Vinge (Dial), one of the most popular books of the year, is a science fiction novel told in a fantasy style. It's long and has a little bit of everything. I liked it, but wish it had been cut by about 100 pages.

Sequels are rarely as good as the original books even though they usually sell better. *Wizard* by John Varley (Berkley/Putnam), the sequel to *Titan*, and *Beyond the Blue Event Horizon* by Frederik Pohl (Del Rey), the sequel to *Gateway*, are both good books, but not as good as their award-winning prequels. *The Wounded Land* by Stephen R. Donaldson (Del Rey), the fourth book in the "Covenant" trilogy (!), is readable, but tries to add to a completed series. *The Magic Labyrinth* by Philip José Farmer (Berkley/Putnam) finally finishes the "Riverworld" series which started out as a classic and has been a little more incoherent in each new book. I couldn't quite figure out what was happening in the last book, and what was worse, I didn't care. I normally like hard engineering fiction, but *The Ringworld Engineers* by Larry Niven

(Holt), the sequel to the award-winning novel *Ringworld*, could not hold my interest.

The most disappointing novels of the year were four books from normally excellent authors. *The Beginning Place* by Ursula K. Le Guin (Harper & Row) was unconvincing, *Lord Valentine's Castle* by Robert Silverberg (Harper & Row) was bland, *Golem*[100] by Alfred Bester (Simon & Schuster) was lousy and *The Number of the Beast* by Robert A. Heinlein was awful. Actually, these four were probably not that bad; I just approached them with too many high expectations.

The Empire Strikes Back, the sequel to *Star Wars*, opened in 1980 to capacity crowds. Although it came in for more criticism than the original, it was easily the most popular sf movie of the year. *Star Trek: The Motion Picture* and *The Black Hole* were failures, both critically and financially.

The science fiction magazine field contracted to its lowest point since the early thirties. There are only four straight sf magazines left—*Analog*, *Amazing*, *Isaac Asimov's SF* and *Fantasy & Science Fiction*. *Galaxy*, *Galileo* and *Fantastic* disappeared in 1980; *Destinies*, the pocket-size magazine, will see its last issue in early 1981. All four of the remaining magazines experienced drops in newsstand circulation. *Amazing* improved somewhat when it was combined with *Fantastic*; *F&SF* made up the difference with a subscription drive; *Isaac Asimov's SF* dropped to 90,000 circulation. *Analog*, sold to Davis Publications—the publishers of *Isaac Asimov's SF*—improved its subscription sales. At 104,000 circulation, *Analog* is the most successful of the digest magazines, but circulation is lower than it was ten years ago. Davis Publications increased the publication of both *Analog* and *Asimov's* to thirteen times per year.

Omni sold an average of 850,000 copies per issue—about three times the combined circulation of all the digest magazines. In addition, *Playboy*, *Gallery* and other large-size magazines published sf. The various games magazines—*Ares*, *Sorcerer's Apprentice*, *The Spacegamer*, etc.—also published sf and fantasy fiction. The publishers of *Gallery* have announced a new fantasy fiction magazine, *The Twilight Zone*, for 1981. The digest magazines could probably survive without much change or growth, but the future seems to belong to the general magazines with a story or two per issue.

John Collier, 78, whose short story collection *Fancies and Goodnights* won the International Fantasy Award in 1952, died of a stroke on April 6, 1980.

Wallace West, 79, who wrote sf for over fifty years, died of a heart attack on March 23, 1980.

George Pal, 72, producer of such wonderful sf films as *Destination Moon* (1950), *When Worlds Collide* (1951), and *War of the Worlds* (1953), died of a heart attack on May 2, 1980.

George R. Stewart, 85, author of the International Fantasy Award-winning novel *Earth Abides,* died August 22, 1980.

Susan Wood, 32, who won several Hugo Awards as a fan and edited *The Language of the Night,* died November 12, 1980.

Kris Neville, 55, author of *Bettyann* and other popular sf stories, died of a heart attack on December 23, 1980.

The American Book Awards, replacing the National Book Awards, started with much hoopla and much dissension. The first year's awards, presented May 1 in New York, included two science fiction categories: Best Hardcover, won by *JEM* by Frederik Pohl, and Best Paperback, won by *The Book of the Dun Cow* by Walter Wangerin, Jr. The sf awards were then dropped from future consideration with the excuse that the field "has its own awards." We almost made the big time.

The 1980 Nebula Awards were presented at the fifteenth annual Nebula Banquet in Los Angeles on April 26, 1980. Winners were: Best Novel, *The Fountains of Paradise* by Arthur C. Clarke; Best Novella, "Enemy Mine" by Barry B. Longyear; Best Novelette, "Sandkings" by George R.R. Martin; Best Short Story, "giANTS" by Edward Bryant.

The 1980 Hugo Awards were presented in Boston on August 31, 1980. Winners were: Best Novel, *The Fountains of Paradise* by Arthur C. Clarke; Best Novella, "Enemy Mine" by Barry B. Longyear; Best Novelette, "Sandkings" by George R.R. Martin; Best Short Story, "The Way of Cross and Dragon" by George R.R. Martin; Best Non-fiction Book, *The Science Fiction Encyclopedia* edited by Peter Nicholls; Best Dramatic Presentation, *Alien;* Best Professional Artist, Michael Whelan; Best

Professional Editor, George H. Scithers; Best Fanzine, *Locus;* Best Fan Writer, Bob Shaw; Best Fan Artist, Alexis Gilliland. The John W. Campbell Award for best new writer was won by Barry B. Longyear; the Gandalf Award for lifetime contribution to fantasy was won by Ray Bradbury.

The 1980 Locus Awards were announced July 4, 1980 in Los Angeles. Winners were: Best Science Fiction Novel, *Titan* by John Varley; Best Fantasy Novel, *Harpist in the Wind* by Patricia A. McKillip; Best Novella, "Enemy Mine" by Barry B. Longyear; Best Novelette, "Sandkings" by George R.R. Martin; Best Short Story, "The Way of Cross and Dragon" by George R.R. Martin; Best Anthology, *Universe 9* edited by Terry Carr; Best Collection, *Convergent Series* by Larry Niven; Best Art Book, *Barlowe's Guide to Extraterrestrials* by Wayne Barlowe and Ian Summers; Best Artist, Michael Whelan; Best Magazine, *F&SF;* Best Publisher, Del Rey; Best Non-Fiction Book, *The Science Fiction Encyclopedia* edited by Peter Nicholls.

Thomas M. Disch won the 1980 John W. Campbell Memorial Award for his novel *On Wings of Song.*

The 1980 World Fantasy Awards were announced in Baltimore on November 2, 1980. Winners were: Life Achievement, Manly Wade Wellman; Best Novel, *Watchtower* by Elizabeth A. Lynn; Best Short Story, (tie) "The Woman Who Loved the Moon" by Elizabeth A. Lynn and "Mackintosh Willy" by Ramsey Campbell; Best Anthology, *Amazons!* edited by Jessica Amanda Salmonson; Best Artist, Don Maitz; Special Professional Award, Donald M. Grant; Special Non-Professional Award, Paul C. Allen. The World Fantasy Convention also gave a special award to Stephen King.

There were, as usual, dozens of other minor awards given to various sf books, authors, movies, TV shows, etc.

Noreascon II, the 38th World Science Fiction Convention, held in Boston August 29 to September 1, 1980, was, to no one's surprise, the largest sf world convention ever held. Six thousand writers, editors, readers, fans and others came together for science fiction's annual celebration. They watched the Hugo presentation, bought art and books, listened to the three hundred speakers who appeared on the multi-track programming, got books autographed, saw an incredible number of movies, attended parties and set a new jacuzzi stuffing record. The working committee, more than three hundred strong, and *all* unpaid volunteers, should be specially commended.

The 39th World Science Fiction Convention will be held in Denver September 3–7, 1981. Guests of Honor include Clifford D. Simak and C.L. Moore. For information on membership, write: Denvention 2, P.O. Box 11545, Denver, Colorado 80211.

The 40th World Science Fiction Convention will be held in Chicago September 2–6, 1982. Guests of Honor include A. Bertram Chandler and Frank Kelly Freas. For information on membership, write ChiCon IV, P.O. Box A 3120, Chicago, Illinois 60690.

SUBSCRIPTION RATES

Charles N. Brown is the editor of *Locus*, the newspaper of the science fiction field. Copies are $1.25 each. Subscriptions in the United States are $12.00 per year (second class), $18.00 per year (first class; U.S. or Canada). Canadian and foreign second class subscriptions are $15.00 per year; overseas airmail subscriptions are $24.00 per year. All subscriptions are payable only in U.S. funds to *Locus Publications*, P.O. Box 3938, San Francisco, California 94119.

RECOMMENDED READING
—1980

Terry Carr

David Andreissen and D. C. Poyer: "If You Can Fill the Unforgiving Minute." *Isaac Asimov's Science Fiction Magazine*, May 1980.

Ross Appel: "Song of Mutes." *Berkley Showcase*, Vol. 2.

Michael Bishop: "A Short History of the Bicycle: 401 B.C. to 2677 A.D." *Interfaces*.

Michael Bishop: "Saving Face." *Universe 10*.

Michael G. Coney: "The Summer Sweet, the Winter Wild." *Interfaces*.

Philip K. Dick: "Rautavaara's Case." *Omni*, October 1980.

Gordon R. Dickson: "Lost Dorsai." *Destinies*, February–March 1980.

William S. Doxey: "Rheeman's Space." *Fantasy and Science Fiction*, November 1980.

Sharon N. Farber: "Trans Dimensional Imports." *Isaac Asimov's Science Fiction Magazine*, August 1980.

Karl Hansen: "Doll's Eyes." *Berkley Showcase*, Vol. 2.

P. C. Hodgell: "Child of Darkness." *Berkley Showcase*, Vol. 2.

James P. Hogan: "The Sword of Damocles." *Stellar #5*.

Bruce McAllister: "Their Immortal Hearts." *Their Immortal Hearts*.

P. J. Plauger: "Virtual Image." *New Voices III*.

Marta Randall: "Dangerous Games." *Fantasy and Science Fiction*, April 1980.

Keith Roberts: "The Lordly Ones." *Fantasy and Science Fiction*, March 1980.

Kim Stanley Robinson: "On the North Pole of Pluto." *Orbit 21.*

Hilbert Schenck: "Buoyant Ascent." *Fantasy and Science Fiction,* March 1980.

Michael Shea: "The Autopsy." *Fantasy and Science Fiction,* December 1980.

Charles Sheffield: "Moment of Inertia." *Analog,* October 1980.

John Shirley: "Quill Tripstickler Eludes a Bride." *Fantasy and Science Fiction,* May 1980.

Robert Silverberg: "Our Lady of the Sauropods." *Omni,* September 1980.

Michael Swanwick: "The Feast of St. Janis." *New Dimensions 11.*

Walter Tevis: "The Apotheosis of Myra." *Playboy,* July 1980.

Howard Waldrop: "Billy Big-Eyes." *Berkley Showcase,* Vol. 1.

Sharon Webb: "Variations on a Theme from Beethoven." *Isaac Asimov's Science Fiction Magazine,* February 1980.

ON THE OTHER SIDE OF TIME AND SPACE

Stories of Fantastic, Futuristic Worlds That Illuminate Universes

Pocket Books offers the best in Science Fiction—
a genre whose time has come.

_____	43684	JUNIPER TIME Kate Wilhelm	$2.75
_____	41593	RUINS OF ISIS Marion Zimmer Bradley	$2.25
_____	82917	ROAD TO CORLAY Richard Cowper	$1.95
_____	82876	A WORLD BETWEEN Norman Spinrad	$2.25
_____	81207	JOURNEY Marta Randall	$1.95
_____	42882	COLONY Ben Bova	$2.95
_____	82835	EYES OF FIRE Michael Bishop	$2.25
_____	43288	THE DEMU TRILOGY F. M. Busby	$3.50
_____	81130	DYING OF THE LIGHT George R. R. Martin	$1.95

170

A.E. van Vogt